THE PARTY WALL

THE PARTY WALL

Stevie Davies

HONNO MODERN FICTION

First published in Great Britain in 2020 by Honno Press
'Ailsa Craig', Heol y Cawl, Dinas Powys, Vale of Glamorgan,
Wales, CF64 4AH

1 2 3 4 5 6 7 8 9 10

A catalogue record for this book is available from the British Library.
Published with the financial support of the Books Council of Wales.

ISBN 978-1-912905-15-7 (paperback)
ISBN 978-1-912905-16-4 (ebook)

Cover photograph: Arcangel.com/Katya Evdokimova
Cover design: Rachel Lawston
Text design: Elaine Sharples
Printed in Great Britain by 4Edge

For Andrew Howdle
poet, painter, friend

Acknowledgements

I am grateful to my agent Euan Thorneycroft, of A.M. Heath, and to my publisher Caroline Oakley of Honno, one of the best editors I have had the good fortune to meet.

Friends have supported me throughout the writing of *The Party Wall*: I thank Rosalie Wilkins, Helen Williams, Julie Bertagna, Francesca Morrison and Andrew Howdle for our years of friendship. I thank Rob and Sue Leek for all their kindness to me. Conversations with the novelist Anne Lauppe-Dunbar have been endlessly delightful and sustaining. Special thanks go to Wynn Thomas, Glyn Pursglove and Ceri Davies for wisdom, invariably salted with laughter. I am more grateful than I can say to my children Grace, Robin and Emily for their support and encouragement.

1

He nursed the wall, propped against pillows, attuned to every reverberation. At first, Mark had whiled away the time with a book. Gradually he left off reading and immersed himself in this quiet act of witness. Strangely, the vigil had no power to bore him. Concentration remained deep and constant as he listened out, or listened in, for his neighbour. There'd been an intermittent scratching or rustling sound he was unable to interpret, but that had ceased. Even when the silence remained well-nigh unbroken for half an hour or so, and he had to get up and stretch or pee, Mark experienced no, or little, impatience. Whatever I can do for Freya, I'll gladly and honourably do, he told himself, grateful for the calm intentness of his spirit. She schooled him. She made him a better person. There was an overarching sense of forgiveness. Not that there was anything Mark should be forgiven for.

He brought lunch upstairs on a tray and ate cross-legged on his bed, to be near to her. The sound of his own chewing blocked off any small noises and he occasionally paused to listen.

Next door's dog broke the trance with a desolation of baying, very near at hand. There was a shriek of 'Storm, no! Get down!' Mark started back from the reverberation; soup slopped onto the tray. He disliked mess and would not normally eat in bed. Everything was in process of change.

Dogs know, Mark thought. Dogs smell the death in a house. But not even the damp snout of a dog can nose out the presence of a person through a wall. Freya's bedroom door clicked; animal feet skittered down the Foxes' stairs. She was locking Storm into the kitchen. Out on the landing in his socked feet, Mark detected her footsteps padding back upstairs. As Freya re-entered her bedroom, Mark returned to his. It was the rhythm of their lives. The soup was tepid. He finished the bread and cheese and brushed crumbs from his sweater.

Mark settled back down again. His body warmth fed the wall and he hoped that a remnant flowed through to Freya. The magpies in Whitethorn Wood set up a quarrelsome churring. Shush! They were the least eirenic of birds. Their violence threatened the songbirds out there, but what could one do? When the predators had finished mobbing whatever it was that had aroused their spleen or appetite, there was a quiet spell, haunted by murmuring. Kneeling, he laid his ear flat to the wall. Was Freya singing to her husband? They say music dies last, and Mark could believe that. The husband's voice had been inaudible for many days.

Now the three of them composed themselves for the long act of waiting and witness, only a membrane between them. This vigil Mark would not have missed for the world. Five months ago, turfed out of his beautiful home, Tŷ Hafan, he'd landed in this terrace of nobodies where walls were thin and neighbours hugger-mugger. He reminded himself that this was temporary, he'd soon be home, with the hope of taking Freya with him. As it had turned out, the move to the crescent had been providential: how otherwise would Mark have come across his darling?

His sole desire was to be close to Freya and open to her. Imagine if this wall were suddenly drawn up like a stage curtain. It would be revealed that he and she were face to face, a metre apart, perhaps, gazing into one another's amazed eyes. His sympathy would flow out to meet her suffering and Freya would know for sure that she was not alone – and never would be. One wished Keir Fox gone but not for selfish reasons. Prolonging the man's life was extending his suffering. And her suffering. And, for that reason, my suffering, he thought.

The bottom line: Mark would do anything for Freya. Except leave off loving and watching over her.

It had come on so suddenly, this final passion of Mark's life. When he'd arrived at the crescent, he'd taken her for an over-age tomboy, whistling on her patio as she tinkered with her bikes. By and by he'd realised that they couldn't all be hers and that she was conducting her business – noisily – outside his home. The gaunt husband, who called himself an artist, sometimes shambled out to stand beside her, shrouded in layers of coat and scarf. With her oily hands, mucky clothes and hair piled on her head in an outsized pompom, his neighbour had seemed just one of the terrace's many nonentities.

How wrong can you be?

Mark had come across Freya in the gallery café, stopped to talk, and glimpsed the depths of her. Her grief. Her need. *Keir,* she said, *Keir* … and couldn't go on. She'd just been told her husband had only weeks or months to live. It turned out that she was educated, quite well read, politically engaged and thoughtful. Near-strangers as Mark and Freya had been, the two of them had talked, really talked. Mark had helped by telling her about the loss of his wife, sharing the insights he'd gleaned in his bereavement.

Somehow, in Freya's presence, Mark had shed much of his crucifying self-consciousness. Which was how he knew: the soul recognises its mate. That nervous tic stills at the corner of your eye; the eyebrows stop working up and down. You begin to like your face in the mirror. And this time, there was no mistake. Gullible as Mark had been with women, betrayed (and had paid for it – was still paying for the trap *she'd* led him into), now there was a quietus to turmoil. A sense of presence.

Timbers shifted, stairs creaked, water gurgled through pipes and, in the echo chamber of an attached home, you had a part in your neighbour's world. In a terrace, everyone connects. That is a given.

Some more than others, of course. He had no interest in the banal little lady on the other side and shut his ears to the signs of her existence.

His phone rang. Oh, not again. The pests! This would be the Museum Gallery seeking a specialist opinion. Why would that be urgent when the cultural artefacts had been entombed in the store for a hundred years? Besides, Mark had received the director's reluctant permission to take an unofficial summer sabbatical, to research a book, provisionally entitled *Authenticity and Provenance*. This would be a big book and perhaps a great one. He'd agreed to pop in now and again when necessary, but naturally he was jealous of his time. *It's you we need:* he could hear in advance the nasal voice of Paltry Patrick, Visitor Team Co-ordinator, so-called – general factotum and gasbag. In one way, the calls upon Mark were flattering. One's expertise was beyond even the most learned of the simpletons at the gallery. He'd risen above the menial circumstances of his childhood to become an authority – a world authority! – on art and antiquities.

Still, since his breakdown, Mark worked strictly part time. What part of 'part time' did they not understand?

On the other hand, the call might be made by the adoring doctoral student seconded by the college. Janine. When he made a motion to rise, the ringing – of course – stopped. It had jarred; he'd lost his place in the book of Freya Fox's life.

Deep breaths. Out there in the wood, cherry blossom frothed and tossed. Nobody had a keener eye for beauty, natural and human. Mark's hands no longer trembled as he brought his ear again to the wall.

*

Freya watched over the undoing of Keir. The once gauntly charismatic face had subsided into a landscape of ridges and shadowed hollows. His brain, burnt-out, remained alive only to fits of restlessness. She'd counted on his leaving in tranquillity, his spirit floating back through the darkening brain towards a final light, where he would find his mother and father waiting to receive him. Instead there'd been this nervous activity, his hand large on the shrunken arm, fingernail scratching at the wall.

Gaps grew between labouring breaths. Keir's hand surrendered its work. Storm had somehow or other managed to paw open the kitchen door and was racing upstairs.

Shush, Storm. Shush now, darling. She let him in. And why not? The Labrador reared on the bed, licked the sick face, sniffed, licked, recoiled, sniffed, nuzzled Keir's neck. The bedroom smelt of acetone, like nail varnish. Storm's nose must be penetrated by explosive smells, an apocalypse of scent, tens of thousands of times sharper than anything humans are capable of. He knew, of course.

Had Keir been waiting for his devoted animal to return? His lungs released a soughing exhalation. Freya waited. Storm drew back, hunkered, quivered. He had failed. He was afraid.

Keir took flight from himself. Just like that. He was gone.

It's all right, Stormie. He's well now.

The locum arrived; scooped up morphine packets. He filled in the certificate. Did Freya want anything to help her sleep? Sure? Was she on her own?

Not alone. I have Stormie. We just want to sit with Keir for a while. The locum left. Freya sat. On the bed lay an effigy of Keir. She was obscurely frightened of it.

The undertakers lifted their light burden. We are so sorry for your loss. Don't you want someone with you?

Not alone. I have our dog. We'd rather be private for a while – then I'll call everyone.

Hanging on to Storm's collar as he strained to follow Keir, Freya watched the effigy being stretchered down the stairs. It took all her power to drag Storm back with both hands. She and the animal struggled on the landing, he half-throttled, she in a fury of depleted strength. The front door clanged shut. Storm surrendered. The two of them observed from the window as Keir was carried down the path.

Freya sat back down on the bed, staring at the dint in the mattress where Keir wasn't. Everywhere lay traces of him, the imprint of his lip on a glass she'd left on the cabinet for a week. The disturbed dust settled. When she got to her feet, she had departed from herself.

5

One of her remained seated on the bed, hands in lap, gaze bent, while the other Freya rose. Faint, she sat back down; rejoined herself.

She tried again. And here she was, quite collected, at the window looking out. Cars, shrubs, blank day, Knots of neighbours, gossiping.

Someone knocked. Freya stayed put, where Keir's recent presence was most potent, the sheets rich with his mortal smell, toxic, terrible, precise and precious. Even the signs of his disease were sacred.

She agreed with Storm, and Storm with her, on their need for intimate privacy. An interval.

The wall Keir had been scraping at wore its old blemishes – dimples, flecks and stains – overlaid with scribble. Impossible to decode whatever message, if any, he'd meant to leave. Perhaps in his delirium, he had imagined he was at his easel in the studio. Or maybe he was making a last ditch effort to escape. A residue of powdered plaster and paint flakes lay on the duvet's hummocks and troughs. Keir had once described a childhood attempt to tunnel out of his room with his mum's tweezers. Freedom, he said: I never wanted to be cooped up, I hated it, Frey, I needed to be out of doors, climbing trees, getting the view from up there. That was Keir. Over time, he'd enlarged the hole at his childhood home. No one had noticed. When his family had sold that house, he'd filled the hole in with toothpaste, which soon, he said, hardens.

Try and dig your way out of a terraced house and you emerge next door, Freya thought. A dead end. Out of one box, into another.

Her mouth was parched. A fly or bee knocked against the window outside and reeled away. Soon it would be time for time to resume. The clock hands would be released. Freya must ring round Keir's brothers, their friends; the news would escape and be disseminated and claimed by all and sundry. Not quite yet. Let me have you to myself. You are mine. She lingered, prey to a pang of jealousy – a sensation so visceral that she gasped.

Eventually it had to be done.

First, open the window to let out Keir Fox's spirit.

A scent of wild garlic and freshly mown grass flowed through. Every bough in Whitethorn Wood across the village green was rocking. Blue-tits and bullfinches dipped and dived between the rippling greenery and the Crouches' bird feeder. Pigeons foraged under the feeder, scavenging what the songbirds dropped. The green lay awash with sunlight.

The guy next door was standing on the path, looking up. His name had completely escaped. With his index finger, he was tapping his top lip – perhaps surveying some suspect tile that had slipped. What's-his-name was a fussy man. Always feared the houses were subsiding, homeless strangers were invading the green, the wood was tainted by ash dieback. When his eyes met hers, Freya stepped backwards, dissolving away from his sight.

The eyes had been soft and ardent and sensitive, like an animal's.

Water, Storm. Come on. He bounded down the stairs ahead of Freya. There was food in his tray. He didn't touch it. But he drank; she drank.

*

Kind neighbours, Terry and Pam, ran Freya to the village, parking down a side-street where they'd wait for her. Their temperamental cat lay snoozing on the back seat. Take your time, dear, they said. Freya walked a couple of hundred metres to the funeral parlour.

Would the family care to place a teddy bear in their loved one's coffin, Mr Knott wondered – or some favourite sweets or tobacco? Many families, he said, gained comfort from this. Freya snorted with laughter.

She apologised and did her best to straighten her face.

'Not at all. I quite understand, Ms Fox. Grief does take us,' Mr Knott soothed, 'in all sorts of ways.'

In his profession, no doubt he saw a great deal of hysteria. Or provoked it, Freya thought, and it made her feel more lively to be entertained by him, in his own parlour, with the top hat in the window, a *prie dieu* and a giant bible open at God knows what. Mr Knott was attired like a boy doll. Freya admired his suit and waistcoat, his silver silk tie, his coiffure, his tan. He was just back, he'd explained, from his hols in the Canaries.

The parlour was stocked with lilies, which always gave her hay fever. Laughter morphed into a sneeze. Mr Knott took a step back.

And Ms Fox's instructions?

No to popping a keepsake in the coffin.

No to a frilled mantle for the deceased to wear. Or had he said mantilla? Definitely no to a mantilla.

No to supplying his best suit. Since Keir didn't possess a best suit or a suit of any description, that was an easy one.

Really, Freya explained, she just wanted simplicity. That had been the reason for the wicker coffin.

'I perfectly understand.' Mr Knott bowed his head. Many mourners preferred wicker, for its ecological advantages. Would Ms Fox like to commune now, with her husband?

He ushered her into the room where Keir was to be communed with. Floral wallpaper and subdued lighting. On the mantelpiece smirked a plaster Madonna, and alongside her lay a rosary. Freya scanned all this before approaching the tressel.

The person in the box was not Keir.

A pang of fear, then the rise in her throat of shocked laughter. For Mr Knott or his operative had plumped up Keir's face and rosied his cheeks. They'd filed his broken nails and painted them pink. The hollows and wrinkles of Keir's face had been filled out. Freya walked all round this artefact, seeking an angle that was not disconcerting. No such angle existed. A simulacrum had replaced her darling. It had made a mockery of Keir. Jesus! In her madness, Freya must have ordered the full cosmetic treatment. Was it offered as a package? She couldn't remember.

Freya laid her hand on the effigy's head and kissed the fridge-chilled lips. How pissed off you'd be with me for throwing money into this fucking pantomime, she thought.

And then she saw it: a life.

The life scurried across its host's wrist and halted. Freya coaxed it to mount her little finger. Instead it detoured, heading for Keir's knuckle, where it stopped again.

'There's nothing for you here,' Freya said aloud.

The life would run into Keir's sleeve and lose itself in mortuary chill. There was nothing off kilter about this concern for a speck of being. To veterans of Earth First, who'd met on the road protests, a miniscule life was precious. Freya grabbed a tissue from Mr Knott's box and edged the creature onto it, lifting it softly.

Freya brushed it off into a pot plant. There you go.

Leaving them both – the dead and the living – Freya stepped out into the glare of the main road. It was like coming from a film matinee into the shrill light of day. Or was she entering the film? Something was very wrong out here. Or back there. Or both. She started over the zebra crossing. Keir has left me, Freya thought. And been replaced by that impersonator. A sense of rejection struck hard. He had abandoned her. Even while she was ministering to him – night and day, day and night – all he'd been concerned with was that scribble he was doing on the wall. A flash of anger against Keir: you took my life with you. The anger was followed by a dark slick of guilt. Whatever should I feel angry about? You didn't choose to go.

From earliest days she'd been a rebel, bolshy, her own person. Keir was proud of her spirit: *Of the two of us, you're the strong one, no question.*

But that was then: before he took her life. In mid-stride, Freya's foot hung suspended. Stasis. The revving traffic ceased to roar. Everything stopped.

Some weird windmill now began to turn its blades in her mind, with incredible slowness. I have been here before, Freya thought, as the street was replaced by a dreamscape. Her foot was still raised. When would it come down? The people on the pavement ahead had all ceased to move, their errands cancelled. Skirts belled, cigarette smoke plumed. Was everyone looking at her? Yes, they'd all swivelled their necks to see what the stranger on the crossing would do next.

Now Freya was – without registering the process of having got there – on the other side, facing an ash tree. Ivy climbed the trunk but its stems had been cloven, to prevent it from overwhelming the tree. She smelt a tang of vegetation. The winding ropes on the ash trunk were just like the protruding veins on Keir's arms. The council workers had shorn right through. What right had they? It was not right.

Was something about to happen? Something apocalyptic? The blades in Freya's mind speeded up. A person in a blue coat flashed past her as if running from a bomb. She should find the neighbours' car before whatever it was that was threatening hit. But which way was the car? Who was her neighbour? Freya spun on her heels; the world whirled in the opposite direction.

But I'm not going to fall, she thought. Don't let go. Just a bit dazed, dizzy, dazzled. The world whirled. The whirl worlded. There was a smell of citrus. Very sour. Can lemons curdle?

At the edge of the park stood a wooden bench. Freya flopped down, leaned back and, closing her eyes, breathed deep, deep. The fugue-like state seemed to be passing. Was this the incapacitating thing (she wouldn't name its name) Freya had suffered from as a child?

Her neighbour, appearing out of nowhere, said, 'Oh, there you are, Freya dear.'

Yes, of course, she remembered now: Pam and Terry had brought her and would get her home safely. Oh, thank goodness. Terry helped her into the car. They'd have a nice hot cup of tea when they got home, Pammie said, and she'd baked some scones.

'It's very hard,' said Terry, starting the engine. He glanced at Freya's contorted face in the mirror. 'It's harder than we think we can bear. But we do get through. We do. You have a loving family, Freya, and caring neighbours.'

2

Scarlet was a startling colour to choose for a funeral. Maybe Freya would change before she left. Mark knotted his tie at the bedroom window, at an angle to the scene unfolding on her lawn. He looked out at dappled sunlight, shadows chasing shadows from the dancing woodland. Through the red ripple of her silk blouse, he could make out the contours of Freya's body – until one of the brothers-in-law obscured his view. Shift, Mark thought: come on, move. Any sighting of Freya was a chance to ponder and cherish her. The brother-in-law obliged, throwing a ball for the dog. The Labrador chased it listlessly, doubling back towards his mistress, ears flat to his head, tail low.

Freya's hair, it was astonishing: a river of glossy chestnut, flowing down her back. He pulled his phone from his jacket pocket. Mark couldn't miss this moment. One – two – three portraits. She was in process of turning, and he had Freya both in silhouette and three-quarters view. Beautiful, the lustre on Freya's face, the mourning in her long-lashed eyes.

I won't even glance at the pictures now, he decided; then I'll have a sad pleasure in store. It was all part of the chronicle of her life. Best to take no more photographs today, though, out of respect.

So would she change for the service, or not? She was not a creature of dour formalities. His dark suit had begun to feel morbid and insincere. The Freya in Mark's mind was persuasive, always: a hint from her could in a trice reverse life-long assumptions. Removing the tie altogether, with a kind of scorn, Mark unbuttoned his collar. The other mourners, apart from the aged, were not in black. We must reject these trappings of a socially obligatory sorrow. Mark sorted through his wardrobe. Yes, this blue shirt; open-necked, with that grey jacket, would work best. He began to change.

Out in the breeze-swept garden, the dog crouched low to the ground like a hunted creature, against his mistress's legs. Mark noted the sunny gloss on the lab's yellow back and on the woman's bare head. Wind lifted Freya's hair, swirled her blouse in sweet commotion. She was not speaking but the throng surrounded her in listening attitudes, like a court around a May queen. Keir Fox's thug brothers stood out by their tallness. They clustered around the nectar of their sister-in-law, who stood with folded arms, in her slippers, on the lawn. Those slippers must be drenched with dew. He imagined her bare feet.

I hear you weep, Mark told Freya inwardly, moving away from the pane and stepping into his trousers. Through our shared wall. Should the trousers be pressed though? Probably, yes. Removing them, Mark set up the ironing board where he could still keep watch. I hear you, Freya, when nobody else is near. I weep alongside you. And it seemed strange that nobody on Freya's lawn recognised the intimate understanding Mark had of his neighbour and how she was not alone – never would be alone, as long as he lived – with her grief.

When he looked again, the mourners had been joined by mutton dressed as lamb. The women wore flowers in their hair like hippies. Osteospermum, if he was not deceived, ochre, scarlet and white. Of course, he thought, as Freya bent her head to receive her own crown, I shouldn't judge: it may be a rather lovely idea, to turn the funeral into a kind of bridal. And of course, Keir Fox had been an environmentalist as well as a modestly talented and highly prolific artist.

Within the babble of this throng, Freya appeared abstracted. Mark read her carefully. Those folded arms defended her chest. He registered Freya's fractional wince from the women's gush and kisses. The dog read her too. It sidled round her calves, mutely reminding Freya: *he is not here but I am here*. Dogs mourned. Mark comprehended that. The Labrador was the key, he saw.

His love of dogs welled up: it all went back to Pearl, bless her.

Mark could not think of the spaniel without a pang of anguish. The loss, after decades, was never less than fresh.

Her silky, rust-red coat. Her gentle slobber. Her intelligent eyes.

He turned from the window and sat down on the bed. Tears overflowed and yet he also smiled, as if to Pearl, to calm and cheer her. She had taught Mark to be unafraid of animal smells despite his nervous susceptibility. But Pearl had shown him infinitely more. She'd nurtured him in the knowledge of the love of one being for another. Across the species barrier, two unloved creatures ministered to one another. Around the back yard of Gran's house, the walls had been a storey high. The clammy and shadowed earth lay in a black mass, sustaining only chickweed and henbit – and those, scantily. A washing line – on which nothing ever fully dried, for no wind reached it – stretched diagonally across the yard.

Out there Pearl had often been tethered, punished for some infringement of Gran's rules. Mark would slink out, wrapping his arms around her gentleness, removing her mess, tenderly feeding her filched biscuits from his palm.

*

Kindness encompassed Freya. It hemmed her in. You could not stem its urge to stampede your heart. It came uninvited, gate-crashing. Kindness assumed rights of guardianship over its victims.

They all claimed possession of Keir. And why shouldn't they? He had loved his friends and attracted so many. Friends, yes, and friends who had been lovers of his, and it had always been possible that they might be again. Keir's boundaries had been indistinct. Now it was as if each mourner had grabbed a garment of his, claiming it was Keir's favourite. Freya had seldom been jealous in her life, not really. She'd hardly known the meaning of the word. Now she seemed to have found out. But what was there to be jealous of?

I am living in a Perspex box, Freya thought. Everyone else is outside ...

... all except you, she thought. Storm nudged at her leg. Stooping to caress his head, Freya sank to her knees, enfolding him in her arms, skirt spread wide over the moist grass. Storm nosed into the dip between throat and clavicle. Amy, one of those who Keir had loved, bent down to her.

Get up, go away, Freya thought, with a fluey sensation. Don't come near me. Especially don't touch me. She felt like slapping the woman. As a kid, Freya had had a hot temper. Love had tamed her but now the temper seemed to want to come back.

Amy laid a hand on Freya's shoulder. The other cupped Freya's elbow, to induce her to rise. Amy's eyes were red. Just beyond Amy stood Rae and her little girl, Freya's niece. Haf, at almost four, had the look of an adorable demon, vital, smouldering. She appeared nothing like Jamie, the only fair Fox brother, and nothing like her older siblings. *She's a one-off job,* Keir had said fondly. Freya's eyes fastened on the child, her dark shock of hair, her comical eyebrows, and the thought went through her: *Keir loved you.*

She allowed herself to rise; stepped away from Amy. She'd heard Amy explain her yellow dress by stating that Keir had adored that yolky colour. Oh, Freya thought, so you decided to come dressed as an egg? She smiled but it was not a nice smile.

They would have a cup of tea, Jack said.

Yasmin had brought cookies. She'd made them herself, hoped they were not over-baked; they were all, so to speak, individually shaped cookies, you might call them rustic. Or you might call them a mess.

Freya could better bear this prattle than the proximity of weepy Amy. And, of course, she'd worn that dress when Keir painted her portrait. Rae stood looking over Amy's shoulder at Freya with a face of humorous sympathy, which she could tolerate, for they went back and back, to earliest childhood. Rae's little girl reached timid, and then proprietorial, hands to stroke Storm's back.

'Mine!' said Haf. 'My dog!'

They had an hour, said Jamie, before they needed to leave.

An eternal hour! To occupy the same cramped room as her old friends, who were looking concernedly at Freya's skirt. Why was she wearing a fucking skirt anyway? Why hadn't she stuck with her usual jeans and gone as herself? The skirt was blotched with wet from the grass and the slobber that was Stormie's contribution. She did not care. What did it matter how she looked? What had it ever mattered? But something had come unstuck and Freya was no longer sure if appearances might be all we had. The wilder life she and Keir had lived together – and it had been a life, they had not been half-alive – was under assault and shrinking.

Of course they all loved him, as how could they not? Her true self was glad they did.

As she moved towards the house, Freya looked up, to recognise her lonely neighbour looking down. He met her eyes and placed one palm flat against the window pane.

*

With Terence and Pamela Crouch, Mark positioned himself directly behind the family pews and apart from the ageing hippies. Who knew what ancient crumbs lodged in the thickets of their beards? Several were local artists of minor gifts and reputation. These he would be giving a wide berth. A melancholy folk singer strummed and sang about tea and oranges that came all the way from China.

Mark heard Pamela instruct her chubby husband, 'Now, don't forget, Terry – a few words but do not, for goodness' sake, go overboard.'

Actually, Mark thought, favour us with no words whatever, please, Terence. He frowned sidelong at the screed his neighbour produced from his pocket and smoothed out. Not that Terence needed a script to support his flux of benign garrulity.

Behind Keir Fox's wicker coffin, the mourners advanced: Freya with her gangsterish brothers-in-law, the flower women, tiny tots, a teenage boy crucified with embarrassment, elderly relatives. They slid

15

into the front pews. Light from an arched window gilded Freya's hair. She was so near him. If he leaned forward, Mark could breathe on her neck. On either side sat a brother-in-law – twin book-ends oppressing a single precious volume. Himmler and Heydrich on a bad hair day, he thought, a high quiff and bald sides in the latest neo-Nazi style.

The folk singer completed his dirge and there was a gradual hush. Nothing happened. No priest or leader of any persuasion popped up. Perhaps a Quaker would appear and inaugurate an hour of speechlessness. Mark imagined the body of Keir Fox in that wicker basket, then he banished the disturbing thought. The thought walked around the coffin and reappeared.

Of course, human silence, Mark thought, is relative. People fidget and cough. Toddlers start toddling. And someone was whispering behind him. Swivelling, he glared into disconcerting eyes of milky blue: an aged face like the Brecon Beacons from the air, all ridges and wrinkles.

Freya rose and walked to the front. Mark put forth waves of tenderness, to enclose her in his devotion, as he did constantly, unseen, but it was as if the pity of the massed congregation rushed forward and fenced her off from him. Tears stood in Mark's eyes.

In a clear voice, Freya thanked everyone for coming to celebrate the life of Keir; it meant everything to her. They weren't here to mourn but to rejoice, she told them, with her voice breaking. Keir hadn't believed in a traditional God but he'd been a child of Gaia, the earth, our mother, and he had gone home to her now, where he belonged. He'd left his paintings as a legacy. There would be an exhibition. If anyone else would like to speak, she hoped they would do so. Returning to her seat, Freya melted into tears. Her back quivered. Mark yearned to settle his hands on her shoulders and just gently press down in reassurance.

Freya's courage and dignity overwhelmed him. If only he possessed a tithe of that dignity. Of course, he had spoken at Lily's funeral, in this same space, eloquently. Perhaps too eloquently, he realised now, and certainly his scripted eulogy had gone on too long.

The whole ceremony had been majestic, packed out with her fellow musicians, a music critic from the *Guardian,* the entire staff of the college of music where Lily had trained. A string quartet had played a transcription of Taneyev's Adagio in C. Mark had created a floral display in the shape of a viola, using a glory of roses he'd grown in the garden at Tŷ Hafan ... he'd harvested the lot ... to make amends ... if in any way he had been at fault ... but he had not been at fault. No. Put the word *amends* back where it belongs, he told himself. The plunge into an abyss lay one step ahead of this word. What had he done, for which he needed to atone? And in any case Freya had released him from this perdition.

Mark shrank from a dangerous edge and, with a sweep of his fingers, brushed dust from the narrow shelf on the pew ahead.

Suffice it to say that Lily's funeral had been grandiose. Freya, by contrast, simply offered a few words from the heart – and that, Mark saw, was the way to do it. It was not too late to learn, even after thirty-nine years in this world.

Well, he'd made two mistakes with women. Lily Himmelfarb and Danielle Jones. Lily was gone and he'd shortly be sending Danielle on her way. But Freya – she was another order of being.

'Wonderful lady,' whispered his companion, leaning shoulder against shoulder.

What did Terence Crouch know of Freya? Sure, he shared the other party wall with her. But that was as far as it went. Mark gave Terence a small, sad smile, which was returned.

One by one, mourners came forward and rambled on about the virtues of the body in the wicker crate. A more original and brilliant soul you could never meet. Sense of humour. Social conscience. Lover of wildlife and trees and bees. Green. Red. Fine husband, caring uncle, faithful friend, *nonpareil* painter. The speakers brought with them pouches of tedious anecdote. Not one had a clue about public speaking but at least they kept it short.

Then the flower woman dressed as a buttercup upped and raved. Oh please.

Gripping a sodden hanky, she sobbed out that she'd known Keir from their second year at primary school. Since the age of six, they'd been *so* close. Keir and she had shared *all* their secrets. They believed they were *telepathic*. They had exchanged *curtain rings*! And Keir was the kind of lovely guy who never forgot or dropped you ... if he loved you, he loved you for life ... this was how he was: open-hearted and generous-spirited ...

Yes, thought Mark: promiscuous.

... you felt he kept a place in his heart for you ... all his *life* ... even after his *death* ... he had left her an aura of *love* ...

Preposterously, Buttercup raved on and on. He could have wrung her neck. It seemed to him that a rustle of discomfort spread, on Freya's behalf, as Buttercup milked her moment in the limelight, staking her claim. Mark was aware of Pamela Crouch digging at her husband with a vicious elbow. What was Terence supposed to do? Rush forward and make a citizen's arrest?

... they'd gone to *Africa* together; they'd suffered *malaria* together; they'd ...

Mark did not wish to learn what else this pair of prats had done together. He coughed, challengingly.

... they'd camped on a *farm* in Devon when they were *seventeen* and the farmer had delivered a bottle of milk straight from the *cow* and they'd washed in a *freshwater* stream ... and most importantly, they'd painted together, she had been his *Muse* ... well, one of his Muses ... and, in a real way, Keir's fellow-artist ... a privilege ... oh, the conversations they'd had about Art ...

Mark coughed again, with more expression. How must Freya be feeling, under this cloud of implication? Her lovely head was down; one could only imagine her expression.

... of course he was a free *spirit*, Keir, he had no use for forms and formalities, he went his own *way*, he did not believe in certificated emotion, he told me many times he didn't really believe in marriage ....

Someone must head her off. There was a rustling discomfort in the body of the congregation. Terence, goaded by his wife, made a jerky motion as if to stand, but Mark had the advantage of his position at the end of the row. He half rose to his feet and put up his hand.

'Excuse me...'

A baby cried out. Someone in the body of the hall shushed either Mark, Buttercup or the baby. Mark found himself striding to the front. The speaker hesitated, flushed angrily to the roots of her blonded hair. I'll faint, Mark thought. No, I'll do this for dearest Freya. He murmured as he passed that he was sorry to interrupt her reflections but time was short. Buttercup gave way, looking concussed, and faltered back to her seat. Job done, he thought.

Turning, Mark took in the massed eyes of the congregation, Freya's in particular. She looked at him with, he was sure, surprised gratitude. Now Mark's loving intimacy must find a form worthy of her.

'Just a few, a *very* few words,' Mark promised, clearing his throat. 'By one who is frankly the least qualified to speak about our dear friend. Freya's neighbours could not allow the occasion to pass without a word being said concerning the dear and good man we were privileged to know – over the garden hedge as it were, by the Crouches on the one side and myself on the other. I speak for all of us,' he insisted, to deter Terence.

But what to say? Mark's heart stampeded; sweat beaded his upper lip. In his panic, he lost touch with the dead man's name.

And then it came to him: he remembered Freya speaking the name so movingly in the gallery café, when she told him that her husband was not well – *Keir, Keir* – he was terminally ill – *Keir* – and oh the music of her voice – *Keir!* – it was as if Mark heard it now.

'Our neighbour, *Keir*,' Mark said, with expressive feeling. 'We speak a name, don't we?' He paused. 'And a person answers. From now on, when we name *Keir*, nobody will respond. But souls live on – and here I am quoting the great George Eliot – souls live on in perpetual echoes.'

He looked round the audience with tender enquiry. Tears stood in Mark's eyes as he heard the pure truth he was speaking, or that was speaking through him.

'In the end, isn't the reality rather simple? Freya's Keir was a good man. Kind. Plain-dealing. Famous he may have been, in artistic and environmental circles – but from everything I witnessed and that Freya has told me, Keir Fox's feet were firmly on the ground of Mother Earth. We valued and trusted Keir Fox as our neighbour and we know we can never replace him.'

Mark's heart was wonderfully eased once he'd started to simplify, adapting his remarks to the capacity of the hearers. But simplicity leads to truth, he told himself.

Mark's proved to be the final eulogy before a brother-in-law – the one he thought of as Reinhard Heydrich, the Butcher of Prague – explained that Keir would be carried out for private family interment. Later a birch sapling would be planted over him and snowdrops and daffodil bulbs. The lovely people gathered here were invited to a gathering at Freya's next-door neighbours, Terry and Pammie Crouch. Freya and family looked forward to seeing everyone there.

Mark sat trembling with elation. I had them all eating out of my hand, he thought. Out. Of. My. Hand. He reproved himself: this was not what it was all about. Of course it wasn't. It was about darling Freya – her peace of mind. In a small way, he had helped ease her ordeal.

As they stood to file out, Terence rather generously murmured, 'Thanks for speaking on our behalf, Mark. I think you said it all. Trusted neighbour, good man. You put your finger on it. In fact all the tributes were grand.'

Mark pumped Terence's hand. He forgave all the chap's foibles. The plump little fellow had no sins. He was an innocent. And after all, people do their best. They mean well. They really do. Mostly. We are all human beings, he reminded himself. Greater apes, a little lower than the angels. Tears sparked. Tears for Keir Fox; for Mozart stricken in his prime; for Keats' tuberculosis, and for Schubert's venereal disease (though this affliction might prudently have been avoided).

He queued to exchange a few words with Freya: best to confine himself to a restrained hug, brushing her cheek with his lips. Was that the next funeral, assembling in the car park? Let them wait.

'Now, if there's *anything* I can do, my dear,' some female was gushing. Oh, get on with it, Mark thought. 'Just email me. Text. Phone. Knock on the door. Any time, day or night. Promise?'

'We're going to shoot off, Mark, to organise the eats,' confided Terence. 'Bless her, Freya looks so tired. Want to come along?'

Freya did look tired. But Mark was not about to forfeit the fruits of his public witness.

'No thanks, Terence. I need the walk. Good of you to offer.'

'Righty-oh. See you shortly.'

Not if I see you first.

Patiently, Mark edged closer to Freya, content to muse on her lovely face and await his turn. She stood erect to her not very tall height. His heart tumbled over. At the same time, there was a pang of stage fright. Should he just bolt and catch up with Terence?

My turn. Crumpling of face. Oh no. Transient gripping of hands. Brief kiss on her hot cheek. Could have kissed her lips but he'd chastely swerved. A glimpse of eyes glittering but focused somewhere past him, or not focused at all.

So kind of you, Mark, to speak those memorable words about Keir. I did appreciate it.

And then he was jostled forward. *Memorable*, he thought: she will remember. That was manna in his wilderness.

The mourners milling on the steps parted to make way as Mark emerged into the brilliance of daylight. He stopped dead, deafened by light. Everyone had stepped back when he appeared. Shunning him. No, of course not. They were showing respectful awareness of Dr Mark Heyward's helpful role in the ceremony.

But the inner voice spoke up: you carry a stigma, it reminded

21

him, always have, always will. I am alone, Mark panicked. I am condemned and cast out. Condemned to survive. Condemned to live in isolation. And now I have made a fool of myself in a public place. He'd been alone from the beginning, abandoned, betrayed, aborted, belittled.

*

Recovering, Mark watched them embrace her, all around, shepherding Freya towards the burial place. A Highlander in Stuart tartan was leading Keir Fox in his wicker home across the interment site, followed by widow, gangsters, gangsters' molls and offspring, and the apparent contents of a care home, complete with a Macmillan nurse in uniform.

He recognised the theme from the New World Symphony, second movement. 'Going Home'.

If Freya had only asked him, Mark would willingly have played a lament for her – for them all – on his oboe. She must often have overheard him practising. He liked to think that Freya listened secretly, receiving the messages he sent through reed and fingertips. The oboe produced just as moving a sound as a bagpipe. Bag, reed, chanter and drone: frankly, who needs all that kit? Way over the top, for the intimate loss his neighbour had sustained. Besides, *pibrochs* and suchlike Scottish music had connotations both kitschy and militaristic, recalling marches, cabers being tossed and sword dances by men in ballet shoes. Even so, Mark was moved by the pipe music, which seemed to call to him – except that it also excluded him, since he had not been invited to attend the private interment.

He drifted in the wake of the procession and hovered at a respectful distance, in the dappled shade of a silver birch.

The body was lowered into the pit. Handfuls of earth, followed by the women's floral crowns, showered down. The birch sapling stood in its pot, ready for planting. This would obviously not happen today. Someone produced champagne and the circle drank to Keir. The mourners laughed and cried; they told stories and uncorked a second bottle. Mark's throat was dry with a thirst that could be quenched by nothing as cheap as champagne.

'My dear wife is dead,' he'd told Freya that day in the gallery café. 'I'm a widower. I have been somewhere near the place where you are standing now.'

Her heart-melting concern stayed with Mark; it had initiated the bond between them. He hadn't made a drama of it. This wasn't about him. He simply wanted Freya to know that he understood.

'My wife was called Lily,' he'd confided, a catch in his voice, so that the name divided into two parts.

'What a lovely name, Mark,' Freya had said gently, laying her palm for a moment over his hand.

'Yes. Thank you. It suited her. Short for Lilith. Lily was a viola player of rare gifts. There are recordings on the internet.'

'I'll look out for them,' Freya had managed to say, thoughtful for others even as she reeled under the shock of her husband's diagnosis.

Now Mark made his quiet way through the Victorian and Edwardian necropolis of detached homes, monuments over which beeches swayed their canopies and blackbirds sang. Pre-Raphaelite angels strummed lyres and pondered books. The wind winnowed their stony hair. It was a delicious cemetery, especially now in the daffodil season.

Mark looked away, as he had taught himself to do, from the area where Lily lay. Her name passed across his mind like a breeze, and was gone.

Twin columns of cypress marked a central path and, walking down the slope between them, you felt you were in Italy. Mark had never visited Italy; would probably never go, although how difficult could Italian be to a Latinist? If he chose to, Mark could pick up the rudiments of Italian in a fortnight flat. But you had to travel to Rome first and the thought of flight made him squeamish. Then you'd have to stay somewhere, surrounded by strangers of all hues, subject to their conversations in the corridor, their television sets booming through the walls. In Rome, you'd need to wear a 'bum bag' and look out for pickpockets. Ordering a meal would be a trial of nerve, let alone the embarrassment of eating it in public.

But a new life was beckoning. So much was possible. With Freya at his side, Mark's shyness would slacken its hold. She'd accompany him onto the plane, chatting lightly, without the least idea that he was phobic. They'd sit side by side, holding hands, the contact reassuring him. Her naturalness and excitement would secure him – or at least, to be realistic, it would diminish the terror of leaving the earth. Once they alighted in Rome or Florence, Mark would be in his element, introducing Freya to classical monuments and Renaissance art works; deciphering them for her. He could foresee the wonder in her eyes.

It was midday and the cypresses cast no shadows. Their spicy scent remained with him even when he climbed into the car and buckled up. The thought of Italy possessed him, with a sense of new freedom, to love, grow, travel.

But the wake was the next step. Terence's wife had prepared the food, so the fare would be sloppy and digestible.

3

Oh, the relief to be free of the crush; to kick off her ridiculous high heels; close the door upon everyone, saying she would change her clothes and settle Storm, and be at the party within half an hour. It's a party, she told herself, not a wake.

Freya had altogether lost touch with her sociable side. I saw him through, I saw him across the threshold, she reminded herself. I'm bound to be drained. It's normal, it's natural. Apart from a dash to the shops or an hour at a café, I was with Keir every moment. Bear that in mind. Freya had given up work as a mechanic at the bike shop without a qualm. But there'd been times when she'd inwardly dissociated from Keir. It hurt and shamed her now to think how she'd recoiled from his skeletal frame. But why be ashamed? She'd kept going until the end – beyond the end – when the dilated pupils no longer queried the great enigma of everything and Keir fled back down the labyrinth of his perishing brain to a final explosion of light, and then nothing.

Freya herself had no face left. Keir had stripped it off in his delirium and taken it with him.

But there were things you had to do after the end, faceless or not. A rigmarole of rituals. Too much talking. There were times when you wanted to blurt, *Fuck off, the lot of you!* Where did that anger come from, especially towards those Freya had loved for so long? She took a deep breath. Be fair, she told herself, be grateful to the folk who go out of their way to support you – lovely people, sincere. You didn't know – until you lost your centre – how people cluster round. Folk you'd never really thought of as friends, people you'd laughed at, even, caricatured and privately belittled. And those people – especially the neighbours on both sides – had been more comfort to Freya than some of their old friends, most of whom Keir had slept with in his time.

Yet that had been with Freya's consent. She'd also been free to love and she had loved. This had never been an issue. Not overtly, anyway. It was part of the agreement you made, the balance between you. After her degree in geological engineering and several years with an environmental consultancy, Freya had left to work from home as a mechanic. It had been her own choice: to be close to Keir, to support his art. *I am my own master,* she'd once informed Amy, who didn't disguise her contempt for women who dwindled into wives.

She wouldn't mind if she never saw Amy again. Bug-eyed Amy. Forever finger-combing her frizzy blonde hair. Amy the mouth. Amy the Muse.

Freya's eyes closed of their own accord. Almost at once she jerked awake. Someone hovering above her had passed a familiar hand across her forehead and brushed the hair back from her temples. Freya looked round.

And woke up.

Apparently she had not been awake the first time she'd awoken. How odd. Now she was. The tender visitor had that second left the room. She'd glimpsed his coat whisking away round the door to the kitchen, just as her eyelids parted. Why was he wearing a winter coat in this balmy weather?

You can get summer flu, she thought, and shivered.

Freya peered into the kitchen. All remained as she'd left it, but atilt and rocking. A smell of rotting fruit, not pleasant, hung in the air and seemed to become more pungent. She glanced in the bowl, which contained fresh kiwis and bananas Rae had brought. *You must eat, dearest.* Rae was lovely. (Had he slept with her too, *because* she was lovely? And not told Freya, which would be breaking their rule of candour and openness? Don't think like that, forget that). Amy didn't matter. Never had mattered. Amy had said, *Keir didn't believe in marriage.* How dare she? And yet that was true, in a way, of both Keir and Freya. But did Amy have to say it? Did she really have to, when one had lost a layer of skin and there was no membrane left between yourself and the world?

26

But, Rae – why did you? Perhaps you didn't. Rae, you are mine, and lovely. And loyal. I will believe that. Rae and Freya were woven into one another's lives.

Of course there was nobody with Freya in the house, there'd been nobody. How could there be? Storm, asleep in his basket, drooling slightly – was he dreaming too? – would have barked the place down if anyone had got in. Even so, Freya couldn't rid herself of the conviction that Keir *had* been here, watching over her. As he would have done, had she been the one doing the dying.

Or would he be committing adultery in the next room?

Of course not. Where did that hellish thought come from? It was not a language they spoke – of marital rules and certificated emotions.

I'm not myself, Freya thought. How would I be, with you in the earth? Humming came from next door, where the wake was starting up. A *wake*? What did that mean? How could you *wake* twice from the same sleep? A nest of sleeps. Her fuddled brain invented specious dilemmas. Not thinking straight. Everything skewed out of true. Freya splashed water onto her face. The stupid mascara ran. A clown's face. Looking in the mirror was like ogling her reflection in a spoon. Wipe it all off then, the cosmetic mask. That was not Freya. My face always looks better naked anyway, she thought. Keir said so.

He should know. Don't cake your skin in muck, he'd said, holding her face between his hands and caressing with his thumbs. Just don't. You of all people don't need disguise. Just be you, Frey. Keir hadn't needed cosmetic enhancement either. But Mr Knott had believed otherwise. He'd plumped out Keir's face and rouged his cheeks, he'd pinked Keir's nails. Keir had not been permitted to appear as an honest corpse.

Keir would have been forensically interested in the planes and textures of his dead face. He had no preoccupation with prettiness.

Next door, the Crouches' sitting-room was warmer than Freya was used to, and overcrowded. Her head swam. The framed watercolour of a fawn gazed with eyes of reproach. Where was its

27

mother, the fawn seemed to ask. Has she been shot? Was it you who took her? Have you eaten her?

An obese golden Buddha kept company on the mantelpiece with a crucifix Terry had whittled and a garish statue of Ganesh, the elephant god. Folk of all creeds, and in varying degrees of need, turned up at the Crouches' door and were made welcome. Terry had left his ministry at an evangelical church to become a kind of lay preacher. Occasionally Freya would catch through the wall a droning that rose and fell and rose again: a circle of prayerful people chanting in Terry's ecumenical sitting-room.

Alex brought a glass of red wine. 'Knock it back, Frey. Keir's favourite red. We're all with you. Have a peanut. Where's Storm?'

'He's in his basket. Snoring away. No peanut, thanks.'

'You OK, sis?' Alex bent and kissed her cheek. He was the Fox who least resembled Keir.

'Fine. Tired.' Why was he calling her sis? Never had before. Presumably reassuring Freya that the link with her brothers-in-law was unbroken. She had no family of her own except her half-sister in Australia.

'Well, you look lovely,' Alex said gallantly. 'What have you done to your face?'

'Taken it off. Why?'

'You look so young.'

Sleeplessness didn't help. At night, in their home, poor Storm could not sleep and so, of course, Freya had even less of a chance. Keir's pet loped around their house, searching. It had been ten days but presumably the beloved scent still lingered and Storm must track the trail until it ran out. In truth, this was only a version of what Freya was doing, hoarding smears, cup-marks, fingerprints. Every night she conserved the traces of Keir that imprinted him upon their home. She could not bring herself to wash the glass that bore his last lip-print. And if this was so for Freya, what did the forest of intimate smells mean to Storm? The essence of the human body informed the dog: he is here, search him out.

Except that this bouquet of sweat and urine was also the smell of fetor, evidence of Storm's beloved's death. She should do some cleaning when she got home. It was her fault that Storm was kept on the edge of his senses.

'Do you want to sit down?' asked Jamie.

'No, I can stand.' Freya had come down off the stilts of her high heels and stood to her full five-foot-two in flats. So that was a gain in steadiness, she thought. I am earthed. When I go back, I must look at that wall. I must examine it. For you were trying to leave a message. You saw something, Keir, dreadful or consoling, and wanted me to know. At that stage, at the end of everything, there was no language. At least, not the language we use as common currency. There was – it seemed a peculiar thing to think – art. Keir had been trying to draw something on the wall. Some final statement, a message from the edge, and if anyone could interpret it, surely she could?

Pammie, with a tray of bakes, urged Freya to eat – just a little something, a vol-au-vent? Or a mini-quiche? They were home-made, she explained. They were tiny and would slip down easily. But no, thanks, Freya couldn't stomach anything. I have closed down, Freya thought, my body is trying to follow Keir's. Later, perhaps.

Amy was a red-eyed waif across the room. Blessings upon the head of Mark Heyward for seeing her off at the funeral. He'd gone straight for her like a human hornet. My God, Freya thought, if Mark hadn't stopped her, she'd still be waffling on, staking her claim to Keir. Rewriting history, with Amy as Keir's true but tragic wife and Freya some kind of homespun stand-in, useful for bringing in a regular income to support his raving genius.

She was angry with Keir for encouraging this yellow parasite. Or at least, not discouraging her. Keir was soft. He could be vain.

The way Mark had knocked Amy off her perch had been inspired – nearly as funny as the march of Mr Knott, as he swaggered down the crescent ahead of the cortège in his topper, swinging a stick. And she'd wondered, choking with black mirth as the car crept along, if Mr Knott intended to perform this death dance all the way? Not on your life. Time is money. Once he was out of the crescent, he'd hopped into a car.

And you too, Rae, with your sad Madonna smile. How can I bear you to be so near? She wanted to push Rae away, hard.

She remembered Keir saying, *Rae has inner beauty.*

And *Yasmin has tender eyes.*

All she remembered his saying about the eternally lurking Amy, was, *Poor Amy is so needy.* It was not said without love. He loved you, Amy, Freya thought, and I should love you for his sake, and because you too have lost an anchor.

But I don't.

She glimpsed Mark Heyward in conversation with Pammie. A shyly awkward man, elbows tight to his sides, holding a sausage roll and not eating it. But shy is deep, she thought. She'd seen what it cost him to speak so movingly about Keir. Torment, almost. And yet, with his profession, he must be used to public speaking.

'I need the *toilet*!'

Nobody paid attention to the urgent young voice.

'Mummy, I do, I *need* the toilet! I need it *now*!' Haf tugged at her mother's jacket.

Rae bent to her daughter. 'OK, sweetpea, but we just went, didn't we? Twice!'

'Well, I want to go again.'

'Hey, ask me, ask Daddy!' Jamie said, squatting down in front of her. 'It's my turn. What are daddies for?'

'No!' Haf beetled her brows at Jamie. 'Not you, Daddy.'

'OK. You're the boss.' Easy-going, Jamie went with the flow, as usual.

There must be times, Freya thought, when even Rae's composure cracks. She remembered her sister-in-law in her earlier incarnation as an ambitious lawyer: hard to credit now. Rae had laid it all aside for children and unpaid work for *Ecology Now*. Keir, not particularly close to his sister-in-law before she'd quit her high-powered job, had afterwards often been round at Jamie's. He'd played with the little ones in the garden; enjoyed long, deep chats with Rae.

About what? Freya had never thought to ask. Rae was quiet, reserved with most people. *All my life I've had long, deep chats with Rae too*, thought Freya, *but what were yours about?*

Rae has inner beauty.

Haf gave up tugging at Rae's jacket and took to yanking at her skirt. *Children are law-givers*, Freya thought, *keeping us in order. Could I ever have been a mother? Was it even in me? I had only the one glimpse, and it lasted three days. Mothering changes you in every cell*, someone had said. *It ripens you. I'll never know now. If you'd been ours, little Haf – if you had – if only you had, and you could have been, or someone like you – Keir would have painted with you, read with you, taken you climbing in Whitethorn Wood, sea-swimming, kayaking. He'd have been a great dad, as he always wanted to be. Perhaps he'd have laid off the wine, stopped smoking, in time for his lungs to recover.*

But she wouldn't think of Larch now.

Haf raised her arms, waggled her fingers to be picked up. She looked so much like Keir in that moment that Freya was haunted. *What was it about her? The eyes. The searching eyes.*

'Hey, why don't I take you, poppet?' Freya suggested, crouching and opening her arms to her niece. A visit to the loo would bring a brief respite from the gathering, an interlude. 'I'd really, really like to. We could do our special dance in the bathroom.'

'Not Auntie Freya! No! Auntie Freya's got *deaded*!'

'Don't be silly, Haf.' Rae looked appalled. 'Sorry, Frey. She doesn't understand. We tried to explain.'

Deaded is about it, Freya thought. 'It's fine, Rae. Of course she doesn't.'

How could children possibly begin to understand? You wouldn't want them to. *But they see the holes in us*, she thought, *they braille-read our scar tissue, they register our fibs and fictions.*

Out of the corner of her eye, Freya followed mother and daughter as they left the room. Haf's small, strong arms snared her mother's neck; her whole body clung to Rae's, as if its chief desire was to clamber back in and reunite fully and completely with her source.

Freya made her way to Amy, pityingly, because no one was speaking or listening to her after her exhibition at the funeral. But was it even her fault? The loveliness of Keir – his originality, his giftedness and humanity – had spread a patina of glamour all around him. Amy had tried to show them in her eulogy that she was covered in fairy dust. And that she was worthy of this lustre.

'What you said was very nice, Ames,' Freya told their friend. 'And I know how fond Keir always was of you.'

Nice and *fond* didn't seem to cut it with Amy. She looked quite affronted. Mortified. *Fond* undermined the claim Amy had tried to stake. But *fond* was all Amy was going to get. And a hug and a businesslike pat, for good measure.

That's you sorted, Freya thought. Who's next? She became embroiled in the giving and receiving of commiserations and anecdotes. So sorry for your loss. So sad, so young. We all loved Keir. Battling cancer. Brave. His pictures. He pruned our trees; it was an art he had, Keir was amazing. Great comrade in the road protests. Fabulous mural he did for us. Time, they say, heals. When my mum died. He should have been on *Gardeners' World*. Once he said to me—

I am not really here, Freya thought. I have left me somewhere else. Next door.

Rae reappeared, daughter in her arms. Haf announced to the whole room, 'I didn't really want to go!'

Laughter. Oh, the darling! Riding high, Haf scanned around, from pride of place, confident in her little drama. Freya registered the resemblance to Keir again, quite clearly. The large eyes, the roundedness of the forehead, that thatch of thick, dark hair, done up in a topknot. And especially the singular arch of the eyebrows.

*

Altogether too many brats. What were they doing at a funeral anyway? You kept tripping over them, especially after the second glass of wine. He never drank at lunchtime.

Pamela circulated with a tray of egg-and-cress sandwiches, cut into triangles. Behind her came Jean or Joan with Kettle Chips, followed by Joan or Jean bearing miniature sausage rolls. Mark helped himself to a sandwich and a roll. The miniature sandwich posed no problem but, raising the sausage roll to his lips, Mark's hands trembled and the attempt failed. It was no joke being paralysed by nerves. All his life it had been the same. Perhaps back away into a corner and swallow it there or deposit the damn thing on a window-sill. There didn't seem to be an unoccupied corner or window-sill. Why not replace it on the silver tray as Joan or Jean bustled by? But they were bustling elsewhere. Mark's horizons shrank to the dimensions of the sausage roll.

'You don't fancy it?' Pamela asked, drawing attention to his misery.

'Pardon?'

'The sausage roll?'

'Oh. Well. Yes. Delightful. Is it vegetarian?'

'Ah, you're a veggie, Mark? Or even a vegan? Dear Keir was not a meat-eater either, was he? *Our* view is that – as long as the animal was happy, and killed humanely –'

'But how do we know that the sausage-to-be was killed humanely, Pamela?'

Now they were both staring at the sausage roll as if willing it to speak.

'I had a very good discussion with Keir about the animals,' Pamela went on.

'Ah?'

'One could speak to Keir directly. Without beating about the bush. He was that kind of person, wasn't he, so much natural

33

courtesy, he could listen. I remember saying that I'm a simple soul and reality is reality.'

Amen to both those propositions, Mark thought, especially the first – and said, 'It certainly is.'

The sausage roll approached his mouth hopefully – but there it faltered, shedding a shower of flakes. Mark's face burned. It was humiliating to be standing here with this half-baked bun of a woman, who went on to inform him of what the Book of Genesis said about man exercising lordship over the animals.

'But we must exercise our lordship in a respectful and humane way, as Scripture tells us,' she concluded.

Pamela was annoying Mark now. He itched. In point of fact he was not a vegetarian but this was provocation. The hell of self-consciousness needling him built towards explosion. He'd managed to agree that Keir was courteous. And then Mark lost it.

'I'm just wondering, Pamela, which version of Scripture you read?' He'd started, so he'd finish. Big mistake, but the fountain of rhetoric would keep gushing. 'One of these semi-modern translations that has abolished all the poetry (and what is the Bible if it isn't poetry?) and rewritten it in words of one syllable adapted, *some* have suggested, to the intelligence of above-average chimpanzees?'

Pamela gasped and took a step back – but stared in fascination from pale eyes at her next-door neighbour-but-one.

Mark strove to collect himself. He hadn't intended to go off like a rocket, but social awkwardness and the company of asses, not to mention personal grief, had been too much for him.

'Well,' remarked Pamela rather mildly. 'I don't know about the chimpanzees.'

'Oh, my goodness, I didn't mean present company, Pamela! No indeed! I was quoting, of course.'

'Quoting?'

'Richard Dawkins. A late flowering of Darwinism.'

'Aren't you going to eat that?'

It was all Mark could do not to stuff the wretched item of

delicatessen down the collar of her cream jacket. Then he was aware of Freya across the room, looking towards him with those beautiful eyes. Oh dear. But she couldn't have overheard. He hadn't raised his voice. And Pamela's dumbfounded look was an expression her face often wore. It was her default, you could say. The situation was retrievable.

Seeing Freya there, as if people had parted to reveal her, was like hearing a phrase of music through a hubbub of meaningless clamour. All around her, the guests chatted. Mark saw clearly how solitary his darling was – and exposed, like himself – as she approached the Buttercup woman, and charitably embraced her. I see what you're doing, he chuckled inwardly: you're quenching her fire. Freya was intelligent and, like him, did not tolerate fools gladly.

He found himself taking a casual bite and chewing it. Rather tasty. Herbs? Rosemary? He'd have another. Freya had done him good, as she always did.

'Well, it's excellent to have a dialogue, Pamela,' he said, detaining Pamela, as she made a motion to slip away. 'A dialectic. You know what I mean. A bit of good-humoured polemic never hurt anyone. And I always felt – you are so right – that Keir understood that principle. Of dialectic.'

Pamela seemed more floored by this Socratic point of view than by the chimpanzees. And after all what was the woman but (as she herself seemed freely to acknowledge) a well-meaning soul with pouched marsupial cheeks and powder in her wrinkles? Why be hard on her? Mark began to fawn. He was lucky, he said, to have such excellent neighbours – and dear Keir had often mentioned what generous neighbours the Crouches were. He quoted Keir to the effect that you could rely on Pammie and Terry Crouch for anything; they were kindness personified. In point of fact, Mark had never addressed Keir on any topic, since the poor fellow had been ill and practically bedbound since before he'd moved in.

Pamela swayed, bemused.

Mark asked her about the delightful brooch, shaped like a cello, on her velvet lapel and remarked that the cello was, of all instruments, the nearest to the human voice. Although the viola came a close second. His dear wife had been a musician. Did Pamela play herself? Was she, like Mark, an ardent music-lover? He smiled at Pamela with all his teeth.

From now on, Mark promised himself to defer to everyone on every subject. This was the only way. It was exhausting to be forever sponging one's own verbal vomit off other people's lapels.

And besides (he felt himself flip from one side of his mind to the other), these were lovely people. Salt of the earth. And some of them were intelligent too. The tall woman with her sandy hair swept back from her face was elucidating some nuance of international ecological law to a circle of dunces. *Ecological integrity* was invoked, *ecological debt*. Only it turned out that the listeners were not dunces. The fellow with the grey pony tail and the frayed jeans, for instance, was saying something about the natural resources of the Philippines. It was a valid concept, he said; very valid.

What was valid, Mark did not learn. Terence arrived, offering more wine. He'd doubtless explain to Pamela later, as the couple debriefed, that Mark, with three or four lots of letters after his name, was an intellectual who hadn't meant to be offensive when he savaged the Good Book.

In point of fact, one had meant to be offensive. It irked Mark to have his jibes soft-soaped by facile do-gooders who hadn't even been to university. But no, he reminded himself, you have just undertaken to be pleasant and sociable. So just damn well be it! He advised Terence to try the *patisserie*, which was excellent, as it could only be when baked by Pamela.

'And Joan,' Pamela corrected him. But she smiled with one side of her mouth, and Mark knew he'd begun to hit the right note.

'I think I'll treat myself to another before they all go.'

Mark gravitated to where Freya was standing with her brothers-in-law. Their brawny handsomeness was intimidating – especially the blond beast, with his blue glance. Hair white as wheat, lashless eyes, albino complexion. These were the sort of men who performed fifty press-ups before breakfast, using one hand only. Mark prepared for another bout of deferring, as he moved into Freya's ken – and she saw him – and reached out to him.

Taking her warm hand in his, Mark squeezed softly. Freya's rings imprinted on his palm. He relinquished the hand, which he would have loved to kiss, allowing his eyes to say what he wouldn't blurt.

'Oh Mark, let me introduce you to my fellow Foxes. David, Alex, Jamie, Will. Keir's brothers. Keir's the baby of the family. This, as you will have gathered, is Mark Heyward, my next-door neighbour. Excuse me: *Dr* Mark Heyward. Thank you for speaking so sweetly at the memorial.'

'A sad pleasure. Good to meet you all properly.'

Four Olympic-standard handshakes.

They were talking about Keir's passionate engagement in Green politics, from his earliest days.

'Before it got to be the done thing,' said the blond horror, the one Mark had named Heydrich, 'Keir was an environmentalist. I always remember – we'd be racketing about in the woods – you'd look round and where was Keir? Stopped behind to check out some mouldy old fungus or collect fir cones or whatever. Never one for sport or lads' stuff, a quiet boy ...'

'I was much the same myself,' remarked Mark quietly.

It was strange how you recognised yourself in the mirror of other people. Now he saw his young self less as the odd-boy-out than as one set apart. A conservationist from his earliest years, Mark's derided effeminacy had actually been evidence of moral strength. The worn soles of second-hand, cobbled shoes were a sign of environmental awareness rather than dirt-poverty. It was a cheering thought. A pearl. He stored it and shone its brightness against the dark sensation of helplessness that rose whenever the memory of childhood surfaced.

'Oh, really?' asked Freya.

'Mmn. I was always told I had green fingers, though naturally I wouldn't claim to be anything out of the ordinary in that way. Not in comparison with Keir.' With every word, Mark gained confidence in the self-portrait emerging in his mind's eye as he painted it. 'No, my efforts were commonplace. But I do still remember the small thrill of planting cress seeds on wet kitchen paper and watching them sprout. On the window sill.'

And as he spoke, Mark did remember: it flashed upon him – the cream tiled sill, the yoghurt pot with the paper and seeds. Or was it cotton wool? He couldn't quite see. But the view into the walled yard appeared in his mind's eye, the washing-line, the peg bag dangling. Even Gran's attention had been caught by the experiment. She'd bent her head over his to inspect the curious little curlicues of cress that grew so fast and willingly that they seemed animated. Together, along a single eye-line, he and she witnessed the small miracles of mustard and cress that gadded into life. You almost saw the shoots wriggle. A couple of days and here we come! Mark recalled the awe that tickled his tummy and made him giggle and want to bend double. He had forgotten all this. And Gran bent her head. She did, she bent her head over Mark's and screwed up her eyes and said (did she say this? perhaps she did), 'Clever boy, Mark.' Or perhaps she said, 'My clever boy, Mark.' Did she rest her hands on the boy's shoulders?

They were all looking at him. At his expression of quiet wonder.

'I suspect your Keir was much the same, Freya,' he finished lamely. 'But more so. Far more knowledgeably and passionately so. Obviously. And perhaps that love for Mother Nature was linked to his passion for painting?'

Everyone was looking at Mark, with softened expressions. The gentler image of his grandmother stayed with him. My clever boy. You can get it wrong about the dead, he thought. You only remember the shadow, allowing it to eclipse moments of light. There must have been such moments.

'And your garden, Mark,' Freya was saying, 'It's so lovely. Keir used to look out on it – I don't think I told you that? He admired the little waterfall and the rock pool you built. It gave him pleasure to see it, when pleasure was hard come-by.'

'I'm so glad.' He *was* glad. She was gracious. He loved not only Freya but Keir and the brothers and Pamela Crouch. A glow spread over the whole room.

'But I don't think you've had a drink?' she went on. 'White or red? Alex, would you mind?'

Opting for white, Mark shook himself out of his reverie and was glad to see the back of Heydrich. The fellow had tears in his eyes, just like the original beak-nosed chief of the *Schutzstaffel*, who was known to have blubbed over classical music.

And perhaps Mark was making it up about the cress seeds. How would you know? Who was around to verify the story? The film clip playing in his mind had ended and there was no way to recapture that sense of blessing. Gran had left behind no written account of her feelings. And perhaps that was a good thing. The old wound throbbed a little more and exuded a pulse of poison. He snapped back into the part he was playing.

He had more to say about his green fingers, his membership of Greenpeace and Amnesty International and his concerns for the ozone layer, but the conversation veered and tacked as it was bound to do on these occasions. A tiny tot was giving the guests far too much information about her toileting habits. Evidently she belonged to the international lawyer and wasn't impressed by her mother's conversation. The little darling rebuffed 'Auntie Freya'. *No*, whined the spoilt kid. *I want Mummy, not you.*

What a brat.

Freya took that well. But Mark's antennae caught the hurt. Everything hurt his friend. Nobody else seemed to recognise the weather in her soul. People came and said their piece about her husband. Why couldn't they leave her alone? The charade of it all.

The kid with the lavatory fixation needed some help from Dr Freud.

The crush in the room intensified. Shunted back against the

party wall, Mark found himself the victim of careless elbows. His face felt like a rubber mask; it glowed with the wine. All the while, the brothers-in-law hovered, saying little. Didn't they have wives and children to attend to? Did they all, except the Jamie guy, who'd fathered the strident kid with the urinary obsession, come singly and have nothing to do with their lives but act as Freya's bodyguard? Presumably the flower women were their wives.

Then through the party wall, he heard it, the howling.

Mark's scalp tingled and for a moment, because nobody else seemed to register anything and the noise abruptly ceased, the outcry seemed uncanny. When the whimpering began, together with the sound of frantic scratching, he understood. Freya had caught the sound too, her eyes filling with tears.

'Storm,' Mark said, cupping her elbow.

'Yes. I'll just go and – if I can get through –'

He parted the mourners, to enable her to make her way through, with a courteous request to 'Just let Freya past. Sorry. Thanks'.

And followed her out of the front door.

4

She struggled the key into the lock. It jammed. I can't get in, Freya panicked. Storm was hurling himself at the door.

'It's all right,' said the kind voice that had followed her through from the party. 'Freya – dear – it's all right. Let me.'

Removing the key from her hand, her neighbour twisted it easily in the lock. He pushed the door slightly open and spoke through the gap, hushing Storm so he'd retreat and let them in.

'There you are, my boy – all's well, all's well. Dogs pick up on everything, don't they? Maybe if we just sit with him for a little, he'll be reassured?'

She didn't think Storm would ever be reassured. He'd smelt the death in his beloved, months before there was the slightest consciousness of pain, long before diagnosis and treatment. Dogs knew so much and had to live with it.

It was a relief to have the reassurance of Mark's calm words. He seemed to understand dogs. Not threatened by them, presumably. Freya was vaguely ashamed of having seen Mark Heyward as a bit of a joke, when she'd thought of him at all. Shy people have wounds to defend. He had nice eyes.

'Yes,' she said. 'Good idea. We'll sit down with him for a while.'

She collapsed on the settee. Storm surged up and slobbered over her face. They trace our weakness, she thought. They scent our grief. It reeks at them. They are alarmed and try to lick it off. While her neighbour went off into the kitchen to refill Storm's water bowl, she took the Lab's comforting body in her arms and listened in to the murmur of the wake, going on without her, through the party wall. She didn't want to go back in there, ever.

'Come on then, Storm,' called the neighbour in the kitchen.

Storm slipped down and loped through the open door. She heard

41

him snuffling up the water. Resting back her head, Freya closed her eyes. So utterly tired and forsaken. Her body gave a spasm. And there was a smell of lemons. How could citrus be an obnoxious smell? But these lemons were nauseous – as if charred on a grill.

Must have dropped off. Just for a moment.

A very minor episode. No one will have noticed. Where did that voice come from? A man's voice, too. Dad's? No. Some medic, way back? If only Freya could go to bed. Take a pill. Take ten pills. Put the light out. But now she had to go back. Back where? In there, of course, through the wall. Where was the weird smell? Completely gone. One arm was numb and her mind swung wide. Through the wall she must go, where the current drama was in full flow, with herself the leading lady. Freya's scattered self rushed together and she leapt up, heart twanging. There were no lemons in the house. Stormie came in from the kitchen and a dark form manifested in the doorway. A stranger: no, not a stranger. Mark Heyward from Number 7. She was glad of him.

'Would you like me to stay with Storm?' he offered.

His face was all practical concern. He'd owned a spaniel once – Pearl – and later on, a black-and-white collie, he said, a rescue dog, and animals seemed to trust him. His collie's name had been ... Blithe. He'd renamed her in hope and done everything to bring healing to Blithe's early sufferings. That was when his wife passed away. Lily. He'd stay, Mark told her, if she thought it would help at all. Because of course the dog suffered at the loss of his master – in his way, as much as any human. Or more: who could tell?

'I could take him for a walk, if you like? Just say the word.'

Freya fetched the lead and Storm tracked it with eager eyes.

'If you're sure it's no trouble?' she said. 'I think a walk will help Stormie more than anything. Ever since ... he's like an orphaned child ... he's been looking for Keir. Tracking the scent. And the scent dies. It hurts so much to see him.'

'Like Emily Brontë,' he said. 'Her dog, Keeper. Bereft without her. We are their life and they are ours. In a way.'

'Ah? Yes, I suppose so. What happened to Blithe?'

'Blithe? Oh, yes. Well, she had a good life. A life – how can I put it? A life glossy with love and wellbeing. What else can any mortal expect? And, Freya, Storm is a life Keir has left you.'

She paused, startled, and looked at him. 'Thank you. So much.'

'For what?'

'For saying that,' Freya said slowly. 'You have a way of putting things. A life Keir has left me. It's true – I'll hang on to that. And thank you.'

It was not only true; it was bracing to hear it put like this – and helped, when so much of what people said was babble. They meant well but all they had to offer were pieties and truisms, or comparisons with losses they'd suffered, so that you ended up commiserating with *them*! Freya paused and took in the understanding in her neighbour's interesting eyes, which held a wisdom she'd be able to draw on, if she could just remain in her right mind. She made a note to listen attentively to whatever he said and store it away.

'I'll leave the spare key with you, Mark, in case you're back before we finish in there. How can I ever thank you? Please would you help yourself to anything you want?'

No thanks were due, her neighbour assured her. When she dropped the spare key into his hand, Mark gave her a blazing smile. The panic she occasionally read in her neighbour's face seemed to have been blessed away by the chance to make a difference. Slipping on her jacket, Freya touched his shoulder lightly before leaving.

*

In that moment of naturalness, he seemed to have happened upon the right words. But somehow, after five minutes, Mark couldn't recall exactly what he'd said. Only that the barriers had gone down between the two of them. And perhaps within himself. *For he is our peace* – the words floated back from childhood Sunday-school classes – *who hath made us one.* How did it go on? *He hath broken down the middle wall of partition between us.* A rush of gratitude brought tears to Mark's eyes. It was a positive sign that Freya could trust him with her intimate world. This was a solemn responsibility he would never abuse. He fondled Storm's ears, at the centre of his neighbour's private space. He would not betray this trust: it was unthinkable.

At the same time, Mark could not waste the opportunity for insight that had landed in his lap. To be useful to Freya, one must understand her better. His eyes roved the walls and furniture.

Frankly, you might have been in Herculaneum, with its gaudy frescos. The dead man's hand was still present. For one wall – and it was the wall the Foxes shared with himself – was decorated with a hand-painted scene of natural abundance – an overarching tree, with birds and red squirrels, in the Expressionist style Keir Fox had affected. The tree canopy spanned the long room: a river of greenery swirling up like vines near the ceiling. Tendrils rather than branches flowed like waves. And this odd but affecting creation was the skin on the other side of Mark's own wall. Who could have imagined it? The blazing colours had faded with time. The paint had been slapped straight onto the plaster – probably some time ago, for patches were flaking. Perhaps the artist had intended the irregularly fading effect. Some comment on Time, maybe.

More likely just slapdash and provisional. And the room stank of stale tobacco smoke.

Fascinated despite himself, Mark slipped his hand into his pocket and took out his phone to photograph the fresco.

And who had stitched the tapestry on the opposite wall? This was a rather clever thing, when he came to observe it closely – portraying the Earth seen from space and surrounded by darkness. Surely that must be Freya's handiwork? Not that Mark had anything against men who sewed – rather the reverse – but it was hard to imagine the scruffy and lackadaisical Keir sitting stitching by the hearth. And besides, the work was detailed, with none of the slap-it-on-and-see crudity that characterised the technique of Freya's husband.

Photographing the tapestry from two angles, Mark went on to video the entire sitting-room, working around debris that had obviously been left by the brothers-in-law – jackets, a backpack, mugs containing residue of tea. As he worked, Storm followed at his heels and Mark spoke to him softly all the while.

Meticulous as he always was, Mark could not bring himself to leave the rest of the house unrecorded. The kitchen was a mess of unwashed pots. The downstairs loo left everything to be desired in the way of hygiene. He didn't hang around, but recorded all that was significant, so as to have a chart of the interior.

'What's up there then, boy?'

He pointed to the staircase and Storm, on cue, bounded up. Mark followed. If anyone came in, he could say, quite honestly, that he'd gone up to fetch the dog.

The front bedroom was the spare one, and filled with junk. Someone had slept in the single bed last night, the beige duvet being rucked and thrown back. That wouldn't be Freya.

Or, of course, it might be.

There had been nights when he had not sensed the presence of Freya and Storm in her own bedroom. After all, would she be able to face sleeping in a bed where her husband had died? Mark had not felt this aversion when he'd lost Lily, but that case was very different. Lily had not been ill. Or not in the way Keir had been. And besides – but there was no need to go there. Presumably Freya had spent some nights here during the long months leading up to the death.

Here, just here.

There is a point, Mark thought, obscurely, at which transgression becomes reverence. I should obviously not be in her private space. And I would not be, in normal circumstances. Love has no boundaries, when it seeks only the loved one's wellbeing. If I slip into the imprint Freya has left, I can know her more fully and love her more perfectly.

But, perching on the bed, Mark resisted the urge to lay his head on the pillow, given that it was more than possible that the sleeper in the spare bed had been one of the greasy-headed louts. He looked round at the clutter. A walking stick with a carved handle. Piles of books. A huge plant – *yucca elephantipes* – very dusty. He inspected it more closely. White, necrotic spots on the lower leaves recorded a death sentence, oh dear. You have been left to die, poor plant. It would have taken so little attention to keep you alive. He felt the soil. Bone-dry, rock-hard. A yucca tolerates near-drought but some water it must have, to survive. Mark fought the yen to water it and set the room's chaos to rights. An occupation for Bedlam, because this was a serious mess.

Dismissing the temptation, he recorded everything cursorily and followed Storm into the main bedroom, where the Labrador mounted his absent master's unmade bed and lay there panting, tongue lolling. The room didn't smell of sickness. Mark sniffed: some kind of perfume. He didn't bother to examine the bottles and pots on the dressing table, just photographed the lot for later, moving on swiftly (having picked up and pocketed the smaller of two hairbrushes) to the bed.

'It's all right, my love,' said Mark tenderly, and lay down beside the bereft animal, feet carefully off the side of the bed, so as not to sully it or leave a trace. His arm lay loosely around the creature's neck. 'You've got me with you now.'

He'd only inhabit Freya's space for a moment. All the while his ears pricked for any sound from below. But Storm would alert him before Mark could sense danger. Dogs know. Know everything; tell nothing. The animal's melancholy eyes gazed at him unblinking. The love Mark had had for Pearl all those years ago, when she was his one and all, throbbed through him.

Across the pillow wandered a couple of long brown hairs. Ah. So this must be Freya's side of the bed – and, with sweet symmetry, it was the side nearest his own on the other side of the wall. When he picked them up and hung them over his hand, the hairs held their wave.

Mark wound the hairs around his little finger, realising that only a cabinet and a wall separated his sleep from Freya's. Nightly they lay like mutual reflections. And she'd be wearing – he burrowed under the pillow – this silky nightie. He ran its coolness through his fingers and nuzzled it with his cheek.

Freya would be reading these books in the light of this lamp. And taking one of these pills – what are they? Ah, yes, Temazepam, old acquaintances – to help her sleep.

Had she tried Nitrazepam, he wondered? Better than Valium for sleep, in Mark's view, but it left you groggy in the morning: on the whole Freya had probably made a sound choice. He could imagine her insomnia with special clarity, since he had been there himself and kept returning. He had helped to calm Lily with Temazepam; it was a very useful medication.

With care, Mark slid the drawer back into the cabinet. Everything was recorded. At least, the essentials.

'We'll go out in a moment,' he told Storm. 'For a lovely walkie.'

Storm reared up, excited; yelped. Whoops, shouldn't have said *walkie*, Mark thought. Stupid mistake. 'Shush, fella, I just need to … *shush.*'

As he opened the wardrobe door, Mark came upon his own surprised reflection in an indoor mirror, as though he'd been exiled to a cupboard and had given up hope of rescue. He dipped one hand into the coolness between two silk blouses, a purple and a midnight blue. He fingered Freya's grey coat with the large lapels and the belted waist, which she often wore and he liked very much. There was still a white poppy from Armistice Day in the buttonhole. Where did you buy these peace poppies? One never saw them sold in the streets. Online, doubtless: he made a note to check.

But why bother purchasing one? Gently, Mark teased out the poppy and put it in his pocket. She'd never miss it.

Long gauzy scarves. He took a green and purple one, rolled it into a tight ball and slipped it into his pocket. There was a selection of pairs of skinny jeans. This reminded him to get hold of some new jeans for himself. And his own pink cords – that he was fond of but suddenly was fond of no longer – must be dumped.

Freya's shoes on the wardrobe floor gave off a fusty smell; not unpleasant though. She wasn't one of these birdbrains who went around bragging ownership of three-hundred pairs of footwear. He knelt to inspect them.

Item: two pairs decent black shoes, small heels.

Item: two pairs winter boots, one being brown suede (or possibly imitation suede), the other black and high on the leg.

Item: one pair open sandals, worn, and if you shook them, grains of sand sifted out. Beachwear. Sand Freya had warmed between her toes.

Item: one pair heavy-duty walking shoes, scuffed, shoddy.

Item: three pairs mangy trainers, in varying states of decay. One newish pair with foam insole.

Item: two pairs of ancient slippers, blue, heels trodden down.

They reminded him of the slippers Danielle used to slop around in. But hers had had bunnies on the front. She'd thought they were cute. Danny probably still wore them, scuffing around the usurped house with – God help us – bunnies on her toes.

Enough of Danielle.

Mark took one of the slippers, bunched it up and pocketed it.

Final item: one pair high-heeled shoes, four inches at least, black leather, triangular toes.

He'd never seen Freya wearing those. They seemed out of character. But that was probably not the case. They were the hidden thing, the valuable inconsistency. Everyone has the equivalent. Mark inserted as much as he could of his right hand into an interior and held it there. The shoe squeezed his fingers hard. He rubbed them to and fro, eyes closed. There was something of a protuberance in the left shoe where the big-toe joint rubbed against the leather. Incredibly silly shoes. If she weren't careful, Freya would be destined for a bunion in later years. Of course Freya kept these shoes for when she might be invited to some formal function. That would be the reason. Removing his fingers, Mark turned the shoe over to inspect its sole. Very little wear.

Scrambling up, Mark slipped his hand into Storm's collar. The second wardrobe seemed to belong to the husband, so he wouldn't bother with that. Freya would need to empty it – if she did it sooner, rather than later, she would better feel its therapeutic effects. There was also the loft. He'd research that on another occasion. Hurry now. What are you dawdling around here for? So much left to do. This may be the only chance you get. At least for a while. Don't throw it away.

For this was love as he had never known it before. That was crystal-clear.

No one could say Mark didn't or shouldn't love Freya. Affection had been secretly budding for the last five months, since he'd first arrived at the terrace. With this death, the bud had blossomed. At first, he'd ignored the tantalising sensation. What started as *agape* had morphed into *eros* – a passionate sense of kinship that made no distinction between body and soul. The Ancient Greeks knew so much. In fact, it had been all downhill from there. This transformed and transforming bond had been nourished by the many gossamer contacts he'd engineered with Freya or that chance had arranged – a bit of both. Such love had its own sovereign laws.

'FREYA – have taken Storm for walk as agreed. Back in hour or so – longer if he doesn't seem properly tired. Rest if you can. M.'

The note was ordinary – friendly, low-key. No endearments. No superlatives. But 'M' was now a shared code, denoting intimacy. On the other hand, it could be read by anyone without suspicion. For the brothers-in-law would be sure to return with Freya, filling the narrow house with wall-to-wall testosterone. When would they be dispersing to their respective gyms? Fastening Storm's lead, Mark closed the door behind him and tested it in a single swift motion. Nobody was about. The buzz from Terence's house had upped a decibel: the wake was still in full swing. Cars remained parked all down the hill. Mark loped off, the Labrador bounding ahead, straining on the leash.

49

He'd take the route to the beach via the cobbler, who doubled as key cutter – a morose artisan with eyebrows, fixing you with a gaze of grave suspicion. As well he might, given that he never knew if the key you wanted copying was bona fide. How, by looks alone, could you tell a thief from an upright citizen? The chap was torpid, like a mollusc, and took his time about everything. He seemed a saturnine leftover from an earlier age – since who, these days, wants his shoes mended?

Actually, that was the wrong assumption, Mark corrected himself, according to the ecological convictions he had espoused. If we are concerned to avoid generating waste, the cobbler and the rag-and-bone man are necessary to recycling. He'd never throw decent footwear away again.

'Good morning,' said Mark.

The cobbler paused to mull this over and came up with '*Bore da i chi*.'

'Well. I'm in a bit of a pickle. I've guests coming – arriving any minute now – and I urgently need a copy. Of this key. Could you do it now? If you would. I'd appreciate it.'

'You mean, this minute?'

'Please.'

It could hardly be rocket-science, Mark thought. Did it take much time or brainwork? The technology belongs to the Dark Ages. The cobbler said nothing as he inserted the key into the machine.

Handing Mark twin keys and receiving the cash, the cobbler leaned across the counter and addressed himself to the dog, in a torrent of ... Welsh? For pity's sake. Did he think Welsh dogs spoke Welsh? What was he saying?

Did he recognise Storm? Was that it?

Confuse him, Mark thought. Be quick on your feet. Adroitly rechristen Freya's dog. Wendy? Don't be ridiculous! This is a man who may not be the brightest button in the box, but who notices and takes note. He'd know a dog from a bitch.

'Come on then, Thomas!' Mark gave the leash a gentle tug. 'Off to the beach! My Thomas loves the beach,' he threw at the cobbler. 'Walkies, Tommy! Good boy, Tomtom! Off we go!'

Storm obliged perfectly, barking wildly. They made a rapid exit.

The tide was in, smashing against the rocks and smacking foam into the air. Mark tossed driftwood into the sea for Storm to fetch. Seeing Freya's pet in his element, he was glad and relieved that he could do something real for his neighbour: the neighbour to whom he had found the grace to be able to say the right, the healing thing. Mark's heart vaulted up and he wanted to sing.

He did sing. *Ein feste Burg ist unser Gott!* Our God is a mighty stronghold!

Luther's words in Bach's great choral cantata would have taken the beach by storm if the wind hadn't got there first. Mark sang at the top of his baritone and the fact that the east wind tore the music from his mouth was no discouragement. He was in the fortress of his heart's truth, the *feste Burg* that was at once defence and weapon. Mark found himself crunching up and down the pebbled shore while Storm charged in and out of the waves – each ecstatic in his own way. Spume skimmed from the surface of the sea and passed over Mark's shoulder. Out in the far reaches of the bay, towards the Point, white horses travelled in to shore.

You needed this sense of an overarching presence fighting for you, Mark thought. From the beginning, he'd been alone.

Once he had been kneeling ... looking out ... in wordless dismay ... but where had that been?... through bars, whether of banisters or cot ... and he had felt (but don't go there) that there was nothing solid (but this is not a thought you can allow) ... his own naked skin was open to whatever threatened out there beyond the bars of the cage or playpen or banister. Abandoned.

Someone was going out of the front door who would never return.

He dropped to his knees on the wet pebbles and the song died in his throat. Abandoned.

For fuck's sake. Get up and at least pretend to be a man. Who said that?

Abandoned was the cruellest word. Another was deserted.

A dollop of spume slapped his face, blinding him like a handful of dirty snow. Someone was always making a fool of Mark – the worst kind of humiliation. As he spat out the foam, he stumbled to his feet. The spume was coloured brownish-cream by some kind of impurity. Presumably it was tar or effluent from the steelworks across the bay. The council was a disgrace. This was known. And nobody did anything about it. And he might have ingested some of this toxin. Fear of pollution raced through his brain: he'd be ill if he didn't take something. What should he take? The shelving unit he'd put up in the loft was crammed with medications. The thought of this resource stabilised him.

However had he got so wet though? Sea water had penetrated cuffs and collar. His hair was wet. Mark was afraid. Of something unstated, a principle of warping and twisting that you could never escape. A coldness that penetrated inside every layer of clothing. Well, some can escape, he thought, but you cannot. You have been set apart.

The only recourse was a kind of black hilarity that frequently and compulsively leered up from the heart of despair. It was useless to him now.

He had forgotten the dog, and reeled around. But apparently the dog had not forgotten Mark. Plunging out of the sea, Storm hurled his entire weight upon him, toppling him, licking him, sprawling over him as he lay flat out on the stones, laughing. Laughing, despite himself.

'Get off, you lunatic!'

Storm removed himself and shook the water out of his coat, soaking Mark again. People were leaning over the rails at the top of the cliff watching. Everybody was staring. He didn't care.

Not-caring was a great gain. To live by your own lights, your personal truth. What did it matter what the herd thought? Mark let Storm haul him up the steps, past the audience, and drag him up the steep hill to the main road. The gawpers, he realised as he passed them, were not looking at him at all but staring mindlessly out to sea. Mark was of no interest to them: good, because they were of no interest to Mark.

But the camera? Had water got into the phone? At the top of the hill he checked. Fine. Intimate secrets awaited him in its depths. He must transfer the pictures immediately to his computer and back them up. Nobody understood the technology. But everyone made use of it. And what was wrong with that? As long as it was done with love and reverence. They blogged and they twittered and they exposed their private lives and even their private parts to public inspection. It was normal nowadays for outsiders to view intimate worlds – everywhere you found intrusions amounting to impieties. Mark was not an outsider: he'd been invited in.

*

'But, Mark, look at your jacket,' Freya exclaimed tipsily. 'You're soaked! Oh dear. What happened?'

'Goodness, it's nothing. We were down by the sea ...'

Apparently there'd been a child – a little girl, about nine or ten – playing too far out in the water. Rather big waves. Anyway, her neighbour said he wouldn't bother Freya with the story. Today of all days. And her brothers-in-law were with her: he mustn't intrude.

'Oh please, Mark – of course I want to hear,' she said, and his modesty touched Freya. She insisted that he come in and warm up by the fire. The stink of charred lemon seemed to have weakened with his arrival. Mark's gentle eyes made her feel safer. Storm looked so much more himself and gazed up into her face in the intense way he used to have for Keir, as though hopeful that Freya could stand in for his vanished master. 'Whatever happened?'

Mark and Storm had waded out to the child. Actually, he said, little Tania – Tania was the sweet kiddie's name – would probably

53

have been perfectly all right without any intervention, but you can't really take that risk, can you? The children of our community belong to us all, don't they? So, just to be on the safe side, Mark had taken Tania's hand and led her in to safety. He didn't want to judge but he did wonder what on earth the parents were *at*, letting a child play in the sea, unsupervised. People were astonishing. He had spoken to the parents quietly when he'd managed to locate them and return their daughter to them. They'd been at the cafe above the beach, of course, eating doughnuts, claiming they could keep an eye on their kiddie from there. Which they might have been able to do – but how did they imagine they'd have had time to get down the forty steps to little Tania, if she'd been swept away?

Anyway, that was nothing. Please. Nothing. It was just lucky that he and Storm had been there. Mark's sole concern now was Freya and how the rest of the occasion had gone. And that she should rest.

'You've got your family around you. I'll make myself scarce. I need a bath and a change of togs. You know where I am.'

He had all but closed the door behind him when he reappeared to say, 'I won't keep bothering you, Freya. Absolutely not. But I'm always there.'

'My god but he's a talker,' said David when Mark had finally gone. 'Endless pratting prattle.'

'Don't say that, Dave. Just don't. And actually I've always found him rather quiet.'

'Really?'

'He's a kind guy. And when he speaks, he says good things.'

'Like?'

'Oh – wise things.' She wasn't going to quote Mark, for fear of hearing him belittled and having the morsels of comfort exposed to Dave's scepticism.

'OK, sorry. I'll make you coffee, Frey. You're in for one hell of a hangover.'

'I'm not drunk,' Freya insisted tipsily. 'Just got a bit of a twanging in my head. Mark's terribly shy, Dave. That's what Keir used to say.'

'Yeah, right.'

Freya had drunk one glass too many. And she didn't drink alcohol, or rarely. It loosened her tongue but made her hazy about what she was coming out with. Her head had throbbed and she'd been glad of the comparative peace that met her as soon as she reopened the door to her privacy. Despite her reservations as to whether Keir would have wanted any kind of a carry-on after his funeral, Freya knew she should have been touched at the memories people offered her. Why then had it felt as if everyone was fighting for a slice of his newborn ghost? She'd felt endangered, embattled, even though everyone deferred to her as the chief loser. Adrenalin had kept Freya going until one condolence too many had sent her reeling towards the red wine. Which she absolutely shouldn't, as a classic migraineur, drink.

'It was kind of Mark to take poor Stormie for a walk,' she told David. 'He was crying – didn't you hear him?'

'*Crying*? What's he got to cry about?'

'No – not Mark – *Stormie* was crying!'

The sound of his keening had been primitive and visceral, a wild creature's belly-howl. Her neighbour had soothed him, leading Keir's dear companion into a healthier place. He was a man with hidden gifts.

The thing he'd said about saving the child: that was moving. The way he'd described it, she felt as if she'd seen Tania herself, in the waves, endangered.

And somehow, as she imagined the scene, she saw little Haf there, in trouble, out of her depth. *No Auntie Freya! I want Mummy! Not you! Only my Mummy!* But Mark had said, they are all our children, Freya, aren't they? They belong to the whole community. Keir would have totally understood that. She could imagine him saying it, in those words. And that was comforting, or would be when she had a chance to dwell on it calmly.

Storm's coat had dried on the walk home. All-in, he slunk over to his basket and his jaws gaped in a yawn. Before his head subsided on the blanket, Storm's eyelids had closed. Live many years, Freya thought, because I could not bear to lose you.

Storm, you are the life Keir has left me. You too are glossy with love and well-being. These words of her neighbour were a lifeline. Only someone more than usually sensitive could have spoken such healing words.

She took a couple of swigs of coffee; hoped to avoid throwing up. She might though, because the room was whirling.

*

Keepsakes. People carted them back from holiday and attached them to the fridge or buried them in a cupboard. Eventually a shard of Egypt, a bauble of Spain found their way to the charity shop or the skip. Mark had never collected souvenirs, but then he'd never bothered with foreign holidays.

Besides, the treasures he'd brought home today were not souvenirs at all. They had more in common with holy objects, but were more endearing.

After his shower, it was time to close the sitting-room curtains and switch on the lamps, though it was not quite dark. No sound came from next door. Mark's hand dithered over Schubert's 'Death and the Maiden' and Dvorak's Piano Quintet, each expressing a music of the heart so ecstatically beautiful that he found it hard to listen without tears. In the end, Mark decided against any music at all. He could listen afterwards, when the music would not be demeaned as background noise. Mark set out his keepsakes on the table.

First, the white poppy. He smoothed its nylon petals with his fingertips. At the corolla was the word 'Peace' in tiny letters. Peace was what he desired above all else for Freya. If he could help her to attain peace, that would make Mark's life not just worthwhile but radiant.

Next, the phone containing a harvest of photographs. Without examining the pictures individually, he imported them into his computer and backed up on a memory stick. Then he backed up again on the Cloud. When your life has been stinted of pleasures, you learn how to hoard them for the future in a state of suspended promise.

Next, a teaspoon from Freya's cutlery drawer. Why he had picked this up, Mark wasn't sure. Nothing differentiated it from any other teaspoon except one's knowledge of its origin and provenance. But it had a history, having been in her hand and perhaps her mouth. He laid it lovingly parallel with the memory stick. It was Freya's, after all. Everything she touched was talismanic. She'd stirred her coffee with it and, from now on, so would Mark.

The green and purple scarf. The hairbrush, containing Freya's hair, her DNA. He put the brush through his own hair and wound the scarf around his neck.

The house key. In practical terms, his most valuable acquisition, the portal to deeper communion.

Oh, and lastly, the ring! How could he have forgotten the ring? Mark's artful fingers had woven the ring from strands of hair. Still wrapped around his pinkie, this miracle had survived all the exertions with the dog. But human hair has greater tensile strength than steel – so why be surprised? *A bracelet of bright hair about the bone*: Donne had written those words about his beloved four centuries ago. The recollection of the line made him shiver. Easing the ring off his finger, Mark laid it on a sheet of white paper, folded the paper and placed it in an envelope, whose flap he tucked in and labelled. Every hair of Freya's head was numbered and equally precious to him.

Best to leave the photographs until tomorrow, preserving the gloss of novelty. Besides Mark was exhausted with emotion and salt water. The poignant ache of sympathy; performing at the funeral; the party, followed by the passionate exploration of Freya's world and the marathon hike to the sea – it had all taken its toll.

After dragging himself to bed, Mark got out again and pushed

57

the bed against the party wall, snuggling closer. He lay face-to-face with Freya, supposing her to be in bed. Impossible, of course, to sleep. The irony of it. Your exhausted brain secretes bizarre thoughts and discharges electricity it can't afford.

He was thinking of the anatomy of ears. Now what was the phrase he was seeking?

The basilar membrane! Yes, that was it.

Mark remembered the diagram of the inner ear they'd studied at Lindenhowe Grammar, himself a friendless runt in second-hand uniform, whose entire attention was focused on his studies. When teachers tested the class's knowledge, Mark's hand would shoot up before the question had been fully rolled out. The teachers' speech patterns were so guessable; his fellow boys were dunces, bar one or two. He'd especially liked the diagrams in Biology, reassessing the messy flesh as a clean and clear geometry.

The inner ear contains three ossicles, Mark remembered, his mind drifting. The vestibular system was a secret place of listening, where outside noises become nerve impulses. Having entered you, the waves become part of yourself. Freya's voice was now Mark's voice, or one of them. The inner world was a weave or braiding of voices. Never again would he need to feel alone or abandoned. Of course he had been beguiled into believing this before, on two occasions, and been let down, but this was different.

Nestling closer to the wall, Mark pictured Freya's body lying within reach of his love, whether facing him or turned away. He tried to imitate her imagined posture – or rather, how he would like it to be. He knew what she would be wearing and imagined the give of her spine, her gentle breathing, her lips relaxing, one arm curved around her head, the tumbling darkness of her hair on the pillow.

How sweet to know that he would awaken alongside her tomorrow morning. If only Mark's near-presence could grant Freya the healing sleep he craved for her. He would gladly give up his own if she could benefit from it – and he was a man who needed the full eight hours or his mood soured. But thinking of Freya was like prayer; it was the relinquishment of self-interest in favour of the good of the other. He would become a human bridge for her and *please use me, walk over me,* he prayed.

As a child, Mark had prayed every night, kneeling at his bedside. His grandmother had observed from the door to ensure he was doing it properly – though how this could be ascertained by anyone but Jehovah himself, supposing him to exist, passed all understanding. At the time Mark had believed Gran could read his mind. Having left school at fifteen, the woman could barely read a book. She was governed, he thought, by fear. Rigid fear. The pauper's fear. They all were. It was catching. They'd infected him.

Pity my simplicity, Gran had taught him to plead, with that harsh tone that reminded him with every syllable of her right to clip his ear if he erred. *Suffer us to come to Thee.* The four Apostles had been stationed at the corners of his bed, two at the foot, two at the head. Mark had been a docile, biddable boy and tried to do the right thing.

He still did; still cultivated the tone of mind, as he phrased it to himself, that found refuge in prayer. The membrane that binds the soul is ultimately permeable, Mark thought. And blessing my neighbour in this way can only do good. The rancid piety of his grandmother had suffused his spirit in a way she could never have comprehended. But Freya would free him.

Mark would not touch himself and profane that tender, overarching shelter he yearned to offer.

5

'You know – if you don't mind my saying so – it's early days,' Freya's neighbour reminded her, as she handed him Storm's leash. 'I kept reminding myself of that when my darling Lily went.'

'And did it help?'

Her neighbour thought for a moment.

'No,' he said, and they both laughed sadly. 'Can't honestly say it did.'

The tonic laughter perished as soon as it was born. The neighbour looked concernedly into her face and brushed the back of her hand with his fingertips. She watched him lead Storm down the path. When they were out of sight, Freya remained standing in the doorway, barefoot in her cotton wrap. Yes, it was the cruellest month. Everything burgeoned – the heavy froth of cherry blossom and hawthorn. Ash saplings forced their way up between paving stones. Over in the woods there was a rapture of birdsong. She shrank from it all. At least their home – her home – was a sanctuary.

Why trouble to dress? Often Freya didn't bother, and skipped showering on some days. God, I must smell rank, she'd think, sitting for half an hour, semi-comatose and meaning to shower, and not doing so but itemising the exhausting list of actions you had to get through to be clean. Glancing out of the window, she'd see the Crouches over the fence, gardening, chatting away. And feel nothing but irritation. Oh, go indoors, you two. They were like twin robots. What one did, the other followed. They hardly had to look at one another to perform the identical action. So fucking complacent. Crouch by name and Crouch by nature.

She pulled the curtains against the Crouches and the light. What am I becoming, she thought? Nasty and bitter. Sour and stupid. Her mind was a blocked drain. They were good, caring people, Pam and

Terry. Keir was fond of them. And they'd gone out of their way to support her. Vegetable casseroles appeared on the doorstep, flavoured and scented with herbs they grew in their garden. An apricot tart appeared, which she'd felt would have been delicious if you could bring yourself to eat it – but then she'd woken in the night, come downstairs and scoffed the lot, and wanted more, and then felt sick. The Crouches' kindnesses to Freya were endless. Why couldn't she feel the easy friendship she had always felt, for more or less everyone? She'd thought of herself as a joyous person. I am degenerating, Freya thought. But surely I'll come up again?

How shall I do my job if I can't feel for people? She ran the bike shop as a business with Dave but it was also work done for love. None of the salaried jobs she'd had in earlier life had satisfied Freya in the way that working with her hands did: building and maintaining those beautiful machines for people. Now she didn't seem to care. The feeling will return, she thought, like circulation to cold hands.

And thank goodness the neighbour was walking Storm. Keir's dog continued to mourn his way around the house. Occasionally he backed into a corner and suffered a fit of violent trembling and wouldn't come when she coaxed him. You are the life that Keir left me, Freya thought, and I'm not taking proper care of you.

Storm could die. No. Not *can*. You *will* die, Storm.

Under the shock of this recognition, a drumbeat of agitation pitched Freya out of the door, plunging her into the street. She flew down the hill, as if propelled, as if Keir's death were chasing her, and caught up dog and dog-walker as they rounded the corner into the green.

'What is it? Whatever's happened, love?'

Whirling round, Mark had her in his arms, hugged up against his chest. Storm, rising on hind legs, pawed her shoulder so that the three of them all but toppled.

'I don't know. I just...'

'My dear,' he said, concernedly. 'You've got no shoes on.'

61

She looked down. Her feet didn't hurt. They were numb. Her neighbour's hand at the small of her back steadied her. It was all right, he assured her.

'I've got you, Freya. I've got you now.'

'I didn't want you to go ... no, sorry, I didn't mean that, I meant, I didn't want – Keir's dog – to go – anywhere. Where I couldn't see him.'

Neither Storm nor he were going anywhere, her neighbour reassured her. Nowhere at all. Why didn't he run back and fetch her shoes?

'No. Don't do that. I don't want you to do that.'

Right, so what they would do was this, Mark proposed. They'd all go home via the green. Then he and Storm would scamper on the grass where she could keep her eye on them from the house – because obviously the dear old dog needed his exercise. Mark would be glad to offer Freya his own shoes, only, with the best will in the world, Size 9 she wasn't. He smiled. And she smiled through her tears. But she was welcome, he went on, to clump up the hill in his Size 9s, and made as if to kneel and untie the laces. Just say the word! She laughed. He laughed. It was good to laugh. Mark squeezed Freya's hand. That's the way, his squeeze said. One moment at a time. We'll get there. You are not alone, you know, you have neighbours.

They walked up the green, behind the houses, and he took her hand when she stumbled. As they walked, he pointed out a flowering cherry that had seeded itself in the Whitethorn Wood, the creamy blossom of the whitethorn, the primroses and bluebells that somehow held their own against encroaching wild garlic.

Freya looked, she saw. The loveliness was still here. Oh, but she'd left the front door wide open. Dangerous. What had come over her? Never, never do that again, Freya scolded herself. Anything could come in. Her neighbour entered behind Freya, wiped his shoes, let Storm off the lead and sat Freya down at the kitchen table.

The kettle boiled. Mark poured her coffee. What a pale face he had. The sole of Freya's right foot was bleeding but it didn't hurt.

He'd bathe it for her, he insisted. Clean and cover the wound. She sat passively and sipped the coffee, which – for once – she could taste. Storm's chin rested on her knees and his melancholy eyes never left her face. Mark was wondering where the plasters were kept. He located them instantly, with what he called his sixth sense. And some TCP.

'You're so good,' Freya heard herself murmur. 'Thank you, but don't trouble yourself.'

'No trouble in the world. Infection in the wound is the last thing you want. We all care about you, Freya. We'd do anything for you. And don't forget, I've been there myself. I was shown compassion: what can we do but pass the compassion on?'

'Yes, but you've been too kind already. Really. Please just leave it now.'

'What is life worth, Freya, if we can't care for one another?'

That was true, Freya thought, and something to ponder, when she was fit to ponder; her neighbour was a fusspot but he had a fund of wisdom. When the big words were needed, he found and offered them without stint.

What is life worth though? What, actually?

As sensation prickled back into her feet and the horror dissolved, embarrassment mounted. Freya pictured herself in her flimsy wrap haring down the hill, landing on this old-fashioned guy who knew her hardly at all. She'd always made fun of Mark from the privacy of their home. Called him the Garden Gnome. How mean of her, how juvenile. He'd seemed odd, in a way you couldn't define. Something about him had struck her as off-key. The boyish hair cut (he'd had it cut stylishly now), the nervous tic (rare now), the clockwork way he'd walked. But suddenly he hadn't been odd. Which in itself was odd. Her head swam.

The fact is, Freya thought, I have not washed, I must – frankly – stink. And he'd be susceptible to odours.

How did she know that? No idea. And this man who didn't like smells was handling her soiled feet. On one knee, this stranger was rinsing a cloth in a bowl of water to wash off her dirt, in a rather biblical way. She winced and pulled her foot back but he didn't let go. In retaliation, the foot seemed to want to kick him. It gave a little spasm but Mark held on.

'No, really, please – I'll take a shower instead,' she blurted. 'But thanks so much. I feel a bit of an idiot now, actually, Mark. Don't know what came over me.'

'Well, don't feel like that. Categorically, don't. Shan't be a sec.'

He towelled her left foot off.

'You should have seen me, Freya, when Lily died,' he said. 'One day I'll tell you about it. Not now. I was wandering from one room to another for days and days. Looking for her. Anyway. I am the all-time expert on going to pieces. You are doing fine, take it from one who knows. You really are. There you are; now the other foot.'

She submitted to his ministrations. Why not? And her submission told her: you have to pull yourself together. You have to allow yourself to weep. Let it all out. You have to realise in your heart of hearts that there is no Keir on this earth. He doesn't exist but he didn't choose to leave you. And Mark Heyward was someone who cared. But now it was time to look Keir's absence in the face.

Freya stood up rather sharply, swerved to one side and the water in the bowl slopped to and fro.

'I'm fine now. Thanks, Mark.'

'That's the spirit. And while you're having your shower,' Mark said, unperturbed, 'why don't Storm and I go and play on the green until he's run off all his energy? If you need us, just holler. We won't be out of earshot, I promise. Does that seem all right?'

*

Throughout the past week, the lovely creature had drawn the two of them closer. Freya and he had patted and stroked the warm, substantial body, standing at either side. Storm was their linking term. Storm knows, Mark thought, that I'm good for Freya, I'm her hope for the future, a very present help in trouble; she can rely on me. And so can you, Storm, so can you.

He thought of Pearl whenever he approached the animal. However bizarre a thought it was, Pearl had been the only true mother he'd known. Pearl had loved Mark with a totality of life-guaranteeing tenderness; and Mark had loved Pearl. He remembered joining her in the dark yard, twilight coming down, when they'd each been put out for some separate misdemeanour, huddling together on sacking, his face against her flank, smelling her loyal and sincere smell until it was his smell. Pearl hadn't whimpered then, and neither had Mark.

It was not ridiculous. Or perverted. Or a substitute. It was love, pure and simple.

Whenever Mark knocked on Freya's door, Storm clamoured for his walk, skittering around at the door. Her dog responds, Mark thought, to the deep true heart in me. Storm helps me find that heart in myself. All their walks were special to both of them. Never the same. It was an honour to be entrusted with a creature precious to the most cherished of women. In a real sense, Storm was becoming Mark's. This was obviously the best thing for the creature itself.

There were times when Storm dissolved into Pearl. They were walking along the lane beside the sea, where the tree canopies met over your head. Pearl would race ahead, then dash back, and off again, and back again. He knew it was Storm but it was also Pearl. And oh, the safety of her company. Celandines stood wide open in the hedgerows, and yellow archangel with its butter-yellow blossoms. The bookish boy had committed to memory the name of each plant – birds-eye speedwell and old man's beard, wild bryony and golden agrimony. The solace of Pearl returned to Mark now, as he walked the dog who was not Pearl alongside the wood which was not Pembrokeshire.

The boy had never minded the cocker spaniel's dirt and secretions. The man was more fastidious. The Chuck-it lobbed the ball for fifty metres and the beauty of it was, you weren't left with your hands coated in slobber: the contraption had a twofold action, releasing the ball and scooping it up. Fellow dog-walkers passed with a greeting and paused to ask after Freya. I am seen as her mainstay, Mark thought, hoping the brothers-in-law would keep away and refrain from muscling in to usurp his place in her life. He'd looked them all up on Facebook: two were firemen (let's hope for plenty of arson to keep them busy), the third was a mechanic who co-owned the cycle shop with Freya and the fourth, Haf's father, was nowhere to be found.

Mark tossed the ball and Storm tore off down the hill after it. A squirrel, sensing the lightning of Storm's advance, scooted up an ash tree.

A problem was, Freya had grown reclusive. In her grief, she hunkered at home, rarely venturing beyond the garden and never into the shed where he knew she stored bikes and tools. She'd cut herself off from work's healing routines. Completely understandable, of course – and in some ways, Mark welcomed her isolation. He would have been just the same. But in the long run – if she kept it up – this would not only prove unhealthy for Freya (always his primary concern) but would bar entry into the Fox house. Mark had explored his personal videos and photographs until they'd become stale and frustrating. Useful, yes, as a mnemonic. Satisfying, no. He'd blown up some details. The handwriting on a note beside Freya's bed was still proving intransigent. This inspired a sense of failure in a scholar expert in teasing meaning from fragments of ancient manuscripts.

There'd been so much to get his mind around while Mark was reconnoitring, that he'd missed this note altogether. The latest software would help with deciphering whatever cropped up in future. Expensive stuff but an investment. It was interesting, getting the hang of the technology. He'd discovered more sophisticated systems whilst surfing the web – a costly and effective surveillance that would act like a film, allowing Mark to keep his eye out for Freya, his wing over her.

Yes, it might be considered transgressive. In certain circumstances, however, a short-term breaking of a taboo may well be excusable, if it's in the interests of the other party.

Well, he might not do it. There was no harm in considering the possibility though: idly glancing at what was available.

And did one want to splash out that ludicrous sum of money? He scrimped and saved, as his grandmother had done – *Waste not, want not* was her daily motto – but every so often, Mark's instinct to spend burst up. A blow-out like a geyser. Why should he deny himself things that everyone nowadays had?

Mark might – in another life – have become an electronic wizard. Who knew that there was a computer scientist in him? Or a physicist! The biography of Einstein he was reading as a bedtime book further convinced Mark of a lost vocation. Quanta and neutrons, dark matter and mc^2 all made sense to him. It was because his mind was open and labile and attuned to the sublime. Mark did not assume, and never had, that common sense was anything more than vulgar assumption.

Einstein or no Einstein (and one must guard against grandiosity), there was no getting away from the fact that he'd sucked the juice from the available portions of the orange, as it were. The camera had served its purpose and he was impatient for a deeper penetration of Freya's world. Until today, she'd never positively invited him indoors. Of course, there'd been nothing personal in that previous exclusion.

Nevertheless she had turned to him now. Unequivocally. She'd pursued him and clung. Mark's arms had held Freya. The yielding softness of her breasts against his chest. He'd rested his lips in her hair. It needed washing, of course. May have been a bit greasy, and there were flakes of dandruff. But to think of Freya in that way was absurd, and he dismissed it – as if a suffering human could be reduced to a hairdresser's dummy. The person mattered, not the presentation. After all, he reminded himself, we are all mortals and formed of the same clay. If you prick us, do we not bleed, etc? In all sorts of ways, Freya was his teacher.

Of course, I can be wrong, Mark thought: nobody knows that better than I do. And maybe I overdid it a bit with the foot-washing. She had seemed slightly irritated. He shrank into himself at the thought of the *faux pas*. Judging intimacy and timing was not always easy. People – he didn't like to say 'women', because of his feminism – had let him down. He'd worshipped Lily – the word was not too strong – reverencing a depth of emotional intelligence and social grace, that had everything to teach a diffident, reclusive man, younger than his age. There'd been the sense of awe when a musician of her gifts and powers chose him for a husband. Why would she stoop to him? But Lily's confidence had been all surface; inside, there was fragility. And, as it turned out, fatal moral weakness.

And she'd kept going away. Upping and offing, he'd called it to himself – and later, desertion and abandonment.

At first Mark had tried to travel with the orchestra on their tours. He'd wanted to help and support her, carrying her bags and ensuring her comfort. But, like kids in a playground game, the ensemble had ostracised him. And Lily said, heart-breakingly: *It doesn't really help me, Mark, your fussing round.* How painful that word *fussing* had been. So she upped and offed without him. Mark had been physically sick the whole week before she was due to leave. *No, it's all right, Lily,* he'd say with something of heroism. *You go. Enjoy yourself, don't worry about me.* He knew she came to dread these occasions of martyrdom. Or else he'd become silent. *This is my work,* Lily pleaded. *This is my life, Mark. You have your work, I have mine.* He'd sit alone at Tŷ Hafan in the evenings and think of Lily in the green dress, exposing her naked shoulder – which was *his* shoulder – to all and sundry. Flirting, partying, taking applause, talking shop with her fellow musicians. It had been torture. When she'd dropped out, that was torture too.

He'd worshipped Lily but she hadn't worshipped him. Lily was a dead end.

The woman after Lily – if you could call her a woman – had been at the larval stage of development, grubbing round blindly for nourishment and in need of a roof over her head. Danielle Jones, of course, had been unable to teach one anything. She'd made Mark's extreme sensitivity, if anything, more painful. She was a haven for gastric bugs which she'd bring home from the nursery. She'd lie in their bed, sweat-sticky, moaning that the sheets *needed changing* and that she felt *so weak* and if only she could *have a bath*, complaining of pangs of longing for *blackcurrant juice*. In paroxysms of disgust, you wanted to run out into the street and never come back. He'd done just that, holing up in his office from dawn to dusk. But the peace had been ruined by his nervous symptoms: throbbing head, nausea, goose pimples, the lot.

Gran had not tolerated Mark's childhood illnesses. Did it count in law as neglect to leave a child with whooping cough for ten hours a day, looking in at lunch time with gimlet eyes?

Storm lolloped back; he dropped the slobbered ball and stood at the ready. A dog is not equipped to pretend. A dog lives in the moment. He knows no shame. A lesson to higher mammals. Mark raised the Chuck-it. Having hurled himself after the false throw, Storm twigged, spun, yowled at the tease and leapt at the Chuck-it.

'There you go, boy!' Off the ball sailed, into the wild garlic at the edge of the wood.

Memo to self: Freya is not Danny and never could be. Danny is callow and stupid. Initially Mark had felt flattered. His wife had not been dead six months. Danielle would visit the gallery at her lunch break and sit in front of a particular picture for half an hour. He'd learned to anticipate the youngster's visits and would talk to her about the picture or object she'd chosen. She'd listen with parted lips, soaking in knowledge. Danny drew Mark out and he found himself telling her about his loss. The soft sorrow Mark was able to express had seemed to dissolve away a residue of the horror he'd been through.

There was not a sturdy enough membrane between himself and others, Mark had once explained to the listening girl. He'd laughed, treating it as a joke: *Empathy will be my undoing*! Danny had

69

confided that empathy was *totally, totally* important for a nursery nurse. You had to understand what the children *feel*. He drew her out. She was flattered that he *took notice*. She was *sooooo* sorry for his loss. She could only begin to imagine what he was suffering.

Danny's true motives had emerged. She'd been on the lookout for a free roof over her head. He took her in. She cast him out! Unbelievable!

Whenever Mark looked back on this episode, he could hardly credit his folly. Like Lily, Danny had known how to drive a man beyond control – and then how to exact a penalty. Oh boy, had she seen Mark Heyward coming! But then, what can you expect if you don't choose your equal? After the honeymoon period of wafting round Tŷ Hafan as if she owned it, a coarser spirit had asserted itself, followed by listless defiance, a puling mutiny. And then she'd shown her claws and fangs.

It was neither more nor less than blackmail.

Anyway, why think of this nobody? Freya was her antithesis. And behind Danny lay the darkness of Lily. The vile colour she'd turned. Colours, rather. Dead meat. He would not think of Lily. The deafening silence after the convulsions. Lily lowered into her grave.

He would reclaim Tŷ Hafan and take Freya there, to lift her clear of her grief. She would love it.

'How are you, Mark?'

Terence had his cat on a lead.

A pussy on a lead! Mark had seen it all now. He rather liked Terence for it. Here was a man who possessed no obvious vanity. Not that Terence had much to be vain about. Still. Who does?

He was anxious, Terence said, in case dear little Pansy ran off.

Pansy the pussy! It was all Mark could do not to chortle aloud. The sight of tubby Terence in shorts and sunhat, urging his six-month-old kitten to walk to heel was priceless. And rather touching. Pammie was eager for the sweetheart to enjoy the treasures of the great outdoors, Terence confided, but anxious in case she got too excited and ran off before she'd properly got her bearings.

'After all, the world is very wide, isn't it?' Terence mused.

'Yes, it is,' Mark agreed.

Or not wide enough, he thought. People infantilised their cats. At heart, mogs were lynxes – and this Pansy, with over-long body and marbled orange coat, looked like a Bengal cat, nearly as wild as its ancestors. Just as wild, but with more hypocrisy. They would gnaw you to the bone if you weren't more use as a lifelong provider of food and shelter.

Pansy eyeballed Storm with quivering bale and there was a stand-off, in which the Labrador failed to assert his dominance over the feral fluff-ball. The kitten arched her back and took a flying run at the dog. Mark chucked the ball again, to release Storm from humiliation.

'You are so good,' said Terence, 'to walk Freya's dog. Hats off to you, Mark. You're one in a million.'

'There's so little one can do to help, Terence. And anyway, I enjoy it,' Mark said frankly.

There was a kind of ease in being natural. It suffused the mind like physical warmth. There was pleasure in the lustre granted by praise. Mark basked, his spirits rose and he felt a fellowship with the sweet-natured chap, whose heart was so clearly in the right place.

'If it helps our neighbour just a tad,' he went on, 'it has to be worth it. And you and Pamela have obviously done a huge amount for Freya. More than me, really. I do wish she could get out though – into the countryside – into nature – don't you? The season is so clement. I'd thought of offering to take her out myself, maybe down to the Gower – Three Cliffs or Pwll Du – or Rhossili.'

'Good idea, why don't you ask her?'

'Oh, I don't know. It might seem a bit ... because there's only the one of me ... a widower ... well, perhaps it would be better coming from Pamela and you?'

'Good thought – I'll mention it to Pammie. A change of scene might be just what Freya needs. Fresh air and maybe lunch. Port Eynon's a nice place for a walk on the beach. Very decent chips they

71

serve, too, in the cafe at the front. You can sit out in the sun to eat them. Also, Pammie tells me, the Ladies is reasonable, which you can't say for every loo on the peninsula.'

'I don't see much walking going on!' chirped Pamela.

She'd straddled the low fence that ran between the houses and the green, wearing what used to be called a divided skirt, as modelled by school hockey captains. Smiling warmly, Pamela linked arms with her husband. Her silver hair was held back by an Alice band.

'Honestly! I send my Terry out to walk the kittie,' she said to Mark, who saw Terence squeeze her arm with the complicit affection of long-married couples. 'And what's he doing? Gossiping with his pal! I don't know! So what's that about toilets?'

The best Ladies in Wales, as far as Pamela had ascertained, was at the Roman village of Caerwent. Immaculate. And very modern indeed. You rarely got the two together. Plenty of space, in case you were in a wheelchair – and all the chrome gleaming and spotless. Terence had informed her that the Gents was equally good.

'I gave it five stars. It makes a difference, you know,' she exclaimed, and Mark kept up the nodding. 'To the whole experience of visiting a place.'

'That's very true,' Mark agreed.

There was much he could have said about Caerwent, a favourite haunt. The fortified walls, the Roman market square, the temple ruins. And Caerleon: the baths, the amphitheatre, the cursus. Concerning the loos, he could think of little to say except to agree – and to add reflections on the principles on which the Romans designed and built their advanced but less than savoury latrines.

'*We* have been to *Rome*, Mark,' Pamela cut in boastfully. 'To visit the Pope.'

'Really?'

'Well, not by personal invitation, of course! We are not cardinals!' She giggled, and Mark giggled along. 'No, a guided cultural tour. Four days, three nights, inclusive. Oh, but it was hot. Sizzling. Never scoffed so much ice cream in all my life. Can you stand the heat? I can't. Still we had those little portable buzzing fans like windmills – they helped, didn't they, Terry? It was moving to receive the Pope's blessing in St Peter's Square and to be – you know – within such a large spiritual crowd. Terry's words. Anyway, we also saw plenty of ruins, including the Cloaca Maxima!' she concluded triumphantly.

Any minute now, Mark thought, she'll be enquiring whether I have been to Rome. I shall say that I am planning a visit later this summer, as a guest speaker at the Sapienza University of Rome. Or I'll remind her that the Roman Empire is right here, under our very feet. But Pamela didn't ask. She stood with folded arms, looking down the green towards the sea and swaying as if she heard some tune in her head.

Storm, leery of the kitten, flopped down at Mark's feet and rolled on his back, legs lazily in the air, to have his belly rubbed. The kitten hunkered motionless, pale eyes trained on the undergrowth fringing the wood. Her tortoiseshell fur burned nearly ochre in the sunlight. Her tail fluffed out like a raccoon's and she quivered all over. Pansy could sense mice and squirrels in their sanctuary and planned to crunch them in her jaws.

'Your kitten is absolutely adorable,' said Mark to Pamela, looking up from where he knelt to fondle Storm.

Pamela beamed, so Mark carried on.

'Truly, you rarely see a kitten with such character. Frankly,' he said, 'I must confess I'm not really a cat person – dogs are my thing, as you know. But Pansy – well – what a jewel! Will she let me stroke her?'

'Of course! She'll love it.'

Mark crouched, placing one hand on the cat's sun-warmed, pulsing fur. He stroked, as if hesitantly, glancing up at Pamela, who nodded. Pansy turned and briefly bared her teeth – fangs rather, coated in bacteria, of course. Cat faeces can kill you, Mark reminded himself, or damage your mental health. *Toxoplasma Gondii*. Memo to self: wash hands immediately you're back in the house.

'Ah, sweet! She's smiling at you, Mark!'

Then in short order, Pansy hissed, spat and swiped at him with her paw. Missed, ha! He'd seen it coming.

'Your dear little Pansy has a mind of her own!' He rose to his feet. 'I like that about her.'

'You're so right.' Pamela favoured him with an impulsive caress on the forearm. 'Come to Mummy then, darling! Do you know, Mark, she can turn a complete somersault!'

'That I must see.'

'Come on, darling, give Mummy a cuddle!'

Pansy took no notice. Crouching low to the ground, her eyes lasered the undergrowth and she wriggled her flanks from side to side. She was readying herself for the kill, Mark saw. Any minute now, watch Pussy pounce.

When Terence proposed to Pamela a Gower joyride with Freya, Pamela thought it a splendid idea and hoped Mark would join them.

'I'd love to,' he said. 'But I'd better see how I'm fixed for the week, workwise, Pam. I've got badly behind, what with one thing and another. The museum is preparing for a big exhibition, objects are being taken out of store for the first time in decades, and I need to work on the catalogue. In any case, it hardly matters whether I go with you or not – as long as our friend can get some needful peace of mind.'

When Pansy broke free, sliding the leash from Terence's hand as she surged into the undergrowth, it was Mark who dived in after her, ignoring the nettles, to scoop her up and restore her to 'Mummy' to stroke and scold.

'Pansy brought us a trophy,' Pamela said. 'Did Terry tell you? Fieldmouse. Still alive. Bless her, it's instinct, after all. You can't argue with instinct. I broke its neck. It's all you can do for them. There are some dock leaves just there, Mark – the sap does seem to help with nettle rash – that's it, rub them on, nice and cool.'

Mark quite liked the bossy molly-coddling, and did as Pamela advised. While the coolness of the leaves did ease the stings, her words reverberated – I broke its neck, it's all you can do for them.

*

From behind the smeared pane, where a fly hung in a rag of spider's web, Freya saw her neighbours as inhabitants of another world: pastoral, uninfected. They were laughing and jesting together, enjoying the air and the company.

Keir loved our corner of the earth, Freya thought. He knew nature through all his senses put together, and the knowledge flowed into his painting. The brush was an extension of his arm and hand. She'd reminded herself – by dashing into the street without her shoes – of how Keir would walk barefoot, to feel the earth better, so he said. He'd take Storm through the woods and down to the beach, unshod. Only the once did he cut himself, on shards of glass, and seemed bemused. How she missed Keir's darling feet.

But what a funny thing to think. His soles were like leather. His toes had spread.

And when the guy next door had done that slightly embarrassing thing of washing her feet, the action had brought Keir to mind.

Keir would have said: embarrassment is the way society polices us, Frey, isn't it? Judge folk by their intentions. Their best intentions, even: we're all much of a muchness when you come down to it. She thought fondly of Keir's hippyish ways. His old and most cherished palette that he'd raffled for Médecins Sans Frontières, which the winning bidder had returned it to him. That was Rae. She'd said: every time you raffle it, cariad, I will buy it back for you – I will always do that – so, hey, try not to bankrupt me?

'Cariad'. Freya had surprised herself by registering a jag of dismay. The novel and fleeting sensation had interested rather than distressed her. They'd had an open marriage and she'd have been content with that, and in many ways enjoyed the freedom. Not least the freedom to have their big bed to herself. Once or twice she remembered thinking Keir was keeping something from her. She'd resolutely turned her face away. Now, without warning, suspicion and hostility to their oldest friends had set in, and this weird sense of a door swinging open. There was nothing whatever left to possess. Not a crumb.

Except the child. But don't think of Haf. Look the other way.

She did look the other way but the image still skipped into view. Haf could approach from any angle, she was everywhere. There was that retching scent of charred lemons again. Nauseating.

Why had Freya allowed his body to be buried in the earth? So far down, unreachable, rotting. What state was he in now? Her mind burrowed into the earth, to see what death had done to Keir, after Mr Knott and his artificers had finished with him. Why not have had Keir cremated, so that she could keep his ashes to herself. Just for a while, she pleaded – just a month, say?

For fuck's sake! What's the matter with you? It's the least environmentally sound way of disposing of remains.

Freya looked out again at the figures chatting on the green. A magpie stabbed with his hopeful beak amongst the violets. A hot gale seethed in the ash and sycamore trees, whipping branches into disarray.

She spoke aloud: 'You did exactly what Keir wanted, Freya. He is where he wanted to be.'

Inexpressibly dear, he was. And stoical. When they were first together, Keir's hair reached well beneath his shoulders. But when it fell out, he hadn't minded – or hadn't shown he minded. But who is going to look after *me*, now that you've cleared off, she demanded, and a throb of anger came, as if Keir had left on purpose. He'd flown the nest. *Right, I've had enough of you now. I'm moving on. You wanted the bed to yourself, Frey? – well, now you've got it.* These were illogical thoughts and would pass through her like a virus. Nothing to be done except to suffer them patiently.

What on earth was going on over there? They were herding Terry's cat, or so it seemed, and hooting with laughter. As one lost hold, another grappled the irrepressible body that twisted and slithered in their hands. And sprang. Whereupon Storm took flight, the ninny, and Mark followed him, with his lolloping gait. Freya smiled: perhaps she would go out. Join them. Just be normal, ordinary. Yes, why not? After all, she didn't smell offensive, now that she'd taken a shower and washed her hair.

When she arrived, there were just Pam, Terry and the cat. They broached the idea of a day out.

'Oh. Yes,' she said to Pam, privately thinking, *I'd rather not be stuck in a car making conversation*. She bridled at the thought of becoming a charity case for her neighbours. Terry was not patronising but Pam (salt of the earth) could be matronising. 'What a nice idea,' she said, insincerely. 'I'd like that. I love the dunes at Three Cliffs.'

On the plus side, it was a place she and Keir had never visited together. Freya didn't want to tread in their old footsteps. Her neighbours were surely right: she needed to be led gently out of her retreat. And perhaps, later on today she'd have a look at the last bike she'd been building.

'Mark may be able to come but we can't count on it,' said Terry. 'He's got a lot on at present.'

They looked down the hill to where Mark was romping with Storm, like a child at play. Freya was not offended. There should be joy, she saw, if anything was to make sense – and this must be a gain for her: what she could not feel within herself, she could see in others and bless. Mark had a secret – what was it? Perhaps she could catch at the hope he seemed to intuit, even in the wake of his loss of his wife. Catching sight of them watching, he waved and began sauntering back, Storm at his heel.

6

A bad dream, oh the worst, *that* dream again, it roiled around your mind – and you shot into wakefulness (but could not move) and knew it was not just a dream but real – oh, it was bad, so bad.

I've been so bad. I've gone beyond.

Nobody helps you, nobody. You're crying out for help and there is no one there.

And let my cry come unto Thee!

There was no one in calling distance and never really had been, or at least nobody to rely on, which was the same – and Mark lay paralysed, clasped in his own arms, eyelids glued shut. Waiting for the axe to fall but it delayed and delayed. Give me the punishment I have earned! Do it now! Finish me off! You wouldn't leave a dog in this condition! For so many years, Mark had endured the darkness of this anguish. Your heart was a galloping stallion. Was it that you were buried alive? Was that it?

Let my cry come unto Thee.

There was no Thee. No mercy existed – you had shown none so how could you expect any?

Get up, Mark advised himself, open your eyes, switch on the light. You are being irrational.

Come on now, it's all right, none of this has been your fault.

Hardly any of it.

Shush-shush: those things *happened* to you and you have had to live with the *dreams* (which is all they are) all these years and the whole thing has made you *ill*, take something. The GP is no good. The last doctor was no good. Quacks, all of them. You have to help yourself. Look here, you have shelf upon shelf of medication in the loft, there is always a remedy.

The contrary voice was remorseless: you are unforgivable. A

parasite, a law-breaker. You know that perfectly well. Where is your contrition? And how could there be forgiveness for a leper like yourself? You'd be better off dead but you're a wimping coward, you couldn't even take the coward's way out.

I won't go in to the gallery today, he thought. I'll say I've got toothache. I can't bear those eyes on me. Like flies crawling around. After all, the job is way beneath my capacities.

If somebody had just stayed Mark's hand. If only someone would hold that hand now, and counsel Mark: how to go on living. But the hand had shot out of its own accord. It seemed to act as if jerked on a string controlled by a puppeteer.

Mark concentrated on controlling his breathing. One survives. That is the penalty. Open your eyes. Unlock your muscles. Fetch the pills. Shivers of electricity thrilled through Mark's jaw and into his rigid tongue and the decaying root canals of his teeth. On the outside, his teeth looked pristine; they were whiter than white, but underneath ... that old dentist, what was his name? – Perks or Perch? – he had been no use whatever, his fingers ginger with tobacco. Anyway, never mind Perch or Perks, he'll be six foot under by now. Tramadol or Oramorph will fix it. Come on, get up. Xanax, I've got Xanax.

Jesus Christ, he was still asleep or wedged halfway between asleep and awake. Call out! Fight! No. There was another way. He remembered now.

Lean in to love, to find your courage, my son, was what the priest had counselled when Mark found his way to the confessional that time and told half a story. His raging remorse had only fractionally been assuaged by the priest's response, for half a story is a dissimulation. Mark had confessed: *I am a guilty man. My wife died. I failed her.*

My son, lean in to love, the priest had urged. *Love will never let you down.*

Freya, Mark said to himself now, and his eyes opened to an answering light at the window: morning had broken. It was a broken morning.

Freya. Dearest.

Creeping to the bathroom, Mark shook, his legs gave, he knelt at the pan as if in prayer, hanging on with both hands; threw up. Over and over, he was emptied out. When everything that was coming had surely-to-God come, he sank down, foetal on the floor. In a cold sweat.

Get up.

I can't.

Wash your paws. The seat is crawling with germs. Don't put your hands near your mouth, it's lethal.

Any more to come? No? Sure? Get up then! You can't? Of course you can!

Antiseptic soap. Hot water. Pumice. No bacterium had a chance after the scrubbing Mark dealt his hands and forearms. Toothpaste rid his mouth of its foul taste.

See? – All well.

He palmed a couple of hydrocodeine tablets into his mouth. Hang on a minute, there was plenty of Oramorph in the loft, saved from the times he'd taken his migraine and spinal pain to Dr Lewis. And there was a reserve kept here in the bathroom cabinet. The back pain was real but intermittent. Mark's strategy had always been to listen out for the approach of pain and hit it before it struck. Dr Lewis, who was permanently harassed, paid him in pills, to get rid of him. He would give you *that* look, say the word *addiction,* but then give in. Mark was not an addict. He was too intelligent for that. Whenever he panicked – which was daily – his fingers, of their own volition, so it seemed, reached out for Oramorph. Hence, he hid it from himself; it was on ration, and he was strict.

He had wasted some on Lily. When she became intolerable, he'd slip something in a glass of orange juice to calm her. Lock the door on the bedroom. Not a cheep out of her for hours. But only very occasionally, because this elixir was hard to come by. And anyway, in due course she did the job for herself with alcohol.

The stuff put a distance between you and your suffering. It fizzed wondrously in your veins. Outwitting oneself was a dodgy business.

Both sides had to know how and when to communicate, in a real emergency.

Today had brought such an emergency. He was not sure why. But the floors, whenever he looked down, lay fractionally atilt. A rectangle of sombre sky showed at the window, and mist rolled past like water.

Breathe, Mark told himself, and the world will right itself. In so far as it ever does. Do this logically. Systematically. Ah yes: he found the bathroom stash, all counted and labelled and lined up, together with a note of the considerable stocks in the loft. Mark reached for Valium, that gentle friend. Of course. But he needed stronger.

One blessed pearl of morphine lay on his palm. He placed it on his tongue with a kind of reverence, a eucharistic hopefulness.

At the very back of his mind he heard Lily speak the words, *Fucking addict.* Sneering.

Speak for your fucking self, he responded, using her gutter language. *Fucking alky.*

Once her career had crumbled, she had degenerated fast, undermining Mark's best efforts to strengthen himself and support her. But he did not feel angry with Lily. No. What did she know? (Nothing – she was dead). What had she ever known of the courage needed by Mark simply to rise every day and face the world?

She never listened, that was her problem. She'd say, *Yeah, I know.* She would look bored and hostile when he told her about his pain.

After a shower, the pulsing in the walls calmed down. There you are, you see, Mark told himself: all you needed was a clean scalp, peppermint mouth, purged stomach. Generally it took all day, after one of those dreams, to lose the lurking terror of her bloody eruption from underground.

Then he caught it, a broken thread of music, the wraith of a voice. Coming through the wall?

Music was calling. He had cried out and a voice called back. Mark stood, naked, ear pressed against the party wall. Susanna's aria from *The Marriage of Figaro.*

81

Deh vieni, non tardar....

Oh come, don't be late, my beautiful joy. As long as the air is still dark. And the world quiet.

What the listener's ear missed, memory supplied. Freya was less than a metre away. The quality of her singing was – frankly – functional. And fragmentary. There were lulls, as if she brooded upon the words or forgot what came next, or was scarcely conscious of singing. Occasionally her voice – a treble like a boy's – wavered, subsided and took up the aria again a few bars earlier. None of that was the point. It was the voice of a beloved spirit that Mark received – and through it, a communication from the invisible world. The very imperfections were consoling. There is mercy in the universe. You thought you were alone, the music said, but you were mistaken: I am here and I am always here. Side-by-side with you. Freya was presumably lying in her bath, relaxed for once and self-forgetful.

Lily's voice had been a powerful mezzo. But do not think of that.

Mark leaned in to love. It reassured him of forgiveness for what, after all, had taken place a very long time ago, when Mark was not the person he was now. Also, and crucially, he was blaming himself for what had been in essence an accident, or a series of accidents, precipitated by Lily's recklessness. Or, as he often thought, her suicidal impulse. She had wanted oblivion.

It seemed altogether feasible that Freya was singing to and for Mark, sending a message through the wall. *Deh vieni, non tardar.*

Mark had been tempered in the fire. Hell goes on forever. You are abandoned in outer darkness, licked by invisible flame. You long to be mortal and capable of death. If you died again, you would land here again, besieged by invisible fire. But Purgatory was limited. You pay for your offence and are gathered in. At the end of the long tunnel, there is the possibility of full and free forgiveness. This was the way to see it. What his neighbour was surely telling him was that his time in Purgatory was up; he'd paid for his fault.

Freya had stopped singing. And Mark was free.

So – coffee! The gathering aroma revived him further. A yolky egg. Toast, yes. Warmly oozing with butter. Thick cut marmalade, dolloped on; manuka honey, with its healing properties. Live yoghurt for the good bacteria, with slicks of strawberry compote. Fish oil tablets.

He would visit Lily's grave in the next week and take freesias, her favourite.

But not today. Far too much to do. This was a day for practicality, for collecting nectar. The Oramorph lullabyed him but it also conferred clarity, or an impression of clarity. Taken occasionally, the medicine lifted the mind to an aerial perspective. Lily, in eternity, would not miss him. What did it matter to Lily if he visited on a Wednesday or a Saturday or not at all? If he brought sunflowers or anemones? It wasn't as if the woman was in hospital. She *had* been admitted to hospital on a couple of occasions, after hair-raising falls, and Mark had not only visited daily but paid for her to be in a side ward. He had devotedly emptied his pockets to succour her.

Oh dear, I'm so clumsy, she'd told the staff, her face pale against the pillows. White light had streamed through the window, as if she were being irradiated. But she looked peaceful too. She hadn't wanted to read or chat, just to lie silently, and Mark had respected that. She felt, Lily had said, secure against accidents. *Story of my life,* she'd admitted to the nurse, shaking her head: *if there's a glass door, you can be sure I'm going to whack straight into it.*

Why am I thinking about that? Mark asked himself. It is irrelevant. Just one of the many foolish tricks that the mind plays in its grief. He bit into toast and honey, and the sugars flooded his mouth: for instance, this yen to ingratiate oneself with the dead, what's that all about? What do they care? They don't give a damn. Why would they?

Too often, he'd slunk weeping to the buried Lily after a night of torment and mooned over the slab that covered her and ought to have held her safely down.

The Crouches were loading the back of the car with an old-fashioned hamper. It looked weighty enough to contain a corpse. Mark stood at the door, holding a tea towel. Poor Freya would be encouraged to tuck into batches of scones and (perish the thought) vegetarian sausage rolls and pickled eggs. Ye gods. He remembered his own travails with the sausage rolls. The pastry would cleave to Freya's palate and load her stomach, when all she wanted to eat, probably, was a light salad scattered with pine nuts, with raspberries and *fromage frais* to follow.

He could see it now. On another occasion, he'd offer her just this menu. Freya would sit in the sunlight in his mini-conservatory at Tŷ Hafan, amongst the geraniums. Sweet peas would scent the atmosphere. Take, eat. He remembered the poem by George Herbert: *Love bade me welcome.* This was how it would be.

Freya was wearing a green hooded top, cargos and trainers, a small backpack over one shoulder. Her rebellious hair was scraped into a pony tail, making her look like a schoolgirl on her first reluctant day. The Crouches wouldn't let her lift a finger to help load what Mark quietly thought of as their hearse. Freya stood with folded arms, squinting against the daylight and throttling off a yawn. Like a lamb to the slaughter, he thought. The pair of them would talk their fragile guest into the ground. While she consumed their fake sausage rolls, they would eat Freya for dinner.

Mark went in and replaced the tea towel with paper and pen.

'I'm working at home on a provenance today,' he explained. 'For my sins. Wish I could come along. Did you sleep, Freya?'

'Not too badly, thanks.'

'Should I look in on Storm for you? I could take him for a walk at lunch time. I allow myself half an hour off or I'd go stark staring mad.'

'Oh, would you mind? Dogs aren't allowed on the beach after April.'

'Do I mind going mad or walking Storm?'

She laughed. It was a subdued murmur of a laugh but genuine. Mark could always evoke a smile from her. It was a knack he seemed to have, even or especially when he came out with some impromptu quip.

'Of course,' he said gently. 'I'd like to. Is there anything you need from the shops, Freya? Just say.'

'No thanks, Mark – I'm fine. I appreciate your kindness. I really do. I hope you know that.'

'We're neighbours. It's what neighbours do.'

'Yes,' she said slowly, and let out a held breath. 'That's right.'

Her shoulders seemed to relax and she glanced towards Terence and Pamela, who were fussing about the alignment of the hamper in relation to the cubic space available in the hearse.

'By the way,' Freya added, 'here's a spare key, Mark. I was going to ask you, actually, if you'd mind hanging on to it for me? In case I lock myself out, or whatever.'

Mark bit back the impulse to say he already had one. The legitimate key now lay snug in Mark's palm. The trust it implied was more touching than he could easily bear.

'Freya, you know, if you don't feel up to going out, just say. Terry and Pam would understand. Sometimes it can just feel – too soon.'

She said nothing; just looked at him with swimming eyes. 'It will be fine,' she said, choking. 'Once I'm there.'

'Sure? You look tired.'

'Thanks a lot!'

'No! You look – oh dear – as lovely as ever – just your eyes are tired.'

'Well anyway – thanks for looking out for me.'

I'll always do that, Mark thought but didn't say. Looking out for you is my way of life and I will never let you down. As he saw them off and returned to his work, a wave of relief crested. Be calm now, he admonished himself. Be gentle, both with yourself and with your friend. Let love come, if it will, in its own time and without strategy. Mark would not force anything.

The party took off for its day-trip. He had engineered it in a subtle way and then assuaged his conscience by suggesting to Freya that she could drop out if she wished. Mark addressed himself to his work. He was sorting through the archive the museum had only just managed to put online in preparation for the exhibition. There was something humiliating about working for a provincial outfit on a part-time basis. But he knew he'd never risk the breakdown he'd suffered at the V&A. In this little Welsh world, Mark counted as a big cheese. He tried to deserve their good opinion and treated all the museum staff with respect; nearly all the time. Those he sneered at, like Paltry Patrick, were too thick to notice.

Mark yawned and stretched. If he went now to check up on Storm, he could have coffee in there. But be scrupulous, he told himself: take your own coffee in your own cup. Besides, Freya only had instant.

Perhaps ring the Crouches first. Yes. Make sure they were far enough away and would not double back, to pick up some essential gingersnaps. No answer. Maybe they were out of range. Then Pamela picked up. The line was poor. A lot of traffic but, yes, they were nearly there.

'Hallo, my boy – my dear old boy.' Mark greeted Storm with sincere delight.

The tail-wagger ran in tight circles to indicate his rapture. Together man and dog wandered into the kitchen. Mark's fingers itched to wash up the pots in the sink and to swab the surfaces with disinfectant. How could people bear to live like this?

But this is not your space, he reminded himself. And in any case, the chaos is a symptom of my poor darling's grief. Closing the door on the mess, he led Storm upstairs. Where did I put the key? He felt in his pockets. Ah, there we are. His fingers surprised him, happening upon the tiny mike he'd hardly noticed himself slipping in there, just in case.

But how languid he felt. There was none of the expected elation at inhabiting Freya's space, just this lassitude – doubtless the effects of the morphine. Not an unpleasant sensation, by any means, but tending to inertia. Whatever he'd come into her bedroom to do or experience, Mark abandoned it, and, sitting on the edge of her bed, removed his sandals. He laid his head back against Freya's pillow; closed his eyes. He felt rather than saw Storm jumping up beside him.

Then nothing until Storm woke him, charging downstairs; the door was rapping.

Shit. Mark leapt from sleep. What if she'd come back and found him snoozing in her bed? Even his powers of invention would hardly have extended to accounting for this plausibly – and in a manner creditable to himself. Although – at once his brain began to run different possibilities – but he switched them off as he quit the bed, smoothing the duvet in one sweeping motion.

Like a shot, Mark was into the spare-room and peeping round the curtain. The top of a guy's head. A blond quiff, greased. Large, rangy geezer in rugby strip. Had to be the brother-in-law he'd labelled Reinhard Heydrich and endowed with the characteristics of that hawk-nosed Nazi psychopath. Evidently he hadn't a key: that was something. Why, if he was thinking of visiting, hadn't Reinhard rung Freya to arrange?

Now the ass was braying at Storm through the letter box flap. *Hiya! Hiya, mate! How ya doing? Hi-ya!*

Storm barked louder. How many times could a fatuous ex-brother-in-law bawl *Hiya* to a canine through a letter box?

Mark kept still. Giving up, the visitor straightened and took a step back.

Any second now, the Butcher of Prague would look up and scan the windows. He did, and Mark smartly withdrew. You would not want to tangle with any of the Fox brothers, each of them built on a grand – grandly moronic – scale. When Mark dared peer down again, the guy had gone. Would he go round the back? The kitchen door was bolted but how secure were the windows? Storm would notify him if Heydrich went round. But nothing. Ten minutes went past. A car door slammed; the ex-brother-in-law drove away. Thank

Christ he had no key. Mark's heart slowed down. He whistled to Storm.

Where to place the mike?

Not in the bedroom: that would be indecent. All one wanted – needed, even – was to be able to keep an ear out so that Freya would never need to be alone. The purpose was beneficent. She was not a natural loner. Downstairs, Mark drew the curtains as he pondered the living-room. Maybe behind a picture? I've never done anything like this in my life, he thought. Stop it now. Draw back. Freya is coming to you anyway, just as Storm has. Probably. Let her come. Give her space and time.

But she might not. She might recover and go gadding gladly on her way. The world would be at her feet. He'd be plunged into a version of the devastation he'd felt when an audience clapped and whistled for Lily, recalling her for an encore.

Keeping the mike in his pocket, Mark opened the door to the store cupboard which wasn't a store-room. Funny to think that his storage space was symmetrically placed against the same wall where he stacked tinned foods, ceiling high, after the custom of his gran. She'd been through the Blitz and, even decades after the War, she'd never overcome the fear of want. Deprivation loomed everywhere in the terraced world where he'd grown up, fear of famine, even though there was always slightly more than enough. When she died, demented and unmourned, he'd returned from Cambridge to find her larder stocked with rusting cans, the back rows decades old, one on top of the other. Every inch was jammed with his grandmother's fear of starvation. Even as a professional with a salary and a pension, you carried the ghost of that fear.

He hadn't realised, on his first unaccompanied visit, that Freya's store-room had been turned into a study, with desk, computer and bookshelves on three sides.

The Botany of Desire: A Plant's-eye View of the World, well thumbed, smelling of cigarette smoke, with pages folded at the edges. A tree-huggers' bible, he thought.

Teaching a Stone to Talk. Good luck with that!

The Tribe of Tiger. Lend it to the cat-mad Crouches.

No. This is the trouble with you, Heyward, he scolded himself, sitting down in Freya's chair at Freya's desk and getting the feel of this intimate space, which almost counted as a secret room. This is you all over. Contempt is your default. If you want Freya to care about you, you'll need to be open. Open to ideas that might seem unlikely, even ludicrous. And, God knows your own head has been a haven for absurdities in its time. The world beyond your wall can shed new light. You know enough about Freya to recognise that she belongs to a counterculture. So you will have to study conditions in this mental world in order to come close to her. See through Freya's eyes, feel with her heart. And take her thoughts seriously. Or how will you deserve her?

Right. The first thing to do was to photograph the bookshelves, with a view to acquiring personal copies. Some could be borrowed from the university library but others he'd purchase on Amazon, as he'd need to annotate them. Second-hand copies would make sense, not only to save money but because they'd appear used, to anyone who found herself pondering his bookshelves.

Storm, having located a bone he'd previously ditched, was gnawing savagely. The dog was happy, and occasionally looked up at Mark as someone who belonged here and belonged to him.

And I do, Mark thought. And shall do, more and more.

He slid open the desk drawers. A chaos of notes, old letters, bills. A pair of glasses that must have been Keir's: long-sighted, the lenses smeared with fingerprints. She needs to chuck these out, he thought. Evidently Freya had not yet felt able to sift and jettison the dead man's belongings: good, because Mark could help with that.

Presumably the Foxes had shared the desk: he recognised documents in Freya's handwriting. And a notebook in another hand, which he pocketed. Scrawl. Photographs. Was this Freya as a toddler? It must be. Bless her, the child's bouncing curls were tied in a topknot, her grin was wide. So touching. The photo went to his heart and into his pocket. Illumination arose in a surprising flash: if she and I had a child, this is how it would look. A daughter, not a son, would be his preference, but whatever God or chance gave.

Did he really mean that? Did he even like children? Mark shook his head ruefully at his own fantasies.

First things first.

He rummaged further amongst the photographs. Blurry Instamatic pictures of a teenage Keir Fox on a motorbike. In helmet. Without helmet. With and without leather gloves. With pillion passenger, female, not Freya.

And here was Fox, posed at some kind of camp amongst trees, arm draped round the shoulder of a half-dressed floosie, his hand dangling over her bosom. Hair down to his shoulders, scruffy beard, hairy chest: the fellow was more than simian, this was Werewolf Syndrome, ha! And women found this attractive? Mark's own chest was relatively hairless. Might he be seen as epicene, not quite a man? But no sensible woman would hold that against you.

Now the Fox was groping another floosie. This was getting tedious. And another. They were all half naked. Now he was waving to the camera, halfway up a tree. Up another tree. Oh, please. Now he was in a scrum with security guards or police, and obviously enjoying the violence.

In six or seven photos, he was shown with an absurdly young Freya, looking twelve years old, an elf of a girl.

Mark would keep a couple of those and cut Keir off the picture. There was something so beguiling about Freya's young self. It was a self you still recognised in the thirty-odd-year-old, tender and unfocused.

Scholarly habits of research came in useful. One thing Mark knew from experience was that the cover does not invariably define the contents. From a buff envelope labelled 'TAX 2011', he extracted a smaller envelope containing three photographs: Keir Fox dandling a jaundiced-looking goblin of a baby, very small, probably newborn; two of Freya cuddling the same infant.

Ah.

Half an hour later, Mark had copied all the images he required, investigated birth, marriage and death certificates, positioned the mike and was ready to depart. As he fastened Storm's lead, the mural in the sitting-room disturbed his eye. Tasteless. Coarse. Imagine living with that swirling horror of vine-like curlicues and twisted branches. Keir fancied himself as an Expressionist. The paint, predominantly green, blue and brown, had discoloured over time and areas had flaked away. Bits of tiny birds – a wren, a bullfinch, a blackbird (and, yes, one could distinguish the species; Fox was not wholly devoid of observational flair) – had fallen off, leaving partial creatures in their stead, beakless or breastless. A cradle hung from a disintegrating branch, beneath a dove's open wings.

This fresco would have to go, Mark thought.

When he and she were united – reunited, he wanted to say – it would be natural to make changes, even before the two of them moved to Tŷ Hafan. As they would. He was leaping ahead of himself but it did no harm to dream.

There was still something ... what was it? Some space he'd missed, which needed to be found. The sensation was like an itch. Retracing his steps, Mark revisited each room and stood in the doorway ticking off possibilities from a mental list. On the landing, he found himself staring at a door to what he'd assumed to be a cupboard. But no, this was the door to Freya's loft. He opened it and looked up the wooden steps. An unmistakable smell of turps. Of course: it was your *atelier*, Keir, where you practised your art, so-called. No time or energy at present to research the studio. Keep that for a future date.

Preparing to leave the house with Storm, Mark faltered. He debated, in a rapid cross-fire and for the umpteenth time, the relationship between means and end, intention and action. Your brain proposes one line of action; your hand disposes otherwise. It was a mystery he'd often pondered and never fathomed. The action decides for you. It had been the work of moments, almost unrecorded in his consciousness, to slip the mike behind the books. He had fully intended (and felt the better for it) not to transgress in that way. And yet he had done so. The Puppeteer foiled one's best intentions.

Go back in, Mark told himself, all but shutting the door.

Remove the device. Stamp it underfoot. Trample it. Then you will not be tempted.

And you won't replace the mike because of the expense – and also because, if you did, you'd have to destroy it again. Mark paused. Storm yanked at the leash. The latch slipped in to its groove.

Get out your key, his right self insisted to his sinister self. Go back inside. Do the decent thing. Come on now. You're having yourself on.

Restraining Storm with his left hand, Mark pulled the key ring from his pocket. Here we are. He inserted the key but it wouldn't turn. The wrong key? So find the right one. But somehow the matter had been decided for him. Mark's left hand restored the key ring to his pocket and his right arm allowed Storm to drag him off in pursuit of beckoning smells – urinous lampposts, chip papers in garbage bags and the smashed finches' eggs of springtime.

*

'I used to come here as a child,' said Freya. 'With my parents and sister. My auntie and uncle had a caravan.'

'Happy memories, I hope?' said Pamela.

'Oh yes, lovely. My cousins and I made up a secret language. The adults didn't know what we were talking about. At least, that's what we told ourselves. I think we were fairly annoying – nowadays we'd be called tweenies. We even had a little dictionary of the invented words. I wonder if I've still got it.'

The three of them trudged up the dunes, against the slippage of sand. Your aching calves remembered the terrain, with its constant subsidence. The more you pushed, the more it gave. Freya admired marram grass. Reeds. Bracken. Vetch. Sea campion. Vegetation that not only tolerated parched conditions but throve and blossomed there. The shadowed flanks of dune lay in deep chill; the sunny side bathed your face in warmth. The rhythm soothed Freya and the exhaustion seemed to have lifted. She launched herself ahead, hearing the couple's conversation at a little distance.

'You know, Terry,' said Pamela, panting her way to the crest of a dune and pausing to take in the view of Pennard Pill, the wide stream curving out to the sea. 'This was a lovely idea of Mark's. I'm so glad he suggested it. We should come out more often, shouldn't we? We're so unfit.'

'Speak for yourself!'

'I'm speaking for you!'

Oh no, thought Freya – she wants to make it a weekly excursion, to take me out of myself. Why couldn't Mark mind his own business? The freshness of the view perished and all Freya wanted was to scuttle home and possess her own space. Before this could be accomplished, there was the hamper to unpack, folding chairs to set out, a three-course lunch to eat with plastic knives and forks.

But Pamela seemed to be following a train of her own thoughts and not to be rounding Freya up. 'You know, I was so wrong about Mark. He always seemed ... oh dear ... hoity-toity. Frankly, rude. For instance, Terry, I told you about the chimpanzees, didn't I?'

'Well, perhaps you got the wrong end of the stick there, Pammie.'

'I don't think I really got either end of that particular stick.'

'Don't forget,' Terry cut in, 'Mark is highly educated. Too highly educated. He knows seven languages, several of them ancient and – dead. It must make a difference to your scale of judgment. A bit of a chimp's-eye-view!'

Freya's heart gave a little lift. The chimp's-eye-view!

'Why?' she asked, turning. 'Whatever did he say?'

'Just trying to remember, exactly.' Pam thought about it. 'Modern translations of the Bible being adapted to the IQ of an average monkey? Something like that. But, bless him, Mark did apologise.

He didn't mean *me*, of course. He was on about that Dawkins chappie. The atheist. And he has been so sweet ever since.'

Yes, the chimp's-eye view, Freya thought. I know all about that. She began to chat as she used to chat, before death blocked her mouth. The three of them waded down the final dunes to the broad flats of the bay as she described the perspective from the tree canopy at the by-pass protest. That first meeting with Keir. Freya had been eighteen, Keir twenty-nine. The movement had been passionately bonded in the tight-knit fight for the forest. Love and trust stretched between the activists like the wires linking the tree-houses. The group's affection had secured and composed her after all the quarrels with her parents.

'Of course, I thought I was immortal. I was eighteen, after all – and a rather young eighteen at that. I had this friend – she was a natural climber. Not like us. She used to say: we were apes once, when we had prehensile tails and hung out in the treetops. Look at my hands, she'd say: eighty-million years swinging from branch to branch formed these long fingers.'

'But they built the roads, of course,' said Pam.

'They felled ten-thousand trees and arrested eight-hundred of us, including Keir. When he got out, we went indoors.'

That was when they'd moved in to the crescent. And painted the wall with its mural. And lost the child.

The sea was way out, across the ochre sand. A piebald horse cantered along the tide-line. Freya knew she would swim. Nobody and nothing could stop her. Whatever anyone said about the currents and rips here, Freya would swim. Despite there being no life-guards. She didn't care.

If she failed to die, she would live.

Freya flew. Whatever came next, it had to be better than what had gone before; just had to be. Planes of water mirrored the three cliffs, which seemed to topple into their reflections. The sea kept its distance. She put on speed. This was where the horse had been cantering, across the corrugated sand. Its hoof prints had filled with water. Over where the beach linked with the next bay, she glimpsed horse and rider, toy-small, vanishing around the rocks.

Freya paused to strip off tracksuit and trainers. She ran into the water as if there were someone behind her, tracking her, overtaking her.

7

'I had a great time,' Freya said. 'I swam!'

Immediately she looked embarrassed at the childishness of her blurting.

'In the sea?'

She laughed. 'Well – *yes*!'

Mark felt daunted. Freya would recover, and be herself. And if he did not act now, he would lose her.

'Of course,' he admitted, reddening. 'Where else? It's so good for you. I love it myself. In the old days,' he swept on, 'everyone swam – the old Gower swimmers; my dad was one, and all my uncles.'

I'm off again, Mark thought. I can't swim, never knew my dad and had no uncles, at least as far as I know. And now that this tribe of alpha males had been spawned, they'd have to be kept alive.

But then it occurred to him: no one should swim at Three Cliffs because of the rips and the estuary flush. Apologetically, he brought the warning up on his phone.

'Freya,' he said hesitantly, 'I don't want to be a killjoy but – it's a death trap. Three people have died swimming there in the last three years.'

Terence's and Pamela's pallid faces told him they had feared for her life – and for their own lives if they'd gone in to aid her. Terence gave him a tiny nod.

'Yes, I knew that,' Freya said serenely, arms folded, looking at the app, only slightly shame-faced. The way she said it told Mark everything about the spirit in which she'd undertaken her swim. She'd played Russian roulette with the rip.

'But Freya – my dear friend,' Mark said, aiming his words straight into the depths of her mind, where the death-wish lurked. 'That was the Lorelei. It would have been so unfair to Terry and Pam. And to your family and friends who care about you.'

'I know. I'm sorry,' Freya said, flinching; his insight had hit home. She shot him a crestfallen look. 'I shouldn't have worried you both. Pammie. Terry.' She held out a hand to each. 'Please forgive me. But it was wonderful. A brilliant day. And I'm fine. How was Storm?'

'Happy as Larry. He's on my sofa, spark out.' Mark opened his door and whistled. No response but sleepy grunting. 'Good thing we're not burglars,' he said as they went in. 'Come on, you dozy thing.'

Storm poured himself off the settee and there was a festival of licking and caressing. Mark put the kettle on. The Crouches would not come in. Mind you, they had not been asked. He saw them lugging the hamper past his window. Freya showed no inclination to return home. She took off her shoes and wriggled her toes in her socks; sand fell out onto the carpet. But it was Freya's sand and he did not mind. He would have minded if it had been Tŷ Hafan. But then Tŷ Hafan was not a house: it was a work of art. Danielle must be removed without more ado.

Freya made herself comfortable and looked round curiously.

'It's very tidy,' she observed.

'Is that bad?'

'No, of course not! But where is all your mess?'

'Obviously – under the bed!'

'That would be it. I love your bronze things. Are they gods and goddesses?'

'They are. Greek. I love them too.'

Athena overlooked Mark's work desk and a sacred oryx was eternally poised to spring from a bookshelf. He would look at them afresh when Freya had left, seeing them imaginatively through her eyes, as if she'd blessed them and everything in his world. Picking up the ornament, Freya weighed it in both hands and traced the geometrical curves with her fingertip. She didn't replace it in the precise position: Mark banished the unease this triggered and forbade his fingers from correcting her mistake.

'It's a goat, isn't it,' Freya said. 'A mountain goat.'

97

'An oryx, yes.'

'So was the oryx sacred too in Ancient Greece?'

'More or less any creature or tree or place could be.' Mark tried not to be teacherly.

'What does the oryx stand for?'

'Passion. Strength. Resource. What you will, really.'

'Yes, I see,' Freya said, consideringly. 'But what does it mean for you personally, Mark?'

'Oh, it means – all those qualities. And just – wild nature itself, I suppose. And – something beyond all that. I mean, beyond what can be limited by words.'

For the first time since he'd known Freya, Mark felt her attention linger, brushing him over and over with a moth's wing. Surprisingly, he didn't feel abashed: this was the kind of conversation that pleased and sustained him.

'And did you get your work done?'

'Not as much as I meant to do. Tea for you.'

She wrapped both hands around the mug and breathed in the scent. 'Camomile and something else?'

'Vanilla.'

'Lovely.' She sipped. Her eyes did not stray from his face. 'So, tell me, Mark, where did you learn to be a mind-reader?'

'Pardon?'

'The Lorelei. Who lures sailors to their death.'

'Oh – well – I don't know.'

'I'm sure you do.'

'Guesswork, maybe? Memory. I remember how I was when my darling Lily passed away. I thought: I'll find the ... portal ... and step through it. You know, Orpheus and so on. There isn't a portal and she isn't on the other side. All the time, Freya, Lily was in myself and I hadn't realised.'

Somehow, in expressing these thoughts, Mark had himself crossed the threshold into a place of equivocation. His falsity came down over them both, a cobweb. You are a fake, you are a ham, Mark told himself. He shifted from foot to foot, rubbing his palms together. Looking down on his hands, he saw them as a pair of fleshy animals, nuzzling together blindly. Orpheus! Strewth! At every moment, he thought, I give myself away. He stopped the hand-wringing. Why had he said that about Lily and portals? What rat seized Mark's goodwill and shook it until there was no life left in it? Anything he said about Lily had to be a killer. My inner rat, he thought.

Freya seemed to lapse; her attention dropped away. She looked spent and drained, and smaller. She'd go and rest now, she said, thanking him for the tea and for taking care of Storm. She dragged herself up from the settee.

Mark washed his cup and left hers where it was. It commemorated Freya with an invisible lip mark on the rim. As he straightened out the kitchen, he couldn't blink away the nagging notion of a portal into another world. His face was wet. What was he crying about? Untruth and depravity. But Lily had died accidentally, of natural causes or by her own suicidal actions, under the influence of alcohol. It had never been deemed her husband's fault. Finally, on the stairs, she had taken that tragic last leap.

This could have happened at any time. It had been waiting to happen.

His intention had never been to cause his wife harm. The very opposite: the way Mark remembered it, he had been shouting at the top of his voice, yes, for Lily was an impossible woman – and, yes, she may have *imagined* he was going for her – but the reverse was true, he had seen the catastrophe coming and lunged out to prevent it.

What he missed was not Lily's presence but the virtue she took with her. A theft he hadn't recognised until the quality was lost. None of it had been his fault.

She had plunged headfirst, like a diver from a board.

Although Mark had gone whistling around Tŷ Hafan, leaving her splayed at the bottom of the stairs, this was not because he didn't care. Shock did weird things to people. They burst out laughing, for instance. He might have laughed. He might have doubled over in paroxysms. To recover his gravity, he might have made himself a cup of hot chocolate and had a go at the crossword puzzle on the kitchen table. Or the living-room table, he was not sure which. He may have had *two* cups of hot chocolate and *twice* gone to try the last two crossword clues. He may have gone round and round, between these two actions and something else.

Calm down, he insisted, nothing has changed. This all happened in another life. Stop snivelling, blow your nose, drink some water, clear your conscience. He fiddled with the positioning of the oryx on the shelf. That was better. Was it? Not really. The more he melted with joyous love for Freya, the more free Lily seemed to be to swim up through the melt-water.

Oramorph, he thought, for the pain.

*

Freya sank down on Keir's side of the bed. Quietly she assembled herself in the space her husband's gangly limbs had occupied. There, you see, she told herself: you can do it. It was the first time she'd claimed or accepted the whole bed as her own.

She curled around one hot water bottle, with another at the small of her back. The icy scald of the sea had leached vital warmth. As the breakers mobbed her, Freya had gone down; floundered up, spitting mouthfuls of salt and sand; gone down again. The sea's two minds had tussled, shoving this way, dragging that. Freya had welcomed it all, her matchstick status, the impersonal forces that generated the maelstrom.

I'm coming now. Be there, she'd said to Keir, surrendering to the currents.

But once the rip took hold, it was a different story. Nothing is as you propose to yourself. You live in a world of gestures, she'd realised as the current yanked her out from land, but who is watching? Who are you impressing? Panic. Freya had fought the cross-bias. In precisely the wrong way. The fool's way. Swimming against the rip. Which is no good. You can't. It sucks you out and, struggling there in those terminal seconds, you foresee the end and its loneliness. And your mistake. You didn't really want this at all. Whatever has happened to you, you want to survive.

I want to live, Freya had thought, with or without Keir.

A light had switched on in her brain. She'd abandoned the agitated breast stroke and did the correct, the counter-intuitive thing, relying on her fish-like freestyle to glide sideways along the rip's rim – outwitting the current, curving for home when its violent energy slackened.

And there had stood Terry and Pam at the edge, with *that* look on their faces. Ankle deep in the shallows, they'd resembled the parents of a teenager nobody dares to scold, the rebellious kid she herself had once been. The kid who, if she was warned against something, immediately went and did it. Pam had thrown her own cardigan over Freya's shoulders and hugged Freya's wet, cold body to her dry, warm one, and hadn't said, *We were so worried,* and Freya hadn't said, *I was an idiot, forgive me.* The wind had dried her fast. Hopping around on one foot to put on a trainer, Freya had felt a fatuous ecstasy. Nothing dramatic: a thin fizz of bubbles rising and popping in her mind.

*

A fury of flies buzzed into his brain through the earphones: static.

He should have tested the device at home. Mark had given precisely no thought to it. This was because he was not a criminal but a decent, straightforward person who took uncivil measures only in emergency. He had a lot to learn and unlearn, Mark saw.

One of the gangsters (he was unsure which as he'd seen no one arrive) was proposing that 'Frey' come and stay with him and Yasmin for a while. Yas would be at work but Himmler or Heydrich would look after 'Sis'. Pamper her. *Pamper* her? Was she a poodle? At least, that's what the fellow seemed to be saying. The abrasive voice came and went amid waves of interference. It might have been the way Mark had set up the system. Ye gods, did you have to take an IT course to understand these things?

From a distant place in the buried past, Mark heard a sardonic whine, a voice of stupidity and meanness: *Oh no, Master Mark Heyward, nothing's ever his fault, is it?*

No, he thought. It isn't. Actually. Very little of what I have suffered is my own fault. He gave the knob a twiddle and the surveillance apparatus beeped. Please let them not have heard that next door.

They hadn't. The guy – who was definitely Himmler rather than Heydrich – seemed to be rough-housing Storm and frankly, you'd be hard put to tell man from beast. Snorts, whoops and barkings made Mark wince and turn down the volume. He imagined the brother-in-law rolling round the floor, with Storm play-pouncing him. You couldn't help but feel betrayed by the dog. Pearl never trusted anyone but himself. Loyalty cannot be extended to natural enemies. All Mark could catch of whatever Freya was adding to the racket was an occasional chirrup.

Game over. He could tell where the pair of them must be sitting, Himmler nearer the mike – and Freya further away, presumably on the sofa.

Oh do, Frey.

Chirrup.

Then something like, *Hey, babes, do you remember ...?* Then, wheedling, *Surely you'd like to ...?*

Chirrup.

Let the girl alone, Mark thought. He didn't catch what Freya said in response to this invitation but it had to have been a 'no', because the sleaze was still trying to persuade her. *At least think about it. Come on, babes, it'll do you good.*

Mark could imagine Heinrich's sitting-room furnished with play station and treadmill, the kitchen cupboards stocked with baked beans and dumbbells. What an oasis of calm that would be for a bereaved woman. Mark fiddled gently with 'Record', though it was hardly worthwhile perpetuating such banality and he'd probably erase it without bothering to listen. Useful, though, as a test run. *Just go home, Moron*, he thought, *and leave her in peace. She won't come. I can tell you that for nothing.*

Gusts of laughter. Freya: *Oh don't, Dave! Honestly!*

And it was good for her to laugh. Whoever coaxed Freya to laugh, one must be glad. Unless.

Unless the pair of them were ridiculing him? The nettle of mockery: Mark shrank from the playground derision that made you sad and scathed and ashamed. And angry. But, worst thing in the world, it made you alone. Alone, abandoned.

Spasms of merriment rose and fell beyond the party wall. Mark turned the volume right down. Now there was just a faint, irregular burbling, which led to a silence. Mark's anger spiralled down into a leaden, everyday sort of sorrow. But not for long. Up gushed the hurtful laughter, worse than ever. Mark's mouth dried out; his knuckles were white.

Why hadn't he foreseen this? Why? Mark abandoned the headphones, ran upstairs, rinsed his eyes and forehead with cold water. Why did it not cross your mind that you might overhear gossip about yourself? The private world was scaled for a reason. Why hadn't Mark considered a backlash, an inbuilt Nemesis, before he set the whole pantomime up?

But curiosity is an appetite: it really is, he saw, as the headphones clamped themselves back onto his head.

No! Freya was yelling, in a screeching voice that went right through Mark. *Don't – don't, for pity's sake!*

Sounded urgent. What was the lout doing to her? Did Mark have to go in and intervene?

But the guy could throttle him with one hand.

You're killing me! Stop it!

So, was he ... tickling her? Mark turned up the volume as high as it would go.

Quiet fell and a tender male voice floated into his ears, amplified. *If you need anything – anything at all, babes – just say the word.*

From his eyrie in the spare-room, Mark observed Heinrich Himmler's departure. A bird's-eye view of the fellow's head revealed a hummock of pomaded hair. Below this tumulus, the hair was shaved off down to the ears. Oh, you beauty, how much do you spend on looking like a cockatoo? The vanity of it. And, Jesus Mary and Joseph, Himmler was growing a beard. His vest t-shirt revealed a tattooed black dragon on his left shoulder and, on his right, the Statue of Liberty.

Her brother-in-law engulfed poor Freya. At least I don't dwarf you, Mark thought. On the other hand, she might enjoy being dwarfed. Himmler's arm lay across Freya's shoulders, hers loosely round his waist. They were chatting; Mark couldn't hear what was being said. Himmler leaned over her for a parting hug and kiss. She seemed to cling; he bent to hear whatever it was she wanted to whisper. Freya had vanished into his SS embrace. Come on now, Mark said to himself, be fair: there is intimacy, yes – but just sibling affection. The guy is shallow and she is deep; she is thoughtful and he's a buffoon. Even so, it gave Mark a qualm to observe their mutual ease. And another three of these unnecessary brethren existed with a claim on Freya. The shortest of them stood an inch taller than Mark.

That's right, off you toddle: Himmler climbed into his car, waved and sped off. When all was said and done, what had this been but a duty visit?

Having disconnected the system, Mark felt more positive. Seating himself at his desk, he reached for his notebook, marbled red and black; the fountain pen, tortoiseshell. With lighter heart, he wrote his way into reverie. Handwriting told the story of passion begotten of compassion; despair yielding to modest hope. From day to day, Mark distilled onto the page his solitary search and preparation for love. Writing brought composure. Flow. Zen. A sense that all things were possible. He'd not only tolerate but welcome the ex-brothers-in-law – occasionally – into the world he shared with Freya.

The kind of jealousy he'd been prey to in the past would not recur. And in that situation, it had been far worse. The whole world had seemed to want to fête Lily – or rehearse with her in his house – or sit for hours talking viola with her in Mark's lounge. Treating Mark like a lackey – or like a wife, for God's sake! – and always that momentary silence when he entered the living-room with tea or coffee. Lily had been *the future of viola,* according to her hangers-on. She'd failed to fulfil her promise and now belonged to the past. By and by Mark had succeeded in banishing intruders, even the bass player who'd shoved his hoof in the door and refused to leave her alone with her husband.

After all this, how did a small tribe of ex-brothers-in-law threaten him? As an only child, Mark had sometimes felt the need for siblings. They could have shared the weight of Gran, played pass-the-parcel with her disapproval. Light dawned, as he wrote: sibling love was a form of *agape* that excluded *eros.* But what he felt for Freya was a form of *eros* that included *agape.*

It was like receiving a message from another world. Your pen unearthed truths you hardly knew you knew. It was almost as if he took them at dictation. Once you'd composed these truths on the page, they led into an enlightenment that relieved habitual fears. For an hour he continued at his desk and, laying down the pen, had the sensation of awakening from refreshing sleep.

From now on, make it easy for yourself, Mark chided himself. If you didn't invent facts, you wouldn't have to put so much work into substantiating them, would you? To buffer himself against dangers, Mark would note down significant inventions in the back of the Red Book. Even so, and despite his formidable memory, you couldn't keep consulting the record when caught on the hop: *Excuse me, I'll just go and look it up!* These inventions were not precisely mendacities – more like the inspirations that accompany creativity. They were metaphors veiling an always elusive reality.

Anyway, whatever they were, they needed reining in: they'd led to the one-to-one session Mark had booked, with trepidation, at the Wales Pool. Having presented himself to Freya as a keen swimmer from a swimming family, he was obliged to substantiate the claim.

*

Standing at the edge of the children's area beside the young instructor, Mark practised converting fear into challenge. The prescription goggles he'd bought seemed to help. He looked the part. Mark explained that what he was looking to achieve, preferably within a week, was a sleek and economical freestyle. It was a problem, he acknowledged, that he was afraid of putting his head under the water, but there must be ways of coming to terms with that? Wills, the instructor, courteous and helpful, entered the pool with Mark. He placed one hand under the arch of Mark's back and told him to lie back on the water. And relax.

Relax? Mark lay back, every muscle in spasm, his head up out of the water. Relax?

'I'm here,' said the instructor. 'I've got you, Mark.'

This was a soothing thing to hear. Letting go some of the tension, Mark allowed himself to lay his head back in the water.

'There you are. Well done – really well done. Now I'm going to take my hand away.'

Mark fought the fear; but then, of its own volition, the fear fled. Remarkable.

Mark was floating on his back, unaided. He basked. The rafters way above shimmered through a mist of chlorine. I am a swimmer, Mark thought. Almost. If he could do this, there was nothing he could not achieve. Almost. But why almost? The water that buoyed Mark rocked, as other learners floundered around. Brawny males, worse than babies, fought the water and panicked. But I can do this, Mark told himself. A few minutes before the hour was up, he was able to propel himself across a width of the pool, using a float.

Will's praise was fulsome. Mark was elated. After all, the instructor should know, he thought, allowing himself to be flattered and encouraged. The clock showed that he had two minutes left.

'I'll try the width without a float,' he told Wills. 'No, I won't try – I'll do it.'

'That's the spirit. Catch your breath first, I should.'

'Right. I'm ready.'

'Go, Mark!'

Mark went. He touched home. In another week, he would graduate to the sea.

8

The lawn she had let grow was laced with clover and tall daisies, wild flowers her mother had especially loved, and Freya loved them too, both for Mum's sake and their own. Self-seeded poppies were showing, and vetches with their curious curlicues. She sank to her knees and paddled her hand amongst cool seed-heads. Storm snuffled around at troves of scent deep in the vegetation.

What to do, Freya wondered, with the rest of my life? I might be only halfway through it.

She unlocked the shed door and was bathed in the warm musk of oil and turps. Here was the bike she'd been building, cannibalising half-wrecked machines for their parts. They lay dismembered where she'd abandoned them in that other world where she knew what to do and how to do it. Freya shut and locked the door.

It's early days, people kept saying. *Be patient.* But the sluggish passage of dead time was tedious. Occasionally someone would appear who brought her to life: Dave with his raucous, campy jokes. Rae and Haf bringing understanding and play. Jamie came, separately from his wife and daughter, and she'd longed to melt into him and then asked him not to come for a while. His eyes were so like Keir's. Terry and Pam were in and out. Immediately her visitors left, she was exhausted and sank further into tedium. Perhaps she could donate her life to one of their causes; do something in Keir's name. That would make sense.

But come home now, she pleaded with Keir: you've been away long enough. And thinking this threw her back – three, four years? It had been early summer, May or June. One morning Keir had stuffed clothes into his duffel bag and said he needed time to be quiet in himself; he was going to Norfolk, for the light. There'd been no distrust between the two of them, ever, and it was only now that she realised how rare and precious this trust had been. He'd bear-hugged her and kissed her mouth, eyelids, cheek. But he'd looked rather strange. Feverish. *I must have felt this at the time or perhaps I didn't*, Freya thought. It was only afterwards, scrolling back, that she'd realised how buoyant and yet suppressed he'd been.

He'd stayed away three weeks. *Miss you, Frey. Miss you like mad.*

In an open marriage, the paradox was that you have to close off parts of your awareness. Freya had had a knack for that. Now the doors seemed to have all banged open. Walls had turned into windows. The windows were hanging off their hinges. She was an abandoned house. Anyone could get in.

Come back now: it doesn't matter what you've done. Freya's thoughts attempted to forge a makeshift bargain with some cold force that did not negotiate.

Freya, she counselled herself, *you have your home. Your patch of earth. Your work. Your friends. Keir didn't choose anyone else to centre him, he chose you. Be comforted.* She sat in shadow hugging her knees, just out of sight of the neighbours' windows. They'd be peering, and whispering, and wondering what they could do for her, and wanting to take her out on a jolly jaunt. *There she is again, poor thing.* At times Freya seemed to overhear the whispers.

And yet it was good to know that her close neighbours were there, alongside, around: Freya reminded herself to appreciate the murmur of ordinary life going on as it had to. Surely this was only a temporary derangement. While it lasted, she should allow the common things to stabilise her. Through the wall you would catch the echo of the Crouches, as they went about their household business: loo flushings, hooverings, a *tra la* through the open kitchen window as Pammie cooked. Doughnut supplier to lost souls. A stream of needy or idealistic people was welcomed daily for Terry's spiritual discussions and meditation sessions. Every visitor arrived with her or his back bent under an invisible cross. Freya wished she could go with them to that door and knock. Help me with this tree on my back, these thorns around my head.

This tree is growing from my rib cage; these thorns are me.

Did those hopeful souls transiently lay down their despair in the Crouches' living-room? Did they pile their crosses at the centre of the circle, with a clatter of timber? When they rose and stretched from their hour of meditation, was the load of each one lightened – and for how long? An hour, a day? Sometimes you heard splashes of merriment through the living-room wall. It rose and crested and subsided in waves. Gentle laughter though, not the hysteria which sometimes gripped Freya. The raging need. The wish to hurt someone. The grudge and resentment, as if she had been reduced to the dregs of her character.

I want to be held, she thought. Tight. But not like that. None of these asexual group hugs or sympathetic back-pattings. When Jamie had visited, she'd seen it in his eyes, the attraction to herself that had been heightened by Keir's departure. She'd felt it too – and, panicking, resisted the pull. *Ersatz,* she remembered her grandfather reminiscing about the War, *coffee made of ground acorns or chicory – a substitute for the real thing, tasting of … acorns and chicory.* Freya thought: I only want Keir's familiar arms to wrap round me and his hairy old legs to twine with mine. I want to snuggle my face in that special place between his breastbone and his throat. The sleep-smell of him, the bones of him, the sex of him. The lovers they'd taken along the way – they'd been lovely, and dear, and she could have called on any of a dozen people to come now and hold her. They would love to hold her. But she wouldn't.

The lovers had helped to keep alive the sensuality between herself and Keir that sprang up in the forest all those years ago, when they'd seen the fireflies dance. In solidarity with one another, they'd struggled with the force of reaction; climbed the elm that had withstood the Dutch elm plague but was scheduled for destruction. Local parents and children came and encircled the tree where she and Keir were living. The postman delivered letters addressed to The Tree House, The Elm, Twyford Down. Perhaps, if it hadn't been for the baby, she and Keir would never have settled together;

they'd have gone on roaming from protest to protest, person to person.

But. The baby.

And if the baby had lived, then again life would have been differently angled. Larch, who survived for three days, would be twelve years old now, she thought: her son and she would have braved this catastrophe together and she would have had the duty of living for Larch.

One of her neighbours had said – it was Mark Heyward – what was it exactly? Something about Storm, who was now butting at her pocket, where he knew she kept the treats. The pocket was empty so she went indoors to fetch a handful, and remembered: *Storm is the life Keir has left you.*

She blessed her neighbour for saying that. It was a seed of wisdom, which contained more meaning than you at first saw. It could grow or not grow. If you planted and watered it, the seed had a chance to yield. She fondled the dog's head and under his chin. Storm stared and panted.

The life Keir has left you. She would ring Rae and go round. Definitely. She would say, talk to me about Keir, Rae, and what he meant to you. I know you loved him dearly and that he loved you.

She could say, I've been thinking odd things, Rae. About Haf. Help me to unthink them.

'Yes, I know, you want a walk,' she said, and watched Storm go mad at the sound of the word. It had been kind of Mark to take Storm out. But there'd been no need. Mark seemed busy and preoccupied. He came and went with a look of settled purpose and smiled as he passed that shy smile she found touching. She heard him through the wall, playing his clarinet and oboe. Magical instruments – and, though she was no judge, she felt he played at a high level. Mark was a private person: inward. Something about him was appealing, and Freya could not now remember why she'd found him off-putting in the past. But then, at other times, she couldn't remember what she liked about him.

Keir had never bothered with a lead for Storm. Man and dog understood one another beneath or above the level of words. As they left the house, Mark Heyward was also coming out; they closed their doors simultaneously. There was tension in his face, which dispersed nearly as soon as their eyes met.

'Off for a walk, the pair of you?' he asked. 'Where are you heading?'

'Not sure yet. Wherever we find ourselves, I suppose. How about you? How is the work on – what was it? – province?'

'Provenance.'

'Oh dear, what a dope you must take me for.'

He smiled. 'Believe me, anything but. I always enjoy our talks. I like to think about them afterwards. But how are you, Freya, really?'

'Well, I'm up and down. But OK, thanks.'

'By the way, I'm thinking of a sea-swim tomorrow,' Mark said surprisingly. 'Let me know if you feel like joining me. I thought I'd go mid-morning when the tide's in. The weather should be fine. Anyway, see how you feel.'

She'd seen Mark leave with his Speedo backpack and return with his hair sleeked wetly back. He looked like a man with a mission. In the old days she'd laughed at the way he proceeded along, looking neither to right nor left. Not now. The thought of the swim pleased her.

The roots of the tree that was growing from her back tingled and seemed fractionally to shrink. They would swim. She would go and see Rae. Soon.

*

The daily training had not helped his mood. Up and down the Olympic Pool Mark ploughed, getting into shape for the trial ahead. Wills no longer buoyed his pupil on a fulsome patter of praise. As Mark tottered out to the showers, over the tiles that swarmed with verucca viruses, Wills had taken to clapping his back and urging him to further, faster, sleeker and more streamlined efforts: *you know you can do it, bro.*

Mark was not Will's *bro*. It was like being patronised by a schoolboy. Nevertheless, he smiled and promised reformation of whatever aspect of his stroke was being critiqued. Mark did not miss a morning. This was being done for *her*. Fatigue didn't improve one's temper. Neither did the elderly swimmers who lumbered along the wrong side of the lane or crashed past in petty triumph, turning the water choppy. He recoiled from the pubescent lads in the shower, jesting about genitals and the volume of pee in the pool. In the sluices, hair and plasters festooned the suds – detritus the attendants made no effort to clear. Mark was in and out of the shower like a shot. But you couldn't not shower.

The training exhausted Mark but not in a good way. He couldn't sleep. He rose unrefreshed, to do it all again. It had better be worth it.

When Freya and Mark were a couple, they'd need to move home, bag and baggage – once what was about to happen did happen. He would not say: *might* happen or *could* happen. The way she looked at him, the appeal in her eyes, promised that Freya was already turning to him. It was only Keir Fox who was stopping them.

Fox was dead. Lily was dead. They had acquired, by dying, a cryptic power.

Once Mark had dipped his head into the fellow's notebook and started decoding, it was like wading through a swamp. Fox had been a parasite on a person of angelic beauty, who'd been forced to endure serial abuse at his hands. Mark had given up reading after a while. Porn – which is what it essentially was – made for dull reading. Repetitive. The writer had no idea of style.

The thought of Freya being subject to this philanderer turned his stomach. She had been forced not only to witness the creep's womanising but even to participate, three in a bed. At least, that was what Mark took the scrawl to mean. It might not. Oh, surely it did not. But even if the record was not to be read literally – *Frey & Rae & me all together. Bliss* – it was still odious. How would it be possible for oneself and Freya to thrive in that polluted space? As for knocking the two houses together, dismiss that from your mind, he told himself. That is just not going to happen.

Of course the notebook wasn't pornography in the conventional sense of that term. It was a testament of love, allegedly, love without possession.

Perhaps Fox had syphilis. Or worse.

Having switched on the car engine, Mark failed to move into the road. He sat motionless, thinking: what if Keir Fox had actually died of AIDS? The possibility of venereal infection and its ramifying consequences turned him dizzy and he switched off the engine. And just sat. One could hardly ask the beloved to take a test for sexually transmitted disease before uniting with her.

For heaven's sake. There would have to be trust. Without trust, what was a relationship? Perhaps he had been a little too cynical in the past. You needed to believe in people. He switched off the suspicion and turned on the ignition again. Even so, Freya and he would need to leave. Mark was damned if he was going to submit to being cooped up in that paltry pen for a moment longer than necessary.

More deeply even than the threat of infection lay uncertainty about sexual performance. How could he possibly match the dead lecher for sensuality? How could a man whose timid body displeased himself hope to please an experienced woman?

Once again Mark switched off the ignition and allowed anger to brew. Up it seethed, hot, hot.

He welcomed its advent. And feared its outcome. Sweating, Mark rolled down the window. Why was he in that shitty little hole in the first place? – a mid-terrace hovel squashed between identical hovels. Everyone closing in on you, minding your business because they had nothing better to do with themselves. Widows and Holy Joes who knew nothing of classical civilisation and, when you mentioned Homer, assumed you meant Homer Simpson. That was the kind of mediocrity that surrounded him. Apart from Freya.

And who had condemned Mark to this hole?

Yes. Exactly. The half-wit who had usurped his beautiful house,

Tŷ Hafan. He had complied with Danielle Jones's unreason, allowed himself to be beaten out of his own property by her accusations and threats – and her trophies, don't forget them. Blackmail was what it came down to. Amazing how he had managed to bury all this in forgetfulness for months now. That spoke volumes for the effect Freya had on Mark. But he must grasp the nettle.

Again he switched on the ignition. But his rage was such that he knew he'd better be prudent and simmer it down, to avoid bumping into the prats who'd hemmed him in. A pity because the surge of frenzy had been checked for so long, it had built up a head of steam. What a pleasure it would be to ram the pair of them. Mrs Teague's Dacia, fore; Terence Crouch's Skoda, aft. Still, think of your own car, he admonished himself. Any dent or scratch would cost a night's sleep and an inordinate sum to the crooks at the garage.

Mark switched off the ignition and folded his arms.

'Everything all right, mate?'

Mate? I don't think I'm your *mate*. That was all Mark needed. Saint Terence in an anorak carrying Co-op bags, stooping at his window.

'Something wrong with the engine? Need any help?'

Mark's eyes fastened on the unctuous face. He was about to yell something he would undoubtedly regret when Terence started babbling about cylinders, pistons and spark plugs. What an ass – *hee haw, hee haw*. If Mark wanted his engine seeing to, he would take the bloody car to a bloody garage, not subject it to the farting bombast of a know-nothing twitting twat. Valves, camshafts and turbochargers. Terence was now describing a mishap he had experienced on the outskirts of Salisbury when the thermostat packed in – well, he remembered it as Salisbury but it might have been Winchester – somewhere with a cathedral anyway.

He'd rested his grocery bags on the pavement to prattle about these engineering matters, about which clearly he knew zilch. Terence bent so that his face jutted at Mark, his bulbous nose being technically *inside* the car window, his little mouth going *clack clack*

clack. And now, by some incomprehensible detour, via a diversion one could not have foreseen, they found themselves in Vienna, the home (as Terence advised Mark) of Mozart, at which Mark heard himself hiss between gritted teeth, 'Salzburg!'

Terence took no notice: he was back in Vienna, having problems with his tyre. It had burst. In the middle of the carriageway. Traffic tootling around like nobody's business. What was a poor Welshman to do? On this occasion he had been visiting the Cathedral of St Stephen, well worth seeing if Mark was ever in the area.

'Ever been to Vienna?' he asked.

'No.'

'Oh, you should, Mark, you really should. So much culture. And Pammie loved the *Kaffee und Kuchen*. German for coffee and cakes. Anyway, I got hold of a garage, after a lot of difficulty, which I won't go into. And, Mark, you may like to know that the German for a tyre is *der Reifen*. Engine is – that's an easy one – *der Motor*. Or it might be *das Motor*. A jack is *der Wagenheber*. I like that one – the wagon-heaver! You can often puzzle German words out for yourself.'

Scheiße, thought Mark. *Du bist ein Aas. Du bist ein verdammtes Arschloch. Du bist ein Garnichts.*

He blew hard between his teeth before saying, 'Yes, Terence, as it happens, I speak German pretty fluently. I read it too. Do you read Goethe, Terence? No? Or Schiller? Rilke? Or Kafka, maybe? Walther von der Vogelweide?'

To each of these queries, Terence responded with a cheery shake of the head, remarking that he was just a common or garden *Wagenheber* himself and left the philosophy to his betters.

Mark switched on his engine and advised Terence to stand clear.

In the mirror, as Mark moved out into the road, he saw his neighbour picking up his shopping bags, standing thoughtfully looking after him. How Mark had managed not to explode at this nincompoop, he would never know. The rage was still on the boil.

But hang on a minute, he told himself, and turned the temperature down to simmer. He reversed smartly back. Idiotic to squander the goodwill he'd spent so long tending. And, fair play, the chap could not help being a dunce. He meant well. If you are not born with a fully functioning brain, that is your misfortune.

Terence was still standing where Mark had left him, with his mouth slightly open, weighed down at each side by the bags. Mark saw him flinch and take a step back as the car reappeared.

Killing the engine, Mark opened the door and got out. He took Terence by the shoulders and said, with tears in his eyes, in a voice that surprised himself by its grovelling deference, 'Terry, my dear man, my friend, I'm so sorry. Did I seem abrupt? I'm a bit upset. Can you forgive me? I'm not myself. Something has happened ...'

'Oh no, bad news – what is it, Mark? Do you want to come in, have a chat?'

'The fact is ...,' said Mark, wondering what the fact was, 'the fact ... is ... oh, I'm sorry, Terry, I can't talk about it.'

'Of course, my friend – of course. And I've been going on and on about I don't know what. Trivia.'

'Not trivia. In no way. I always enjoy our heart to hearts. And our lighter chats. It's just. Oh dear. I need to go!' Mark shook Terence's hand cordially.

But the phrase somehow made him want to cry. *I need to go.* A child holding himself, desperate for the loo. And no one is listening. They never are. Rigid adults tower above you and move like clockwork, according to their own laws. *I need to go.* He would be chastised when the inevitable happened. There was nothing you could do. A moment's release and then the hot wetness in your underpants, the soiled shorts, the sensation of helpless shame, the penalty exacted. A storm of tears threatened; his face worked.

Concerned, Terence offered to drive Mark wherever it was that he needed to go.

Mark hastily blew his nose and forced a grin. 'No, no, I'm perfectly all right – it isn't so much what has happened as what *may* happen as a result of what *has* happened – if that makes any sense?'

Confounded, Terence assured him that he understood perfectly.

117

'And,' added Mark, as a final sop to his neighbour's piety. 'What I was doing when you first saw me was – praying.'

'Prayer,' said Terence quietly, 'helps us so much. I am so very sorry to have interrupted.'

'Not at all. Our little chat has done me good. And isn't human communion a form of prayer? Bless you, Terry.'

Mark switched on the ignition. And left. In the mirror, Terence could be seen waving with both hands. Apples were spilling out of a carrier bag into the gutter.

*

The rage had slackened to such a degree that Mark virtually dropped the idea of visiting Danielle at Tŷ Hafan. What roused it was the fogey dawdling along the coast road – slow, slow, slow – who stalled at the traffic lights, holding up a queue of cars. Mark sounded his horn and sounded it again.

Nothing. Not a dicky bird.

Mark got out, tapped on the pensioner's window and explained, 'Green – Means – Go!'

The fogey and his wife both shook their heads and pointed, mouthing that the light was red.

Yes, it was *now!*

Mark flounced back to his car. He could feel himself flouncing and felt that it was ridiculous to flounce and that he would have scorned anyone else who behaved in this way.

The lights changed again. Here we go, he thought. At last.

But here we didn't go.

This time he'd had enough. Mark jumped out and approached the non-driver, banged on his bonnet and bawled, 'The light's green! Wake up!'

The old geezer was a shrunken toad, mottled and cadaverous. Nearer ninety than eighty. Should not have been allowed on the road. Probably had cataracts. Dementia. He wheezed some retort, after which Mark could not be responsible for what he said. It had to do with nursing homes and eugenics.

When the guy behind Mark appeared at his elbow and began to accuse Mark himself of being either plastered or a frigging tosser, the two of them enjoyed a loud exchange of views, whose gist Mark remembered afterwards but not all the detail.

Meanwhile the liver-spotted source of contention drove off and disappeared.

Mark headed for Tŷ Hafan. There had never been the least question of marriage or co-ownership. He had explained this fully and frankly to her when she moved in: Danielle was young, with her whole life ahead of her and considerable earning power, potentially. If she should leave him ('Oh but I never will, my dearest') – yes, but if she did abandon him ('But I won't') – if for any reason, the partnership failed – she would have no rights in Tŷ Hafan or any pecuniary rights in anything whatever. Tŷ Hafan was Mark's home, left to him by his wife, and must remain with him, intact.

'I never expected anything! Of course not! Why would I?'

'But just in case, I thought I should make it clear, Danny.'

'I completely understand, my dear old darling,' she'd assured him breathlessly, perched on his lap. Kissing the top of Mark's head, she had begged her dear old darling not to speak of it any more.

'Less of the *old!*' He'd laughed and ruffled her ginger hair.

'Young, then. My darling boy.' Kisses. 'I will never leave my darling boy.' Kisses. 'I adore him.' Gazing into his eyes: 'Why don't you know that, Mark?'

'I do really, but I've been badly hurt in the past. And I'm serious, Danny. Please listen.'

She'd ceased frolicking. 'OK, I'm listening.'

Mark had felt bound to hammer it home, so that there could be no possible dispute if trouble arose. And in order to be completely fair to Danielle.

'Tŷ Hafan is my inheritance from my ... from ... you know.'

Lily, unworldly as she was, had died intestate, so that Mark inherited both her house and the terraced place at the crescent. At that time it had housed a tenant he'd speedily got rid of. As he would get rid of Danny, if things did not work out.

'I know you don't like it, Danny, when I talk about Lily – but honestly and truly, there is no need to be jealous. Even so, I cannot consent, ever, to divide or sell this home, not because I am avaricious but because – this was the most sacred tie of my life.'

Danielle, glad of a pad to perch in, would have agreed to any terms. Mark had reassured her that he trusted her implicitly.

And when – those things – happened between them, he'd reminded Danny of her agreement.

Who could predict, just by judging the egg, what chick or reptile would emerge? Danny was staying here, in this house, until she was fucking-well ready to leave! Or he'd find himself in court! And for more than these bruises! Someone must have put those words in her head. Mark had recoiled, morally shocked. But what could he do? He'd gone to pieces. *Six months,* he said, *and then you go. I am disappointed in you, Danielle.* She had proved foxy as her hair; childish as her freckles. Bruises flowered on her white skin, even if you only brushed her lightly or took hold of her arm, to reason with her. Privately, Mark had always wondered if she inflicted damage on herself – because he certainly couldn't be held accountable for those prints.

Oh, by the way I've photographed them and left copies with friends.

He nerved himself, navigating the twisting lane, to meet the dramatic sight of Tŷ Hafan on the breast of the rise, white and gleaming. The unique Art Deco house was curved, with a gracious sweep like a signature in stone. He parked and sat for a bit, taking deep breaths. The home from which she'd driven him affected Mark strangely, as if he'd once dreamed it and woken to find it real. The conversation with Danny must be carefully handled. Her six months was almost up. And she was not as tough as she had pretended. He took a couple of codeine. Play to her Sunday-school side, he reminded himself. Her nursery-nurse, butter-wouldn't-melt side. Danny liked to think well of herself.

There was no doubt that it had been all his own fault. He'd lost his head, running from Danny's bruises and the spectre of Lily Himmelfarb lying at the bottom of the stairs, and the possible reopening of the question of how she'd got there.

Locking the car, Mark climbed the path to his own front door. Danielle of course had never acquainted herself with the uses of lawn mowers, garden forks or hedge-trimmers. The lawn was a wilderness.

But. On the other hand.

He paused to take stock of the self-seeded flowers amongst the grasses. Cornflowers. Ragged robins. Daisies. Freya loved wild flowers and her lawn was something of a meadow. Perhaps keep it like this, Mark thought – an ecological paradise, if you looked at it like that – for, under Freya's influence, this was how he was beginning to think. At least, it could be a controlled version of a wildflower meadow. Bees could freely visit. Butterflies. Hedgehogs. Freya might want to have a hive in the garden when they moved back in. Or even two. There was plenty of room.

Things were looking shabby, with a growth of moss up the walls. Window-cleaning, gutter-clearing and doorstep-washing would be necessary before Mark brought Freya here. He rang. No response. The doorbell was probably broken. He couldn't hear it chime. Checking the side door, he peered into the dining-kitchen window. Nobody there – but a light had been left on, wasting electricity.

Returning to the front, Mark got out his key. If she'd changed the locks again, he knew a way to wriggle in through the pantry window. Tight fit but one was slender. This would be a last resort, since no posture could be more humiliating, should anyone happen to pass by and accost his back end. Still, he'd done it before and could do it again. He'd not put on weight since the hatch episode.

Mark turned and there she was, at the gate with a bag of

shopping, wearing a summer dress, floaty, floral, sleeveless. She'd grown her hair.

'Danny! – I didn't mean to startle you. Sorry if I have. I just thought I'd come by and – maybe, if you don't mind – talk.'

She sized Mark up, keeping her distance. 'What about?'

'First and foremost, to apologise.'

Danny's look told him: yeah, you've apologised before. Grovellingly. Literally on your knees. About ten-thousand times. The first five-thousand, I was taken in.

'I know, Danny, I know.' Mark responded to the sceptical look. 'But I've had time to ponder – and I understand everything better now. I get it, I really do. Would you let me come in and try to lay things out? In a friendly way. Then we can sort out how to organise the future. Or at least, make a start.'

She nodded. And they were in the house.

'Go through, Mark. Coffee?'

The effect this space had on him was profound. The panelled walls of the hall, the high ceilings, gave the area a sepia look, like an old photograph. This was a theatre in which two of his life's great tragedies had worked themselves out.

The first on those stairs. Still here, just the same, as if awaiting a final act. Oh Lily, my Lily, he thought, you're still here. You're still dying on the staircase. Oh, my darling. And you will never know how I loved you, worshipped you.

Mark's gaze locked on to the door leading downstairs to the cellar, where she had threatened to hang herself, for there was a meat hook in the ceiling of the Edwardian underground kitchen. Presumably whole hams or sides of beef had once hung from it. In his mind's eye, Mark could see right through the cellar door, down the stairs, into the kitchen with its black range, the meat hook and the dark pane. It came to him that the memory he'd had of whistling after Lily died, laughing, doing the crossword and so on, must be a false memory, born of trauma. He could not conceivably have behaved like that.

Mark was impotent to move past the staircase and the cellar door.

The dim light cast by the chandelier caught in her bright hair, as Danielle turned round to see why Mark hadn't replied.

He had his hand over his mouth and tears sparked at the back of his eyes.

'What is it?' she asked. But not sympathetically. Danielle had come, he knew, to see his easy weeping as the entrance to a trap.

'Oh, nothing. Just – well, being here – brings back – things I wish I'd done differently.'

'Ah.'

What the fuck did she mean, *Ah*? Was *Ah* an appropriate response when you bared your soul and implicitly took blame for catastrophes for which they were both responsible? I'll *Ah* you, if you go on like that, he thought. But no. No, he wouldn't take offence. Danny had meant nothing by it. Probably. She was nervous. And even if she had, it was time for research and rehabilitation rather than judgment. Do not fall back into old patterns, Mark counselled himself. Show Danielle that you have changed. Meet as fraternal equals. What a good phrase.

In the kitchen, light poured through the high window onto the flowers in a milk bottle on his old oak table. Lily's old oak table. Everything had been Lily's originally, her family home for three generations. In a curious way, Lily was more present than Danielle. Tenderness and terror rose together, those incompatibles. Yet he did not wish her undead. Mark shook, sweating, and had to rest against the table. The floor seemed to heave.

'Could I sit down? Glass of water.'

She brought the water, which he grasped with trembling hands. 'What is it, Mark?' Danielle asked, more gently. 'Are you ill?'

'Yes,' he gasped. 'I'm ill.'

'You mean actually ill?'

She knew what she called his hypochondria inside out, of course she did. She'd seen him sweat and faint, gnaw at his knuckles until they bled. There was nothing Danielle had feared more than his symptoms. At the same time, he'd never put it on. And yet in the paroxysms of genuine suffering, he had seen himself faking, as if another of his selves hovered somewhere clear of it all.

'It doesn't matter,' he said, genuinely panting for breath. 'Not your problem, Danny. I'm coming round. Just hang on a minute. Breathe, breathe.' He patted his chest. 'I'm fine. You mentioned coffee?'

She would have been expecting a deluge of complaints, Mark knew, and his present restraint might imply that there was something seriously wrong. Never the brightest button in the box, Danny had been caring, very caring early on, almost stiflingly caring, so that he'd felt like one of her nursery charges. She'd seen and addressed the hurt child in him, offering all the balm she knew how to offer. That had been real. But also offensive. Who wants to be seen, or seen through, when it comes down to it? Who wants to be treated as infantile when one is the other person's superior, with a certain standing in the world, achievements, letters behind one's name?

Danielle had something more impressive about her than before. A centre of gravity. She'd put on weight, Mark saw, in a good way, for she'd been skin and bone with not eating. Now she had something like a figure. In fact, with her new confidence and even – was it? – lipstick, mascara – she intrigued him.

Who had given Danielle the flowers? Certainly shop-bought. Danny would not buy them for herself. And the dress. Wasn't that beyond her budget? It was cut on the bias and swung elegantly as she moved. And a coffee machine. Where did that come from? As the machine perked and she put away her shopping, Mark viewed and valued the purchases. Far too much for one person.

'You're still working in the nursery, Danny?' he asked.

'Yes. And you?'

'Still at the gallery, yes. Just part time, of course – because of my chest. We've had some interesting new acquisitions. I remember how you loved the Gwen John lady holding the cat. We've acquired a tiny masterpiece, a picture of a corner of her studio.'

124

'What's wrong with your chest?'

'Oh, nothing to worry about. You're looking well.'

She placed the coffee in front of Mark and took the chair opposite. She'd remembered, then, exactly how he liked it. She'd poured none for herself: obviously she didn't intend to play this as a social occasion. Danny's gaze was calm and straight as he'd rarely seen it before. Only a tremor in her lower lip indicated apprehension. He guessed that she was controlling her breathing. Her hand was on her mobile phone. She waited. He waited.

'I hope life has been kinder to you, Danny?'

'Did you want to say anything in particular, Mark? I have an appointment in half an hour. In fact someone is coming to collect me.'

She was more or less a squatter in his property; a parasite, a leech (how had Mark let it come to this?) – and there she sat coolly telling him to hurry up, she had better things to do. But really, wasn't this just fear? She wanted him to know (it was probably fiction) that there'd be someone at the door any minute.

'Well, yes, of course,' Mark replied. 'The six months are almost up and we need to make arrangements for you to vacate.'

'Vacate?'

'Have you found yourself a place of your own?'

'I've not given it any thought, Mark.'

'We agreed, in a civilised way, I think, that you would remain for a specific period, to give you time to look around for somewhere that suited you.'

'Civilised?'

'Danny, what has happened to you?'

'Happened to me?'

He kept his temper, reined it in, despite the vapid way Polly Parrot kept echoing his phrases. Taking a sip of coffee, he smiled. It must have come out as a leer. For evidently Danielle did not like the smile very much, as she picked up the mobile and placed her thumb over what was doubtless her list of contacts.

'Danny – dear,' he coaxed. 'No need to be alarmed. I come in peace.'

'Don't call me Danny. And don't call me dear. I'll leave when I'm ready, Mark,' she said evenly. 'I'm recovering.'

Theft. The woman had stolen his world. And was intent on gelding him. The word *geld* was unexpected but let it stand, he thought: let it stand. She had crept round him when she was nothing but a scrawny kid – an airhead, banality on legs – and once she had inserted those insignificant legs under his table, she'd played on his worst instincts until she had something to hold against him. And now she was blackmailing him. Mark understood the mute challenge: if you oppose me, I will have you arrested and charged, I have all the evidence, how would you like to spend years in a prison cell?

Again Mark checked himself. Important to challenge Danny obliquely, subtly – find out where she was in what she used to call her 'journey'. She seemed to have no idea how perilously close to an edge she was forcing him to come.

'You seem very different, Danny.'

'Could you not call me that.'

'Call you what?'

'My name is Danielle.'

'Yes, of course. Sorry, Danielle.'

'If you want to know, I've had therapy, Mark. I'm still having it. Twice a week!' she proclaimed. 'I practise yoga. And I have friends now. Friends I can rely on.'

Mark had difficulty keeping a straight face, imagining Danny on the psychiatrist's couch. And as for the yoga: the cat pose, the lotus pose, the corpse pose, the one-leg-up-the-wall pose – imagine her on her mat with the other ninnies, the gullible adherents of claptrap. At the same time, Mark was aware of the onset of a fierce bout of sweating. Where was his handkerchief? Where? Here we are. He wiped the wet from forehead and philtrum. I'm going to have a panic attack, he thought.

126

But then a blackbird trilled outside in the long back garden, thrilling, virtuoso. They both turned their necks and saw the bird, on a bush a metre from the window. A blessed ordinariness descended.

'Oh, my goodness,' said Mark, craning. 'He's still with us. Is it the same one?'

'Yes, I think so. I feed him around noon when I'm here and he's got so tame. He seems to know the time of day to the nearest five minutes.'

They both rose and stood side by side at the window.

'They're wonderful, aren't they?' said Mark. 'Quite haunting. It's as if we had usurped the bird's territory rather than the other way round.'

'I know. I love him.'

It was surely the same bird that Lily used to feed. Or perhaps the offspring of that blackbird. She had been able to emulate its music – and vary upon its repertoire – so precisely that, on spring mornings when Lily went out and practised bird calls, the blackbird had sung back to her from the copper beech. Mark remembered the golden dawns in the garden, Lily's long shadow and the copper beech in purple bud. The beginning of an idyll. The fluting recitative between bird and woman had become ever more complex and ingenious. When Lily had died, a unique voice perished. The pity of it. Danielle of course knew nothing of this.

Mark stood at the window listening with his heart. His pulse calmed and he'd half-forgotten Danielle's presence when she said, 'I'm not saying that I won't leave, Mark. I will leave when I'm ready.'

'Fair enough,' he agreed, turning.

Danielle's head swivelled. Her grey-green eyes squinted, dazed at his amenable reply, into the sunlight.

Had she got a boyfriend and did they couple in Mark's king-sized bed? The guy sprang up in Mark's imagination, an amalgam of the Fox brothers. Beefy and pea-brained. Did the boyfriend eat at Mark's board? Were there parties? Drugs? There would have to be surveillance.

'When you're ready, Danielle,' he said evenly. 'Let me know. Of course I understand – and I don't want to turn you out with nowhere to go. It's just that there's something I need to do with the house – not for myself. For the sake of someone – who needs a roof over her head and her family's – but I can't say more. I'm sorry to have seemed abrupt. You stay until you have found somewhere.'

'You're OK with that?' she asked, with something of her old timidity.

Got you! he thought.

'Take your time, Danielle. I have total respect for your sense of honour.'

She blushed.

'I know you'll do the right and decent thing. I understand now how I pushed you. It was indefensible. But – just to let you know – I've had therapy too.'

'Really?' Her mouth hung open.

'Yes. Funny, the symmetry. We must have learned complementary things – about ourselves and each other.'

'That's good to hear, Mark.'

She was eating out of his hand, the mobile phone forgotten.

That's right, peck away at the crumbs. Keep swallowing. He had awakened her shame. After all, Danielle certainly realised she had no right to hang about in his house, that he'd done her no real damage and that her blackmailing was despicable. It would be altogether better for everyone – especially for *her* – if she saw the light and got out, of her own volition.

Passing through the hall, Mark glanced up the gloom of the stairs with their faded scarlet Axminster. A dark dazzle of propositions flashed through his mind.

There had been no blood. It had been a clean fall.

There'd been no need to replace the valuable carpet. But it could do with a professional clean.

She had been a sick woman. In more ways than one. A sudden death was merciful, probably.

He paused to advise Danielle to lock the cellar door at night. Just in case. She couldn't be too careful. Safety was paramount, he reminded her. Did she go down there much? There'd been break-ins in the area, hadn't she read about them? Was Danielle careful to lock the windows at night? He watched the gathering dismay cloud her face and begged her not to worry, he'd always been a bit of a fusspot, and he didn't want to frighten her – just to make sure she was all right, safe and secure.

'I know you don't feel I have a right to care about you – or for you,' he said. 'But – forgive me – I do care that all should be well with you as you move into your new life. I owe you that, at least.'

'I hope your chest will soon be sorted,' she said, in parting.

It was almost too easy – as if Danny had been waiting or asking to be thrown off balance. Rattling round like a pea in a very large pod, the silly little person must sometimes have misgivings about the scale of the world she was camping in. The creaking of the timbers as the house settled for the night. Rain clattering on the bay window. The whoop and skirl of wind in the gutters. Arousing Danielle's susceptibilities was child's play. She was a puppet leaping in agitation with each twitch of the string.

She darted her hand out to turn the key in the lock of the cellar door. Mark raised his hand in valediction.

9

Freya woke to the stench of animal organs charring on a barbecue, with a hint of burnt lemon. How could people tolerate the invasiveness of that meaty smell? It was far too early in the day for a barbecue.

It was the smell of cruelty, she thought. People settle for cruelty. It's what we do. That's the kind of ape we are.

Maybe someone was burning car tyres in a garden? Throwing up the casement, she stuck her head out. No smoke anywhere. It couldn't be indoors, could it?

As she cleaned her teeth and swilled her mouth, Freya's mind swung above the basin. The smell had faded, but she felt a bit weird. Spacey. Raising her head, she looked into the mirror's eyes. Get a grip, Freya told the alien image. She'd obviously regressed to the insecurities of adolescence. Perhaps it was the weed she'd smoked last night. That would be it. Today's swim would help, definitely.

When he came to pick her up, Freya's neighbour was quiet and withheld. But then, so was she. There were too many words in the world. Too much blah from too many mouths. All speech fell away into the void where Keir lay and also Larch. Try to put all this weirdness aside, Freya told herself as Mark parked. Or don't even try: just do it.

Teenage girls in bikinis flaunted their shy beauty on the steps to the beach. Lads at the group's edge yelled with laughter. Would Larch be at that stage now? Whatever would he have found to rebel against, with parents as permissive as Keir and herself?

Freya paused on the bottom step. *Larch, you lived for three precious days and for those three days I was your mother.* Had she spoken those words or just thought them? Her son had opened his eyes to the puzzle of light, received drops of milk on his tongue, whimpered a little, closed his lids on it all and taken his leave. This was his life-story.

Mark seemed more than usually diffident. When Freya kicked off her flip-flops, he bent to undo his sandals, miming. There was an odd kind of gracelessness, Freya reflected, about Mark's physical movements: was he happy in his own skin? She thought not. Poor soul, he had sustained hurt and fought to ensure that pain did not damage him.

Straightening up, Mark looked into Freya's face and caught (she was sure of it) the strangeness that buzzed around her today like swarming flies. He said nothing. But she knew he read her. His antennae brushed the surface of her grief. One could almost be afraid of him. Her neighbour had insight, she thought, a power of divination: why wouldn't that be scary? Plus, Mark had a tendency to speak the truth. Truth-tellers were rare. And should be rare. If we all went round flaying each other with honesty, we'd be skinless.

Sand sifted warm beneath their soles. The sea was mint green, the sky pearly, the tide creaming in. Three dads and a babble of kids were building a sand elephant, with a head-dress of pebbles and shells. Its trunk curved out, a metre in length. She paused for a moment to admire and praise it, and Mark followed suit.

Later, when they'd decided on their spot, in the cavern mouth, Freya remembered the kiddie he'd scooped out of the waves that time – the first time he'd taken Storm for a walk, the morning of Keir's wake. She mentioned it to him.

'The child?'

'The little girl you saved? Tania, wasn't it?'

'Sorry?'

'Tania. The parents weren't keeping an eye out and you ...'

'Oh – yes, of course – Tania,' he said, recollecting. 'I was miles away. Yes, she was a sweetheart.' He paused. 'Not seen her since. And it's odd you should mention her – because there's something I've been meaning to tell you. If I may. I don't usually talk about it.'

'Yes of course.' Actually she meant – squirmingly – no. Don't.

Keep it to yourself, whatever it is. Don't unburden yourself on me, just don't. Not here, where I can be free of dark concerns.

'Well, I don't know. It's –'

'You can say anything, of course you can.'

Better get it over with, Freya thought. Just nod and commiserate. How hard can that be? A butterfly – a red admiral – was fluttering around the rocks. What sustenance could it hope to find on the sands?

'I had a daughter, Freya.'

Had she heard correctly? 'What?'

'A daughter.'

'I'm sorry – you said – did you say? – you *have* a daughter or that you *had* one?'

'Her name was Fern. She didn't live long.'

The chiming in her head: Freya didn't like it, it was uncanny. Something was definitely burning. The kids came down by twilight and made fires from driftwood, and cooked sausages. How come the smell lingered even when the fires were black and cold?

A breeze lifted Freya's hair and let it fall. Fern. Larch. Each named from nature. She saw herself reach out a hand and place it over the back of Mark's for a moment.

What he'd said about Storm came back: *Storm is the life Keir has left you.* It clicked now. Mark *knew* this; felt he had the right to tell her because he'd been standing somewhere near to where Freya was standing. They didn't meet one another's eyes but looked out to sea. Freya's heart went out to Mark. At the same time, she was aware of shrinking further into herself. Her shoulders hunched and she gathered her knees into her chest and rocked.

'Keir and I had a son, Mark. He lived for three days.'

'Ah, yes.' He nodded, without surprise.

Which rattled Freya. She stared. Greasy skin. That was why his age didn't show; there were no wrinkles, he'd never age, he'd always appear a child. How old actually was he? Something about Mark was not right. She didn't *like* him, was the feeling. But how could

132

she be thinking like this? She often turned to him instinctively. The conflict flashed through her and she rushed out with, 'You *knew*?'

'I guessed. Somehow. Uncanny. I don't know how. I didn't exactly guess – just, when you said, just now, I somehow wasn't surprised. Do you think – perhaps – people ... I don't know ... pick up echoes?'

'How old was your daughter – when she – ?'

'Fern was just short of a week old when she left us, Freya.'

He swallowed. His Adam's apple worked up and down. He spoke with calm dignity.

'Fern was born with a hole in the heart and had a bungled operation. But what I was going to say, if it doesn't sound crass – or mealy-mouthed – over the years I have more and more experienced – a sense of presence. Isn't that strange? Presence. Not so much that I lost my child as that, if I was once Fern's father, I still am her father.'

Freya sat silently, allowing this to sink in. His face was working. Mark had divulged a private agony and she had thought, *I don't really like you.* Sometimes the feelings that bubbled up in her were like sores filled with her own pus. They had nothing to do with the world outside as it was. A tic spasmed under Mark's eye. His head was tucked down, in a posture, almost, of shame, or as if someone were about to strike him. *I still am her father.* This was more than a form of words. It was wisdom.

And I am still your mother, Larch, she thought. I shall always be your mother.

A single oystercatcher cruised the bay, skimming the water, vaulting high, swooping, on and on.

'Does it hurt to talk about Fern?' she asked him gently.

Tongues of water spilled in. Children larked. Babes-in-arms lamented. A warm wind rose and ballooned the beach tents until you thought they might take off.

'Yes, in a way it does hurt. But no – talking to you doesn't hurt, strangely. Not at all – although I've almost never spoken about Fern before. But you can ask me anything.'

'So may I ask ... Fern was Lily's daughter?'

'Lily's, oh yes. Ours. Yes, Lily's.' He choked on the word. 'But don't let me upset you by talking about Fern – I wouldn't for the world – I just thought – '

'I know. Thank you.'

Again Freya reached out her hand and placed it on Mark's arm, holding it there. The arm was warm, brown, hairless. How thin-skinned you are, Mark, she thought. He'd been wringing his hands unconsciously but now he stopped and leaned towards her. Rather suddenly, he folded Freya in his arms. She accepted the embrace and kissed his cheek. Drawing back, they looked one another in the eyes – embarrassed now, uncertain – before their gazes swerved away.

'Come on, let's swim,' she said.

They stripped off, storing their clothes on a ledge. She waited while Mark fitted on his goggles, apologising for the delay.

Past the kids spanking one another with seaweed they sped, past floating paunches and bobbing heads.

When Freya looked across, Mark was freestyling out. In a straight line. A classic crawl, slightly rigid, but it moved him along. The determination with which he swam made you feel he was making straight for Ilfracombe, across the water. She followed and passed him. He passed her. Then they floated and you sensed, lying on your back, rocked on this great bed of water, that the two of you were in danger of falling asleep, into an endless safety.

*

He felt afterwards, with jaded satisfaction, that he'd accomplished everything he'd set out to achieve, and half killed himself in the process.

In actual fact, Mark had done more than he'd planned. At moments he'd felt that he might have over-reached himself: the tale of Fern had come unbidden and fully formed. It was an aspect of Mark's dangerous virtuosity. Rather brilliant, like a poem. And when he recovered from the stress of it all, he'd be able to cast his mind back and taste to the full the sweetness of Freya's response. No wonder he was utterly spent. Jesus Christ, the icy sea raising and shrinking your balls. Ache, ache. Sheer hell. There'd been mounting panic as he'd sped out beyond his depth. Afterwards it had taken every ounce of energy for Mark to lug his carcase up the steps and the hill to where they'd parked. He'd really thought he might pass out. And then idiots had boxed him in, forcing him to inch back and forth to clear their cars.

Shivering, Mark had made it home, only to find that some of Terry's visitors had usurped his parking place, forcing him to park at the bottom of the hill. As he floundered along the path in her wake, Freya all but skipped. It was not that Mark had failed to train for the sea-swim. Of course he had. Even over-trained. But the perishing cold! In his marrow. In his liver. What was the temperature: 15 degrees or so, according to the life-guard, but it felt like zero. Freya didn't seem to feel the cold. How could people actually enjoy this torture? He'd kept his nerve, remembering in the course of the swim every tip Wills had given him at the pool. Invaluable chap. You don't fight the water, you rest on it. You make yourself into a fish.

What if she'd had to life-save him? – which of course she'd be perfectly capable of doing. Imagine the ignominy of being ferried in to shore with hypothermia by a woman who swam like a bloody dolphin, to end up wrapped in tinfoil by a life-guard.

To cap it all, Freya had been inclined to chat out there, as they floated well beyond their depths. He'd been dumbstruck. Frankly, she seemed a bit out of herself. Looking for the seal, she said. The seal that liked to play with swimmers, and would get so near that it would lick your toes if it felt like it.

The seal would lick your toes? That would be all Mark needed, a toe-licking fucking seal.

'Have you ever swum with seals?' Freya had wanted to know.
'No.'
'Oh, there's nothing like it in the world.'

135

'I can imagine,' he'd gasped. Surely his extremities were turning blue. If the seal came along and nibbled his toes, he'd not feel a thing.

Where Freya seemed to be experiencing rapture, Mark had had to focus on mentally repeating relaxation formulae and clamping his teeth to stop the chattering. Still, Freya, enclosed in her bubble, hadn't noticed. She'd taken his silence for fellow-feeling.

Would he ever be warm again? With two hot water bottles and a winter duvet, Mark burrowed down and, unexpectedly, slept.

When he woke, the sun had crept round and the afternoon was nearly spent. Mark's garden lay in shadow but a lozenge of golden warmth lingered at the edge of Freya's lawn. And there she was, lying on a recliner, dozing, thighs slack, in shorts and t-shirt, driven back by encroaching shadow to this luminous triangle. A book lay splayed on her lap. The Crouches' swine of a cat, Pansy, was taking the opportunity of doing its business in Freya's border, erect tail quivering. Venture into my garden, you little bag of crap, he told it silently, and you will feel the attentions of a high-pressure hose pipe.

The animal looked up and caught Mark's glare. They eyed one another with equal bale and the Bengal cat gave in first, scrabbling back over the fence into its own garden. Storm slunk out of the bushes where he'd taken refuge.

Freya slept on in the retreating amber sunlight. Her lovely hand dropped down over her thigh and was gradually swallowed in shade. Peace, she had peace. And, yes, Mark thought: you see, I gave her that. I rescued my dearest friend from the grief of that adulterous house and gave her a chance to come out of herself. I did it, alone, as I am always alone. I laid my story of Fern alongside hers of Larch.

Who else would have kept this vigil for Freya, watching over her, listening out for her, devoted to her security and health?

The invention of an infant daughter for himself and Lily had been sheer improvisation. And, given that the fable had come to him in a flash, he must be careful how he elaborated on it in future. Maybe don't.

But its effect had more than vindicated his researches into Freya's privacy. It had enabled Mark to minister to his neighbour. Thank you, Keir, for recording it in your notebook! For years that loss had been fresh in Keir Fox's mind. Without his allusions to 'L', the meaning of the mural would not have been as obvious to Mark: the babe in the basket, hanging on a branch of the painted tree? Rock-a-bye baby. The cradle rocked. The wind blew. The bough broke. The cradle fell. Down came baby, cradle and all.

Mark had located the birth and death certificates of the baby. The death of a child: what sorrow lay buried there. It would be with you all your life, never lessening – on the contrary, it would remain at precisely the same level. Especially if you could have no more children, as he surmised Freya and Keir could not have had. He remembered the complex look she had given her niece's irritating kid at the wake, the way she'd crouched down and offered her open arms. No, said the kid, and swatted Freya away: she only wanted her mummy. Now, poignantly, Mark had been able to enter into Freya's loss by dreaming up his own dead child. In this sense, it was no lie. A true fiction. Fictional truth. For the invention led straight into reality. Fern opened up a path to Larch.

NB, Freya had not confided the name of her son, so Mark must remember, until she did, not to refer to it.

Memo to self: good idea to research the internet for sites about dead babies and then write it up. I shall need to know how dead babies are cremated and interred. Also I need to inform myself on open-heart surgery for neonates.

Mark was hungry now, and more relaxed. Anchovies on toast, a sharply interesting taste, followed by fresh peaches. Afterwards he listened to Mozart adagios, eyes half closed. He allowed himself to replay his memories of today. Freya. She'd touched Mark's hand, brushed it with her fingers and held it in a light clasp. He mimed her touch, to arouse the memory. He clasped his left arm with his right, and the skin came to life. He draped his arm around a cushion to recall the moment of embrace. My God, he thought, this is really happening to me – I knew it would, but at the same time hardly dared to hope. Freya had permitted him to embrace her, cherishing her in a deep and tender stillness, like this with the cushion, and she had – of her own volition – kissed his cheek.

So why this shadow darkening his heart? Was it shed by the threat posed by Danielle? Not really, for Mark would surely find a way to shut her mouth.

Shut your mouth, shut your flaming mouth! Those were words that had spelt threat of punishment for the boy. But, he reminded himself, the boy was now a man. And the man was not on the receiving end of such words. No, the man was in a position to punish insult and injustice. Talk them down. Shut their flaming mouths. Shut them up. Shut them out. Shut them in.

So, yes, it's all right, Mark Heyward the grown man told himself, the undigested anchovies in his stomach turning over, it's fine, it's good, you are in full control.

Well then: Danny. She was in the way. She was, in point of fact, directly in the path of oncoming traffic. Mark had gone some distance towards removing her: for her own sake, as much as anything. In the end, Mark was ten times as bright as Danny. He knew her every weakness. He had observed and listened, and on various occasions he had recorded her whining phone calls, noting her capacity to blame herself. Who could be afraid of a nursery nurse? A section of the Red Book was devoted to analysis of her character and actions. Mark understood how each nerve connected to another and how they webbed together. He could anatomise her inner self, what there was of it, with a scalpel.

That was how it had been, until he had come into collision with Danny's bad side, turning her into a harpy.

Until he'd lashed out and called her those names (names he'd hardly known he knew), she'd danced to their agreed tune. I lost control of her, he knew, because I lost control of myself. That has been my Achilles heel.

There was little left to fear from Danny, who was already on the back foot. He smiled at the memory of how easy it had been – knife through butter – to penetrate her defences by referring Goody Two Shoes to her own sense of honour. To think of herself as behaving like a harpy would offend her. She was someone who needed to like and approve of herself.

No, it wasn't Danny who curdled his spirits. Not directly.

Freya's physical presence had frightened Mark, arousing fear of – well, admit it – sexual ineptitude. Her physique was statuesque. He'd torn his eyes away from her loveliness, quivering with anxiety, as he changed into his swimming togs, staggering about all over the place. Freya had stepped unconcernedly out of her shorts, stripped off her t-shirt. It was not that he'd thought her immodest, but that he'd been intimidated by her ease. What was the term? *Punching way above your weight.*

The phrase *sexual ineptitude* rose in his mind and had him cringing. He was almost tempted to give up the whole quest, settle for evicting Danny, retreating to his lair and burying himself in the gallery.

How could Mark ever convince this experienced woman that he was a man? That's what it came down to.

One had to believe that Freya had retained an essential purity despite the hands that had crawled over her skin like flies at the behest of the porn-brained, pot-fuelled husband. But crawl they had. Fifteen years of bedding down in stained sheets with Christ-knows-what human filth. And those people would have explored every variety of sexual practice. He couldn't even imagine what these practices might have been. Compared with such *canaille* – male and female – Mark was virginal. And Freya, though quintessentially pure (almost), must know everything there was to know about sensuality. For her, uniting with Mark would be like coupling with a pimply adolescent.

Virginal. As Danny had been when she came to him. He'd been able to dominate Danielle because, frankly, she knew no better. He'd understood that she hadn't a clue. It had made Mark feel imperious but he'd also been so kind, so soft and understanding that he all but *became* her in his sensitive care for her comfort.

It was all marvellous, as far as the unseasoned Danny was concerned. *Oh, don't change*, she'd breathlessly pleaded, when her lover expressed concern about his powers and the limitations of the position – *I love everything about you – and what we do – it's perfection – because it's just us two*. He'd begun to accept her state of thraldom as his right. And when she'd withdrawn, like a slug with salt on its tail, wanting a single bed in a room of her own, he'd felt it at once. The rejection. The abandonment. Desertion. Those evil words surfaced from the pit where they'd hidden out. And then he'd withered. The magma of an old and incorrigible rage had seethed up.

But how come Lily had failed not only to satisfy but to enlighten Mark? She'd slept around before they met, so how come she'd left him as she found him, timorous in sexual matters? Don't go there, Mark told himself. Thinking about Lily's body led inexorably to a cadaver at the base of a stairwell.

It led to the smashed fragments of a viola in the road.

Things needed cleaning.

Wherever Mark's eyes roved, there was a coating of dust. A dullness of dust. Nothing checks it. When you cleanse your surfaces, the danger is that you simply shift dust around. Nobody can ever claim to have got on top of it, nor the mites that thrive on it. The women he'd known took a cavalier attitude to mess. They seemed blind to it. Good thing he was a feminist and believed in doing his own cleaning and disinfection. Theirs might be a rational view though, because, even if you devoted your entire life to cleansing, it would be useless. Pollen and dander, dirt and fibres, human cells and mould. Invisible creatures and the bacteria that inhabit them, revelling in drifts of scurf and draff. Even with the dehumidifier and impermeable bed covers, the laminate flooring which he made sure to damp-mop, Mark was aware that the stuff accumulated.

He got out his dusting rag, dampened it and began, methodically, to clean. This generally helped to temper stress. A superficial clean was as good as Mark was going to manage at present, wiping down ornaments, pictures and surfaces, without attempting to deal with the book shelves. His beloved books were farms for bacteria. Most of his collection had been left, perforce, at Tŷ Hafan. He'd always insisted that books be kept out of living spaces – which was practical in a spacious house like Tŷ Hafan but, in a hovel such as the one to which Danny had condemned him, what option was there but to store them in the lounge? And his was an antiquarian collection. Termites, cockroaches, bookworms, silverfish, firebrats, book lice, book mites – you name it – had all infested these volumes over centuries. They'd devoured the glue and leather, minutely staining the pages with excreta. Then they'd died and rotted. The naked eye couldn't see them but you knew they were there.

Yet Mark loved his books, passionately. They were his pride and joy; he was their child. They'd fathered his mind; mothered it when nothing else nourished him. No matter if you had a whole book by heart, the physical object was what you yearned towards. He had a Kindle but that wouldn't do.

Saturday mornings, cross-legged in the children's section of the local library, had been Mark's chapel.

Of course there were steps you could take to cleanse and preserve ancient volumes: the process of decay could be delayed – at best, arrested. This he worked to do. Freezing books in polythene bags was a tried and trusted remedy. No larva, pupa or egg could survive ice. And weren't books the mind's proper food? Didn't they in some sense belong in a freezer? Decay or no decay, he luxuriated in their scent and texture.

When Mark glanced out of the window again, Freya and Storm had gone indoors. She'd left the recliner where it was, and what if it rained in the night? He might go out later, fold it up and bring it in.

*

'Aye,' Terry said to Freya from his patio as she went in. 'Poor chap was in a frightful tiz. Kept turning the engine on and off. In the end, he told me something bad had happened.'

'Oh dear. He seemed fine this morning. Did he say what the trouble was?'

'No, he wouldn't say,' said Terry. He looked at her and took a deep breath as if to add something but thought better of it and turned the conversation. 'Do you fancy a courgette or two, Freya? Mrs Teague passed on an overflow. They are trying to be marrows. What am I saying? – they have succeeded! – they *are* marrows! Joking aside, it was neighbourly of her. She gave us ten.'

She received twin giant courgettes, one on either arm. Pam threw open the kitchen window to advise stuffing and roasting.

Freya wondered, as she went indoors, what it was that had so upset Mark – and thought she knew. Bless him, he was a lonely soul – and he brooded in his solitude. There was something childlike about her neighbour – a quality that, despite her inexplicable moments of recoil, called out to her through the intensities of her own grief. He'd apparently sung in a cathedral choir as a kid, until his voice broke. You could imagine the surpliced boy with earnest eyes and treble voice. Freya had an idea that today might be an anniversary of Mark's daughter's death. He'd never shared the experience with anyone before – but he had confided in her. So Freya had been of use to him – which was good, because she was otherwise of no use to man or beast.

The quirky thing was, Mark had seemed cheerful. Was that the right word? He'd felt relieved, perhaps, of the burden of trauma.

Storm ate lustily in the kitchen and she heard the bowl skidding round the floor, with a tinny echo. *Storm is Storming,* she thought. The echoes bounced round the borders of her mind. Everything felt a bit odd, a bit off; it had been like that all day.

Perhaps there was about to be a storm. She carried her tray into the living-room. And the oddity, the offness, increased. Freya glanced over at the fresco she and Keir had painted all those years ago. Their babe was still there, rocking in his basket, waiting. Waiting for what? Other folk watched the television as they ate: Freya watched the fresco. Things were moving on the fresco. Well, they weren't actually, but if you stare, they stir.

Staring and stirring.

The pair of words blurred and blared.

I'm hungry, probably, she thought, trying a forkful of mushy courgettes. It tasted like nothing at all. The sweet potato on the other hand tasted sour, citric? Water. Wash it all down.

There was something she believed she knew. About Rae, about Haf. The frescoed branches flowed and swirled. Freya became dizzy watching them. Her fork paused in mid-air.

The leaf canopy pulsed. Or was it her eye throbbing? Freya's face bulged weirdly on one side. Something was coming. It was coming. A bad thing. An old thing. Approaching. She'd been here before. How could you avoid it? She abhorred it. There was no evading it.

The leaf canopy crashed out from the wall, branching into the room, boughs heaving, leaves thrashing. The whole wall smashed open like a window and the outside came roiling in. A fork clattered down. The tray tilted. Her glass, sliding to the edge, toppled. The baby in the basket tossed violently in the gale that streamed through Freya's living-room.

Was the door open? The window? Something was due to arrive. Was it already here?

No, this was wrong. Something *had* happened, long ago, and was being repeated. She'd been here before. Freya detected this by the smell.

A face formed in the curlicues of the boughs, a green face, cartoonish, bulbous. Must be a left-over from some dream or drug. She could make out the body now too: a mass of twiggy bones. Freya felt her eyeballs roll back in her skull but could still make out the festooning greenery and the face.

Aura. Ictal. Seizure. Those words ticked through her head from early childhood. Mum, curled up beside her on the big bed,

143

cocooned her in a tartan blanket, saying, *There, Freya darling. Soon be over.* Oh Mum, come back now, I really need you.

Blitzed. Zapped. Zoned. About to pass out. About to splay, thresh, thrash about, pee herself, crack her head on …

… an animal bent over her, rough-coated, wet-tongued, panting.

A figure came through the wall. It emerged, with a little popping sound, like a tadpole from spawn.

'Oh, it's you,' she overheard herself say, matter-of-factly. For it all made sense now. Everything made sense. 'Where on earth have you been, Keir? How did you get in to our painting? How did you get out of it?'

Her husband bent over Freya and made to stroke her forehead with both hands. Somehow or other the caress never arrived.

'You came through the wall,' she exclaimed, wonderingly. The veins in her temples, palms and the arches of her feet fizzed. Her tongue, too large for her mouth, seemed like a plug against the palate and yet flopped about all over the place.

Keir stood over her, younger now than when she last saw him – for he was tumbling head over heels into the past – and somehow luminous, although his lank brown hair fell forward over his face, shadowing it. Lustre poured from starry eyes.

'Hang on a sec, don't go away,' Keir said and turned to shove the invading vegetation back.

*

'Hang on. Don't try to move, Freya. Really – don't. I'll call an ambulance.'

'No need, Keir.'

Then, he thought he heard her say, with stumbling tongue, 'Came through the wall?'

Does she think I'm him then?

Thank God for Storm, whose howling and scrabbling had alerted Mark.

144

He hadn't even been listening in when Storm's call found him; not even, for once, consciously thinking of Freya. You can get weary, after all, not of love itself, but of intense arousal. He'd been engrossed in cleaning, squirting wax polish onto the table, involving himself in a fine mesh of droplets and that rather pleasant smell. He'd heard himself humming arias from *The Marriage of Figaro*. Mark was Cherubino, the adorable girl-boy. Then he was the revolutionary servant Figaro, striding around in manly breeches. He'd raised his voice sweetly to sing the Countess's '*Dove sono*'. Polishing the wood with pathos, he'd enquired, falsetto, as to where had gone those beautiful moments? Where were those sweet promises sung by lying lips?

Storm's frenzy had broken into Mark's trance. When he'd dashed in, Freya was on the floor by the hearth. Had someone or something struck her down? Heart attack? He knelt, lifting Freya's head onto a cushion, searching out a pulse.

'No need, Keir,' she repeated quite distinctly when he proposed calling an ambulance. Her eyes were wrong, looking straight through him and out the other side. There was a swelling on her forehead where she'd hit the hearth.

'Freya. Dear. I'm not Keir.' He lunged at Storm, who was nuzzling her hands, whimpering. When the dog resisted, Mark shoved him back.

'You came home!' she said.

'Yes, I came.'

'You really did!'

'I had to come. Wherever you are is my home.'

Who was Mark to wreck her moment of blissful recognition? Everyone needs illusions. She wanted Keir so he became Keir. Simple as that. The wall between them, whatever name she called him by, had melted. They were in each other's lives now.

'Yes, it's me,' he whispered, lips at the shell of her ear. Storm butted him hard with the dome of his head and had to be thrust back again. 'I'm here with you, Freya. I'll never leave you.' He kissed her forehead, avoiding the injury. 'I want you to have peace now, my sweetheart. Move on with your life. Nothing is lost.'

Mark could not make out what she said in reply. She seemed to be sinking. She smelt of urine. He hadn't called the ambulance. Must call it. Without delay.

But first, make sure to plant your loving message where it can never be forgotten.

'Dearest,' he said, kneeling, in his persona as Keir. 'Let Mark take care of you now. Forever. Mark loves you. Mark will never let you down. Mark.'

No response. Was she – dying? No, don't die. Just when I've found you and you've found me.

'Stay with me, keep awake now, Freya,' he commanded, scrambling up. He dialled. Storm was all over Freya. Gran would have rubbed Pearl's nose in a crap-heap for less.

Did you growl at me, pal? I wouldn't if I were you.

Within minutes the paramedics appeared. Mark had the presence of mind to grab Freya's keys, bag and mobile phone, making it clear that he'd accompany her.

Ten minutes there; A&E; suspected epileptic seizure; EEG; MRI scan; waiting in corridors.

No, I'm not her husband. Her closest friend, next door neighbour. The nearest to next-of-kin Freya has. Mark repeated this, with variations, until he came up with the word 'partner'. I am her partner. May I stay with her?

Of course, of course.

Waves of pathos washed over Mark as he held Freya's hand in the side ward, minding neither the pain in his coccyx nor the urge for sleep. Let Freya live and be well. This was all he wanted in the world. Nothing that had gone before had mattered as Freya's wellbeing mattered. At Gran's bedside he'd kept vigil in a stupor of grief, waiting for a few words of tenderness and counsel that never came. Now Mark's head swam with exhaustion, for something was simmering in his memory and he lost his train of thought. Whatever was rising from underground threatened to uncover thoughts that could not be thought.

I will not think those thoughts, he told himself, so sternly that they fled.

Freya opened her eyes. She looked at him and knew him, he was sure of that. And slept again, her mouth open. As dawn was coming up, she surfaced.

'Hallo, Freya.'

'What on earth are you doing?'

'You're in hospital, love.'

'Ow, my head.'

'You fell.'

'I had a fit?'

'Something like that. A seizure.' Was *seizure* a kindlier word? Were there any softening words for this complete loss of control? Should he have said *episode*?

'No. Not *again*. Had this as a kid.' She sat up, urgently, captured his hand. 'Did you phone anyone?'

'Not yet, love. I didn't want to leave you alone. Who would you like me to call?' He took her phone from his pocket.

'No one.'

'Really? Are you sure?'

'No one needs to know. Did the neighbours see? They must have seen the ambulance? There was an ambulance? But don't tell them, don't say a word to anyone. Tell them I ... I don't know ... I had a fall or something. Did they see?'

'Oh, I don't think so. It was all very quick. Well – if you're sure, Freya, I won't tell anyone.'

'So – promise me.' Her manner was oddly vindictive. What was she afraid of?

'If that's what you want – of course I promise,' he said. 'Absolutely. Hand on heart. No one needs to be told or will be told.'

A tear leaked from the corner of her closed eye. He thumbed it gently from her temple.

147

'It's OK, dear Freya. All over now. You are safe. All well.'

He knew what to say because these were words Mark had always needed to hear. Saying them to his beloved Freya was like hearing them spoken to himself. Even Mark's voice sounded different to himself, more like a woman's; how strange.

'There's no reason to think it will happen again. Truly. The neurosurgeon said medication would help and anyway it might well be a one-off. From extreme stress. I took notes. But he will tell you himself. Perhaps you can sleep now, Freya? Try to sleep.'

'But will you stay?'

Mark stayed.

10

Home again, and thank heaven to be at her own hearth, with her back turned to the painted wall. Mark had built the log fire up high. She'd turned to him. He'd been there. She could rest on him.

And – the main thing – Mark could keep a secret. A bit of an outsider, he was very private. Whatever Freya asked of him, he would carry out, to the letter. She couldn't cope with people's exasperating concern. The way they'd look at her, gossip, weaken her into – God help us – an invalid. She was the girl who beat up the school bully in the playground: no one had messed with Freya Vaughan after that. Then the net had dropped over her – the fits and fugues of epilepsy that struck without warning. She'd become a kid who could no longer rely on herself to remain in the same world as everyone else.

Shame troubled Freya nearly as badly as shock, together with a kind of itching boredom. Losing control of yourself – even your bladder – was demeaning. You never knew when it would trigger. Her epilepsy had made Mum and Dad cosset her, which Freya disliked. And then, for no obvious reason, the episodes had ceased.

So this could be a one-off, the product of violent grief. No reason to suppose it will recur, the medics said. Are you sure? No, we can't be sure, but it is very possible. She took a grain of comfort from *very possible*.

Mark had driven her home, picking up a pizza on the way. They'd talked, mercifully, of other things. It came out that he'd never bought a pizza before. What, never? See what you've initiated me into!

He'd diverted her with mundane things. And he'd made her laugh. It turned out that Mark was an exceptional mimic. Who'd have guessed? His Margaret Thatcher! Somehow, he even managed to look the part. The way he played her – *The Lady's not for turning!* – somehow endowed him with a blonde wig and a blue suit as he handbagged his foes. *Oh don't! Oh please!* He'd stopped at once, his demeanour changed, and he became Mark Heyward again, anxious in case he'd gone too far. *No, no! Carry on!* He took up the same sentence – it was to do with Saint Francis bringing peace and groceries to the Falkland Islands.

He'd succeeded in halting the flood of darkness, making everything feel more normal. You never knew how blessed ordinariness was until you lost it. Freya didn't even think of Keir, although she was aware of not thinking about him. They'd watched a spy film and she'd nodded off in the middle. When she came to, the credits were showing.

'We can see it again any time,' Mark said. 'I won't spoil it by telling you how it ends. I was glad you could rest.'

He'd fed Storm. Now he made hot chocolate for them both. Should Freya ask him again to keep quiet about the fit? No, she thought: I can't keep going on at him – I'll trust him.

'I could stay tonight if you're at all nervous,' Mark ventured. 'On the couch. No problem. No? OK, but just knock on the wall if you want me. Or ring. Here's your phone. I took the liberty (hope you don't mind) of setting my number as priority in your Contacts. Here. Is that OK? I'll call for Storm in the morning if you want to rest up. I'll let myself in if your curtains are closed. Look after your dear mum, Storm – right?'

As Mark left, a jittering emptiness surrounded and invaded Freya. She almost recalled her neighbour and begged him to stay. She couldn't look at the mural. It would need to be painted over; even or especially the baby must go. She could not bear the baby. In every sense, the baby could not be borne. It must all go. The way the words chimed in her mind reminded Freya of a Closing Down Sale: *Everything Must Go.*

Keir had returned to their home but in such a creepy way. All that whispering. *Ssss-ssss-ssss:* sussurations right into her ear. He mustn't come again. Of course she knew now that it hadn't been Keir but some hallucination of her own. That didn't really help. Freya was tired, tired. She kept dozing off; waking with a start and looking round. The episode had cast a pall of dread over familiar things.

Don't look at the baby.

There was a can of white paint in the shed. Blank it all out. How had she and Keir tolerated the commotion of patterning all these years? In fact everything in this house needed calming and ordering. What a mess it was. The restless jazz of furnishings. Clutter. And, frankly, Freya thought (without summoning energy to do anything about it, not now at least) a bit grubby, shabby. That would be how her neat neighbour must see it.

Here's your phone, Mark had said. He would understand and perhaps advise. *Call me.* Freya's thumb hovered above the screen. Just go round, go to him, she told herself. He won't mind, he understands.

*

When Mark opened his door the following morning, Freya rushed full-tilt into his arms.

'I've got you.' He rocked her, crooning. 'Come in now. I've got you, Freya. Nothing bad will be allowed to happen to you, nothing.'

'It has! It has happened!'

You saw how Freya had been as a child, mouth squared up, tears rolling down scarlet cheeks.

'Yes, but you've got me now, cariad. To lean on. Whatever happens, you're not alone. I'll be with you every step of the way. If you want me to be.'

'I do! I do!'

Like wedding vows, Mark thought, and half carried Freya, sobbing, into his living-room. But in reality it was himself he lifted. He was lighter than he'd been for years. He knew by intuition what

151

to say and how to say it, what to do for her and how it should be done.

He fried an omelette for her breakfast and afterwards she insisted on drying up while Mark washed. Looking along the same eye-line at the trees and the palaver of magpies, they chatted as if they'd known each other forever. She pointed out a bullfinch, pink-breasted, on the fence. When Pansy came sleeking along the margin and got into pouncing posture beside the undergrowth, they both laughed: you could *see* her hiss.

Freya's spirit was sapped, he saw – near to tears all the time, not bothering to stanch them. He would not take advantage of her. This is my moment, Mark thought, to enter into a new world of loving-kindness and fellowship.

He would be her human bridge: just as he had been *ein feste Burg* to the little girl in the sea at Rotherslade. He could see her now, wading out from the shallows, skirt tucked up into her pants – and himself plunging after the child, with Storm swimming alongside him. Taking her in his arms, lifting her out of the swell, he'd calmed her, for Tania had just been beginning to feel alarmed, realising her isolation and frailty in a world of impersonal forces. She'd been shivering with cold so that when he'd set her down on the sand, Mark had draped his jacket around her. With no concern for the soaking of his clothes. She was a child, and needy, and Mark was an adult, who understood, and cared, and felt the truth of what he'd later said to Freya, that children belong to the whole community. We are all their uncles and aunts. And Tania's negligent parents, of course – the underclass – were stuffing their mouths with chips in the cafe, obese and vulgar. What chance did the offspring of such lax parents stand? He had spoken to them sharply in restoring their daughter to their care. Why have children if you aren't prepared to devote your life to tending them?

Hang on, there had been no Tania, Mark reminded himself.

But if she had existed, he'd have acted exactly as he'd imagined. And in reality there were so many Tanias in the world, children left to their own devices, wandering off the safe path for want of someone to guide and guard them. He'd sung *Ein Feste Burg* on the seashore in the wind. Mark could be a safe stronghold for Freya, and perhaps for the Tanias of this world, able to use the pain he had suffered as a child to give him insight and the power to heal.

He was in some sense glad of – reliant on – Freya's weakened state, but not in an exploitative way. It was almost as if she now suffered for both of them, draining his heart of its toxic need. Mark took refuge in Freya and experienced a new purity. How odd, because superficially it was the other way round. Standing there, side by side, as he passed across the steaming plates, he felt she was attaching herself to him in a life-guaranteeing way. A very present help in trouble. He felt – it made him smile sadly at the paradox – taller.

Rappings on Freya's door seemed to go on half the day. Then, as often as not, the visitor would knock on Mark's door. Neighbours, family, a couple of females in slashed jeans, about Freya's age, had heard of the ambulance and were anxious that Freya's phone was switched off. To each he explained that Freya had taken a bit of a fall and needed to be checked for concussion. She was resting now. Resting where? Oh, resting here, he responded, as if it were a matter of course. But she was fine, he assured them, thanking them and asking that they give Freya a bit of space: 'She would be grateful for some quiet time to herself. Perhaps you wouldn't mind gently letting people know?'

Then there was Amy. Oh god, not you, he thought, and opened the door just sufficiently to speak through the gap. He gave her the same answers, a little more curtly perhaps, but not discourteously. It was raining, her hair was soaked, but he did not invite her in. No, Freya wasn't seeing anyone at present. He repeated the message about the need for *quiet time* and *giving space*. What part of that did the woman not understand? He shut the door before she had grasped the concept and saw her face at the window peering for a view. He drew the curtain.

'Thanks,' said Freya, hiding in the kitchen. 'I don't want to be ungrateful. But you're right, I just need time to breathe.'

'Of course you do,' Mark purred. He laid his arm round her shoulders and squeezed, drawing her for a moment against his chest, then letting go – but she stayed close. 'Of course you do, love. We will never get Keir back,' he murmured, as if he had somehow been a third party to the marriage, which was not entirely fanciful because he had inserted himself into their world with all his imaginative potency. 'But we will keep Keir's spirit with its ... with its wings over you. We can do that.'

And really in speaking this gibberish he had gone too far. *You are so glib,* a distant voice reminded him. *Glib is your second name.* That must have been Lily, because Danny (who still needed to be dealt with) would not even have been conversant with the word *glib* and its oleaginous implications. However, Freya noticed nothing amiss. Her sharp mind had softened, Mark saw. Confidence grew as they slipped back into her house to sort things out.

Down to business. Mark helped bag up Keir's most personal possessions. Freya explained that she'd felt unable to jettison anything. This of course Mark already knew from his siftings of evidence. She showed him the drawer containing Keir's specs; the cabinet with his shaving things. Personal and intimate items. She'd just left them in place. And of course Mark had been through this process before with Lily. Surprising how much detail there is in a life, all assembled with elaborate care and dispersed in half a day.

Mark reminded himself to appear ignorant of the layout of the upstairs rooms and to ask for directions as to where everything belonged. On the top landing he paused at the loft door, remembering this as the one place he had not explored. It stood ajar.

'Should I ...?' he asked her as she passed with a black bag.

'Oh no. Don't open that, please, Mark.'

'It was already open – I thought ...'

'We won't. Not up there. I'm not ready to ...'

'Of course.' He hastened to comply and soothe. Presumably Freya had decided to go up but felt daunted and couldn't summon the courage. It increased one's curiosity to see the private world that lay up those stairs. 'Just say the word when you want to ...'

'It's just ... it was Keir's studio, Mark.'

'Sorry – I hadn't realised. We must leave the studio until you're completely ready, love. Don't cry now, dear Freya. It's hard but we'll get through this. We will. There's a time to every purpose under heaven.'

The quotation from the Book of Ecclesiastes had maybe been a bit rich. Over-egging, Mark thought. But, as it turned out, not over-egged at all. He heard Freya working downstairs, singing 'There is a season, turn, turn, turn ...'

In the study, he pocketed the miniature mike. With any luck, and the exercise of good judgment now, in the future there'd be no need to overhear anything. Where Freya was, Mark would be. Of course if it became necessary before that time, Mark could easily reinstate the device.

'Mark, I've got something for you.'

'What is it?'

'Please have Keir's watch. Take it. I'd like you to.'

She slipped the watch – a cheap old thing out of the Ark – into his jacket pocket. You had to wind it. Mark tried, embarrassed, to return it. She strapped it on his left wrist.

'Really, you shouldn't. I mustn't.'

'It's just a *thing*,' she informed him, and the life was fleetingly back in Freya's voice. Her fingers as she fiddled with the strap were warm on his wrist. 'And now it's your thing, Mark. So don't make a fuss.'

He wanted to say, *I'll treasure it, Freya, I really will,* but, suspecting that this would qualify as a fuss, kept quiet and accepted the trophy, different in kind to the other trophies he'd collected. One day he would jettison those – apart from the fragile ring made of her hair. The teaspoon he'd rather randomly picked up could go back in her cutlery drawer now. It was important to hold oneself to standards of probity.

155

But he might keep it all until he was secure of Freya and she'd joined him at Tŷ Hafan. Yes, he would keep it.

Mark ran most of the bags to the Air Ambulance shop and was thanked by a weary-looking helper, who bunged them one after the other into the sweat-smelling back-room. She looked at him dolefully, as if too many folk insisted on dying and their relatives failed to wash their clothes before dumping them on the shop. In other circumstances, Mark might have expressed a view on her manner. But bliss had dissolved away the acrimonious feelings bubbling under the surface. He smiled, sympathised, and left, feeling that he had made a new best friend.

Driving the rest of the stuff to the recycling centre, he lobbed the bagged bits of Keir Fox into the appropriate receptacles. Done.

On the way home, Mark stopped off to buy paint. Interior decoration was one of his skills: in the right hands, it could count as an art form. He was often called upon at the gallery to advise on wall colourings. In the domestic sphere, too many people thought in terms of magnolia. Or they aspired to a kind of Regency Wedgwood blue or apple green, which shrank a small space into something even meaner. Freya had requested white – but perhaps she'd like the elegance of this dove grey? He could always exchange it if it wasn't to her taste. Once they'd painted the Freya side of the wall, he'd do the Mark side to match. In any case, white walls reminded him of lavatories. He found Freya slumped on her sofa, hugging a cushion. At first she seemed doubtful about the dove grey paint, or maybe just indifferent. She was watching the news with the sound turned off. Her face looked dead. Mark hoped she wasn't ill again.

'Oh, that's fine, Freya. Of course. I just thought – that white sometimes glares. But what do I know? I'll take this back and exchange it. No problem at all. Back in half an hour. And I can start the job as soon as you like.'

'But – well, maybe try it? It may grow on me. God,' she said. 'These politicians in their masks. What am I doing, watching this?

156

You don't need to hear what they're saying, you know it's lies and evasions.' She roused herself. 'Let me look – yes, let's try the grey. It's a peaceful colour.'

Freya didn't want to be *glared* at by the wall, clearly. It had been a well-chosen verb. She came over, tucking her hair behind her ears. She'd washed it, he saw, it was softly uncontrollable. Sunlight through drops on the window caught Freya's tired face in a sudden prism. He'd never seen any distress as lovely.

'It's a shade I am quite fond of,' Mark said. 'Gentle and not in-your-face.'

Freya was content to be guided. Yes, she liked the colour and was impatient now to get started and eclipse the swirling drama on the wall.

In point of fact it needed replastering but Mark kept that to himself. Important to act expeditiously to cover the imagery she'd begun to find hateful. Give Freya a clean start, he thought. Obliterate the so-called artist and his pretensions from their shared world. For it was Keir Fox they were about to bury together.

The dead should not control the living. He believed that profoundly.

As Mark took the roller to one end, Freya peeled off her sweater and prepared to start on the other. Out of the corner of his eye Mark watched, curious to see how she would approach the problem of the baby. She seemed to be working round the detail. As she raised the roller, he loved the lift of Freya's breasts through the eggshell blue t-shirt. He even liked the sweat marks under her arms. He hoped she liked his. When she raised her arms, a hint of midriff showed.

Freya worked methodically, keeping the paint even, but leaving an ellipse round the baby like a nimbus or aureole. Or like an egg.

Might she ask Mark to do that for her – eliminate the child?

Refuse, he cautioned himself, as you initially refused the tatty watch. Only accept if she's adamant. Nobody can do that for Freya without risking a kind of sacrilege. She must do it for herself. All Mark could do was support. He thought of sacred images in

157

churches – Madonna and Child, the Pietà – painted out by Reformation iconoclasts and revealed centuries later in restoration. Mark wanted Keir and Larch to disappear and stay disappeared. It was in Freya's interests that this image of loss should be lost – but it would not be directly accomplished by him.

Mark bent to refill his tray. When he looked up, Larch had left the painted world and that was that. The shadow of the sling that bound him to the tree survived but would not outlast a second coat.

He made no comment. They worked in silence and met towards the middle.

'So what do you think, Freya?' he asked, standing back. 'Is the colour OK? Completely up to you. If you don't like it, nothing's lost – it can do the job of an undercoat.'

'You were right, Mark. Thanks.'

This was the turning point, he knew, the second chance that life had granted. Providence had offered Freya Fox to him but one must actively cooperate by working to channel the goodness of Providence.

*

How on earth did policemen on surveillance duty keep awake? Or stalkers loiter for hours in bushes outside the quarry's home? What kept them awake?

Mark had brought supplies and consumed the lot within forty minutes but was rationing the flask of coffee. He'd had the foresight to bring a bottle for urine and wipes to keep his hands hygienic. Mozart as ever soothed the soul. This was necessary, given the level of vexation involved in observing your own property going to the dogs. His hands were kept fidgeting by the compulsion to snip the hedge and wipe bird shit off the bay window.

Was she in or not? A light burned in the front-room that had been Mark's study and would be his sanctuary again. Danny always assumed that someone else – some grown-up – would pay for

158

electricity and gas. Twenty minutes crawled past. Mark kept his attention nailed to the door and windows of Tŷ Hafan. When melting thoughts of Freya threatened to intrude, he blocked them.

Mark trained his binoculars on the guy approaching his front door, a podgy consumer of Big Macs. He was delivering leaflets, despite the fact that the notice clearly stated: NO UNINVITED TRADERS, NO NUISANCE CALLERS.

A crocodile of small children and their helpers toddled hand-in-hand round the bend from the village and along the beech hedge. The column seemed never-ending. He remembered the Eliot line: *I had not thought death had undone so many.*

Shit. One of the carers was Danny. Don't look this way. She didn't. What was she doing? Opening his front door: letting the tribe into Mark's house.

Mark had time to video the tail end of the procession before the door closed. There would almost certainly be a regulation against bringing nursery kids into private property. Ha! Got you! There'd have to be inspections and insurance: health and safety. As the door closed on the last infant, Mark let out his breath. There was something unnerving about witnessing the commandeering of your property, as if you were an observer hanging around after your own death. Observing perfidy, you were barred from intervention.

One-and-a-half mortal hours later, carloads of parents turned up to collect the kids and their helium balloons. So they must have given permission for their offspring to infest his house. The kids looked the worse for wear and Mark prayed they hadn't been sick on his carpets. Danny, waving her guests off, stood at the door and kissed each child goodbye, flaunting a pink party dress with a sash. She looked like the Christmas fairy or a pink meringue. He waited till the meringue had finished waving and shut the door.

How to negotiate all this? It would be tricky. Danny had evidence of what she called his violence and, feeble as she was, she was a weakling with an advantage.

Mark sat and drummed his fingers on the wheel. Rain pulsed on the roof. A van drew up; another visitor. Tall and lean. Jeans, black leather jacket. A belated dad come to collect his child? Or a boyfriend? *The* boyfriend? Mark was sure she had one. Wearing her like a glove puppet. Dancing on his fucking hand. If so, this was probably not the guy. Danny came to the door, greeted him, disappeared again and handed over a black bag which he slung into the van. What was in the bag? Something of mine, he thought, which she was disposing of like junk to a charity.

You didn't intend to take any action and then you found yourself precisely where you had decided not to go.

Danny had changed out of her frillies into pyjamas – he recognised them – and those old sloppy slippers with the bunnies.

'Danielle, I was passing and I wanted to run something past you. Only if that's convenient. I don't want to bother you. And – oh, sorry – I see you're resting.'

He turned as if to leave and, after a fractional pause, she stopped him and invited him in. Invited him in! To his own damn house!

'Are you sure?' he asked meekly. 'I can come another time.'

Mark held his peace about the guy with the bag and the seventy times seven brats. As he came through the hall, he pretended not to notice the spillage at the base of the stairs, which might have been any liquid: at any other time, he'd have knelt to sniff it. He refrained from noticing the discarded party poppers, the ripped wrapping paper or the food trodden into the living-room carpet. That carpet was Egyptian. It was old. It was unique. He had used to lay a runner from the door to the sofa, to spare it. The Art Deco sofa had been laid end to end with easy chairs: one could imagine the shrieking horde of tots vaulting from seat to seat. It was a supreme test of patience to abstain from restoring the furniture to its proper place.

Danny, caught off-guard, had to confess, 'Bit of a mess, I'm afraid – one of the mums has gone into hospital in an emergency and her little boy, Rhys, would have missed his birthday party, so I ... well, stepped in.'

Her nervously pleading glance spoke volumes. Mark elected to be gentle in pursuing his advantage After all, Danny was still young. There was time for her to learn and grow. And, if Mark was honest with himself, as he always tried to be, he had not always done his best by Danny.

'Poor wee mite,' he said softly, to emphasise compassion, and shook his head. But why had his voice taken on a Scottish twang? Correcting it, he went on, 'That's so hard. I hope Rhys's mum will be all right?' He looked concernedly at Danny's watchful face and saw her anxiety descend the scale by a wary ten per cent. He added, 'That was kind, Danielle. Really kind.'

'Lara suffers from kidney disease,' Danny explained, exhibiting a further ten per cent decline in angst. 'Reading between the lines, I don't think the prognosis is great. Unless she can get an exact match.'

'I'm really sorry. A friend of mine suffered with that. It was unimaginably painful.'

Mark thought of telling her how he'd offered his own kidney, which had proved, sadly, not to be a match. How the friend had a daughter called Tania, about seven years old. He decided against opening the door to this parallel world: enough was enough.

'I hope the little chap enjoyed his party, even so?' he asked concernedly.

Danielle could not disguise her astonishment at Mark's sympathetic attitude. She stared, wrapping her dressing-gown around her, tightening the belt, and was lost for words, before reassuring him that Rhys had thoroughly enjoyed himself, despite all. But what, she wondered, had Mark wanted to run past her?

He explained about his new partner.

Her pregnancy.

Her teenage children. The need to accommodate the whole family. And Pansy, their beloved Labrador. The impossibility of housing them all where he was staying.

How, although the baby was not biologically his own, Mark was determined to love him or her as his own. It was the least he could do. Well, actually – if it made any sense – Mark loved the unborn

161

babe already. If it was a boy, they planned to name him Luke – and (he hesitated: *girls' names? girls' names?*) Tania, if she was a girl.

He explained that the counselling sessions he'd already mentioned to Danielle, with this lovely lady psychotherapist, were continuing. She – Val – was wise, he said, but also sharp and didn't spare him. She was originally from Sweden and her methods and techniques were Scandinavian. Val had helped him strip away his protective layers – and, among other things, revealed in him this tenderness for children, which he'd never suspected.

What is more important when you come down to it, he asked Danny solemnly, than children? She nodded agreement.

He often thought of Jesus saying to the disciples, 'Suffer the little children to come unto me, for of such is the Kingdom of Heaven.'

Danny nodded again. It was beautiful, she said. She loved that passage. The disciples had tried to shoo the children away but Jesus had rebuked them.

'It has been a lesson to me,' Mark said, humbly.

'I can see that.'

There were things he felt remorse about, Mark acknowledged, accepting a cup of coffee. He didn't specify, but, turning his head away as if in shame, looked towards the reproduction of the portrait of John Donne (which needed straightening, also dusting). But you can't go back and adapt the past – you can't, you wish you could, but you can't. And basically you just have to get on with making your life more *decent*, more *listening*, more *understanding*.

Danny was now nodding at every other word. She appeared spellbound. Her expression reminded him of how she was when they first became close. Even Janine, his idolising research student, did not come as close.

'Well,' Mark concluded, tearing his eyes away from John Donne with that long, wan, lop-sided face and his hair like spaniel's ears. 'I'll shut up now. I just wanted you to know why I felt I needed space, Danielle. But I leave it all to you. Pressure is the last thing I want you to feel. I know you will do the right thing for everyone.

162

Val advised me to be completely open with you. I told her I'd been so lucky to have you. And it's true, I feel it. I have been such a know-all. Pontificating away at you.'

She grinned, and he saw how his acknowledgment released something in Danny that had started as hero-worship but soured into grudge and then loathing. Her resentment now flew out of the window (which needed cleaning. Presumably she had told the window cleaner not to bother, she could do it herself).

'Yes, but you've taught me so much,' Mark continued, trowelling it on. 'And I tell myself it's never too late to learn. A pinch of humility,' he admitted with a wry smile, 'never hurt anyone – least of all a dry old academic with too many long-term chips on his shoulder. And – well, thanks – for listening, Danielle. For just being you.'

There were tears in both their eyes. They put out their hands; their fingertips touched.

'And – it's no excuse, Danielle, please don't imagine I'm hiding behind an excuse – I've done too much of that – but when you and I first came together, I was deep in mourning. I blame myself for not realising that I was in no state to form a new relationship – although I suppose that was part of the grief. I wasn't thinking properly – in fact I think I was mad – genuinely – out of my mind – after Lily's death. But what I can't forgive myself for – can't ever make up for – is that I subjected you to my craziness, even though you were always so dear to me.'

'There's nothing you should reproach yourself for, Mark. You've found healing.'

'Well, *finding* it. But even so.' How Danny loved to confer forgiveness. It was part of her Christian heritage. 'Even so, there is no excuse. And I am being helped in all sorts of ways. There have to be second chances.'

'Oh, I need those too. I really do.'

'The thing was – I don't know if I should say this – but – she died here, you see, Danielle – in this house. Of course you knew that. But I think the house was the unbearable thing. It seemed to record the horror of it all. She was in the very walls. Or rather, her death was. But that's gone now, for me.'

This was the haunting note he thought best to leave her on. As Mark made his way back to the car, he was taken up in the sentiment of his story. He pegged it down at the edges, to ensure he wouldn't forget any details. He was sensible of a kind of elation at the hatching of this narrative, not because it was full of surprising inventions but because there was something genuine at its core. Not quite sure what, because having babies with Freya was a no-no. Chaos, nappies, racket. Even so, there was a symbolic resonance in what he'd heard himself say.

And Danny hadn't been a bad kid, especially in the beginning.

If Mark knew her at all, she'd now be prey to pangs of guilt, wondering if somehow she'd driven him to whatever it was she thought he'd done to her. She'd be questioning her right to keep this comfortable haven from a family in need. As a child Danny had attended church twice on the Sabbath and gone on to lead a Sunday-school class. She'd want to believe that a sinner could amend his ways. She'd been a Brownie and a Girl Guide, earning badges for knots, baking and helping senior citizens across roads. Danny had rescued nestlings that had fallen out and cooed over them: if they'd gone on to die of her ministrations, at least she'd done her best for the darlings.

Oh yes, Mark thought: unlike Lily, Danny was a do-gooder. You didn't easily grow out of that.

And now she'd vowed to give Mark a date to vacate as soon as she possibly could. She'd stood at the door in the bunny slippers, arms folded across her chest. She was sorry, she'd bleated, so sorry, for the mess and pain. And Mark wasn't solely responsible, no one person could be, it takes two, she'd admitted, summoning clichés of self-reproach.

Where Danny had kissed him on the cheek, she'd left a trace of contrite tears.

The demons beneath had no chance against a second coat. Under the onslaught of dove-grey paint, they gave up the ghost.

Freya made coffee and brought it through. However long was it since she'd just flopped down and lost herself in a book? Since Keir's death it had been hard to concentrate. Stormie sprawled on his side, eyes half closed, and she stroked his sleek back. He was a picture of peacefulness, having called off his compulsive search for Keir.

Freya's old liveliness might never return but surely she could hope to live without constant turbulence. Reading should bring calm and focus; it always had, from early childhood. Dad had read with her every night. She loved huge books into which you could climb and be lost for six weeks on end. Where was her old copy of *Middlemarch?* That had always done Freya good. Its binding had failed and the dog-eared pages had to be secured with a rubber band. She tried the opening sentences, with their branching clauses. From the clauses dangled phrases. As Freya traced the twigs, she lost the boughs, and the structure tossed in a mental breeze. One by one, leaves dropped out.

A wail broke from her: she heard it with dismay. Was another attack coming on? Up to that moment she had felt well and hopeful. Prepare yourself then, Freya told herself; go to the loo, empty your bladder in case you're about to have another fit. Losing control was a humiliation she dreaded. She lay down on the bed, her mobile on the cabinet. Should she call Mark?

Nothing happened. Nothing kept on happening for so long that boredom set in. She went downstairs and confronted the wall. If you're coming, Keir, just bloody get on with it. She stared at the wall. But the wall was blank. The second skin of paint had eclipsed the underlying designs so thoroughly that no outsider could have guessed what lay beneath. The smell was just wet paint, nothing sinister.

Lighten up, she told herself; keep sane. Where was Mark? His car was not there so presumably he was at work. Should she ring him? He would come if she called, whatever he was doing.

Opening the window, Freya heard the murmur of passing people, car engines, the whine of a strimmer. Mrs Teague, with her carrying voice, was explaining to someone – presumably – from the council that, yes, of course she was sure she'd seen a rat.

'Rats! I know what rats look like! It was as big as a cat,' she told him. 'Actually, no: a dog.'

The rat-catcher collected a trap from his van. He would set it under this bush here, he explained. There was poisoned bait in the trap.

'I've heard them in my loft,' complained Mrs Teague. She didn't seem to be speaking just to the rat catcher but to the cosmos in general. 'And I know they're in the wall spaces. I hear scrabbling. At night. The moment I put my head on the pillow, out they come. They sound as if they're in the wardrobe. You'd better lay down poison in the loft too. Can you manage to put it in the wall cavity?'

No, he couldn't, the rat catcher said. The wall spaces were sealed: that was how wall spaces were supposed to be. A wall space was not intended to have entrances and exits. Then it would not be a wall space, he went on, but a wall corridor. He promised to try to locate the rats' point of entry and seal it off. The pest control officer seemed a patient guy, accustomed to householders' hysteria.

So that was probably it, Freya thought. The noises coming through the walls are just rats. She caught (what she'd never perceived before) the dread in Marion Teague's voice, disguised in the cringing despotism she exercised over her narrow bounds. Marion feared that creatures might come bursting through – or die and putrefy in the wall spaces, where no rat catcher could reach them, filling the house with stench.

'If they die in the wall space, it takes three weeks for the smell to go,' the rat catcher explained. He was trying not to gloat over the power he exercised over his customers. 'Nothing we can do about it.'

'Oh *no.*'

She is a widow, thought Freya, as if this were a piece of news. Mrs Teague had already lost her husband when she and Keir first moved in. Now I see, thought Freya. At last I see. All because of the rats, I get it. The light of recognition flickered briefly in her mind.

Out popped Pam Crouch and offered the services of Pansy. Vermin soon cleared off when Pansy was around. Pam could offer Marion a nice bowl of cat urine. No sooner would the rats scent Pansy's pee than they'd vamoose: you wouldn't see the blighters for dust. She suggested placing this miracle liquid in the loft. Terry would do it as soon as he came home.

'No thank *you*,' said Mrs Teague, who could obviously imagine all too clearly Terence Crouch wobbling his way up the loft steps with a bowl of cat pee. 'I prefer the poison method.'

Normally Freya would have gone out and reminded everyone that poison takes time to kill its victim; the stricken creature runs out and dies in the woodland and the corpse gets pecked by a crow and the crow dies, and so on along the chain. And Pansy would be endangered. She went as far as the door and somehow couldn't face opening it and meeting the eyes of pitying people. This was not like her at all. I'm not myself, she thought, but surely I shall be again? If I'm not myself, who am I?

She remained dithering there, between intention and inertia, until Mark came home.

11

Was Freya up yet? He'd caught no sounds through the wall but what could you tell when the dawn chorus in the woodland was so deafening? It was a madhouse over there. They were rutting and warring, nesting and laying. Squirrels were abroad on egg hunts. Birds were warning one another off their territories. They sang their throats out, at the first sign of light. Standing at the open window dreamily listening to the drumming of the woodpecker, Mark tried to isolate the bird. You couldn't. Its rapping echoed round and round, a whirlpool of sound. This was a halcyon time: he'd become himself – unprecedentedly – released from impersonations.

Freya had turned to Mark and he knew, with scarcely a shadow of doubt, that he'd been able to answer her need. She seemed at last to understand – it had been staring them both in the face for months – that in some core way they were alike, they were kin. Nothing was said but he read in Freya's softened glance, in the attitude of her lithe, ripe body, that she was finding in him a version of what he had discovered in her.

Yes, he was wounded himself. Mark had always known that. Such wounds fail to heal with time. Red and inflamed, they seep pus, which pools in the heart. You learn to subsist with them but time makes no difference. Time is a fiction. There is no time, none whatever, in that dark place of offence. When Lily left him, the priest had counselled, *Lean in to love, my son: love will not fail you.* The message had transiently stilled his hunger like a communion wafer on the tongue. But then it dissolved, becoming a platitude.

The wound had started to heal, he was sure of it. The platitude blossomed all over again into wisdom.

For when Mark leaned in to love, so did Freya. There was symmetry. Even symbiosis. Freya trusted him to keep the secret of her epilepsy: nothing would drag it out of him. I am the same as my lovely Freya in so many ways, he thought; she is me. Not in a claptrap mystical way. Mark's hollowness had begun to fill; his cup brimmed as he helped Freya meet the days and nights of her mourning.

There were numerous practical things Mark could do for or with her. He accompanied her to the solicitor for probate. Keir Fox had died intestate: they'd looked high and low, in case he'd bothered to leave any indication of his wishes. Typical, Mark thought, of a woolly-haired idealist. The guy had never bothered with building up a pension or purchasing life insurance. Jack of all trades, Keir had odd-jobbed as a builder, landscape gardener, hospital porter, with spells on the dole – and occasionally sold a picture. Fundamentally the guy was a bit of a sponger. Not to mention his womanising. But don't think about that.

Mark was careful to say nothing to criticise the improvidence of Freya's husband. It was not for him to comment: he was scrupulous about that, holding himself severely to account.

The search had acquainted Mark with most of what remained unexplored in Freya's little universe. The sole unvisited area – apart from a shedful of bikes, was the loft. He'd maybe mention this to Freya and offer to have a look round on her behalf – or just go anyway when she was asleep in his house. Freya was always tired. An afternoon nap seemed to help.

His fingers had fossicked out three personal notes from a file of Keir's. They'd been in sealed buff envelopes marked with her name and the phrase: READ AFTER MY DEATH.

Mark had pocketed them. For Freya was a woman perched on a narrow ledge, above an immense drop. She was an epileptic who needed support and a calm environment. Drawing on his own terrors, Mark could imagine hers. Anything might unbalance her, let alone some random message from beyond the grave. Mark had pledged himself to guard Freya's safety and he would do just that. Later, at home, after carefully studying and photographing the letters, he'd burned one of the three originals, to spare Freya further emotional upheaval. And also because of its PS about 'the guy next door'.

The other two messages he locked into the reliquary that housed his tokens, a growing hoard: the ring woven of her darling hair, the white poppy, nightie, reading glasses, teaspoon, slipper, and so on. These were simple things, of intrinsic worth to nobody but himself. The third letter, however, had been a time bomb. Keir had been less dense than he appeared.

Together they'd painted Freya's house until its surfaces were brought under control. Sips of bliss came Mark's way when Freya's eyes warmed to his smile, and she accepted a cup of tea or handed him Storm's lead. At work, Dr Heyward had been affable, charming, conciliatory; even in meetings where his small explosions in the past had become a mini-tradition like Roman candles on bonfire night. He'd clapped Paltry Patrick on the shoulder and congratulated him on the preparations for the exhibition. He'd typed up and printed all the provenances to save the secretary trouble.

'You look happy, Mark,' she'd said, thanking him.

'Do you know, I am happy. And how about you, Carrie? Did you go away anywhere nice for your hols? Or are they still to come? I've rather lost track.'

He'd sat down and chatted with her for a quarter of an hour, listening and responding – without self-consciousness, really wanting to hear and interested in what she had to say about Crete and her grandchildren on the beach.

'It's so important, isn't it,' Mark said, 'to switch off and take time just to dream. Or play, with grandchildren, or swim, or even spend time doing nothing. We're all so driven, aren't we? – we hardly give one another the time of day.'

'You're so right. And have you plans to go away?'

'You know, Carrie, I've come to the conclusion that being happy is a holiday of itself.'

She'd beamed. As he wandered down the corridor to his office,

Mark found himself thinking of Carrie kindly, as a friend, an equal, someone to pause and share time with. And he must not forget that Janine would be coming in to consult him shortly: he looked forward to her visit. After he'd answered his emails, Mark would get ready to shop for himself and Freya. Happiness would be waiting for him at home.

Freya would kiss Mark's cheek as he carried in the shopping. They'd unload it together. He'd made no effort to coax her out of doors, except on necessary trips to the solicitor and into his own place when she got sick of seeing the same four walls. Exposed to daylight, Freya seemed dazed and muted, and she screwed up her eyes against the light. He'd made sure after that to remember to take her sunglasses if they had to go out. No doubt she dreaded another episode.

Well, if it came, Mark would be there. And he knew the drill. He kept close and, on necessary trips, shepherded her rapidly towards the car, past the neighbours who bustled out, wanting to know how their dear friend was, and would she like to come in for coffee or tea, cup-cakes or flapjacks, or be taken on a nice shopping trip to the industrial park?

In a real way, these people, who thought they meant nothing but good, were bloodsuckers. It wasn't their fault: it was how they were built. Terence was the worst; Terence he was beginning to find objectionable. The fellow was nowhere near as harmless as he liked to appear. And as for Pamela, comparison with the chimpanzee was not in her favour.

Yesterday there'd been a minor scene. As Mark dealt with his emails, the memory of Terence's impertinence threatened his peace of mind.

Terence had actually laid hands on Freya.

'How are you, my dear?'

The guy had taken her arm in its thin white cardigan and would not let go. For a moment, Freya had been the rope in a tug of war, Mark guiding her forward at one side while Terence detained her on the other. The thought had occurred to him that the fat little fool fancied their neighbour. Fancied her! Ha! What would Pamela make of *that*? Terence's life wouldn't be worth living!

Terence, mirrored on the surface of Freya's reflecting sunglasses, had enquired again how she was.

'We're fine, thanks. Doing great, in a bit of a hurry, do excuse us,' Mark had heard himself respond, smilingly steering Freya onwards.

Terence had let go, no option. Mark had noted the guy's rattled look in response to that *we* and *us*. But Freya and I are *we* now, Mark thought: get used to it. Once Danny had vacated Tŷ Hafan, he and Freya would be quit of this place and its population of pious parasites.

'Where are you off to, Freya dear?' Terence had asked, keeping pace.

'We're just on our way to do some errands,' Mark had replied, at the same time as Freya, appearing rather stunned, murmured, 'The bank.'

'And how are you feeling now, love?' the leech had persisted, addressing Freya, despite the fact that Mark had already responded to this question and manoeuvred them to within metres of his car.

'I'm OK, thanks, Terry. Doing quite well. How are you and Pammie? I've not seen you for a while. I've been rather –'

Mark had opened the car door. For a moment, a wave of the old nauseated indignation had risen and he'd felt like throwing Freya in, buckling her up and slamming the door, especially as she had now removed her sunglasses and was looking at Terence with naked eyes. The trite little troll had begun to tell an anecdote concerning the really cute things one of his cousin's toddler nephews had said about eating toothpaste off the toothbrush, and Freya was chuckling.

Casting her head back, she'd let out a loud laugh – a guffaw, almost.

No need to overdo it, Mark had thought waspishly, but quickly recovered himself. It was good for Freya to laugh. Of course it was.

Nobody who loved his darling Freya could begrudge her that release. And it was also rather brave, given her situation. However, Mark had reminded himself: Terry doesn't know about Larch, she has told no one but me, in total confidence, which I shall never betray.

'Sorry not to be able to stay and chat, Terence.' Mark had given his neighbour's shoulder a friendly rub. 'Good to see you. Very. Have to dash. Catch you again.'

This time he'd avoided 'we'. He'd shown courtesy and indulged the fusspot's right to fuss. Terence hadn't seemed impressed. He'd looked disgruntled. *Get over it, chum,* Mark had thought as Terence cast on him the flicker of a cold and suspicious glance. *Not quite such a saint, are we?*

And be careful, I should, he silently advised: Mrs Crouch would be less than delighted to learn that Mr Crouch nourished 'feelings' for the widow next door.

They'd driven to the bank. There was nothing Mark didn't know about Freya's finances. And he could help, being shrewd with money – except when he wasn't. His occasions of spectacular blow-out were rare, sudden ruptures in his settled habit of economy – and obviously would not occur in relation to Freya's property. He'd noted with interest that she had savings in her own name. An ISA and a bond. That implied to Mark that she had not quite trusted her husband and had taken practical steps to secure herself.

Her head was generally screwed on. It implied that this weakened, suggestible state would not last forever. Important, therefore, to give the attachment between them a deep, strong root, now, while the soil was pliable. In her current needy state, Freya had said to bring his gallery work in and do it in the study if he would like to. He'd accordingly deposited his second laptop and some files on her desk, which was now their shared desk.

Mark understood so well why Freya breathed a sigh of relief at reaching home and shutting the door behind them. He threw the bolt, while she ensured that the curtains were closed and the lamps on. A ribbon of daylight where the seams didn't meet was the extent of Freya's compromise with the sun. Nothing odd about this: it was something Mark often did himself. The two of them were, within this capsule of time and space, all in all to one another.

There was nothing Mark wouldn't do for Freya: almost nothing. Every morning he knocked at seven and left her at about ten-thirty in the evening. If he'd pushed – or even pressed lightly – he could have stayed overnight.

In her bed. With Freya. Made love to her. Stayed at her side, perhaps, for good.

Thinking of this possibility, his breath came fast, in snatches. Desire and dread were first cousins – kissing cousins.

Last night he'd slept deeply, through what must have been quite a wind, for in the woodland, hawthorn and whitethorn blossom had fallen like snow and the green was strewn with broken branches. He thought: I can never leave or lose Freya. My Freya. Mine for life. That *mine* tasted sweet. I'm home at last, he told himself. The woodpecker dinned a percussive head into its decaying tree. Finches and blue-tits dipped and dived between their cover and a neighbour's bird table. This was a lovely site, the green slope and Whitethorn Wood, but of course it was not one's own. Privacy here never went unadulterated. Mark saw himself and Freya as pilgrims passing through this over-populated terrace. Once they were installed at Tŷ Hafan, Mark could introduce Freya to his blackbird and the copper beech with its purple darkness, the wrens' nests in the beech hedge at the bottom of the long curving lawns. A detached house would be an island for their love.

He tapped lightly on Freya's door and, still in her dressing gown, she let him in. She'd been crying. For hours and hours, to judge by the half-closed state of her eyes.

'You didn't sleep, *bach*?'

Freya shrugged. 'Thought I might try an afternoon nap today, Mark.' It was her way of confessing that she'd spent another roiling night – but that she might manage some rest, if he stayed around and kept watch. 'What about you?'

'I was all right,' he said stoically, ruffling Storm's head. The dog startled him by growling deep in his throat and baring his teeth. 'Hey, what's up, Stormie?'

Mark was hurt. He bent to Storm and put out his hand to be sniffed.

'It's only me,' he said. 'Your old friend. Your forever friend. And I don't bite.'

The dog quietened right down. No wonder Storm was temperamental, bombarded with all the pheromones of stress and fear and sadness pouring out at him. Mark still felt a little hurt at his reception. 'I'll take you out shortly, boy.'

'You should have come in, Mark, if you were lying awake,' Freya said. 'Did you hear the owl in the wood? They sound like babies crying and they seem so near.'

He nodded ruefully, as he would have done, had he been disturbed by an owl.

'Next time, ring, won't you?' Freya went on, 'and we can keep each other company.'

His heart beat high but Mark quashed the excitement. 'I'd a lot rather *you* rang me, *bach*.'

'Yes, but I don't want to disturb you.'

'Please disturb me!' He took her transiently by the shoulders. 'What am I for? Disturb me! OK? I've brought my work, as you suggested.'

He opened his laptop and hung one of the new sweaters over the chair back. Keeping open the door to the living-room, Mark was aware that Freya had placed herself where she could see him.

'Don't tiptoe around, Freya,' he told her, without turning. 'It's companionable to have someone there while I work. It really doesn't affect my concentration. Somehow or other it makes it easier to write.'

'What are you working on?' Bringing coffee, she lingered and he felt her bending over to look at the screen; heard her breathing.

'I'm sketching out some thoughts – about the Rosetta Stone. We have a fragment in the museum of an even more ancient stone with trilingual translations of Egyptian hieroglyphs. So we'll be making a feature of that at the exhibition. We call it Baby Rosetta.'

'That's fascinating.'

She drew up a chair and Mark took her through a video of the Rosetta Stone and its inscriptions: a diversion for her grief, if nothing else.

Even if Freya opened the laptop in his absence, she'd glean nothing that should be kept private from her. Having deleted all memory from the hard drive, Mark had restored the programmes: the computer wore a brand-new face. But obviously one wouldn't wish to offer her a mindless blank. If Freya had the curiosity to open the computer, he should confer glimpses into his heart of hearts. He'd sifted out, revised and imported email correspondence and documents from his main computer. Some files Mark had created especially for this laptop – thoughts on nature and environmentalism, whimsies really, but he felt she'd appreciate the sentiments, as he did. He'd enjoyed the creativity of the exercise. Mark had also copied poems for her to read – a Shakespeare sonnet, a translation he'd made of a Goethe lyric – with his own marginal comments. It had given subtle pleasure to prepare this external mind for Freya to ponder if she chose.

'Please don't feel you have to keep me company, Mark,' Freya said. 'You've got your life to live.'

He looked into her face as she straightened up. If only she knew. The shadows under her eyes were almost black. Had she eaten anything this morning? He chided himself for not ensuring she was well fed. Freya was a bird with two broken wings. How could she feed and tend herself?

'I've imposed on you enough,' she said. 'There must be things you need to do.'

'Well – yes – there are. You don't understand, Freya,' Mark said, getting to his feet, taking her hand between both of his. 'What I want to do is what I'm doing. There's nowhere I'd rather be than here with you. Nowhere in the world.'

'I feel so weak. But I'm not a weak person, you see.'

'You've been exceptionally strong. Way too strong.'

'You think so?'

'I know so. It made you ill. And don't you think ... that ... episode ... was trying to give you a message? Sometimes we have to just touch home and stay cwtched up in hibernation for a while, or so I've found. Where's the shame in that, Freya?'

She listened and entered his arms and he rocked her. So gentle, so easy. Anything Mark was inspired to say or do proved miraculously to be the real and right thing, speaking to Freya's condition from a fund of healing wisdom he'd hardly known he possessed. Afterwards, reclining with Freya in his arms on the settee, fully clothed, lullabying her with heaven knew what whisperings of comfort, Mark buried his face in her dark cloud of hair and breathed her in, somehow unsurprised, knowing that this was where his entire life had tended. There was no going back. Softly they drifted to sleep together.

*

And then Lily came and breathed on him. Her breath carried a rank whiff of the grave. Her dismembered viola screamed at Mark. Mark bellowed and reared up off the couch, flailing. Freya woke with a shriek and Storm bayed.

The room was a welter of terror – and the two of them were terrifying each other, he saw, as he sobbed there in the middle of the room while the television showed silent faces mouthing at one another – dead stars in an old film that revolved in the same loop whether you watched it or not, and he looked across where Lily – no, Freya Fox, not Lily – had stifled her shrieks and striven to raise herself from the couch, but Mark had batted her aside, whereupon Storm flung his body upon her and dragged his tongue over her face (not Lily's, it wasn't Lily) and leapt off the couch and, unthinkably, bared his teeth, ears erect, tail high, and snarled at Mark. The animal guarded his darling against some obscenity that was at large in their world.

How calm it was, lingering here in the moonlight, Keir's dog at her side. Storm nuzzled Freya's calf, huddling his flank in close. You could not feel unsafe in his company.

Moonlight creamed over the still trees and cast an intricate shadow from the maple Keir had planted when they first came to the crescent. It had been a miserable-looking sapling, unlikely to thrive, which had shot up to a height several feet taller than Keir. Its purple leaves astonished the eye every spring. Strangely, Mark's panic-stricken outburst seemed to have brought Freya's scattered self together. She'd never been a whining, cringing kind of person, never. That just wasn't her. Keir had always said Freya was the stronger and braver of the two, by far.

Something tickled at Freya's memory: Keir had said he'd left messages, a little cache of letters – but wherever had he hidden them? How could she have forgotten something so important? They'd been through the desk drawers so they couldn't be there. Maybe in the studio? That was the most likely place. Keir had written them in the last stages of his illness, when it was apparent he hadn't long to go. His voice was a ghost of itself but his mind remained lucid: partly the drugs but also the crystallisation of certainty about where he was bound. The jettisoning of hope was not a bad thing, he said: you were lighter for it. He'd dreamed of packing his old knapsack for a journey, the khaki canvas one he'd had at the road protests. It was here somewhere, he'd said. In some pile of my old junk. One afternoon Freya had come in from shopping to find Keir licking an envelope – and he'd said, *read these, my lovely – afterwards, not before.*

Tomorrow Freya would hunt and squirrel them out. Meanwhile it felt good to stand in the friendly dark, outside her anguish.

No light showed in Mark's windows: with any luck, he'd have got over the shock of whatever had hit him, and gone off to sleep. Jesus, what a turn he'd given her. She could hardly believe the power of that bellowing: a slaughterhouse noise.

He'd given so much of himself. How kind her neighbour had been, bending over backwards to answer Freya's needs. His rule of thumb, Mark had said, was that friends should be human bridges for one another. That was a lovely phrase amongst many lovely phrases. He had the gift of the gab and she'd occasionally had the feeling that his words ran before him; he raced along behind, wherever they led him. Mark had thrown his words ahead like a footbridge over a ravine – but people are just people, aren't they, Freya thought; our feet are clay and we shouldn't be asked to function as bridges for too long. Such intense identification with her grief was bound to arouse Mark's own trauma – and Freya had the feeling he'd be better off – they'd *both* be better off – if they took a few steps back from one another.

He wouldn't like that, a quiet voice told her. No, but he'd have to accept it.

Going back over the scene, Freya recalled how he'd leapt off the couch and slapped the side of her face, unintentionally of course, as she realised later. Then he'd rounded on her, demanding, *Why the hell are you looking at me like that, why, answer me, why?* She'd replied that it was just the shock of being woken up and being hit like that, and he'd sobbed, incomprehensibly, *You're going to leave me! I know you are!* And pushed her back.

It was Mark's dream talking; must have been. He couldn't have been properly awake. Well, his eyes hadn't been closed but they were dead. Was he even seeing her at all? She'd guided him back to the settee, where he sat, head in hands, convulsed. *I've always tried, I've tried so hard, I've tried my best to be the best – and look what's happened, look what's happened now!* On and on. What was all that about? She'd kept her hand on his back, massaging as you did with a child, murmuring reassurance, stifling her yawns, her cheek hot with the slap. And then, when Mark had seemed to be calming down, there was something about a coal hole and he was crying aloud again: *God God God, no no no!*

But what she'd thought was: *Nobody hits Freya Vaughan and gets away with it.* Her maiden name, her true name. *Do that again, boy, and you will get the same back but harder.*

Then, to cap it all, there had been Terry knocking, and Pam, in their dressing gowns, with torches and anxious faces. As she answered the door, Mark had shut up.

All that shouting: they'd thought Freya was being attacked. Should they call the police?

'No, it's all right,' she'd whispered, embarrassed, as they sidled in. What on earth should she say in explanation? 'It's just – Mark. He had a dream.'

As if that made any sense! Why would Mark be having a dream in Freya's house? Should she say, *But we weren't in bed or anything?* She'd choked a laugh, for this was all so mad, and what would Keir have made of the pantomimes she'd taken part in since his death? But Terry had slipped past her and was in the living-room. Through the open door, she and Pam had watched Mark wipe his face on his sleeve like a child while Terry knelt and said, 'Come on now, my friend – Freya's got enough on her plate – come in to ours and sit with us a bit. You can bed down in the spare-room if you like.'

He'd offered a nice cup of tea and a ginger biscuit, which Mark, rummaging out a handkerchief and blowing his nose, had refused with a dismissive wave of his free hand.

But what was it Pam had said?

'There's something badly wrong with him, dear.'

Not quite those words but that was the gist. Pam had delivered the judgment in a tone that carried a note of warning and was quite unlike her normal charitable self. In Pam had sashayed, wearing her cherry-red dressing gown, and carrying what looked like a car tool as a weapon. She handed this to Terry, whereupon – so it appeared – she apprehended Mark by grasping him under the armpits and hauling him up.

'Now, whatever it is, Mark dear,' Pam had chided – and he'd gaped at her, stunned – 'you can come in and tell us, dear. Or not tell us, just as you choose. But we should all leave poor Freya to rest, don't you agree?'

Without waiting for an answer, Pam had escorted Mark into the hall. Like a felon under arrest. Like a scolded child, his face all blubbered. Terry, following with the car tool, said to Freya, 'Stay safe. Ring if you want us. Bolt the door.'

On the threshold, the ejected visitor had stirred from his trance; he'd turned to face the three of them there in the wan light. Murmuring an apology, he'd explained that he'd dropped off, watching television – and he must have had one hell of a nightmare, no idea what it was all about, he was fine now and would go home and get some kip, as long as he wasn't needed? No, I'm not needed? Are you sure? They all assured him he was not needed.

'Then farewell!' He'd vanished, with a wave.

Although Freya could not see that the sky was lightening, the birds in Whitethorn Wood presumably could. One or two experimented with tuning up. In the south-west, Freya spotted the Plough – and Orion's belt told her where to hunt for the Milky Way and Sirius. We are stardust, she thought, craning her neck, quoting Keir who'd liked to quote some old Sixties song, we are golden, we are billion-year-old carbon.

The billion-year-old atoms of Keir were everywhere now. He'd gone home.

Solitude was one thing, isolation another. The first she had little experience of but could live with if necessary; the second – no.

Stormie scampered in and waited at the bottom of the staircase as Freya locked and bolted the door. I should be with people. And why be ashamed of telling folk I love and trust about the epilepsy? It's just an illness. And why be afraid of Keir's lovers, and jealous, and bar my house to them, and to Keir's brothers, who are my brothers? What can anyone steal from me?

For Keir was everywhere. Hold on to that. Keep coming back to it. Keir could be traced and tracked in every molecule of her world.

12

Oramorph: that was the answer.

Mark was not needed; they'd stated categorically that he was superfluous. In the great sum of things, he was excess to requirements.

The agony felt physical; it skewered Mark's chest, a serrated blade. Nerve-pain forked, his prick felt as if it would ejaculate shards of pain, his gut spasmed. Cupping his genitals with one hand, he clasped his belly with the other. Oramorph would open out distance between his mind and its thoughts as it eased Mark's body's paroxysms. But what then?

For Lily had broken through – broken out – broken in. Again. What, in Christ's name, did you have to do to kill the assault of the dead?

Oramorph offered hope of transient help. But what about the soundless seethe of archaic pain beneath the immediate pain?

Valium. He'd stockpiled the stuff, concealing it from himself, restraining the yen to raid his stash, shit-scared of running out of supplies. He'd staged a theatrical event at Dr Lewis's surgery when the fellow had threatened to adjust the repeat prescription and wean Mark off what he called his 'addiction'.

Addiction!

The demeaning word was hardly out of the quack's mouth than Mark had swung into action. After a couple of minutes of his patient's loquacious frenzy, Dr Lewis's head had drooped and he looked as if he'd gladly have paid a fee to have him depart and never return. In any case, the quack was only a step away from clinical depression himself, as witness his demented hair and the suicidal expression that was his default. As it turned out, Dr Lewis was quick to pay up, in the currency of an open-ended repeat prescription.

He'd slapped on Temazepam for good measure. *Anything to keep you quiet, pal, take 'em all in one go while you're at it,* Lewis's expression had said. *Care for some hemlock?*

Mark hadn't given a damn what the fellow thought of him: doctor and patient are natural enemies.

He'd assumed Lily would lie quiet now that he had Freya. But no, it didn't work like that. Lily returned with her bad breath, just to taunt Mark with her threat to leave him! How did that make any sense?

Go away.

No.

Yes. Go away.

All right, I will.

No, don't go.

I'm going, I'm leaving you, get used to it.

Don't leave me.

And she will leave you too. She doesn't need you.

In life, Lily had known exactly how to spite Mark. Her boundless malice! And most of it unconscious! He'd told her this and she'd shaken her head as if he were a lunatic. Then she'd begun to believe it and be ashamed of the hateful feelings she harboured for her husband. Good; reality had dawned, and she couldn't stand it because Lily liked to think of herself not only as an artist, and therefore entitled to privileges, but as a *decent person.* In the end, she'd been pitiless. She'd fought him tooth and nail – but passively. Her musical gift lay in spectacular ruins. Her silence and the mute viola had accused him. You still heard her sing occasionally, when she thought you were out or in the cellar, a ragged remnant of her voice's splendour. *See, you've killed my voice,* her muteness had said. No, you've done it to yourself, he'd respond, and you've left me the sole breadwinner in the household!

There'd been occasions when Mark had acknowledged culpability and it drove him wild, rolling round on the floor, begging Lily, his beautiful Lily, for absolution. He quite clearly recalled the view from the carpet as he lay on his stomach, in a performance he recognised at the time as extravagant. He remembered the sight of her bare feet with their crooked little toes, and how he'd felt so sorry for the imperfect toes and pitied them and reached out for them and tried to kiss them.

At which she had ... laughed! And kicked at him.

After her death, you could not silence Lily: for one thing they still played her recordings on local radio. And she'd burrow up to announce ... this contradiction in terms ... her intention to abandon him. Then she'd lie low for months at a time.

He'd forget Lily, and think, *that's it then, I'm free.* But there festered a nameless sense of foreboding. She'd found out the trick of opening a two-way door between opposite threats. Like a cat flap. In the last six months of her life, she'd seemed to Mark to be something like a feral cat, prowling here and there when she thought he was asleep, with her searchlight eyes, her disfiguring scars, her unwashed hair and her hoarse, smoky voice.

The precious stash of medications filled the shelves he'd erected up in the loft – near the entrance – and overflowed into a packing case. Mark creaked his way up the metal ladder to release the trapdoor. Something thudded across the wooden floor. A rat? He didn't care. Ten rats? He still didn't care. All that mattered was the stuff. He scrambled a container from the case, with shaking hands. Even in extremity, Mark was proof against the temptation to ransack the hoard. This proved he was not, never would be, an addict.

Your heavy limbs become inert.

You sink down into the mattress.

Peace was what he craved. But his mind was ajar and terrible things were butting at Mark's consciousness. Another ten milligrams, or rather twenty, should do it. He fell back, foetally curled, beneath the duvet. And waited. Every muscle was lead, his eyelids were sealed, but the mind declined to close.

As clearly as if it were all being staged in the present moment, and for the first time, Mark saw Lily when she'd begun to degenerate. Yes, he told her, but you did it all to yourself. Also, you had an illness. You can't lay that at my door. And besides, you are a hallucination.

After all the love – the worship, not too strong a word – Mark had poured out onto Lily – the cash he'd lavished on her! He had shown special concern after her stage fright or mini-breakdown or whatever it was had caused her career to falter and then collapse. After all her promises to listen to his needs and to understand why he might sometimes be possessive, and that it was only his vulnerability talking, she'd started to loathe him again. Sensitive understanding wasn't much to ask. Was it? Ask any man, he will lose his temper from time to time. Help me, he'd beg Lily, after one of his abject sessions, to be the best person I can be. Help me to put you first – by putting me first.

She'd promise anything, in the aftermath of a row. Just for a bit of peace. Well, Mark had understood that. Peace was a condition he'd always craved. But Lily's promises were worthless. He'd heard her on the phone to one of the many friends and admirers he'd had to deal with. *Mewling and puking,* she'd told the phone. That meant him: Dr Mark Heyward was being dismissed as a mewler and puker! They'd just rowed and he'd apologised handsomely. She'd only twenty minutes ago promised to be more alert to his needs, more caring and sympathetic, to share everything with him, never to blank him out. And what was the bulletin she was delivering on the phone to some Dick or Harry, some fatuous flautist or bassoonist? *Mewling and puking.*

How could Lily have disintegrated so swiftly, when he'd loved her so profoundly, unless the weakness was in her from the start? The distance between the way she'd appeared when he'd first heard her play Blumenthal's *Caprice*, in that astonishing emerald green silk, one shoulder bare – and the stupefied wraith who drank too much and ate too little, cut herself and slopped around in grubby pyjamas: how had this come to pass?

Perhaps one had after all to take one's share of blame. I was not

185

always an angel, he acknowledged – nobody is. Mark always apologised when he knew himself to be in the wrong. He did so copiously, with tears and self-abnegation. In fact he would over-apologise. He would follow her on his knees. But it strained credulity to imagine that he was always the one in the wrong. Life was not like that. It takes two, doesn't it?

You could have bottled the woman's endless tears and used them to pickle herring. A soak in every sense. With the best will in the world, you became immune to it after a while.

That morning. Lily had been all but out of it. She'd swayed on the landing. What had she been taking in the night? Possibly he'd helped her sleep with some of his precious Nitrazepam.

She'd tottered past and into the kitchen; poured coffee with a trembling hand, elbows tight to her narrow chest. Her skin had been bad; one of her lower teeth became discoloured because she didn't brush properly and refused to see the dentist. Her imperfect mouth came back forever after in dreams that terrified him.

But that morning – that awful morning – he'd tried jollying her but that hadn't worked, so he'd laid his coaxings aside and sought to cheer her in more practical ways.

Her watchful face.

It all started by his offering to wash Lily's hair for her. He'd suggested softly, *You'll feel so much better, love, when your hair is clean, won't you? Let me give you a hand with it.*

But how had this unleashed the tempest? It was not clear. Perhaps it had not been clear at the time. Something compulsive seemed to have got loose in the house and it fought itself in ways no one could reasonably have foreseen.

Shoulders slumped, Lily had slouched into the bathroom like a kid in a sulk. Mark had followed her in and closed the door. He hadn't locked it. One wall was entirely faced with mirrors and there seemed to be two Lilies in the room. He'd suggested she remove her long-sleeved t-shirt so as not to wet it. He'd wash it for her – and her pyjama bottoms, just slip it all off.

Was that wrong? Surely not. It had all been meant innocently and helpfully, and Mark was Lily's husband, for God's sake.

He remembered the vehement shaking of her head – or was that later, or another occasion altogether? It all bled together in memory like spillages of paint – because those months had been so chaotic and meaningless and tedious, as events sped on, in loops and spirals, with a logic that had never appeared then and couldn't be discerned later. Perhaps it had been another occasion when she'd shaken her head, childishly, and tried to slip past him to the door.

Here we go, Mark had thought, but he knew he'd reacted temperately and said something like, *Fine, just a thought.*

Besides, had he wanted to expose to his revolted eyes the grid of cut marks on her arms? Probably not.

After some cajoling – he did not bully her – Lily had submitted to his gentle but insistent request to bend over the bath.

Bend over.

I said, *bend over.*

And remembering that he said *Bend over* was not a good thought.

It went back and back, that phrase. Bend over. Over a chair. Once on the stairs. Over my knee. Pants down. Hollering. Screaming. Leather belt thrashing down on the boy's backside. The suppression of humiliation and rage.

Bend over.

He knew he hadn't intended anything perverse. He'd meant it in a jocular way – or, no, a neutral way, it was an ordinary phrase. In fact he'd carefully tested the water: too hot? *Just say the word. Too cold? Just right?*

The beginnings of arousal as he'd stood behind her.

Bend over.

He'd rinsed Lily's greasy hair (however did she let herself get like this?) and begun to shampoo, fingertips kneading her scalp. She'd held still and let him minister to her. Perhaps she was, against her will, enjoying the massage. It's always hard to resist a head-massage.

He'd bent to nuzzle the back of Lily's wet neck. Rinsing out the lather, he'd reached again for the shampoo.

And she'd gone. Just as she was, hair dripping. Pelted down the stairs. Into her music-room. That wonderful room which he'd later taken over as his study. Vaulting after her, Mark heard the key twist in the lock. Heard the bolt being thrown.

Hey! Hey, open up!

Nothing. He was fired up, he was going in there, she was not keeping him out.

He'd rattled the doorknob, which came off in his hand. He remembered standing staring at the thing. And then a tumult in his head, somehow to do with the fact that the doorknob had come off and everything in the house broke at the slightest opportunity and then you had to call a man to fix it and the man didn't come when he said he would and you wasted time and … standing there holding a fucking doorknob, while the hall chandelier flickered, Mark lost it. He did clearly remember how he felt himself lose it. The winy sensation. Blood flooded his head. Oh, the relief as rage surged from red-hot depths. He heard himself yell but what he was bawling, he had no idea. Perhaps there were no words, just a primitive roar of outrage – or maybe it took the form of protesting that his wife's behaviour was the living end, why the *hell* couldn't Lily just be civilised? Something like that.

She has never really loved me, Mark had thought. This was a distinct and incontrovertible memory. The atrocious pain had slammed in, releasing a shock wave. A live wire had scorched lips, bollocks, soles of feet. His fist had battered the wood of the door, with its grain and whorls. And all this while he hadn't lost his erection, far from it. He'd taken several steps back and hurled the doorknob at the door. Overarm, like a cricketer. The crash had satisfied and that was all.

Silence.

Ah: but there was another entrance to the music-room! Although it had no windows, this was the least impregnable room in the house. You didn't remember that, did you, Lily? Ha! Not as bright as you think you are, not by a long chalk!

In the kitchen Mark, breathing hard, had paused to drink half a glass of milk and fetch a screwdriver from the tool box. The music-room connected to the kitchen by a hatch he'd painted shut. Mark had worked to free it, which took a while, but at last he slid it open. All this he recalled clearly.

She'd gaped as she was confronted by his grinning face framed in the hatch. Yes, Mark thought: that's caught your attention, Miss Himmelfarb. Your sanctuary has become your cage.

Hitching himself up, Mark had inserted his shoulders and squirmed his hips through diagonally, panting with effort. Just made it – and he was – in. No membrane intervened between the two of them.

The look on Lily's face as he straightened up and caught his breath! He recalled that quite clearly too.

She'd gaped wide open, as if about to sing, he could see directly into Lily's skull, he could see the fillings of her teeth, he had her now – although for a moment, unsure what to say or do, Mark had felt a bit of a fool. He felt the same now; his face burned on the pillow. It had run through his mind to grin and prance and make a prank of it. Cut a caper. Silly me! Just messing about, didn't mean to frighten you! He could have defused and aborted the farce, for farce it had been and even at the time he'd been aware of that. The afflatus had been slowly subsiding when Lily made a cardinal mistake. She reached for the phone.

She was prepared to call an outsider in. And that was it.

I saw you. Bend over.

Round and round the rugged rock – desk, rather – the rude and ragged rascal ran. Round and round the ... round and round ...

Afterwards his red rage was not spent, he had not even managed anything. He'd just chased her round the desk. Maybe her screaming had triggered it. A ridiculous non-event. What had set off this pathetic ejaculation he had no idea. His mind blanked.

And was it on the same day or another that Mark found himself loping out into the garden with Lily's viola, which he lobbed over the wall into the street, where it lay in the path of headlights on the rain-swept, darkly shining road, and Lily rushed forth in panic to retrieve it?

He had not expected a car to be coming along the lane at that time of night. How could one have predicted it? The lane was often free of traffic for hours at a time.

She had certainly asked for it. But he pitied the viola. It was an AE Smith model, unique amongst modern instruments, bearing the luthier's chisel marks and a glowing varnish. Mark had blocked the door as she'd returned. Lily had just stood there, saying nothing, cold, calm, not crying. Abashed, he'd stood aside, speechlessly as she carried the smashed beauty in. He'd remembered his Julius Caesar's *Gallic Wars*: *In tres partes Gallia divisa est*. Gaul is divided into three parts. He may even have uttered these words.

Later, Lily had gone back out into the lane and gathered what she could of the smaller fragments, flattened by vehicle tyres. She'd collected every visible splinter, swaddled them in a blue cloth and hugged the bundle to her breast.

Later still, Mark had been contrite as he'd never been before. He'd felt so ill, even though Lily had driven him to it. He seemed to remember taking too many Xanax and sleeping for a long time.

Weeks later, he'd asked, 'Where is the instrument, my poor darling?'

Lily had said she'd not attempted to have the instrument restored; she'd chucked the remains in a skip, was how she put it, casually, as if it didn't matter. After her death, Mark had looked for its shattered body amongst her effects, in case she had lied, but could not locate it. He'd wept for all that perfection, violated.

Was it on another occasion altogether that Mark's heel had stamped on Lily's phone and ground it to smithereens?

All he knew was that there'd been a series of explosions in the past. But the past was not over, never would be over, for the explosions kept on detonating, their wrath was never spent, it was still discharging lethal air particles travelling faster than the speed of sound, the blast wave driving out shards that were only just reaching him. The physics of terror.

Asking what had happened when was pointless, there was no chronology, one knew that but one kept asking. For instance, when was it that he slammed the jangling door and she trapped her hand in it?

He'd released and opened the door; sucked her and her shrieks indoors, into their shared vacuum. Mark could not now recall why any of this had started, given that his sole desire from the outset had been to tend his wife lovingly. To further her career. To cherish her gift. To give her tenderness such as she'd imagined (after one or two disastrous affairs) no man could offer or sustain. Ice. Swelling. One finger bent and swollen and purple. A musician's hand. Trapped in the door. Terrible accident. Straight to A&E. Let me stay with my wife, please, she's in severe pain. I will speak for her, she's in shock, aren't you, darling? Give her something for the pain. Well, you're the medics, aren't you? You're paid to know! Are you all right, cariad? For goodness sake, hurry up! Musician. Her bowing hand. Bless her, she caught it in the door. X-ray. Broken? Oh no. They'll tape that finger to the next finger. Mute, she was, holding her hand up as if to answer a question in class. Does it throb, darling? When will my wife be able to play again? Not for a couple of months?

I'm so sorry, he'd sobbed at home, over and over. Every time, which was all the same time. *Oh Lily, dearest, precious lamb, how can you forgive me?*

When he'd offered to take the viola to the restorer, she replied in an oddly flat voice, *I hate you, Mark.*

I hate me too.

On his knees, he'd fawned and crawled. What did she want him to do to make up for it, he'd begged her? Her injured hand seemed to point to something meretricious floating in the air.

Anything, anything. Seriously, I will do anything.

191

Pack your stuff, you lunatic, and go. This is my house, not yours.

Lily didn't explicitly say this more than the once. But Mark had read the message in her eyes whenever things came to the boil. Of course, packing one's bags and moving out was what one couldn't under any circumstances do. The couple had thrown in their lot with one another, they had made eternal vows, and he had given up the maisonette to share Tŷ Hafan with his wife. Marriage was a serious venture. Your property and possessions were now one single commonwealth. Lily's earnings had been sporadic; frankly, she'd always counted as a dependant. Whatever she earned, she'd kept. He'd paid all the bills, without complaint. And latterly of course she'd brought in nothing whatever and he'd supported her. Besides, Mark had restored, painted, decorated, carpeted, furnished, gardened, cleaned, thrown himself and considerable resources into the building. At the gallery, he had initiated a research project into Art Deco art and architecture and did everything in an authentic way. Lily might have been born at Tŷ Hafan but, morally and also (he'd always assumed) legally, it was no longer exclusively her house. Even the law was clear about that, he'd believed, although the law favoured wives over husbands.

In the aftermath of their spats, Mark would sometimes retreat to his study (at that period the second-best room in the house) and write letters admitting responsibility, assuring Lily of his remorseful love, promising to do everything to set their house in order. He'd made notes and charts in his red book for organising future conversations. In the letters, Mark would take the fault squarely upon his own shoulders and promise reformation. He'd see a psychotherapist if this was what she wished, anything. *Only do not leave me in this pit.*

He'd tried to explain how his heart had been broken early on. She knew that anyway: he'd told her often enough.

See how you like it in there for the night, you little swine.

That came back.

Thick darkness and the chemical stink of coke and coal. Crawling out when *she* opened the lid, a child chilled to the bone, face black as a miner's, knees bleeding black where you'd stumbled when she pitched you in.

Seven years old is old enough to know better. Isn't it – isn't it?

Saying *Sorry, sorry, Gran – yes, I was bad, but I won't be bad any more.* Not always comprehending what he'd done that was bad – but willing to own up and make any promises.

You pigeon-chested little git.

Bright light lanced the git's screwed-up eyes as he was manhandled into the bathroom. *You are lucky to have a bathroom,* she would say. *Now clean yourself up.* The git scrubbed at his hands with a pumice Granddad had brought back from Pompeii after the war. The git liked the pumice. He liked the nail brush. He had to be clean. He wanted to be clean.

Once the echo had been aroused, Mark had to kill it. Writing drew the poison, converting it into inky patterns on the page. Letters to Lily would effloresce into eloquent and expressive testaments, written in fountain pen. The pen nib analysed the depths of his own turpitude ... his malfeasance ... his transgression. A warm stream of verbal solace bubbled out, assuaging self-abhorrence. In the act of confession, language drew the sting of truth. He'd explain that, although he knew he'd never deserved someone as exquisite and special and talented as Lily, he also knew he loved and honoured her – and that from then on, she would know it too, for he would be a different person, if she would just give him a chance. On and on his pen would glide, vowing amendment. Lily was the centre of Mark's world and, without Lily, Mark would perish.

He'd go on to imagine and describe the manner of his own death-to-be. Healing tears brimmed and fell on the absorbent page, blurring the ink and rippling the paper. The writing would focus and compose Mark. He'd sign and read through. Rarely if ever had those messages reached Lily. In point of fact, he couldn't recall one occasion. It wasn't necessary, for they'd done their anodyne work, setting him straight. Besides, a canny self of Mark's stood apart and recognised that written confession, however eloquent, was imprudent. He'd set light to the epistles and – for weeks or months at a time – be purged.

Had it been on the morning following the hair-washing episode, or the viola, or the trapped fingers, or some other row, that – to help Lily comprehend the depths of his sorrow and the origins of his frailties – Mark had explained, choking, that he was the boy who had been shut in the coalhole?

'Yeah, I know,' she said, with a listless indifference that sealed her fate. 'You told me before.'

13

The girl hesitating at Freya's neighbour's gate said, 'Excuse me, this is Dr Heyward's house, isn't it?'

'Yes, although I'm fairly sure he's not up yet,' said Freya.

'Really? Not up yet?' The girl seemed fazed, as if all the clocks in the world had stopped. They both assessed the closed curtains of Mark's house. 'Are you sure?'

'Doesn't look like it. Can I help?'

'So – is he ill?'

'No, I don't think so. Why?'

The girl, auburn haired, freckled, a student presumably, grinned with one side of her mouth. It was just that she'd never known Mark oversleep. Never once in all the time she'd known him. She had an arresting face, open and gentle, with pale lashes and eyebrows, and premature frown-lines in her forehead that you wanted to smooth away.

Probably not a student then, Freya thought, given her familiarity with Mark's sleeping habits?

'Well, I can just put this through the door,' the young woman said. 'Then I won't have to ... It's a key. To his other house.'

'His *other* house?'

'His Gower house. I've vacated.'

'You've – vacated? You were his tenant?'

It was a long story, the girl said, and heaved a sigh. Then she laughed and shook her head.

'So – I'm Danielle,' she said and waited to see if the name shed any light. Anyway, she was moving in with her boyfriend, they had a top-floor flat in Cardiff. A bit cramped but they were lucky to get a halfway decent place at short notice; you have to start somewhere and she was looking forward to it. She struggled to shove the bulky

195

package with the key and whatever else it contained through Mark's postbox.

'I can give that to Mark when I see him, if that helps?' Freya offered. 'I'll be back by lunch time and I'm sure he'll be up and about by then. Or else – I've got his key – I can just put it inside if I miss him.'

Danielle handed over the package and watched Freya lock it inside her own front door. Her eyes, pale green, curious, lingered on Freya. As they were about to part, the visitor said, 'Excuse me – hope this isn't a cheek – but you're not the ... lady with three children Mark is ... looking after?'

'Mark? Looking after three children?' Had they got the same Mark? Was another Dr Heyward living in another street of the same name, with a sort of crèche, owner of twin houses? 'Well, he looks after my dog from time to time but I don't know about any children.'

'Oh sorry. Of course you're not. Although she has a yellow Labrador too, apparently. Your lovely dog is a Labrador, isn't he? That's why I ...'

'Yes, Storm's a Lab. But – whereabouts is the other house, if you don't mind my asking?'

Twin Marks, two houses and a pair of identical Labradors?

They fell into step. Storm didn't care which way they walked; he was happy to hang around at the bus stop, a trap for chip wrappings and a site of panoramic urine smells. As he snuffled around, Freya extracted information from Mark's tenant, involving astounding feats of undercover altruism on his part. It fitted, in a rather weird kind of way, with the Mark she knew. Or didn't know. She gathered that Mark had, after his wife's death, befriended this young woman, a nursery nurse, and housed her, absenting himself from the property.

To abandon your home to a needy person, Freya thought, would be an extravagantly benevolent gesture. And maybe she had muddled what Mark had told her. There was something hesitant, agitated, about the young woman's manner. On the other hand,

Freya had already felt the intensity of her neighbour's power of sympathy. That ability to identify with others' needs, added to the delirium of grief, might have led Mark to offer this girl a roof over her head, securing Danielle a home whilst enabling himself to recover in a space that wasn't a constant reminder of his wife.

'I'm going to make a new start. I just want to leave ... all that ... behind.'

What was *all that?* The girl chattered away about the future. Her new home. She couldn't wait! From the sublime to the ... minimalist. Living in a single room had its advantages, she said. Definitely.

'Provided you get on with the person,' Freya hazarded, laughing. 'Extremely well?'

'Oh yes. Leo's as gentle as a lamb. He's really, really gentle.'

Odd thing to say, Freya thought – almost as if she were reassuring herself. She conjured up a muscle-bound bully.

'That's good,' she managed. 'Gentle is very good.'

'No, it's not.'

'Pardon?'

'Gentle,' said the girl, 'is everything.'

'Right. So – does your boyfriend work with children too?'

'Oh no, he's an electrical engineer. Kind of solid, you know, dependable. Not too much imagination.'

'You don't approve of imagination?'

'Sometimes, not.'

'Our first home,' Freya told her, 'my husband's and mine, was pretty imaginative. It was a tree!'

'Wow! That is so cool!'

The stranger was ignorant of Freya's loss. She had never heard of Keir or of the road protests and she knew nothing of death. She was unconscious of the vast, dark burden on Freya's back that bent her double with the effort to bear it. Such innocence freed you somehow. She explained about the system of wires that linked the treehouses. The security men with the cherry pickers, the bulldozers and the saws, the hundreds of arrests.

She'd seen this look of wonderment on other faces: it envied you for having lived so fully and freely.

'So, did you get on each other's nerves in the treehouse?'

Freya grinned. 'Never. We were all in love.'

The girl nodded. She was in love too. She thought she knew what Freya was talking about but, in point of fact, she couldn't.

'We were all in love with one another,' said Freya. 'All of us with all of us. And with the trees. And with our cause. We were fighting for our lives and the trees' lives.'

'And did you succeed?'

'No. They destroyed ten-thousand trees.'

'So – when you left?'

'Everything is harder at ground level, isn't it? Anyway, all that was a long time ago.'

Freya had turned the conversation, trying for an eye-line on the business of Mark's pregnant partner, the three teenagers and the dog. What had all that been about? Apparently the other house had originally belonged to Mark's wife.

Poor Lily, the girl said. She'd never met her – but had found traces of Lily everywhere. She'd found a smashed musical instrument in the loft. Not a violin, though that's what Danielle had assumed at first: a viola. She had the idea that it had once been a beautiful instrument – and perhaps valuable. All the parts – the split front and back, the pegs and so on – were wrapped up like a baby in a blue muslin cloth. The bow was snapped in two. She'd found ... well, all sorts of stuff. It had spooked her out a bit. She'd put it somewhere safe. And there was something ... she wanted to forget ... and bygones should be bygones ... though perhaps she ought to say ... but the bus came, and Danielle had got on before she'd been able to convey the nature of the something.

Presumably it was out of grief for his wife, Freya thought, as she and Storm walked away from the bus stop, that Mark abandoned his home. Freya understood how you might go mad with loss, enough to flee your home. There'd been moments when she'd felt like accepting Rae's invitation to stay with them, and Dave had offered too. She'd thought of selling up, getting on a train or plane, disappearing. But she knew you shouldn't. Not too soon anyway – because at present Freya wasn't Freya and there were no bearings.

Their home had settled down now, somewhat – but it's more like a tent than a building, Freya thought, flapping and billowing in any wind. The memory of how the wall had pulsed out at her, flailing the tentacles of trees in her face, slapping them over her mouth ... it frightened Freya even to think of it, although it had been a hallucination and nothing to do with the real world, and – she told herself – I must keep calm, calm, look outwards, not in or back.

Passing the wreck of what used to be the premises of the wrought-iron maker, she paused. The workshop had lain derelict for some time. Foxgloves and buddleia had gained a footing in the ruins – feathery ferns too, and brambles. She'd even reached in through the wire last year and plucked a handful of blackberries. The buddleia had yielded a tempest of scent. Butterflies had been drawn to it, commas and red admirals flocking together like blossoms on the blossoms. This summer, demolition and reconstruction were underway: the walls were down, the foundations exposed. The building's time had come and you started to forget the architecture of the place, and its use – for instance, hadn't there been a door on the first floor, where the wrought iron goods would be lowered onto carts? She looked up into the blue air, to the approximate position where the door had existed that nobody could ever enter.

What would Mark do with the home that remained full of Lily? She must have been remarkable. Freya had never bothered to listen or to look Lily up on the internet. In fact, so self-engrossed had she been, that she'd never really asked questions about his wife. What was her surname? Heyward, or did Lily keep her own name? Was it a comfort or a torment, or both, when Mark heard one of her recordings? The guy, shattered by grief, had not recovered – look at how he'd broken down last night, shocking them both under the onslaught of that nightmare. Mark hadn't properly woken up when

Terry and Pam arrived in their dressing gowns to turf him out. What Pam had said was surely unfair. And he didn't mean to lash out at me, of course he didn't. I could have reassured him, Freya thought, I could have helped him wake up gently, couldn't I, once I'd recovered from the shock? After all, he's done as much as he can for me.

She remembered emerging into the silvery garden after Mark's hysterical fit, her cheek stinging: the mild quiet of the night and a full moon eclipsing the stars in half the hemisphere. It had been the first calm time she could recall since Keir went.

What was it she'd glimpsed out there? Something restorative. A kind of clemency. It had been as if Freya had passed the pain sideways to Mark Heywood. You carry it now. Your turn to go mad. She'd stepped out of the maelstrom into a region of greater sanity, such as she'd lived in with Keir.

Thank heaven Freya had found Keir and taken him home. After their initial concern over the age gap, and Keir's long hair, and then the baby, Mum and Dad had grown to love Keir as their own. People did. Keir was older and – as it turned out – wiser. He could be quiet; he listened. The two of them had looked out towards friends and the causes dear to their hearts, none of which would go away.

*

Hallo, Lily.

You were close by all the time, just around the corner, a small, thin person with long straight hair, sleek, tucked behind your ears. Nine videos. Solos and quartets from 2006 and 2007. Several posted after your death in 2011.

Lily Himmelfarb had not been flamboyant; there was virtuosity without showmanship. At least, that seemed true in all the films but one. Lily disappeared into herself and closed the door. Even in the Tchaikovsky solo, 'Passion Confession', there was a simplicity and inwardness in the way Lily played. That was how it seemed to Freya. Lily bragged no stage presence. She left it to the viola to speak ...

... except in the modern piece where she raised the roof.

Lily in green silk. How could you play that fast and furiously? Bow strings broke and floated adrift, catching the light. Who cared? Lily went for it. There was clapping, stamping, shouting. Lily flung her arms wide and laughed, viola in one hand, bow in the other, and took her bow, and the applause kept on coming.

*

When he woke, Mark was paralysed. Sleep had been violent. No sooner had his head sunk into the pillow than a fury of unconsciousness ploughed him into depths beneath depths.

It was morning, was it? Mark could not move. Daylight tantalised the curtain edge. Women's voices floated up. Someone tittered. The voices receded.

He slept again. A dog barked.

Through the wall, Lily was playing her fractured viola. On and on, but muffled. The strings were tormented by the bow and all they could deliver was pain.

Every time the music ended, and he began to sink back into sleep, the instrument took up its burden again.

Who, if I cried, would hear me among the angels' hierarchies? And, if one of them pressed me against his heart, I would be consumed.

Who spoke those words? Was it Rilke? Was Rainer Maria Rilke also, then, unforgiven?

No, it was the Oramorph speaking, and whatever else Mark had taken. The music had stopped. Probably he'd dreamed it.

He raised his head to peer at the clock face; could make little sense of what it was trying to tell him. Had the clocks gone forwards? Or backwards? Mark's skull subsided into the dip in the pillow and he soothed himself with the thought that he could rest now – drowse comfortably, doze for as long as he liked, as lazier people did at weekends. Why not? It was lawful. It was ordinary. There was no depravity in this at all, whoever claimed otherwise.

However many hours later, the sun had set. He yawned and stretched; switched on the lamp. There was a feebleness, a languor, but no paralysis. That must have been a dream or he'd been lying awkwardly on his arm and it was numb. Had Mark slept away the entire day? Were there things he ought to have done before it was too late? Well, for once they would have to be left undone. He wobbled his way downstairs through the gloaming on the stairs. Peered between the curtains: twilight and a streetlamp on, casting a coppery aura round the elliptical shape of the hornbeam. No need to open the curtains: leave them be. For one day, let the eyelids of the house be sealed. Answer to nobody. Admit nobody.

Mark made tea, picked up a note from the doormat and came back upstairs.

Back in bed, he read Freya's message. She hoped he wasn't unwell; hadn't liked to disturb him but if he needed anything, just to let her know. She'd accepted an invitation to tea with a friend, followed by a concert, so her phone would be off for a couple of hours in the evening. She was staying overnight but could look in on their way home if he needed her, about 11? By the way, someone had brought round a package for him which wouldn't fit in his letter box. It was in Freya's hallway if he'd like to pick it up – otherwise she'd deliver tomorrow. Her name. No kiss.

To a concert? That was new. Had she gone alone? Was she even musical, in the sense of *musical?* He'd heard more Bob Dylan renderings through the wall than *music.* If Mark had known Freya would care to go to a concert, he'd have taken her himself, he thought. Not that he ever went to concerts nowadays but it was something he was always intending to do. Staying over with *a friend?* So – not the brothers-in-law, who would count as family... Who then? One of the flower women, presumably. Well, whoever – the bird had flown. Nothing to be done about that.

The important thing was that next-door was guaranteed to be empty all evening. Storm would be snoozing in his basket so it was wholly appropriate that Mark should drop in and ensure he was fed, watered, accompanied and taken out to relieve himself. There was no sound, so Storm was probably asleep. No immediate hurry. Mark rested his head back on the pillows and closed his eyes, laying his hands flat on the duvet, palms downward. Enjoying the composure of his mind, Mark breathed deeply and relaxed in the haze of the Oramorph aftermath. All shall be well and all manner of thing shall be well. The words of Mother Julian of Norwich floated in his mind.

Mother Julian had lived in a wall. An anchoress's needs would be pared down to the barest minimum sufficient to support life. The cell would stink but the nun wouldn't be self-conscious about the human stain. Everyone stank in those days and, in any case, one's own smell is always more acceptable than another's. Mark tried to imagine the anchoress as she would appear to pilgrims. A pop-up counsellor in a window of her wall, Julian had been available to mother all comers. Some would have entered the cell for therapy but most would queue to consult her through the grille.

There'd been times along the years – and this was one – when Mark had allowed himself to muse on the possibility of tracing his own mother. This should not be too difficult. The occasional blissful dream had prompted him to set out in search of her. The opposite of a wet dream. A Madonna-dream.

But maybe not. Why upset yourself by chasing black holes? On the handful of occasions when he'd actually set out to track her down, Mark had experienced a mental backlash so shattering that he'd run yelping for cover. The real thing to fear would be if the black hole turned round and wanted to know you – pursued you through Genes Reunited and Somerset House – and manifested on your doorstep.

Good afternoon, darling, I'm your black hole.

He sniggered. For some reason, terrible things seemed dryly amusing this morning. Or rather, this evening. For he had skipped a day. In his mind's eye, Mark's mother resembled a bag lady, with a version of Gran's work-worn, haggard face. She smelt of fag smoke and had lived on the dole. He'd have half a dozen half-siblings in an array of colours. What could they have to say to one another? In what possible tongue might he and this black Madonna converse? What words could she come up with, even supposing her to be a form of intelligent life, to draw the sting of her desertion? *I was so young*, she'd whine; *your dad didn't want to know, he was a bad egg; I had no income; I had to let you go, dear; it was for your sake; I felt rotten about it; I've always loved you* (snivelling, catching crocodile tears in a tissue, peeping to see if she'd persuaded you that she was a true mother who'd been forced to abandon you and wondering if you could lend her a few quid). This living cliché would come up with the sob story he'd heard on TV series in which professional nosy-parkers track down other people's long-lost relatives. No thanks.

In Gran's house, his mother's name had been taboo. The tacit agreement was that Gran had had no daughter; Mark no mother. There was no photo on the sideboard – or anywhere else, as he had established when his grandmother died and Mark had sorted her few possessions.

He knew what the name was though. Sharon.

In the generation after hers, this name had become fashionable and common. Sharons were two a penny, along with Traceys. But when Mark's mother had been christened, the name had been understood as biblical. He had no recollection of his grandfather, the miner, but he knew he'd been a Methodist, a bible Christian, and the probable source of this name. Occasionally, if you thought that name – *Sharon* – almost hiding the thought from yourself – *Sharon* – there came a sense of something endlessly tender. A presence, just out of view, like a scent. Getting out of bed and stretching, Mark opened the curtains and looked down the darkening garden. The pale, cup-like flowers of *Hibiscus Syriacus* he'd planted along the fence, in her memory, still glowed faintly. *I am the rose of Sharon and the lily of the valleys.*

All shall be well and all manner of thing shall be well. And if you had not forsaken me, all would have been – if not well – better than as things stand now.

Mark turned away and began to dress, keeping his breathing steady. To continue with this train of thought was to tempt the darkness to open its box of horrors. Happily, the events of the previous night had somehow been voided from Mark's mind, as when you have a gastric bug and it all comes up and that's the end of it. You feel clean again, with a healthy appetite. Until the next time. A respite.

Opening Freya's door, he scooped up the bundle from her doormat and called to Storm. No response.

Freya could hardly have taken a dog to a concert, so presumably Storm was spending the night at the friend's. In the kitchen, Freya had left a tin of biscuits open on a counter-top. Home-made, he thought: had she baked them herself? Surely not. This could not be imagined. Possibly the offerings of Mrs Pamela Crouch. They did look good and he felt hungry. Freya wouldn't mind if he took a few. Wrapping a couple in kitchen paper and pocketing them for later, Mark brought a couple more into the living-room to munch. They were good – a hint of ginger and a lot of chocolate. Mark sat down in the easy chair Freya preferred and switched on the electric fire, before opening the package.

Out tipped the keys to Tŷ Hafan. After checking that they were all there, he tossed them up and snatched them from the air. A heady, jingling sensation. After one more toss, he stowed them in his pocket, patting it. Danielle was gone. She was gone for good and all!

The pleasure made Mark aware of how ravenous he was, for of course he hadn't eaten for twenty-four hours. There was more stuff to look through in Danny's jiffy bag but it would wait. What did they have in the fridge? He went to check. Plenty of Cheddar, odds and ends of Stilton and Brie, hummus that was still in date, baby tomatoes, Pamela's famous chutney with a handwritten label. In the cupboard, Mark found seed bread: excellent, and not stale. Perched on the kitchen stool, he munched happily, like a husband in a long marriage who happens to arrive home early and enjoys the quiet time, knowing his wife will arrive home in due course. His happiness – filling his belly, thinking of nothing much – felt blessedly ordinary and when he'd finished, he looked round for something sweet. An apple or a tangerine would do.

At last Mark's luck was turning. He took the Satsuma with him into the living-room and opened up the rest of the package. Ha! Danny had vacated Tŷ Hafan, leaving no forwarding address. Thank you, God!

An illiterate letter from her went into several pages. Life's too short, Mark thought. The first few lines, however, persuaded him to read carefully.

Let that be an end to the relationship, Danny wrote, her feint at a grown-up style belied by her round script and frequent underlinings. She deeply regretted her part in the fiasco. Fiasco! Good word, Danny! Since Mark's last visit, she had seen that the blame was not all one-sided. Danny had never meant to exploit Mark by squatting in his property – and, if she had, and she could see it looked like that, she apologised unreservedly but she had been upset, very very upset which was understandable considering – anyone would of been (would of!) – and she would never want to take advantage of anyone, it was against everything she believed – and at this point her syntax wobbled about and confused itself before skidding to a full stop.

On firm ground again, Danny stated: 'Here are your house keys. They are all there.'

Fine, but Mark's first action would be to change the locks. On she went, prattle prattle prattle … but the next part shocked him. His heart beat up into his throat.

'Please find Enclosures.'

Danny had enclosed prints of the photographs of her bruises, all of which she had now deleted from her mobile and computer. Obviously Mark would have to trust her on that, she pointed out.

Although he had definitely <u>meant</u> to hurt her and these injuries had <u>not</u> been inflicted <u>accidentally</u> – Danny was confident Mark had not intended to assault her <u>so badly</u>. She would give him that, and she knew he was sorry but on the other hand it was good he was getting <u>counselling</u> from this lady Val and hoped he would <u>carry on</u> because <u>we all need to be in control of what we are doing where other people are concerned</u> and Val sounded very <u>wise</u>.

Danny was a girl of inexhaustible platitudes.

Trust you? Mark queried. Yes, actually I am inclined to trust you, Danny, even though it would have been the easiest thing in the world for you to have retained copies of these images as insurance. Personally, I would have done so. Or you might have broadcast them on the internet to revenge yourself, a thought which brought one out in a sweat.

But, yes, I shall (within reason) trust you. For Danny would want to be free of the *fiasco* – but, even more, she'd need to square her own behaviour with her Christian principles. The guilt she'd carried from her cradle was a dark treacle liable to spread revoltingly all over her conscience. He'd seen it in action. Clearly, the blackmailing way she'd retaliated against what she perceived as his misdemeanours (doubtless egged on by some moronic pal) had been unacceptable by her own standards.

Danny began to conclude her long, paragraph-free screed by stating that she had <u>discontinued</u> the phone number he knew – so would he please <u>delete</u> it. She had deleted his number. *I will sign off now.*

But then away she went again, with a PS and a PPS. <u>Let this be a clean break</u>, she wrote, and we can both 'gleen' (spelt wrong) wisdom for the future from our past mistakes. I wish you well, she burbled, with your new family, and I hope they will be happy at Tŷ Hafan and that all will go well with the <u>Birth</u>. (The birth? Oh yes, Mark remembered, my 'partner's pregnancy'). It is a perfect family home, Danny wittered. She had cleaned and tidied to the best of her ability and taken nothing that was not strictly her own.

In other words, there'd be a litter of Danny's leavings throughout the house, which would require disinfection: the droppings of an unruly mouse. Well, this was not news and Mark rather looked forward to cleansing the place and making it his own again. Again? Frankly, Tŷ Hafan had never yet belonged to him as sole owner, in any meaningful way. At last he would enter into possession of the property that had come down to his wife through her family. He'd be free to wander round his own garden without being overlooked. There'd be no party wall. No voyeurs or eavesdroppers.

Mark would just give a cursory glance to the photographs Danny had enclosed, before dispensing with them. Why Danny had printed and enclosed them he had no idea. To punish him one final time?

The blown-up images slammed into his eyes. They were windows into a past he had quit. His hands trembled.

Danny's skin was perfect. So fine and freckled and young. No flaw except what their disputes had left. Bruises on her throat showed finger marks. Was that a bite mark on her upper arm? No, it couldn't be. He crumpled the image. How in Christ's name could that have happened? Saliva collected in his mouth and he swallowed.

Were those really his tooth prints in the pearl-pale skin? He ran his tongue-tip around his teeth. Plaque encrusted them, despite regular flossing. You could not taste plaque. It built insidiously and ended in cavities. What had Danny said or done to drive Mark into a frenzy so total that he had been out of himself, he was someone else, a pit-bull off the leash, an automaton? He could not recall any such occasion. Which in itself was frightening.

But not as frightening, Mark told himself, as it would have been if he had remembered.

The spaced-out calm he'd been enjoying was dissipating. Holes gaped in the veil of oblivion. Don't let the holes expand, he thought: all *that* belongs to the past. Look here: Danny has put it behind her. Generously and graciously and sensibly. She knows it was as much her fault as mine. So I shall do the same. We have lived and learned!

He almost laughed aloud now, for Danny would so have approved of this truism. He could just see her, listening and nodding solemnly, her doll-like eyes wide.

Locating Freya's matches, he set fire to the pictures over the sink and washed away the ash. Then he bleached the sink. That part of Mark's life was finished. No token or witness remained to tell the half-true tale. And after all, anyone can make mistakes. We all do. No one is a saint. Let him who is without sin cast the first stone.

He could not now imagine what had possessed him to take in that callow kid: a palpable mismatch. They had always been unequals – and, to be honest, that must have been the initial charm of the relationship – although Mark did not remember feeling particularly charmed. He had talked a great deal and Danny had been a thirsty listener. She'd sat in his office, leaning forward, lips parted. She'd followed him round the gallery, asking questions. She'd lurked at the front entrance at the end of the working day, explaining that she'd just been passing. Mark had tried to oblige and had given of his best. Her calf-love had turned Mark into a milch cow, an udder of information. More, more! And he'd delivered. There'd been times when he'd been kept talking so long that he'd hardly known what he was saying and felt inclined to tip Danny out of the open window.

To be fair, her adoration had been a solace. Of course it had. Someone had needed Mark, looked up to him as a strong and protective presence, compassionated him and, when he wept, wept too. In other words, babied him. A gush of tenderness poured into his heart as he remembered the reassurance Danny had once offered. If he was upset during the night, she'd stay awake with him for as long as he needed, promising not to allow herself to sleep before him. She'd pinch the flesh of her wrist to keep herself awake. Of course, she could do without sleep, being young and strong. Somehow or other, Danny had also managed, in those early days, to be awake before him and he would come into a world safeguarded by her mild solicitude.

After what Mark had been through, the extremity of his loss, to be adored and nurtured by a gentle nobody had been balm.

Until it hadn't been.

Not so very long after she came to live with him at Tŷ Hafan, the ointment became an irritant. Danny's silly little eyes seemed to be forever watching Mark; her dogged attentiveness had palled. He'd wanted to switch her off. Fold her up and pack her away like a puppet until she was wanted again. He'd realised that Danny was practising on him – a scholar in his late thirties – the skills she had learned in her nursery-nurse training. A form of control, in point of fact. No man, however unhappy, wants to be treated as if his nappy needed changing.

Well, Mark thought, it was an innocent misdeed on Danny's part. He'd been remiss in failing to see what had been staring him in the face from the off: their incompatibility. Eventually Danny had uncoupled from him, affronted, petulant, bewildered, before revealing herself to be not only an empty vessel but also a female animal with rather sharp claws. There is a hypocrite deep down in any cat. Witness the Crouches' malevolent Pansy who sleeked round its owners' legs, despising the pair of them. In the case of Danielle, the milk of human kindness had thinned and soured more or less overnight, or so it seemed. But let Danny go, Mark told himself. Forgive her as she has forgiven you. She is young, she'll recover.

Why was he sitting here in Freya's house anyway, giving thought to someone who, sad to say, had never been truly important in his life?

Mark looked round the quiet sitting-room – already a home from home. He tentatively thought of it as *ours*. His pockets were stocked with his wife-to-be's biscuits! He was cosily occupying her chair! Keir Fox's mark on the living-room had been in large part obliterated with the painting-over of the fresco. Granted, the mess was still there. But, sealed in the wall, it had vanished from sight – justly so, for it had contributed to Freya's fit. Mark had created a safe space for his beloved, where she could temporarily rest and begin to recover. And recovering Freya evidently was. She'd gone out now – and he ought to feel – and therefore did feel – that this was a positive sign of returning health.

Well, if Mark was honest, he didn't feel this, he felt the opposite, but it was something he could say to himself in the hope of conjuring an appropriate generosity of spirit. There was no denying that Freya's gadding off gave him a twinge. She was establishing a modicum of confidence, a centre of gravity.

Nevertheless, Mark thought, Freya is an epileptic. That episode has radically insecured her. She needs me. I am indispensable. And I'm the only person who witnessed and is cognisant of her affliction (which she considers to be a shameful secret). I'll be there to break her fall and hide her away from prying eyes.

Who had she gone off with though? Where was she spending the night?

And then again, it was a mite disconcerting that Freya had managed to bump into Danny and taken in the package meant for him. What had they said to one another, if anything?

He fished around for ways to angle the story of Tŷ Hafan. Danny was a fantasist, would be his theme. Lovely girl, but she imagines things. A serial fantasist. She was my lodger at Lily's house. That was how to put it. And of course Danielle was head over heels in love with me, he'd go on. What an idiot I was, not to see it coming. Could have kicked myself. You have to understand, Freya, I had not long lost my wife. I was utterly at sea – and I may have made some questionable judgments. I felt for Danielle, though obviously there was no question of my returning her feeling. Different generation. A children's nanny, with a piquant fondness for art. I tried to give a hand when she was in a fix. From what I could gather, poor Danielle had had a difficult childhood – to put it mildly – and several times had attempted suicide. And in the time I knew her, she'd self-harmed. I also think there was a boyfriend who was, how should I put it, not the most predictable?

That was the way to slant the story, if it came to it – and especially if any of the photos still turned out to be extant. And indeed, it was – or might be considered – a version of reality.

Had Danny told Freya what was in the package, aside from keys? The supposed evidence of his misconduct? Mark's face burned at the thought that she might have blabbed about the pictures and what they recorded. Purported to record. But surely not. In her note, Freya had said, quite casually, '*someone* called'. No name. No sense that this was anything more than a practical transaction (which, after all, it was). Freya's note to himself was affectionate and concerned. Mark concluded that Danny had accused him of nothing. After all, though garrulous, she was a girl of her word. If Danny said she'd put the whole thing behind her, she would honour that undertaking.

Still, it left your teeth on edge. Had he got rid of every single trace of the pictures? Just go into the kitchen and double-check.

And, of course, Mark had done the job meticulously. He sluiced the sink once more. It was a whole lot cleaner than when he'd arrived. Freya wouldn't notice that.

But what if, in his shock, Mark had accidentally let fall one of the pictures beside the chair or in the waste paper basket – and Freya came upon it? What about the vile one of the bitten neck that he'd crumpled up in his shock? What the hell had he done with it? Tossed it aside or burnt it with the rest? Think, think.

Be methodical. Deep breaths. Mark searched every inch of the living-room. There you are: worrying about nothing.

So what to do now that one had the house to oneself? All its spaces were familiar and he doubted if there were anything new in Freya's world to discover. So perhaps dwell on some small area, for instance, the bookcase? There may be forgotten notes secreted between the pages of books. Truffling them out would involve a lot of work for probable meagre benefit. Or: Freya's laptop. A richer and more interesting prospect. Mark had long ago picked up and memorised her password but never felt safe to investigate. Now he had plenty of time to browse and a memory stick in his wallet.

212

And, yes, such conduct was honourable. All Mark did was done for her sake.

Her laptop didn't seem to be in the study, where it was usually kept. Upstairs, Mark glanced into the spare-room, then into Freya's bedroom, where a ruck of duvet on the bed and a silk nightie spilt on the floor suggested ... no, of course it suggested nothing of the sort. Absolutely not. Mark would have known if there'd been someone in the house with her.

Would he though? He sat down at her dressing table, forbidding his fingers from lining up her pots and removing the hairs from Freya's brush. Most of last night and throughout today, Mark had been completely out of it. He would have heard precisely zilch if the whole tribe of Fox brothers had been heaving dumb-bells and executing press-ups in here.

But don't panic or jump to conclusions. The mess simply showed that Freya had dressed and left in a hurry. Also – truth be told – like both the women Mark had known intimately, she was relatively indifferent to neatness and order. Women he felt some contempt for – What's-her-name next door the other side, for instance, the widow – were forever out bleaching their patios, so perhaps Freya's disorderliness was some kind of feminist reaction against patriarchy. Mark could sympathise, if so. But in Freya's case, it had more likely been the effect of living with Foxy the eco-warrior. If we're not careful, we become like our partners, he thought: so many relationships boil down to a *folie à deux*. Keir Fox had been a latter-day example of Pliocene man, handy at flint-knapping and cave-painting, unfamiliar with the uses of deodorant and shaver.

Already it was difficult to feel that Freya's husband had ever existed in this house. Or anywhere else. It was as if Keir Fox had been swept away with a ferocious broom. Mark remembered rushing the fellow's personal effects into black bags and heading for the Air Ambulance shop and the tip. He trusted he had not done so with importunate haste.

NB Mark had only acted in Freya's best interests. Better she suffer an acute pang than chronic misery. If you've dislocated your shoulder, you want someone to snap it back into place rather than to haver and let you drag it around uselessly for all time.

He paused at the door to the loft. Ah. Yes. Never been up there. Mark tried the handle and it turned, opening into a dark stairway, stairs with rickety bookshelves all the way to the top, where there was another door. This would be a perfect time to glance round. Light on.

14

They had known each other forever: since nursery and school and then again at the road protests, at university and on into the weave of adult life.

Together Freya and Rae bent over the cot. Haf's curly dark hair rayed out around her. The child's cheeks were flushed and she had the paw of her cuddly monkey in her mouth. Her rest cast a spell over the dim room. In the rain-forest that Keir had painted on the walls for Haf, thrilling creatures paused and waited, suspended in the midst of their roaming and climbing and flight. Startled sunflowers opened their eyes wide. Haf still needed her daytime nap, Rae whispered, and got grumpy and over-tired if she missed it: then she couldn't nod off at night.

Deep, deep under: a sweet oblivion.

Storm had loped up behind them but seemed to know not to make a sound. He too stood looking into the cot, nostrils distended, breathing in the child's sleep. Normally Haf was a good sleeper, Rae whispered. Good eater. Good shouter. Good jack-in-the-box. Good everything. She picked up the cuddly green snake Haf was fond of and returned it to the cot.

'Knitting up the ravelled sleeve of care,' Freya whispered.

They both smiled as they returned downstairs, remembering Miss Cooper teaching them Shakespeare. They'd all revered her. She'd never needed to lift her voice to keep order. No sooner did Daphne Cooper appear on the stilts of her high heels, her suit smart over her voluptuous figure, than a listening hush fell.

'Balm of hurt minds, great nature's second course,' said Rae. 'I remember almost the whole of *Lear* too, because of Daphne.'

'You were a terrible Macbeth. Abysmal. You played him as a lamb that had lost its mother and its mind.'

215

'I know. It was madness, the way I bleated and squeaked. Everyone just fell about. And do you remember how I begged Daphne to spare me the part and she refused. Took me aside and said it was in me to do it, violence and betrayal and ambition were in every one of us? Put yourself into it, Rachel, grasp that dagger, she said: each of us is a potential killer. Find the murderer in yourself – and *then* apply the revulsion. That really stuck in my memory. It helped me, actually.'

Everything is in every one of us, Freya thought: the deadly and the kind. That was a lesson that took some learning and perhaps she'd never wholly manage to accommodate it. She did remember Miss Cooper saying this to Rae. It had been a poignant – a learning – moment. Rae's profession had required her to toughen up but the softness survived. All Rae's movements were gentle. Freya had somehow forgotten how dearly she'd loved her. Always I could say anything to you – and you to me, always. And then we couldn't.

The old pulse of conspiratorial tenderness passed between them – its echo, rather. From nursery days, Freya and Rae had known each other's hands by touch: braille-reading hands that stole out to clasp one another in times of crisis. Their touch said: I am still here with you, I have never gone away, I never shall. But was that real, still? Was anything real, now that Keir was dead? How could you know? The living-room, scattered with toys, was quiet. As Rae went out into the kitchen, the space blurred in a film of tears that gathered on Freya's eyes and did not spill.

When Rae brought tea, Freya let hers stand. She would not have been able to pick up the mug without shaking.

'About Haf,' she managed.

Rae focused, very composed. She didn't blink. She waited.

'It's … her eyebrows!'

'Her *eyebrows*?'

'They're so like Keir's!'

'I hadn't thought. Are they? Yes, perhaps they are. And like her dad's. And, I hope, a bit like mine, Frey, in amongst the mix?'

Freya's angled question had been partly answered by indirection, partly deflected. Rae was trained as a lawyer, after all. Or perhaps she simply didn't register what Freya was implying. Freya took a deep breath, to launch her question again.

For some reason, she hesitated. The thrumming of her heart. Qualms in her gut. Most of all, this seething in her brain. And. No, please not. Lights like flares sent up from within into her eyes, danger, danger.

Swerve. Don't broach this now, while you are half mad with grief. Only half mad? Hardly half: double mad. Step back. Qualms, no. Calm, calm. Not seethe. Breathe. Yes, breathe, that's right, breathe, breathe it away. You can.

'What is it? Are you all right, Freya? Are you faint?'

'Yes, faint, I'll just put my head down, faint.'

If she told Rae about the epilepsy, if she shared it with her, wouldn't that ease the secret terror she was locked in? The wall of division would surely come down. If she said, *I've had an epileptic fit, Rae. Just the one but it has terrified me. I've not been able to tell people – well, only one person. It's warped everything. It's always spinning just off the edge of vision.* If it became a story Freya could tell about herself, mightn't that make it easier to live with? But the news would leak. They would say, *Poor Freya, all this time she'd been having fits and we never knew! What can we do for poor Freya?*

Was she about to have one now? Or was it simply the fear aping the symptoms? Breathe, breathe.

The quietude the previous night reminded Freya of itself; the pause in the garden with moonlight equally a version of shadow, a version of light.

No fences, no boundaries. Keir's darling heart diffused everywhere. This was what Freya had intuited.

We are stardust.

Keir loved you. What more do you want?

I want his child. I want our child so badly. Rae has a child who looks a bit like Keir.

Beyond the delusions sounded another voice, her next-door neighbour's at the crescent, as if speaking aloud in the room. She couldn't recall the occasion but he'd said something to the effect that children belong to us all. It wasn't, or shouldn't be, a question of preferring one's own DNA.

Keir would have said, *Yes, my love, yes, exactly, listen to what Mark is telling you.* Keir would have been grateful that someone could comfort Freya with words that sounded so very like his own. Only Keir had gone further, into realms most people would find laughable: all creatures are our family, right up and down the chain. He'd never liked it that she'd sneered at the fussy ways of their neighbour. Having lost a child himself, Mark had every right to moralise. He knew how longing had power to curdle you, twisting you out of true – unless you could, somehow or other, convert grief into loving energy and blessing. Mark had chosen the thorny second way.

'It's Larch, isn't it?' said Rae amazingly, on her knees, stroking Freya's hair back from her forehead, face against face.

Racking sobs. Blubbered eyes. Nose running snot. On and on. Rocking one another. You could not tell whose tears were whose.

*

For some reason, the base of the door wasn't flush with the landing floor. You had to step up as if clambering into a wall. Mark switched on the staircase light. Trapped in the narrow stairwell floated a chemical smell: a build-up of linseed, mingled – perhaps – with turps? Sickly sweet as linseed was, it attracted Mark and confirmed that Freya had kept Keir Fox's studio sealed.

She'd sequestered this room, not only from Mark but from herself. The loft door opened easily. He groped for the switch and turned on halogen spotlights, which presumably had been used to augment the daylight from the north-facing dormer.

Something large, blue, ugly and tentacular leapt forward from the easel. Presumably Fox's last-gasp effort.

Mark's glance swept the chaotic work space: bookcase, portfolios, oils, palettes, mess, dust, shadows. A couch lay like an animal carcase draped in a seedy looking throw. Canvases were stacked back to back around the walls. Strewn on the floor lay a debris of leavings – crisp packets, paper bags, a cup with a tide line of brown gunk. The guy's last drink perhaps. That rather got to him and he looked the other way.

Well, Keir Fox's time had come. And to do him justice, the guy had been true to his art. What more, Mark asked himself, can be asked of us? Seating himself in the artist's place, Mark lifted the palette in his left hand and the nearest brush in his right. He itched to have a go. Not that much could be done to temper Fox's last effort. It was beyond remedy.

Mark's knowledge of visual art was compendious – but the practice? It was never too late, surely? He'd always liked to sketch. In childhood, he'd been a *Wunderkind* who might have taken any path. Even his grandmother had wondered at his brilliance. Mark had had the potential not only to be a scholar but a novelist, poet, composer, visual artist. The seeds lay dormant, awaiting their moment.

Fox had left the brush crusted with a crud of dried paint, dark blue – a product of the mix on the palette. Ultramarine. Cobalt. Prussian. Violet. Chrome green. The brush had not been cleansed since its last feint at a daub, as vitality drained from the failing brain and hand. It was rock-hard. All the brushes were.

'So where did you keep the turps, my friend?' Mark heard himself enquire aloud.

Dirty bottles and jars littered the floorboards, amongst discarded crusts and other detritus. Fox would have been in the habit of reaching blind for whatever he wanted and dropping what he didn't.

Mark had attained – all but – his heart's desires. Tŷ Hafan's keys were locked in his safe; both Lily and Danielle had departed; a new love and a new life offered themselves. Dante's *vita nuova*. There was time to enrich his own creative life. Start now. Why not? The turps was clouded with foreign matter and, when he swirled the crusted brush in the liquid, the crud didn't want to budge. Wiping the brush on a rag, Mark sorted through tubes of oil paint and squeezed worms of blue and green onto the palette.

Perhaps there had existed in Fox's mind no concept at all, just the compulsion to go on painting: to coat the world with his identity, even as identity disintegrated. The picture is whatever you make it into, Mark told himself. It's for you, as a fellow artist, to judge. Or rather, not judge but, yes, co-create. Perhaps this canvas was a representation of Fox's own death, a creature spasming in its death-throes, angry and flailing. He squeezed out a variety of blues, testing them at the base of the picture. The bristles had set so hard that the brush was unusable for anything delicate.

Give up, Mark told himself. The disease is inoperable. The thing's an eyesore: a waste of time to try and correct it. He thought of the fresco Fox had inflicted on his wife downstairs – trees with waving tentacles, dragging your gaze every which-way, unsettling the viewer. That was the sort of flamboyant style that typified Fox. Mark put down the brush on the palette, and got up for another look round.

The Foxes had an extensive skylight. He straddled the stacked canvases and prised it open. What a view across the darkness of Whitethorn Wood, over the allotments, to the lamps around the bay, leading to the lighthouse: a bracelet of curving lights. Cool night air bathed Mark's face and rustled through the leaf canopy. The joists of the house creaked and he jumped.

Don't worry, he told himself, retracting his head: she's not coming back tonight.

A slam and a judder scared the breath out of him. Fastening the skylight, he swivelled round. A row of framed canvases had slipped, dislodging one at the end. Of course it was because Freya couldn't bear to confront the pictures that she'd avoided the attic, perhaps even erasing its existence from consciousness.

The pictures! For goodness' sake! Mark hadn't even bothered to glance at them. Kneeling, he began to pull the canvases from darkness, one by one, into the circle of light.

*

An hour later, he had glanced at – oh Christ – dozens of the pictures.

Nudes. Beautiful nudes, for, yes, it turned out that Keir Fox had the power of portraiture. He possessed an eye and a hand and a heart. A sandy haired woman, voluptuous, reclining. His sister-in-law, if Mark was not mistaken. Keir's brothers, all recognisable, each seen with love and light irony. An elderly woman's face, her quicksilver hair brought forward over one naked shoulder, eyes full of laughter.

But chiefly Freya, oh Freya, most graciously beautiful and opulent and painted with a passion Mark recognised for a searing moment as entirely beyond his reach and experience.

There was terror in her beauty; a puerile feebleness in himself. He would not look any longer, Mark told himself.

He could not look away.

Tearing his gaze from the images would make no difference. He had seen what he had seen, and the vision was in him, and would be in him forever. The afflatus had perished, Mark's illusion of his own potential genius. The erection he'd had – on and off – ever since coming upstairs had flopped.

There were more of the portraits, more and more, an apparently infinite sequence.

And then the sketches. Sliding open a cabinet drawer, he came across a portfolio. Charcoal, ink, pencil sketches slid out, miracles of understatement.

A few casual lines expressed her, Freya in motion, Freya in her moment. And Mark must have them. He could not leave them behind. The sketches were, in a strange way, already his own.

*

He startled at a commotion in the belly of the house.

The front door slamming?

But surely the sound must have come from the Crouches, returning from some pious late-night singsong? Or was it a car door? How had Mark managed to lose all sense of time and danger, up here in the studio, reflecting on mirrorings of Freya? He replaced a canvas against the stack, gently, gently. Getting to his feet, he stood listening. Nothing.

Best be on the safe side and turn off the light.

Remove your shoes. Tiptoe. Softly.

There was absolutely no one down there; he was imagining it – but if there is, she certainly won't come up here, he thought. She never has, why should she now?

With the light off, the studio was pitch black. Like a coal hole.

The black was solid, it wedged him in. But it's all right, Mark told himself, caressing one unseen hand with the other: that can never happen again. You are in nobody's power. In any case, people don't have coal holes nowadays. They don't have eye-watering smoke in the sitting-room, they don't have soot on curtains, they don't have ash in the grate: they just don't. He forced himself to dwell on the obsolescence of coalmen, miners and bunkers: there were laws nowadays against smoke pollution, there was green energy, and in any case *she* was dead, years ago, she could never punish a child again.

No good: he could still smell and taste coal dust – carbon and hydrogen, sulphur and nitrogen – in his throat. Filth clogged the boy's nostrils, but he must not cough. Or wheeze. Mark's panic-stricken bronchial tubes closed; a gob of phlegm tickled. A handkerchief! Quick! He felt in his pockets, found one and spat into it, blew his nose as silently as possible, breathing through the cotton.

Better?

No, not better, because Mark distinctly heard the coal mound shift, over there, across the void. Lumps of coal chinked as the mound settled. A silent scream built. Tears bled from his eyes but he must not sob aloud, there were penalties for crying; crying is what babies and girls do, he was a Nancy-boy, he was a mollycoddle, a milksop:

This is what I have to put up with, day in, day out, what is the flaming use of you, I wish someone would tell me that, have you any idea what you cost to keep? I wish you'd gone to Barnardo's.

But there is no coal mound, Mark's adult self repeated.

No hole. No void. No rancorous old woman.

You yourself have just chosen to turn off the light, Mark! It was *you!* You did it to make yourself safe. And you are safe. You can reassure yourself by running your finger over the switch.

See? That's right. Here's the switch, OK? All you have to do is flip it and *fiat lux.*

But someone might see, he might give himself away, if the light went on? Although two doors intervened between attic and landing, a hint of light might leak through and betray his presence. Counter-intuitively, this notion calmed Mark's terror; it returned him to the dimensions of the present. The coal hole collapsed into the vortex of a long-outlived childhood. The fear of exposure was so welcome that Mark found he had no need to reassure himself by pressing the switch.

If necessary, he would remain in the loft all night. The couch on which the models reclined would be comfortable ... enough. He wouldn't sleep – but did that matter? He'd slept nearly round the clock; his mind was alert. He'd need to pee. Well, there were plenty of jam-jars. Nothing up here to drink, obviously, but Mark's pockets were bulging with the biscuits he'd taken.

When he lay down on the couch, he'd be embarking upon a kind of vigil. To lie awake in her space, metres above Freya, keeping watch: wasn't there something blessed about that? For Mark was not alone. The muffled sounds from downstairs were traces of presence. Darling Freya was in the heart of the house. They were together.

15

Your own chair is so welcoming that it counts, all by itself, Freya thought, as a creature comfort. It gives to your shape and, in that sense, remembers you. Even the patches of wear and small stains are intimate.

I need to be grateful, she thought, for the small things and not take them for granted – well, they are not small: the privilege of being fed and warmed and sheltered.

Flopping down and yawning, she fondled Storm's head, as he rested his chin on her knees. For the first time, the house felt peaceful and welcoming: Freya would sleep tonight. Well, sleep better. And if I don't, she thought, planning for the possibility of insomnia, I'll read. Read something real and nourishing, and make the time valuable. Hot chocolate first perhaps – and some of the biscuits Pam had brought. The Crouches were beyond kind: she'd learned to accept generosity without the sense of beholdenness that converts a gift into a burden.

Being with Rae had done her good. They hadn't gone on to the concert: too tired, with eyes pouched from all that useful crying. I'll start regaining balance now, Freya reassured herself. Every day, I'll fall down, get up; fall down, get up. That's how it's done. And one day I won't fall down. As she waited for the kettle to boil, her face in the dark pane was a shadow you could see straight through, to the electric green stare of the Crouches' cat prowling the lozenge of light cast by the kitchen window on the lawn. Pansy froze and stared with searchlight eyes that appeared, in this optical illusion, to be set in Freya's own head.

She put her feet up and sipped the chocolate. Storm had decamped and was snuffling and scrabbling around upstairs on the landing. She called up to him.

He gave a yelp, carried on snuffling and didn't come. Probably he was looking for Keir again. How long would Storm's hope survive his master's death? At least he'd stopped the shivering and howling that must be the equivalent of human crying. A wraith of Keir's scent must have survived: when she'd put on Keir's old brown jumper, Storm had been all over her. And she could smell Keir there too. She'd never wash it.

Why had they been so quick to bag up Keir's darling clothes and take them to charity shops and recycling? She had proceeded in a spirit of butcher-like gutting of the house – working to keep up with Mark. She'd disembowelled the dresser and kitchen cupboards, while her taskmaster had scooped whole drawers of old clothes into black bags. She'd released sour smells of decay – her own ankle boots unworn for a decade and some boots of Keir's, caked in mud, keeping company in a cupboard with ancient shoe polish and cookery books, their dust jackets coated with grease and dust. On and on, her neighbour had ridden her, brain fogged, back aching, mouth full of pins and needles: *What about this? You don't need that?*

Still and all, it had to be done, never mind how. Mark had ensured that the painful task was completed in a single action. Freya soothed herself: put it behind you, like the embarrassing delusion about Haf. A waystage on the road to sanity.

Today the little girl had adored the dog and Freya had adored the little girl. Haf's hostility had evaporated. Once fully awake, she had seemed pleased to see her auntie and they'd completed a puzzle together, kneeling on the floor. She was full of quips and kisses. Then another puzzle, and another. Haf's arm had been draped round the Labrador's neck, fingers caressing his silky pelt. How silly of Freya to have taken to heart the little girl's outburst after the funeral. It was natural that a child of that tender age should need to wrap herself around her mother. Haf had sensed, without comprehending, her parents' heartbreak over Keir. More than once, she'd apparently come upon Rae and Jamie weeping. They'd not even realised she was in the room. How long had she been there? What had Haf overheard? And then, of course, one lies, said Rae, we panicked and pretended we were not very sad, only a little bit sad, it was all OK really, come and snuggle down here with us. That was bound to be unsettling for a little one.

'We are the walls of their home, aren't we? We can't be seen to break down.'

But the lies are worse, Rae knew. In the end, she and Jamie had sat the child down and broached the truth in a more honest way; tried to anyway. How do you know what they understand? Then they'd all gone down to the beach to play a cool game of football. Rae had sensed that they'd turned a corner.

And all the while Rae talked, Freya was remembering that Keir had written: *Rae has inner beauty.* Rae's inner beauty was still there, pouring out on Freya in this barren world. There were paintings of Rae, and sketches. Freya felt ready to see them. She would go up to the studio soon and look.

Still, it was a relief to have come home for the night, away from these intensities, skipping the concert. There was something unnerving about Rae's antennae. Years of practising law had taught her to read faces and minds. Her warmth saturated you but at the same time she would slip in shrewd caveats. Don't be too trustful of people's motives. Well-intentioned people – she surely meant poor Amy – can be a bit parasitical. They suffer chronic lack themselves and suck out food wherever they can find it. They prey on needy people. They try to isolate you. Don't let them.

Yes, I know that, Freya thought – everyone knows that. And in any case, I'm not needy, I'm grieving.

Amy hadn't turned up since she'd appeared after the funeral. She'd confined herself to torrential emails which Freya skimmed. Amy dwelt on the way Keir had trusted her as his confidante. He relied implicitly on her discretion – and he'd been right to do so, for Amy had never – would never – let him down. In some of her screeds, Amy reprised little scenes between the two of them, complete with setting and dialogue. A major theme concerned the portraits Keir had made of herself. Some of these, she wrote, were and had remained *private* between artist and sitter. But perhaps Freya would like to see *some* of them? Amy would be more than willing to share.

It had dawned on her, Amy wrote, that she had functioned for years as Keir's Muse, his twin, his other self. Keir had many times said so.

Yeah, we know, thought Freya: you have many times told us.

The emails became ever more grandiose. Amy had been as important to Keir, she realised, as Camille Claudel to Auguste Rodin! And the reason for her primacy in his life was of course that she was not simply a model but a *fellow-artist*. Like Camille. Also like Gwen John. These artists had been Rodin's equals, as Amy – in a different art form (what art form? Origami?) – had been recognised as Keir's equal.

This would have come as news to Keir: Freya could imagine the expression on his face – twitching with amusement, rueful, queasy. For he prided himself on his modesty and acknowledged his limits. But how could someone so attractive be without an alloy of vanity? Keir's feet were, in one way, on the ground; in another he was blissed-out by everyone's love. Of course, Freya thought, he drank too much red wine. There was no knowing what Keir might have blurted when afloat on a warm tide of red.

Getting no answer to her messages, Amy shot to kill. 'I don't mean it personally, but ...' Freya could imagine her thin, pointed face as she sat at her tablet with her fingers poised. It was well known, Amy wrote, that Keir did not believe in marriage. This did not mean that Keir didn't love his *wife*, she hastened to add. She didn't mean that at *all*. Freya, you were closer to him than *anyone*. Just that he felt the institution itself was *anathema*. Especially to an *artist*.

Each time, Freya felt irked, clicked 'Delete' and pitied Amy. In many ways it was not her fault but Keir's. He'd been lovable and pliable, because his conscience twinged at the thought of hurting women. He had hurt women. But he'd never rejected any friend or past lover. So he had a bloody great collection. Everyone had a claim on him. In their kitchen, Keir had sat and hearkened to Amy's woes, even when she drove him mad and wasted his time. Passing an open door, Freya had glimpsed them at the kitchen table, a bottle of red between them, Amy leaning forward, Keir lounging back.

His goodbye hugs and kisses had looked, if Freya was honest, more tender than might have been wise. She'd had the feeling that Amy hungered for the kisses, and invented scenarios to elicit them. Her heart had suckers. What Keir could offer, after their brief affair, never appeased Amy. Playing on his vanity, she'd tried to live on his gestures of fellow feeling, and turn them into little worlds of hope, when they were not much more than bubbles Keir blew. Amy, an irritant, failed to endanger Freya, then or now.

So Rae was wrong about that. For who else exploited her in that way? Her next-door neighbours maybe seemed to thrive on others' need. But bloodsuckers? No. She was surrounded by kind and decent people.

Freya let it go. Her mind drifted, dishevelled. The house uttered its familiar creaks, shudders of joists and pipes – homely sounds that never distressed Freya. Upstairs, Storm was still skittering obsessively over the uncarpeted landing. Freya closed her eyes and almost nodded off. Best get myself to bed, she thought, hauling herself to her feet and climbing the stairs.

'Come on then, lovely.' She bent to him, where he lay stretched on the landing and panting. 'Or are you planning to stay there all night? He's not here, you know.'

She gave his collar a tug. Storm raised his head, bathed in the outflow of tenderness she brought him; licked her face devotedly but showed no sign of moving from his chosen spot. He whined at the studio door.

Freya crouched. 'He'll never be here again,' she said, looking into his eyes, fondling his ears. 'He won't come back, we know that, don't we? But, darlingest, I am here.'

*

It was one thing to propose a night's vigil in a chilly loft that stank to high heaven. However cunningly Mark positioned himself on the couch, his feet inevitably dangled off one end, while his head jammed up against the other. You couldn't turn over. Mounds and dips mined the exhausted couch. Most daunting of all was the squirming suspicion that Keir Fox had shagged (it was the only word) his sitters on this piece of decrepit furniture. That was why it had seemed prudent to leave the dingy throw in place rather than using it as a blanket. You did not know what revolting traces might be revealed upon the upholstery.

On the other hand, one could not be sure that the throw itself had *ever* been laundered. This thought made one itch.

The exalted feelings that had possessed Mark fled with the onset of cramps and nausea. In the end, he had to get up to stretch his back and of course the boards shouted out with a volley of creaks. He had no idea how much time had passed. The night framed in the skylight appeared faintly lighter, so he judged from that and from the occasional chirps of waking birds that dawn could not be far away.

He'd heard Freya go to bed hours ago, coaxing the damn dog away from the loft door. Saying, *darling, darling.* He clearly caught the endearment and its cajoling tone. He'd heard her in the bathroom and the cistern flushing. Another call to the dog. *Darling, darlingest.* But what happened next was uncertain. He wasn't clear that the Labrador had quit his guard post. Storm had smelt Mark's presence and would continue to register it, and the part of the canine brain that lit up would stay alert. All night, if necessary. The dog would sleep with one ear cocked, if it slept. Mark knew from listening in on his own side of the party wall that Storm often shared Freya's bed. He'd always tried to avoid dwelling on this unhygienic practice, trusting that the animal reposed above and not beneath the quilt.

There was no sound whatever from downstairs. One could cautiously conjecture that the dog had given up its watch. Storm was familiar with Mark, in any case, and used to his presence in the house. He hadn't barked, just whined and scratched at the landing door. That was reassuring, in view of the fact that Mark had lately noticed signs of reservation in the animal – not quite hostility, more ambivalence. Mark had not taken the time and trouble (given the pressures he was coping with) to allay Storm's fears and pacify him. He'd always been quick to recognise signs of imminent rejection but, on this occasion, had proved slow to address them.

A dog was a simple organism. Dominate it, feed it, cosset it: the dog is yours for life.

Perhaps there was some way to divert Storm's attention if the worst came to the worst and the dog waylaid him. Mark's mind recurred to Pearl. What would have worked with her? But Pearl had been as cowed as Mark by the punitive atmosphere of their home. Her spirit was crushed, with a fear so deep that it never rose to aggression. Pearl whimpered, slunk, shook. Only with Mark were her fears partly allayed; she'd allowed herself to frisk and gambol with him, though always with the sense that she was looking over her shoulder. Pearl would never have stood up as his protector. Well, let's face it, he thought blearily, she didn't. When Gran took the belt to Mark, where was Pearl? Under the bed, cowering. She was acquainted with that belt. Her spirit had been broken long ago.

But, bless her – ludicrous as it might sound – Mark was Pearl's pup or no one's, as certainly as Romulus and Remus had been sucklings of the wolf.

Just one snarl or lunge from Storm would awaken Freya. And then what? A surge of terror. Screaming. How could Mark explain his presence? Perhaps he could say something like: *I heard a scream! I think you must have been calling out in your sleep, love. I was worried about you. Thought you might have had another attack. So sorry, Freya, I knocked and you didn't answer. So I let myself in with the key you gave me. Terribly sorry. Are you all right? Oh good, I'm so glad.* If

Mark took the portfolio with him, of course – and, yes, however idiotic this was, the sketches were going with him – that would be hard to explain away. The sketches belonged, of right, to him. Who else adored Freya as Mark did? In amongst the mess up here there must surely be something to wrap the portfolio in. He switched on the light and located a supermarket bag.

One thing was sure: he wouldn't be staying up here another minute. Everything in him craved the sanctuary of his foam mattress and pillow, his laundered and ironed sheets. Time to creep downstairs and let himself out. Make sure, he reminded himself, when you open the front door, that no one is around – the milkman, for instance, delivering to the ancient ladies of the crescent.

Tying his laces together, Mark hung his shoes over one shoulder. Ready. He padded to the door in his socks. It opened soundlessly. On the staircase, he took his time, keeping tight to the wall.

He listened at the second door. Nothing. Clasping the handle in both hands, he twisted, a fraction at a time. Listened again. Nothing. Now pull: that's it, just an inch.

His eye at the crack stared straight into Storm's.

Shitshitshit. The animal's eyes were wide, showing their whites, mouth open to blast out a bark. Any. Minute. Now. Jesus. But don't panic, act normal, act natural, you are familiar to him, you are her friend, you are his walker, you have every right to be here. Think think think.

Think.

Mark thought. His pockets were still stuffed with broken biscuits. Opening the door another couple of inches, he scrambled out some fragments and offered them on the palm of one hand.

Shhh, Mark whispered. And gave Storm his friendliest smile. They understand Shhh. They understand what a smile means. Darwin claimed dogs could smile. He should know. Shhh. Smile. Shhh. Smile. Biscuit, lovely biscuit.

The door stood open far enough for Mark to slip out sideways. Storm was eating and looking up for more. I'll pretend to eat one

231

too, thought Mark. Man and dog ate together, mutely, until only crumbs remained. Shhh, Mark whispered. Shhh. And smiled. He scattered the last crumbs on the floor, for Storm to lick up; pointed to them. Stepped out. A midnight feast.

'Basket,' Mark whispered. He cancelled his smiles, to indicate that the game was over. There was a faint growl in Storm's throat. Shhh. Mark pointed toward the stairs. 'Basket. Go.'

Storm understood. He obeyed. Mark heard him lollop down the stairs. Easing the loft door shut, he turned the handle and let go. Done. Brilliant. Bloody resourceful. Mark flew above himself. Who'd have guessed it would be so simple? He was ready to leave now.

But her door, partly open, detained him.

Just one look, a single glance. I cannot leave without checking on her, he thought. In all conscience, I can't. Freya has no one to watch over her. She is alone and defenceless, lost in grief. And afflicted by a neurological illness. Freya had made him promise: 'Don't tell anyone. Give me your word.' She'd trusted him to turn away her so-called friends and her husband's relations, to keep them at arm's length. People were possessive of Freya, and he understood that but they must not be allowed to swamp and suffocate her. Mark would not let her down. Anything might happen to her at any time.

Jaundiced light spilled into the bedroom from a bare bulb at the end of the hall. Mark stood in the doorway, accustoming his eyes to the dimness and his ears to the rhythm of the sleeper's breathing. She lay sprawled on her stomach, facing away, an arm crooked around her head. One leg stuck out from under the duvet, up to the knee and he could see the dusky sole of her foot – soiled, because Freya went barefoot in her house: no slippers, no socks, even. The vulnerability of his darling Freya shook him – thrilled through him.

At the same time, this woman could have been anyone. She was a piece of female flesh in a darkened room. It daunted Mark while it excited him. The room's breath reached him where he stood in the doorway: it was stale. Those sheets would be impregnated with nights of sweat. He didn't notice that she changed them all that often. When the neighbours flew their duvet covers like flags in the wind, the Foxes were at ease with what he had heard the husband calling 'clean dirt'.

What am I thinking of? Here I am, a guest in her intimate privacy, and I'm perturbed by the state of her washing!

If she opened her eyes and saw him, the spell would be broken. The damned Crouches on the other side of the wall would be calling the police. But Mark couldn't persuade himself to depart. Freya had yielded him this privilege of sharing – with trusted eyes – her innermost world. It was a beautiful thing; he had not deserved it. And in fact, there was a sense of the sacred.

Setting down the bag with the portfolio, Mark took a cautious step into the room. He couldn't not. Freya sighed and gave a slight snore, or snort.

He smiled at that. Who'd have thought Freya snored? It tickled him. So sweetly human and endearing. Her private self lay open to him. Every hair of her head was numbered. Her guardian angel could not have felt greater or more chaste tenderness or a more devout desire to succour and protect.

For all that, a pulse of excitement beat up hot and thick. Your groin tightened. You dared another step. Another. Until you were silently poised inches from the bed, looking down in tender wonder at the mass of dark hair on the pillow.

Her shadowed face could not be seen until – he recoiled – she rolled onto her back, towards him.

In alarm, Mark moved back a pace.

She murmured something. Was she dreaming? Of himself, perhaps? Of how he stripped naked and slid in under the duvet and reached his arms around her?

The duvet had slipped down and exposed her left breast.

He could not *not*. The palm of his hand could not *not*.

It reached down and cupped, as softly as breath, Freya's breast. But immediately came the disaster.

No. Too soon. There was no stopping it once the spasm started; shame sent him plunging silently out of the room, along the hall, down the stairs, where he skidded to a halt; rushed back up to grab the portfolio, skimming down the stairs again, past the fuddled dog, key fumbling in the lock, hearing the half-asleep call from upstairs – 'Storm? Stormie?'

The dog broke into a frenzy of barking. Out, out Mark bolted, locking her door, unlocking his own, snivelling and reeling, ramming the portfolio of sketches into his bureau, hanging on to the back of the settee to get his breath, showering and lathering, putting on fresh pyjamas and firmly tying the belt of his dressing gown.

Next door, the dog went mad. And Freya was up and about. Through the wall, as he put the kettle on, Mark heard her scolding Storm, sounding really cross. God, he needed this cup of tea. She hadn't a clue that anyone had been there. Mark wondered vaguely whether he should go and knock, ask if everything was all right? Freya might need him, if she'd been scared. But no, Mark thought, yawning, I'm absolutely whacked.

And what if the Crouches came snooping round with their do-gooding torches and their snide comments (oh yes, he'd heard, he wasn't deaf), which did not say much for their Christian charity. *There's something wrong with him!* Pamela had a carrying whisper. It came in fruity bursts from her silly little mouth. And frankly, she had never forgiven him for his remarks about the chimpanzees. Which he did not regret. Darwin had passed the Crouches by. *Something very wrong!* Yes, but not with him! Mark was not pharisaical, he was no hypocrite. The Crouches were sealed in unctuous religiosity – so keen to admonish other people's flaws and blind to their own power mania – for that was what it was.

The pair of them – particularly Pamela – needed to go on retreat, in a monastery as far away as possible, to fast and contemplate their navels.

And who knew what lascivious thoughts lurked in that chubby

cherub? Mark had seen the way Terence looked at Freya and leeched onto her. The wonder was that Pamela seemed impervious to it.

Mark hummed, dismissing the Crouches, as he carried a cup of jasmine tea up the stairs to bed. The dawn chorus had passed its prime and the day had begun. No sound could be heard from Freya and Storm. His darling had no idea she'd been visited. All was well. All was better than well. Something had been accomplished, a line crossed.

He'd been too nervous, obviously, far too overwrought, to have been able to offer Freya anything substantial, had she awoken and wanted him in that way. Mark was not going to let that humiliate him. How could it have been otherwise, considering the tremulous shock of sudden arousal? She'd sprung her nakedness on him when she'd turned over and exposed her breast. There'd been no possibility of preparing his mind for that impromptu moment. At least he'd not been timid. Mark had been, in his own way, bold.

At the same time, his body had preserved his and her essential chastity. That was the way to look at it. Premature climax was his spirit's way of signalling to Mark that now was not the time. Having come so far, he should wait for Freya to catch up consciously.

I'll sleep now, Mark told himself, brushing his teeth. Freya has granted me the power of sleep.

16

The night would have been peaceful if Storm hadn't ripped it to shreds. Sleep was balm, was health – and for once, Freya had slipped easily into its still waters.

What the hell was the matter with Storm? The dog had dragged her into consciousness, scrabbling in the hallway, rushing up and down the stairs – a rampage she tried to blank out. He'd ended up barking his head off. When Freya had stomped downstairs, he'd been hurling himself at the front door – which she'd forgotten to bolt. As she tried to control him, chiefly by yelling at the top of her voice, Freya had heard the knock.

A pang of alarm had gone through her. 'Who is it?'

'Don't be afraid, Freya. It's only me. Terry from next door.'

Well, Terry was harmless. A little voice had come worming through to ask: was he harmless though? How did anyone know who was harmless and who was not? Be careful. Storm didn't seem to be taking kindly to the guy at the moment and he was generally a decent judge of character. She'd put the door on the chain.

'What is it, Terry?' she'd asked through the gap. Storm had lunged and she yanked at his collar.

'Just wanted to make sure you were OK, Freya. Sorry, love. If you're fine, I'll go –'

She'd unhooked the chain and opened up. Terry had been standing in his striped dressing gown, his kindly features smeared with yellowish light from the street lamp. He'd had a book in his hand. Pamela had not been with him.

'How long have you been there, Terry?'

'Oh, just this minute. Storm was barking and I heard you call out.'

'I don't know what came over him.' She'd apologised for waking

Terry for the second night in a row. 'I'm going to have to get my neighbours ear plugs.'

'No problem, Freya. As long as you're all right … I was worried in case … well, the upset last night. Anyway, you know where we are. Just knock on the wall if you want us.'

Having announced his departure, Terry had waxed conversational. He'd explained that he slept rather lightly – encroaching age, no doubt – with one ear open. But he actually enjoyed waking in the early hours because that was a rather spiritual time of day, especially at this season, perfect for meditation. He'd listen in to the dawn chorus and he liked to read the poems of Henry Vaughan.

'Ah, I don't know his work,' Freya had said lamely.

'You should, you should. He was Welsh, you know. Brecon.'

'Oh?' She wasn't ever rude to people but she'd felt a bout of rudeness coming on.

'And Henry also was fond of the dawn chorus. In fact, there's a rather marvellous poem about it.'

Jesus Christ. Showing an interest in mystical verse in the early hours of the morning was a chore, but Freya had taken a deep breath and made a feint at interest, praying that Terry would not feel inspired to read a few stanzas aloud. If only Storm had started barking again. You never bark when I need you to, Storm. Terry had hesitated. The inclination to fill her in on his beloved poet had been written all over his face. Freya's stagy yawn seemed to help him resist the impulse. He'd creep back to bed forthwith, Terry had said, now he was sure all was well: Pam was snug as a bug in a rug and she'd be none the wiser. She'd tell him off for yacking on people's doorsteps, if she knew.

''Bye, Stormie,' he'd said. 'Look after your mum.'

Terry had bent, offering his hand to be licked. Storm obliged.

'There's so much we don't know about the creatures,' Terry had remarked, straightening up. 'Dogs are supersensitive, Freya, aren't they? Well, and cats, of course. We think our dear little Pansy is positively clairvoyant! Anyway, enough of this – and no more night capers for you, my lad.'

'Thanks, Terry,' Freya had said. 'But, honestly, if you hear noises, just please ignore them, OK? I can cope fine.'

She hadn't wanted him or any other fusspot turning up on her doorstep in the early hours of the morning. Had he got the message, though? Why hadn't he wanted Pammie to know he'd been knocking on her door in the night?

Freya had flounced back to bed. Too early to get up, too bloody late to sleep again. She'd still felt pissed off with her neighbour. But she hadn't been rude, had she? It was odd how people came nosing round you when you'd been visited by death. They wanted to give you comfort – yes, but weren't they also drawn to the drama of it all and fancied a role? Perhaps Rae had seen something in Terry that disturbed her. In any case, wasn't there an element of *Schadenfreude* in the attention given to the bereaved? The angel of death had passed them over and dropped in on you instead.

Am I getting rather nasty? Freya had asked herself.

She'd nodded off again and, waking, felt less rancid, more rational. Start again, she thought, why not? Just do it. She found herself in the garden, getting out her road bike, wiping it down, oiling the chain. Now, get on with your life, just go, speed away.

Mark's curtains were closed when she cycled off to the farmers' market. They were still shut when she returned. She'd relied on him in her lowest moments, even stationing the poor guy downstairs, to somehow guard her afternoon naps. He'd helped with finances, probate, removals, illness, everything. Like a brother. And just because of his agitated behaviour the night before last, and Pam's unkind insinuation, Freya had recoiled.

Perhaps Pammie was deflecting anxiety about Terry onto their neighbour.

She put the salad stuff away in the fridge and ate up the last morsel of cheese, mildly surprised to find so little there. Mark was actually quite sexless. Perhaps that was the source of the peculiar blankness she sometimes sensed in him. Freya had occasionally wondered if he might be gay but couldn't bring himself to acknowledge it. On the other hand, think of the passion the poor guy still had for Lily.

The viola videos had released something in her. They'd said, go out and live and listen, there will be clues, you'll get your balance back. Lily had sent her to Rae, allowing the two of them to talk as they used to, face to face.

What business of Freya's was his sexuality anyway, for God's sake?

She'd never paused to ask Mark about himself. Not really. His private history had come out in glimpses, when he sought to place his own story alongside hers, for her benefit. Friends should be human bridges for one another, was Mark's maxim. A one-way bridge this had been, so far.

She knocked softly. No answer. And harder. Nothing. I'm being a bit of a Terry, she thought, stepping back. Probably Mark had come down with a cold or was just tired and resting. He wouldn't want to be disturbed. She'd always thought of him as a shy, retiring person – almost a recluse. There was so much he didn't say or show – and that should be his choice, surely. Freya wavered.

What kept her hovering was the memory of poor Gaynor, Mark's predecessor. Marion Teague had conducted a feud with Gaynor, accusing the ex-deputy head teacher of deliberately throwing dead leaves over the fence to litter her patio. To Marion, Mother Nature was an ever-present threat to the perfection of her paved garden. Sycamore seeds drifting over from Whitethorn Wood were apprehended as they settled and before they could gain a foothold. Faced with leaf accusations, Gaynor had given short shrift: *The wind blows leaves, Mrs Teague. The wind bloweth where it listeth. Quarrel with the wind if you must pick quarrels. Or have a cup of tea instead.* After months of witnessing this simmering dispute, Keir and Freya had been entertained by the sight of Gaynor on early autumn mornings, dumping scarlet leaves over the fence in fistfuls.

The closed curtains somehow brought all this back. As the girl who'd been Mark's tenant had said, it was out of character for him to sleep in.

Gaynor had remained for five days dead in her bed.

Nobody had noticed. They'd all passed by on their oh-so-important daily business. Freya remembered the shock and Keir's remorseful face. He'd cleared off to the studio and she'd opened the hallway door, to hear him weeping. Freya hadn't gone up: that was Keir's space. The lady had been lying metres from them, on the other side of their party wall. She'd been characterful, satiric and original. It turned out that she'd died of a heart attack. But she could probably have been saved. There were bloody scratch marks on the adjoining wall, where she'd tried to summon help. Gaynor had no one. The delay in finding her was a speaking image of human isolation, community indifference.

Storm had known, and tried to alert them. Days before the body was found, he'd taken to howling at Gaynor's door. Freya had been busy and harassed that week. Also, she'd been conscious of a niggling toothache. Keir had been more or less living in the studio. He'd bed down there when a work was reaching a pitch, crumpling his lanky form onto the couch. Neither of them had taken notice of what Storm was telling them until their own noses registered a smell. Freya had called the police and the ambulance. You couldn't ignore closed curtains after that.

And besides, there was something in Mark that made you wonder how he could bear to live with that degree of pain locked inside him. This thought shot through Freya. She'd never put it into words before. *He's been telling me something. I've never attended to it. Something about his childhood.* She hastily fetched his keys.

Best to check. And Freya felt easier, as if at last she was seeing the world outside herself again.

She called round the open door. 'Mark! It's me, Freya! Are you all right?'

No answer. The house was dim and cool. She peered into the living-room: immaculate, as always. A blue vase of freesias on his glass-topped table caught a ribbon of sunlight where the curtain seams didn't meet. She'd seen Mark arranging the flowers. The bronze Greek archer on the shelf flexed his bow eternally at the geometrical mountain goat, preparing to spring to safety. The one would never fulfil his aim; the other could never escape. The Persian rug: Mark had explained the meaning of the imagery, fascinatingly, though she'd forgotten what he'd said. He was learned, cultured. Everything in his world had its proper place and related to a web of arcane meaning spreading back and back into the past.

The kitchen light had been left on, which wasn't like Mark, but everything else was in order. A bundle of asparagus had been positioned on the counter, parallel with a leek and a knife. On the chopping board lay an onion. She smiled at the symmetry. He'd planned to make soup today.

At the foot of the stairs, Freya called his name again, without reply. So maybe he was out? Still, she ran up just to make sure, tapped on his bedroom door and peered in. Mark was lying on his side, one arm thrown out. He didn't stir.

No, she thought, oh no. No, please. There was a box of pills on the bedside table. She recognised them.

*

Someone had violated his hermitage. Mark's heart raced but his eyelids were sealed, as if gummed together. Horror loomed. Don't look. It's all right, it's all right, there's no one – a dream – an old dream, a stale dream, nobody can get in.

His breathing calmed. There was no one. How could there be? There couldn't be but there was.

Mark shot awake to the presence of a shadowed face above him and the touch of a hand, shaking his shoulder. For a moment he panicked and batted it away.

'It's OK, Mark – it's OK. Just checking you were all right.'

Freya's hair cascading down enclosed his face like a curtain. It was dark in there. When she raised her head, light dawned.

'Freya. You're here.'

'Thank God you're OK.'

Why was she thanking God? Drug-fuddled, Mark felt vacant apart from this shock of what might turn out to be joy. Freya sat down on the edge of his bed. She looked as if she were about to cry.

'What is it, love?' Propping himself on one elbow, he reached out to take her hand. 'Has something happened?'

How long had Freya been here? What had she seen? Had he left the sketches out? Had she twigged that he'd been rooting round in her loft?

'I don't know. I thought ...'

'What did you think?'

'Your curtains were closed, Mark. I thought I'd better check. The pills ...'

He followed her gaze to the bedside cabinet; took in the pill box and the time – ye gods, midday! He leaned over and switched on the reading lamp. Passing his hand over his face, Mark tried for the right words and tone. Whatever did he look like? These pyjamas – like an old man's – never meant for show.

'Freya – dear Freya. You thought I'd done away with myself? I would never do that to you.' He smiled. 'No, I'm afraid you're stuck with me. Don't cry. Don't, love. Come here a minute.'

He sat up and folded Freya in his arms, turning away his head because if your mouth tasted this sour, your breath must smell. She moved away, saying, 'I'm not crying. It was you I was worrying about!'

Mark's bladder was bursting. A sick sense of embarrassment came over him, caught offguard and exposed as he'd made sure never to be since childhood. But the mechanisms of his mind were beginning to function. Mark recapped, fast.

Last night. Visit. Research. Studio. Biscuits. Dog. Bedroom. Escape. Sketches.

The sketches were in the bureau. Had he closed the lid? Yes, but not sure if he'd locked it. He had definitely disposed of the plastic bag in the recycling.

Now Freya had come to *him*. He received her, of course, as an eternally welcome guest, though he'd have preferred to have had notice. Mark's mind travelled back more cogently over the night's events. The upshot of his having been in Freya's house seemed to be that Freya was now in his house. He all but laughed at the dream-like dance of symmetries.

She did look as if she were about to cry but perhaps she was just expressing concern. The light was dim.

What would help her and release him from embarrassment? Practicality. Common sense. Of course. Mark let her go, whilst keeping hold of one hand.

'I don't think I've ever mentioned, have I, that I have a chronic back problem, Freya?'

She shook her head. And now she was feeling rather a fool, Mark could see.

'Perhaps I ought to have mentioned it,' he went on. 'Thing is, I've learnt to live with the pain and mostly I hardly notice it. Once in a while I need to take a strong painkiller. But only occasionally. Really. And I'm so sorry you've seen the meds, Freya, because – am I right? – I think they must bring back ... difficult memories?'

She nodded, distressed. I must remember that, Mark thought, and be sensitive. Must not mention or display meds. He saw her chagrin. She'd begun to feel better, stronger. She'd slept through the night. Mark knew that because he'd seen it with his own eyes. But Freya was discovering that it took years to recover from a death. If you ever did. *Difficult memories.* Mark could read her so well that he could practically see those memories stream across Freya's mind; the weather in her face told him all he needed to know. She'd been feeling stronger and now she'd come adrift. You'd only need to blow on her and Freya would quiver and relapse. He was in love with her sorrow. It made her so reachable. As she sat there, her hand on his duvet, he thought how small and slight Freya was.

243

'So – it's just your back?' she asked. 'Nothing worse? Sorry, I don't mean that a bad back isn't excruciating ...'

'Just my back, I promise.'

'How is it now?'

'Much better, Freya. Sometimes it frees up when I'm asleep.'

'Oh, that's good. And the night before last? When you had that ... awful dream, or whatever it was?'

'That dream?'

'In my house?'

'Freya, surely you have realised?' Mark tossed the problem across to Freya because his brain needed a moment to consider what it was that she should have realised. Quick, quick.

'I don't think so, Mark. Oh dear – realised what? I've been so bound up in my own troubles – or maybe just thick. Have I missed something obvious?'

'You really didn't notice?'

'Oh dear. Notice what?'

The answer came like a revelation, all the more clear because it was in a way true. 'I suffer from PTSD, Freya. But it is getting easier.'

'Ah. That makes sense. I'm so sorry.'

'Don't be. I've had counselling. With Val. Val is tremendous – highly experienced and wise. I don't know where I'd be without her. The flashbacks get fewer and fewer – but I'm afraid you came in for one that night. I can't remember what I came out with – I hope it didn't frighten you.'

Freya half nodded, half shook her head. There was a pause while she took in this information.

Val was such a standby. So real had she become to the eye of Mark's imagination that he knew how she dressed, the exact area where she practised, her age and education, her very faint Swedish accent. He could track her expressions and gestures. Mild-mannered she might be but this was a powerful woman, with unnerving acuity. Val's hair was blonde (naturally so, being Swedish) and straight, cut in a longish bob, laced with inconspicuous streaks of grey: it swung as she altered the tilt of her head. She wore expensive dark-framed glasses and stylish grey suits. Val had been trained in a holistic school and took careful note of one's every mannerism. Her brandished pen reminded him of a fencer's epée. By this unconscious habit, she told him of leashed aggression – and in fact she was the sort of person who might belong to a fencing club. In their mutual observation, the two of them duelled for truth. They were well matched. Val had rarely come into contact with a client as acutely insightful as Dr Mark Heyward.

She understood now, Freya said thoughtfully. Her face spoke of pity and relief.

He reached across and, shutting the pill box in a drawer of the bedside cabinet, smiled and said he hoped that weight was off her mind. One day, he promised, he would tell her about it – but now was not the time. They shared a moment's quiet. He was thinking that his bad back would offer a pretext to miss the next occasion of sea-swimming. What a shame he hadn't thought of this before. If you wanted nightmares, that had been a nightmare. His skin goose-pimpled at the thought and he shivered.

'Can I ask you something, Mark?'

'Of course. Ask away.'

'Just between ourselves. What do you think of Terry Crouch?'

Mark was ultra-careful. He refrained from labelling Terence a pious fraud and Pamela a two-faced busybody. Cautiously, he enquired why Freya asked, and learned that apparently – on cue – Terence had come creeping round in the early hours, instilling unease. Claiming to have heard noises. Damn prowler must have just missed me by a whisker, he thought. God Almighty! In future, do not take undue risks. Ever. Mark's palms sweated and he wiped his free hand on the duvet cover.

'Whatever did he want?' he asked mildly.

'Oh, just to make sure I was all right.'

'Ah. Yes, that sounds like Terence.' It is all said in the tone of voice, Mark thought.

'He said he'd heard Storm barking. Didn't you hear the racket?'

Mark shook his head. 'I'm afraid I was spark out, Freya. Storm *was* barking, was he?'

'Yes, but I had a rather anxious feeling ... I hope I'm not being unfair ... probably I am ... I wasn't quite awake ... that Stormie was making all that rumpus because he sensed Terence there all along. Please keep this to yourself, Mark. I'm afraid I may be doing Terry an injustice.'

'Was Pamela with him?'

'No, Pam was asleep apparently. Terry told me he was often wakeful in the night and he'd heard a commotion. He was up reading poetry. He'd brought the book with him.'

'As evidence!'

She grinned but said, earnestly, 'I've always thought of the Crouches as the salt of the earth.'

Mark thought biblically: *And if the salt has lost its savour, wherewith shall it be salted?* He made ready to desalinate the Crouches in the most subtle way.

'You want my honest feeling? I may be wrong, Freya, but I'm never sure about Terence. Not completely.' He'd planted the suspicion but then he softened it and made a partial retraction. 'I think he means very well. I really do. And Pamela too, though she can be a bit prickly, maybe. They are enormously kind and charitable.'

'But?'

'Pardon?'

'There's a *but* coming.'

'Well, let me just ask: did you feel afraid last night?'

'Not really, no. I just felt, I don't know, a bit uneasy.'

'So maybe trust that instinct? For your safety's sake. When we're alone, we have to be careful.'

She nodded and no more was said about it. Freya would wait downstairs until Mark was up and showered. Maybe the two of them could do something together: the day was still young.

The embarrassment at being caught unawares in bed subsided as Mark put on his dressing gown. Freya called upstairs, something about asparagus, and he heard her laughing in the kitchen. And that was delightful – to be teased by the one you loved, in your own home – which was in a real way Freya's home – or rather a way-stage on the way to Tŷ Hafan. (Danielle had gone.) Mark whistled a few bars from *Eine Kleine Nachtmusik*. (Danielle really had gone.) As he replaced the razor cartridge before shaving, he made sure to stow his new inventions in mental pigeonholes – and at the same time, match them with the existing narratives. His memory rarely or never let Mark down. But that was in part because he went over and over the diverse weave, pulling the pattern together. And he should write all this down in the red book.

Three headings basically. Number One: *I suffer from PTSD*. Not really a lie...? Important to emphasise that the condition had been treated and was well on the way to being resolved. The symptoms Mark had exhibited or might in future display were vestiges of an old condition. The blade glided over his cheeks.

Number Two: *Oramorph for chronic back ache*. This pain (which had once been real) must be understood as intermittent and not debilitating. It would be self-defeating to present himself to Freya as past his prime. He rinsed the blade. Looking at his semi-shaven face, Mark thought: Terence and I must be approximately the same age, give or take, but he is bulbous and I am svelte. These epithets brought an amused grin to Mark's lips and the contrast inspired unusual optimism about his appearance. Obviously, Mark thought, I'm not a fitness narcissist like Himmler and Heydrich. I am decently fit, despite the fact that I never knowingly go near a gym.

And Number Three, of course: *Val*. Both to Danielle and now to Freya he had introduced this figure of a wise woman who'd counselled and redeemed him. A kind of confessor. Mark's face now was cleanly shaven; no nicks or redness. He patted on the coolness of aftershave. He'd developed the characterisation of Val over the course of time, as he'd got to know her better. She was someone he valued, who had set him straight on much in his life that beggared explanation. And how strangely grateful he was to Val, considering that she was not a real person.

Or not yet real. Or not substantially real in the way that the reflection in the mirror was real, as it flicked a comb through its hair, still boyishly abundant – well, perhaps thinning at the crown but not blatantly so. Taking Terry as a template for incipient baldness, Mark was not even at Stage 2 on a scale of 10.

From downstairs wafted the aroma of frying onions. That was it: Freya had found the ingredients and utensils for the asparagus soup and was preparing lunch.

*

'So, you have your house back, Mark.' Freya broke open a warm roll and dipped it in the soup. 'What are your plans? Will you move back now?'

He saw her noting his hesitation. Freya was observant. Not much escaped her – except when everything did. She looked rather radiant. He'd never seen her eat with such a good appetite. Rain drummed on the porch roof. Blackbirds were pecking around on the turf and the plants were getting a good watering. At Tŷ Hafan, he would plant and tend something glorious for Freya: Red Eden roses, perhaps, clambering over walls and trellises, heightening the senses with intense scent – or the velvet glamour of Black Baccara, where scarlet meets black. He would say, *These are for you, my precious girl.* But Freya had never seen Tŷ Hafan and he must get her there before he allowed fantasy to harden into plan.

'You know,' he said, 'I've not really thought about moving back. I've been so happy here, Freya, alongside you. It feels like home.'

'I'm glad.'

'But Tŷ Hafan is rather a beautiful house – or so it seems to me. It's a bit of a one-off – an Art Deco house, not pretentious in any way – but curious and special. You feel that people have been happy there. And I gather you met my lodger?'

'I did. Nice young woman.' Freya looked at him with suppressed curiosity.

Danny did not seem to have told her anything worrying.

'Very nice. But going through a bad phase at that time. She was homeless, you know – I expect she said. And I needed a breather from Tŷ Hafan – too many memories. So the temporary arrangement suited us both.'

Freya nodded. He felt there was something else she wanted to ask. But she let it go. He didn't have to enter into an explanation of how Danny was a fantasist and a self-abuser. The less said, the better.

'I'll go round,' he said, 'and see if anything needs to be done. Young people can be a bit careless, can't they? I'd enjoy showing you the house, Freya, if you'd care to see it. The garden, especially – and the view. I think you'll love that. I can see you climbing my copper beech.'

They both laughed.

'Never climbed a copper beech before,' she said.

'A first for you then. So you'll come?'

'Of course I will. I'd love to see your home, Mark,' she said warmly.

'The garden's a bit of a wilderness – Danielle, bless her, hadn't much interest in it. Although she enjoyed the bird life.'

17

She had vacated. Mark exulted at this thought as he set out in the car to reconnoitre Tŷ Hafan. Unless he bumped into Danny by accident, which couldn't be ruled out, he'd seen the last of her. A clean break, Mark thought: always the best way. Long ago, he'd fathomed that beneath Danielle's confused defiance had lurked the fear of being obscurely in the wrong.

Hers was not the kind of mortal fear with which his wife had stated he – what was her melodramatic verb? – *impregnated* her. He remembered the expression on Lily's face when she'd caught herself blurting this. She'd clapped her hand over her mouth, taken a step back and looked round for somewhere to run. By this time, Lily was sodden and didn't know what tasteless phrases she was going to spew at him. Be fair, though, she'd wrought Mark to such a pitch that his language was also a bit of a lava flow. By that time, Lily's talent was out of the window. She'd ditched it to spite him.

Occasionally Mark had obtained some relief from her vagaries by sacrificing one or two of his hard-won sleeping pills. He'd ground them up and put them in her tea. Oh, the relief when you knew she'd be out of it for the next twelve hours. He would melt towards her then, sitting and contemplating the remnant of pale beauty that had never quite faded.

Even in her decline, Lily had remained deep and complex. Her inner light – as she'd liked to call it when she briefly joined the Quakers – was never extinguished. Mark was not sure that it was quenched even now she was dead. Danny, by contrast, weighed less than a matchstick. All along she'd naively wished, as she put it, to be *the best possible person I can be.* She'd obviously been egged on to cause trouble by some creep she'd now gone off with. Lily however had forfeited all contact beyond their four walls. This was what

Mark had always wanted – but by that time it was too late. He could not respect her. Despite the passionate tenderness Mark had offered his wife, the core of Lily remained obdurate. He'd been willing to abase himself if he had exceeded the mark or to assume the blame for her faults. In her egotism, she'd chosen to abandon Mark to forces they both knew to be life-threatening.

You see, he thought, I'm still wrangling with her. She has power, even in her ruin.

He had not meant to bring Lily into the picture as he drove towards Tŷ Hafan. The stifling humidity, even with the window down, seemed to release his demons. Lily would lie low for a while, until she intuited a gap in his defences. Then she'd rage out at him with beak and talons.

Mark's hands sweated on the steering wheel, inching forwards towards the roundabout. There was a cyclist, some old biddy in a helmet, passing him on the inside. He snarled the engine and gestured, honked the horn. The crone gestured back. They shouldn't be allowed on the road. Look at her, wobbling. There should be some sort of road test for cycling grandmas.

The lights changed; the grandma sprinted off and then wove through the slow traffic on to the roundabout. Red socks on a grandma! An odd thought: he would outwit Lily by taking a longer route round to Tŷ Hafan. Irrational anxiety built up when you repeated an action. So change your habits! Mark knew this. It was what Val might have advised. The grandma signalled left. Go on then, off you go, fuck off. She's kitted out for the Tour de France.

Lily was still circling, her ragged vulture wings spread wide, carrion dangling from her bloody beak. Violent, implacable.

That vengeful quality had always been there. One heard it in her music: the vicious assault of bow on strings. Mark recalled the concert in which Lily had devastated a viola bow. Berio's *Sequenza VI* – the loathsome buzzing of a trapped hornet. He'd felt sick to the stomach. She, of course, had enjoyed herself; adored playing the hateful piece. Their marriage had just begun to fracture. Mark had

251

been sure she was playing it against himself. He remembered the way her arms opened to receive the thunder of applause (what the hell were they applauding? The murder of harmony?) Broken strings had flashed out into the light like a mare's tail.

Shouts of *Magnifico!*

But this was not about Lily. Mark refused to allow himself to be preyed upon. He stopped in front of the little park with the pond in front of the museum. Swan-shaped pedalos were moored at the wooded island; a pair of cormorants perched at the edge, stretching their necks sideways, a double-act in a mime show. He smiled. The geese, for once quiescent, sat grouped on the turf. The water's surface lay unruffled, mirroring the island's ash trees. It made for an idyllic scene: the world as it ought to be. Mark sucked a polo mint and thought of Virgil. *Otium,* ease; the *locus amoenus,* the pleasant place. The classics always cooled one's mind.

So why not go in to the office first? The working world had receded. Mark had hardly given it a thought. In the somnolent trough of mid-summer, there were many visitors but none of the big boys would be around. His office would be mercifully cool.

As Mark hurried through, Paltry Patrick was conducting a guided tour of the collection of Palaeolithic knapped hand-axes and scraping blades. He was explaining, boomingly, that the Red Lady of Paviland was a man!

He paused for mirth.

And, he said, not a Neanderthal! Some of us, he quipped, have more Neanderthal in us than others!

Mark waved, lowered his head, and charged through to the gallery and his office.

A knock on his door jolted him as he stood, hands on hips, looking out of the window. Ah! Janine! How are you? I'd been wondering how the great work was progressing! Come in – do – and tell me all about your visit to the Bodleian. Janine had been seconded from the university to research for her PhD under Mark's supervision. She apologised for taking up his time, and Mark was

252

able to shake gold dust all over her. Janine had his full attention for the better part of two hours. It was a rare kind of happiness, this touching of minds. Mark relaxed into the truest self he had.

He made her coffee and the two of them sat companionably, minds cruising over subjects of kindred interest.

Perhaps he could buy her lunch?

'Oh, no, thank you ever so much, Mark. I've a dental appointment and then I'm going to write all this up.'

'Another time then?'

'Yes *please*! This has been amazing. I can see now where I've been going wrong and how I ought to proceed. I'm so glad I knocked but I hope I didn't interrupt something important?'

'Janine – what am I for?'

Charmed, she stammered out how lucky she was to have Dr Mark Heyward as her supervisor. Not just *the* authority on her subject but incredibly kind and thoughtful. She knew that researchers from all over the world would give their eye-teeth to sit at Mark's feet. Janine appreciated his help more than she could say.

Mark cut her off, waved the praise aside, explained that he was nothing more than a medium, a bridge. What he had been taught, he was passing on. He felt touched, and humbled. Janine reminded him of what really mattered in life, the intellectual pursuit that had from earliest days salvaged and centred him, convincing even his grandmother that he was something out of the ordinary.

The idea of becoming a visual artist and hanging about in lofts now seemed risible.

Othello's occupation lay here, in the sphere of the mind. Most of Mark's colleagues (not all) might be second rate, and one or two frankly third rate, but there were these dawning stars amongst the young with whom to share knowledge. It had made all the difference to his wellbeing to assume his professional self for Janine. The way eloquence bubbled up never failed to surprise Mark – especially when a listener appeared out of the blue. You were stimulated to make creative, off-the-cuff connections. The chance to illumine a mind already bright and curious and committed was a gift to a teacher.

This is my kind of fatherhood, Mark thought. In the next generation, there would be a cluster of disciples to pass on his insights. How had George Eliot put it: *Souls live on in perpetual echoes.* When Mark Heyward was dust, Janine Macpherson would be passing on to a new generation of young people something of himself. He was grateful for her gratitude.

He tried to explain these thoughts to Janine. She seemed to be listening with her blue eyes, which were moist and avid.

It flashed through Mark's mind that, now Danielle had decamped, and once he had cleaned Tŷ Hafan, he could invite Janine to visit him there and profit by his armchair wisdom. She also had the intelligence and taste to appreciate the culture of the house. It was heartening to reflect that even Freya was not the only woman to whom he might have a bond.

When Janine left, and he'd called out *Good luck with the dentist!* the nightmarish sensation had ebbed. In his mellowed state, Mark looked with pleasure out of the window at the summer trees, heavy with foliage. Was there a hint of yellow autumn? He replayed the morning with quiet interest: that feisty old cyclist, for instance. Mark hoped that when he got to be her age – sixty, seventy? – he'd be a tithe as active. Why should feistiness only be for women? Not that he'd learned to cycle, but it was never too late. This was the kind of thing a dad would have taught Mark. He saw his boyhood self on a tricycle, powering along, followed by a watchful young dad in corduroy trousers and shirt sleeves.

But I am my own parent, Mark told himself. He would not be self-pitying. Today was the beginning of a new life. Live it.

Janine had sparked a train of ideas he would enjoy sketching out. Turn off computer. Sheet of best paper. The old magic fountain pen. This little beauty never let Mark down. Tortoise-shell body, fine nib.

The riddle of the Knossos labyrinth: Mark would never travel to Crete but imagination winged him there, to the unearthing of those prehistoric clay tablets a century ago. Janine had visited and some of the observations she brought back had tickled Mark's brain. Since the deciphering of the Bronze Age Aegean script, a community of scholars across time had passed the puzzle from one to another. The meaning of the code might look prosaic: records of harvests, goods, animals and offerings to the gods. Mark's modest contribution linked this distillation of the mundane to the world of Odysseus, Nestor and Agamemnon. Start small: think big.

His blue-black handwriting flowed across page after page. Almost in a trance, Mark allowed thoughts to crystallise. After an hour or so, he screwed on the pen's cap, gathered up his papers and locked them in the top drawer of his desk, without reading over. In that way, the writing surprised you the following morning, as if it had been taken at dictation. Now for a tuna sandwich from the cafe, which he'd eat outside in the shade. After that, let's see what treats Danny has left behind at Tŷ Hafan, he thought. Yes, I'll drop in and take an inventory. It was easier now to be forgiving.

You were just a lass, he thought. You were doing your best, Danny. Before you let yourself down. It struck him that Janine was better qualified in every way to thrive at Tŷ Hafan and to benefit from his patronage than Danny had ever been. She had the intellectual calibre. She was thirsty for knowledge. If everything with Freya fell through – despite Mark's devotion – there were still avenues open to happiness. Ordinary happiness, such as he saw all around him.

The real terror was to be left with nothing and nobody. The motherless immensity of the world appalled him: the high-walled back yard without Pearl. But that was not going to be Mark's destiny.

He parked in front of the home that had been restored to him. Its white facade shone, the curving bow windows flashed in the sunlight; white blossoms around the walls looked festive, bridal. In the little valley below the house the roses had run riot. And all around was green spaciousness, fields upon fields on three sides and over the road the conifer plantation. Inside, well, the place was bound to be a bit of a mess but Mark was ready for that.

255

Firstly, the gate was sagging off its hinges. What had Danielle been doing? Getting her little band of brats to swing on it? Never mind. Secondly, the hedges had sprouted madly. Easily sorted. Thirdly, the undulating lawns were a jungle, sown with dandelions, dock and creeping Charlie. Nevertheless, Mark could see at a glance that uncommon wild flowers had also self-seeded. Freya would cherish those. A litter of cardboard cups and plastic bags had blown into one corner. Where on earth had those come from? The work of a minute to clear.

He'd move his most important possessions this afternoon. Papers, computers, medications. And do a quick clean round.

Stooping, Mark tugged at a stem of creeping Charlie. No use at all. An inch tears off the mother plant and the rest laughs at you. The ivy reminded him of Terence Crouch. Smells minty; is poisonous.

*

Her neighbour was carrying cardboard boxes to his car, preparing for their visit to his house. She'd never seen Mark in shorts before! He liked to be covered up. But then the heat was stifling.

Where was the electric fan? Freya had opened the windows and lowered every blind without much effect. The bedroom was worse than downstairs. It would make sense to sleep down there tonight. Last year there'd been a heat wave in June. In the sultry weather, Keir had found it tough to work in the studio, complaining that the houses hadn't been built with nice cool cellars. The electric fan was still up there, presumably.

Freya didn't falter. She was through the door from the hall without giving it a thought. Bounding upstairs two at a time, she entered the space she'd evaded.

Some marvellous, unfinished thing greeted her on the easel, blue and purple.

All Keir's paints and tools, canvases and bottles lay strewn where he'd abandoned them. Hot, trapped air was dense with the musk of paint and turps. Freya threw open the dormer as far as it would go and poked her head out. Vanilla scents wafted up from the gardens. A dog-walker shuffled up the green. Whitethorn Wood was dead still.

She withdrew her head. Canvases had tumbled on their faces. Freya bent to right them.

Oh, Rae, it's you.

Her friend looked out from the canvas. *Rae has a beautiful spirit.* Over and over again, Keir had tried for the elusive quality he discerned in his sister-in-law, never quite content with the result. But this was lovely. Rae was an implied, fleeting presence – in motion, a mystery. Had Keir intended to leave the work unfinished? Or had he run out of time? Whichever, Rae was there. In what was shown – an eye, part of her mouth – and in what remained unexpressed.

Pictures were ranged around three walls, stacked upright, face to back. A hundred, easily. When was a life over? She would not hurry. Nobody had seen these works. He'd given versions to sitters but what remained was fresh to the view. The canvases were Freya's now, to browse for the first time, like everything else in his studio. She sat down on the couch with the portrait of Rae held upright on her knees.

She kissed the picture, which expressed both of them, Keir and Rae, and 'Thank you', she said aloud.

All this was Freya's inheritance: not only the pictures but their friends and home, and this space, containing the tackle of his trade, brushes and palette knives and oils, turps and white spirit, lying exactly where Keir had left them. She put down the portrait and, resisting the impulse to hunt through more canvases, seated herself at the easel.

Swirls of colour, purple and blue, with spots of yellow and green, radiated from the centre. Keir had made the image throw itself forward and free from the canvas. So this was your final work, she thought. What did it represent? The last time she remembered Keir working up here had been months ago.

Freya picked up what she supposed was the last brush Keir had used, clogged with paint. And the paint was wet.

No. It couldn't be. She dabbed the back of her hand. A blue streak.

She shook her head. Perhaps something to do with the heat? Some quality in the paint? That must be it.

18

A sensation of miracle lingered, a gloss on everything. From where she sat in Mark's car, the sky was almost too intense. Her skin tingled, a shimmery sensation like flu. Was it a good feeling? Freya was unsure. There was an aura of presence.

Something is playing with my mind, she thought, and I am apparently letting it.

They crossed the common and she relaxed as he drove, the engine purring, her companion quiet, exchanging with her a gentle smile before letting her be. He seemed to know Freya needed to breathe. He wound down the windows before she asked. Closing her eyes, she let the breeze flow across her forehead. She opened them as she felt the car twisting down windy lanes.

'I'm taking you the long way round,' he said. 'The scenic route.'

What should have taken ten minutes, straight across Fairwood Common, lasted half an hour. Freya didn't at all mind. Was the bracken turning towards its bronze autumnal colouring? Wild ponies glanced up from cropping the grass. Through hundreds of years they'd lived and bred here on the hard grazing of brambles and gorse. I'd like to walk through the wild, she thought dreamily, or run, rather, out and away, and leave the crescent behind; leave myself behind. Yet she enjoyed the lassitude, glad to sit passively with her hands in her lap, and be driven.

Tŷ Hafan. At last she'd see the house Mark was so attached to.

Perhaps she'd mention the paint that had not dried and how it seemed so magical: Mark would be able to hazard a notion of how that might happen, the chemistry of the thing. For there must be a rational basis. Freya had no conscious belief in the supernatural. Cause and effect: that's the law. Cause and effect doesn't spook you. When we die, that's that: Keir and Freya had agreed on this without needing to debate it.

And yet. And yet.

The heat seemed to melt one's logic and distort perspectives. The sense of Keir's survival beat mothy wings round Freya's mind. Commonsense condemned the moth as an illusion: wet paint must have a rational explanation. Or perhaps Freya had made it up? But this streak of blue was evidence she carried, written on her body.

The right side of her head pulsed. Not a migraine, please. Or worse. No, because she heard herself talking in a perfectly reasonable way.

So maybe the paint's failure to dry was something to do with the humidity of the space, the nature of the oils? I'm definitely not going to wash you off for a while, she thought. Every so often she peered at the hand. Glancing sideways, Mark saw her looking.

'Not long now, Freya,' he said. 'Nearly there.'

'Oh, I'm not looking at my watch, don't worry,' she said, and explained.

Mark's hands on the wheel gave a judder. The car swerved, then slowed down.

He was surprised and attentive, hazarding no opinion of why the paint might still be wet. There was no explanation that he could think of. He recalled that she'd mentioned the studio, a very special place obviously, which he would love to see one day, he added carefully. Perhaps Freya could show him? – when it felt right to her, of course. Not before.

'Yes, of course,' she said.

But she wouldn't take her neighbour or anyone else up there. Not for a year and a day. Or ever, maybe. Not until her thirst was quenched. The studio was private space. The memory of Keir's last, unfinished canvas flashed, blue, upon her inner eye. The unexplored paintings stacked round the walls waited to offer themselves. The loft was like a library. She would never be finished with reading Keir, never.

Mark turned into a winding lane with high hedgerows, leading to the village. They passed old stone houses, a post office, newsagent, pubs, a hotel and a nursery, 'Daisy Chain'. Presumably that was where his lodger had worked. Freya remembered the girl but the name had escaped. Pale, freckled, red hair pushed back behind her ears: *gamine* was the word. She'd looked about fourteen but must be in her mid-twenties. One could, in a way, understand Mark's taking pity on her. Yet it had been an extreme thing to do.

'What was your lodger called, Mark? The young woman you took in?'

He swerved slightly again.

'Sorry. Oh yes – Danielle. Danny was a rather needy person. Her boyfriend beat her, poor lamb. She had a crop of bruises.'

'Oh *dear*. She did say something about the boyfriend.'

'She did?'

'Something about how he was not imaginative. And how that was a good thing.'

'Well –' For once, Mark seemed to be at a loss for words. 'Anyway, all's well that ends well,' he managed, closing down the topic.

But what was it the girl had said about a lady with three children Mark was looking after – or had looked after? The pregnant lady with a Labrador. Maybe Danielle had been muddling various people up.

I'll ask him, Freya thought, and didn't.

She glanced again at her skin with its blue daub. What had been the subject of Keir's last painting? It had appeared abstract but Freya knew his methods. Everything he did was rooted in nature. She closed her eyes and discerned the beginnings of a face: some creaturely life was stirring behind the wall of canvas.

Tŷ Hafan was at the edge of the village, Mark was saying – well, they called it a village but really the place was a dormitory to the city. He loved the privacy and apparent remoteness of his home.

'Far from the madding crowd,' he said, and she caught the nervousness in his voice. 'And here we are! *Voilà!*'

A white house was built above a curving slope. The broad bay window overlooked a lawn that fell away to the base of the garden where four trees had been planted, Mark said, when the house was built. An oak, a copper beech, an ash, a larch. A path with a railing looped its way down the incline. On three sides lay farmland, on another a fir plantation.

Danielle, Freya thought. That had been the girl's name. He'd called her Danny. She had not conjured up in her mind's eye a house as imposing as this.

Mark opened the door. He returned to the car for boxes of papers, files and IT devices, which he was transferring bit by bit, for when he moved back in. Mark's face was flushed and he was saying something about stained glass. The uniqueness of Art Deco architecture. The principle of the labyrinth. He needs me to admire his house, Freya knew. Well, she did admire it – who wouldn't?

'Oh, my goodness,' she exclaimed in the hallway. Books rose to the ceiling. Portraits. 'What a lovely space, Mark.'

'Mais oui! Merci bien, mon ange! Entre dans mon petit château, s'il te plaît!'

Her host seemed to have turned into a stage Frenchman. His eyebrows had worked up and down as the key disputed with the lock: Mark was obviously seriously nervous. He ushered her into the front-room with its green view. He'd bring coffee; she was to make herself at home.

What Freya couldn't get her head round was however Mark could have brought himself to move out of his *petit château*, leaving this place to the young lodger: the nursery nurse – who had praised her boyfriend as lacking in imagination. A peculiar thing to say. Freya had nearly laughed aloud for who could tolerate a boyfriend without imagination? The girl's face had been solemn. There was something not right.

Grief had driven Mark out of Tŷ Hafan, obviously. Freya could understand that need to bolt. She felt it now, as if knuckles were thrusting into the small of her back, saying *Go, just go home.*

'Shan't be a minute.' Mark's voice, still frazzled, came from the kitchen.

Go, just go home.

'No hurry,' Freya forced herself to call back. 'I'm enjoying the view.'

The broad expanse of window and many bevelled mirrors bounced light to and fro, brightening the room despite the dark wood panelling. Mark bustled in with a tray and set it down. The fragile cups had wasp waists and geometrical designs. They were Art Deco, apparently: works of art. Mark was explaining that he normally kept them locked in a glass case and used mugs like any sensible person. But this was a special occasion, very special, and out they must come for Freya's first visit to Tŷ Hafan. The first of many such visits, Mark proposed, smiling, pouring. She was to regard this as her second home. The biscuits he had baked himself. A bit on the rustic side, he apologised, and definitely not Art Deco.

The coffee tasted bitter. She turned a grimace into a skewed grin.

Mark had spent yesterday afternoon at the house, reclaiming the place, as he put it. He showed her round. Her head spun. A white grand piano shone in the adjoining room. The lid was raised and a score lay open. Schumann. *Träumerei.* This must have been where Lily practised. Her name was not spoken.

'It was my parents' home, Freya,' Mark said.

'Oh, really?'

Hadn't she gathered, way back, that the house had been in Mark's wife's family?

'My great grandparents built it in 1928. Look, here's the date – you'll find the date in every room, sometimes carved into the panelling. 1928 was their wedding. There are all sorts of nooks and niches and ingenious recesses built in. Like this. Press on the panel, Freya. Just there. That's it.'

A drawer slid out on a magnet. She was intrigued.

'That's so clever! It must be wonderful to live in a house that has belonged to your family for generations.'

'And a responsibility,' Mark went on. 'There is a responsibility, isn't there, to the past? The truth of the past.'

'Did you know your great grandparents?'

'Goodness, no, Freya. Long before my time.'

'Your grandparents, perhaps?'

'No. Anyway.' His tone was curt; his forearm made a brushing motion on the mantelpiece, as if he'd happened upon unsuspected dust. 'Do you think Storm would like it here, Freya?'

'Oh – well – I'm sure he would.'

'I was thinking of his running free in the garden. I've strengthened the fence and he wouldn't be able to get out.'

'I suppose not. But Storm wouldn't try to get out, Mark, would he?'

'No, but if he did –'

'He just wouldn't.'

Why am I being so argumentative? she asked herself. He's only trying to be polite. But I don't like him, she thought. I've never liked him. She was feeling a bit dizzy.

'Funny though,' she blurted, and stopped sipping the indescribable muck he had served her. 'I thought the house was in your wife's family.'

'Oh yes, but we were first cousins, Freya.'

'Ah.'

'Anyway.' Mark's sleeve executed another sweep of the mantelpiece as he dismissed the subject. He sat down again and raised his cup. 'Do let's drink up and we can look at the upstairs rooms. I think you'll find them interesting. I've tried to be faithful to the Art Deco theme with the soft furnishings.'

'I've had plenty, thank you. I'm a bit coffee-ed out this morning.'

Did she really have to view his soft fucking furnishings? The house was like a museum: lovely, but dead.

As they climbed the stairs, Freya thought with a qualm: this must be where his wife fell.

Lily. Did you fall here, Lily?

She looked back over her shoulder, off kilter, letting Mark go up ahead. Keir gone. Lily gone. Turning, Mark reached for Freya's hand, as if it were the most natural thing in the world to steady and guide her. The pressure seemed to indicate that, where they were going, there was no turning back. Everyone else had gone but the two of them had not gone. You are going nowhere, his grip told her.

I've strengthened the fence, he'd said, *there are no gaps; he wouldn't be able to get out.*

Silly, Freya thought, leaning on the banisters overlooking the stairwell, to feel so rattled. Her mouth tasted metallic. The coffee had tasted disgusting. Her gaze was toppling into something that was not there. Was she falling asleep? Such a fall could not be broken? It would break her. Language was losing its bearings.

An arm insinuated itself around her shoulders and the strange man in long shorts was asking, face up close, smelling of peppermint, was she feeling all right?

Why was he always sucking on mints? Suck suck. You never actually saw him put them in his mouth. Suck suck. Of course, she reassured him, of course she was fine, Freya gasped, she'd just been admiring the drop.

What? Why did I say that? she asked herself. The drop!

He looked concernedly into her eyes.

She corrected herself. 'The fall.'

'The *fall*?'

Words kept tumbling out. If she carried on like this, Mark would know Lily was on the tip of Freya's tongue. She forbade herself to say the name Lily. Lily was a beautiful name and asked to be voiced. Lily had been a gifted musician, herself a living voice. Lily had been in the public eye, much talked about. Lily had worn a green silk dress for that amazing encore, off one shoulder. Walls of silence interred the name Lily. To Lily something inexpressible had happened: a fate so unspeakable that it had blanked the name Lily.

'Did you say *fall*?'

'No, no, of course not. Or rather, yes. Oh dear! But I didn't mean that kind of fall.'

The chandelier in the hallway winked and spun. Freya gripped the balustrade with both hands while the world whirled. She sought to laugh off her blurtings.

'No, I meant the fall. Autumn. We went to New England in the fall. Have you been to New Hampshire? You should go.' *You should go*. Or I should go, Freya thought. Because frankly I'm not feeling comfortable, I'm breathing shallow, you're far too fond of me, I feel shaky. *There's something wrong with him,* Pam had proclaimed in a carrying whisper. Politeness is a tyrant. Embarrassment rules us, it makes us false. What she should do was to ask Mark to drive her home immediately. Instead she kept rabbiting on about the bloody fall. 'I love it when the trees turn.'

He did too, Mark agreed uncertainly. He'd sometimes wondered about a trip to Connecticut, say, or Vermont.

No, you haven't, Freya thought spitefully. You've wondered no such thing. Something in here smelt off. Who was the pregnant partner with the three teenage children and the Labrador? Should she ask? Or was she about to faint?

'You're not well.'

'No, I'm not. Could you –?'

'Of course, dearest – of course. Don't worry now, I've got you, you'll be fine.'

'I wish you wouldn't –'

'Wouldn't what, my love?'

'Nothing, never mind.' She wished he wouldn't keep mauling and coaxing and calling her *dearest* and *darling*. It was like seeing the obvious answer to a sum. You'd been staring at it, doing your mental arithmetic and getting a different answer every time, and then, too late, seeing how it added up. It was not even a difficult sum. A child could have worked it out.

'All right, sweetheart, it's all right. Easy does it.'

He seemed to dance her along, as if performing the Gay Gordons. They were in a bedroom. A master bedroom. The guy was saying something about an *en suite* bathroom and loo. Over there. He'd leave the door open.

266

Just lie down, Freya, that's the way.

She didn't want to lie down. She resisted lying down.

He helped her to lie down. Was that better?

It was a foam mattress, absolutely new, she'd be very comfortable, the prattler prattled. And it was cooler in here, sometimes the heat affects us adversely. He'd close the curtains in case the sunlight affected her.

In point of fact, she was glad he'd drawn the curtains. The dimness was less oppressive than blue dazzle. Freya's right temple throbbed. She was in a cold sweat. So perhaps he was right and she should not be standing up.

The man had gone, but not before he'd spoken the word *episode,* followed by the phrase, *fugue state.*

Back he came with a glass of water. She needed to go home, Freya explained, propping herself on an elbow. She'd be better in her own home. Ah but, with respect, the guy didn't think she was well enough.

'You don't look good,' he said, perched on the bed.

Well, you don't look fucking good either, she thought.

On and on the mouth babbled. Have a nap, it suggested. The doctors at the hospital had advised that if he recognised certain symptoms, he could help her avert a major attack by doing as he was doing now. They'd suggested he give her two codeine tablets to take at the first sign of an episode.

'I'm not having an – episode. I'm not in a fugue state. I'm tired, that's all.'

The man, the bloody man, was offering tablets on the palm of his hand.

'I think they meant that codeine might help to avert ... anything like that.'

She was not going to take the codeine and that was that. Freya's mind flicked back to the hospital. She remembered now: she'd heard Mark Heyward telling the medics he was her partner.

'Your *partner*, Freya? No, no, the nurse had assumed I was your husband. It was all very frantic, it was surreal.'

'I heard you. I heard you say it.'

'Freya – dear – have you any idea how upset I was? I may have said – almost anything. I really thought you were dying. Look, I'll leave the codeine here. Another sip of water? How do you feel?'

How did she feel? She felt like upending the glass of water over the guy's clucking head. He was doing his best but his square-jawed, concerned face was up so close that it felt like a fucking Face Invasion. She could see the pores in his greasy skin. The metallic taste in her mouth made her want to retch. If he wasn't careful, she'd throw up all over him. See how he liked that.

Why am I being like this, she asked herself. Nasty, testy. And he's just taking it. He's trying to help. Isn't he? I'm behaving like a teenager. Am I? Something is not right and I think it's me. Or actually it's you, Keir, isn't it, it's you, after all.

She accepted another swig of water. Her head flopped back.

'Take no notice of me, Mark. I do really need to go home.'

'Of course, Freya. Let me help you up. We'll go now.'

She tried to rise but giddy weakness forced her back.

'I'll drive you home, love, as *soon* as you've come round. Unless you want me to call a doctor now? Should I? Perhaps I should.'

He got out his mobile phone.

'Just say the word. What should I tell them? I mean, symptoms. No? You don't want me to? You're sure? Am I being a terrible fusspot? It's my besetting sin. I'll be in the study when you want me. Or in the garden.'

*

Ought one to lock the door for Freya's security? He'd never forgive himself if she stumbled out on to the landing, all groggy from sleep, and lost her footing on the stairs.

Best to turn the key, just to be on the safe side. He'd keep coming up to check. Pity there wasn't a baby alarm. He could have brought the listening system, if he'd thought.

Mark washed Freya's coffee cup and rinsed it, before scalding it with water from the kettle. For safety's sake, he dried it with paper towels and polished with a clean cloth. The same with the biscuit plate. No trace remained. She'd drunk very little. But she'd eaten two biscuits.

Freya's phone lay on the counter top. Better to keep it down here than leave it to ring and disturb her rest. As if on cue, the phone vibrated and gave a restless little squirm. No sooner had the caller given up than a text pinged in.

Barbie at mine babes midday U comin round?

Dave the illiterate ex-brother-in-law. Mark deleted.

The paint on the blasted canvas had not dried! Jesus Christ! Of course the damn paint had not dried! Because he'd been up there fiddling about with it!

And now she had it down as a miracle! She was displaying a paint mark on her hand like some sort of holy relic or stigmata. Ludicrous of Mark to have gone up there messing about with the dead man's stuff. But how could anyone have predicted that Freya would go up to the studio directly after he'd visited? Maybe it hadn't been coincidence. In her sleep, she may have unconsciously registered the small sounds that betrayed his presence.

What to do now? Freya could be asleep for hours. Nothing was working out as planned. Far from becoming tranquil and malleable, she'd turned peevish. And this was how it was: you were doing your absolute best for people, bending over backwards to please – whereupon they let fly at you for no reason. You cringed and shrank into a helpless blob. Or else you lashed back and put yourself in the wrong. But what you actually were was a manblob. Utterly mortifying. And to think this manblob had dreamed of lying down beside his darling Freya, taking her in his arms, soothing her to sleep, so as to be there when she awoke to find herself looking into his rapturous eyes as into a mirror.

Instead of that, she'd turned huffy. She'd accused him of calling himself her partner. Well, what else would you call someone who had not only saved you, but accompanied you to hospital and spent the entire night at your bedside? Who had walked the dog, cooked the meals and even knelt to wash your feet! But no, one's efforts went unvalued. The tender scene Mark had envisaged was out of the window.

Freya's bad temper was odd. Shouldn't she have been drowsy and tranquillised?

And here was another odd thing. Did Mark even like the woman? Occasionally he smelt smoke on her breath, a whiff that nauseated him. He'd seen her in her back garden taking drags from what looked like a roll-up. Cannabis? People who took illegal drugs sickened him. Freya's teeth were slightly stained. You wouldn't want to kiss an impure mouth. For a jaded moment, he wondered why he was bothering with this woman.

How old was Janine? Twenty-four or five. He could check in the records. Beautiful mouth, white teeth. An elegant thinker. Very like himself.

For all his doubts, Mark reminded himself that Freya was his guest: he'd better just go upstairs and check she was all right. Maybe just pop your head round the door, Mark advised himself, and assess the situation.

Fast asleep. He could have hollered *Boo!* into her ear and Freya would not have surfaced. Seeing her here in his bed, so slight and vulnerable, pacified him. Freya lay curled up, one arm cradling her head.

That's right, rest, sleep, be calm, little one.

Like her? Of course Mark liked her! Loved, adored her. He dismissed all thought of Janine. Freya was a beautiful, complex, wounded human being. Mark's legs went to jelly. He would not dare to lie down beside this treasured creature until she begged him to – and this – not because he was craven and pathetic – but out of a proper decorum and reverence. Mark was unworthy of Freya, he knew. This self-abasement gave him a curious pulse of satisfaction.

The thing was, Freya had actually drunk a little of her coffee –

so what she'd swallowed probably induced confusion. He'd had similar symptoms himself, several times, after taking opioids. Dr Lewis always emphasised the necessity to remain within the prescribed dosage. Probably the old guy popped any number of pills to get through the parade of sad sacks coughing in his waiting room. The GP's eyes were baggy with fatigue; he looked only just alive. The thought of Lewis was accompanied by Mark's realisation that he must urgently reorder, now that he had spent a quantity of his savings. For morphine was a form of currency. In imagination, Mark fled to Lewis's surgery and rehearsed his request. *Terrible back pain, it's the only thing that helps. I can't manage without it. As you know.*

And Lewis knew. Of course he knew. He had on various occasions suggested more scans. Physio. Counselling. Yoga.

So far, Mark had never quit the surgery without a prescription. After all, he was *Dr* Heyward. A General Practitioner is no more than a referral agent. He is not even an authentic doctor. A real doctor has a doctorate. Did Lewis have a doctorate? He did not. The term doctor is an honorific for medics. What do we pay them for? Mark had never articulated this view explicitly to 'Dr' Lewis. But he'd made it clear from his public manner, even while begging for pain relief.

The pain was indubitable. There was no lie involved in demanding some palliative. Lewis would concede the prescription. Just to get rid of me, Mark thought, don't worry. What he would do now was to saunter down to the rose garden and gather some of the beauties that had just come into bloom. He would bring his guest armfuls.

If you grind the pills to powder, of course, he thought, fetching gardening gloves and secateurs, you can't know how much has been ingested. He ticked himself off, relieved that Freya had rejected the extra medication. After all, she was asleep, wasn't she?

He must have got something right.

*

Two magnificent silver swans – almost ceiling high – reared up on the curtains, breast to breast, wings held back. They uplifted themselves against a background of blue-black, spangled with silver stars. Freya, in a fog, stared at the cosmic swans. She'd smoked some weed after finding the wet paint in the studio: it had left her groggy, though it usually mellowed you. And now she was visiting the *petit fucking château* of Mark Heyward. It all came flooding back. Shit, she'd more or less passed out on the landing. She had a vague memory of finding her host repulsive. Kafka's insect. Had she said anything unkind? Mark had been forbearing, considering.

Were the swans about to fight or mate? How could you tell?

Freya got up and dragged her fingers through her hair; yawned; used the loo and splashed her face with cold water. Each swan occupied one curtain. She parted them and gazed at Mark's view. Better go downstairs and apologise. She'd call a cab to save him driving her home. Frankly, she'd had enough. Her own life called as it had not done since Keir went.

The door was jammed.

Freya twisted the knob and yanked: nothing. She returned to the window. There he was at the bottom of the hill, busy amongst the roses. She knocked with the knuckles of both hands, tried the sash. The bloody window didn't open. He couldn't hear. What was he doing? The bushes were massive, heavy with blossom, pink, yellow, scarlet.

She'd left the phone downstairs. Shit. Just wait; he'll come back in a moment – and then I'll be off. She calmed right down and had a nose round.

*

Freya did not find it. It found Freya.

The cubby hole was in plain sight. It appeared empty but Freya's hands felt their way to the back. When she reached right in, out came a package wrapped in a blue muslin cloth.

A violin? No, of course not: a viola. *Her* viola, Lily's – venerable, precious and smashed. The glorious instrument had been destroyed. The bow was in two pieces. Good God. Someone had gathered up every shard.

Don't drop any of it, Freya told herself. It needs to be kept together, even though it must be beyond repair.

Lily, did you do this? How *could* you do this? Why?

To create that ruin you'd have to hold the instrument by the stem and bash it against the wall, wouldn't you? If so, it would have been a form of suicide: this instrument had been Lily's whole life. Freya was holding Lily's life on her lap. Lily would never have got over the loss. She must have been having some kind of nervous breakdown. She'd done herself an irreparable injury.

With trembling hands, Freya spread the muslin on the bed and laid out the fragments. She returned to the window. What was he doing now? Pruning, apparently. Secateurs flashed. Had he noticed that she'd woken and drawn the curtains? Presumably not, or he'd have been hotfooting it back.

She closed the curtains again. The swans resumed their intimate stand-off.

Freya sat alongside the remnant of Lily's life. She placed her hands around what remained of the viola's curving waist. Such mortal damage could hardly have been caused accidentally. If it had somehow fallen to the floor, there might have been a scratch, a dent. But what if the viola had somehow fallen over the banisters into the stairwell? Or it had been accidentally dropped out of the window? Was that conceivable?

Or what if Lily had been holding it when she fell to her death?

No, because how would the remains have come to be interred here? Her brain still felt foggy: think, think.

Freya tried to remember what Mark's tenant had said about Tŷ Hafan. It hit her. Danielle had said she'd come upon traces of Lily everywhere, despite the fact – didn't she say this? – that Mark had tried to scrub them away. Actually though, Danielle hadn't said this.

Freya was remembering the way Mark had sailed out of her own house with Keir's belongings, leaving her no time to consider and decide what should be recycled, what should be discarded and what should stay. She'd gone along with it unquestioningly, as if programmed.

Danielle had definitely mentioned the viola. She'd found it, trussed up *like a baby*. Didn't she say in the attic?

Danielle must have brought it down and stowed it here in the cubbyhole. Mark wouldn't have been told, he wouldn't know, he doesn't know. The girl had lived here in the wake of the accident and snooped around and clearly, in the end, couldn't wait to get away. Danielle had given the breathless impression that anything was preferable to staying where Freya was now. A garden shed would be a palace! Again Freya was making it up. Danielle had said no such thing. But her body had been trying to speak. Hands unstill, forehead furrowed even as she smiled, swallowing her words back into a choked throat.

What if it was not Lily who'd caused the damage?

No, that was unthinkable. Mark was a lover of music. And he was habitually careful with all objects, even those lacking obvious value. They were a collector's hands; he had curated this house! She'd seen the care with which he handled the Art Deco cups, setting hers down on the coffee table, watching her drink. The coffee had been vile. Perhaps the coffee was Art Deco too and had been curated. For sure, Mark would not have preserved a smashed instrument.

She tried the door again. You have locked me in. There had better be a good explanation.

Was he coming? Freya peered round the edge of the curtain. They guy was still gardening, partially obscured by the copper beech. He'd piled a mound of blossoms beside the path. She'd never liked cut flowers. And seeing red roses, with their flagrant symbolism, somehow triggered the realisation: *he's wooing me, he wants me.* Well, of course she'd known that, hadn't she, it was hardly news, but she'd ignored it. When Jamie had said, *Careful, lovely, with him next-door sniffing round you,* she'd insisted, *Hey, Jamie, not fair, Mark's a good friend.* Jamie had given her an if-you-say-so shrug.

Rae had said, *Watch out for bloodsuckers, Frey – they prey on needy people.* Freya had thought she meant Amy, and perhaps she had.

Well, I'll go home soon, Freya thought, and you'll be going with me, lovely broken creature. She took the remains and – with all possible gentleness – swaddled it again in the blue muslin. Danielle had known. She'd seen what Lily had bundled up and concealed from sight. Where to stash it now?

Yes, he had curated the house. And now he wants to curate me.

A tap was running in the bowels of the house: Mark was back. He'd be filling vases and arranging flowers. It was an undervalued craft, he'd said. Give every bloom its due, like notes in music or poetry, don't you think? Freya replaced the viola in the cubby hole, sliding it right to the end. Her backpack was downstairs. Once Mark released her, she'd grab it and make an excuse to come back up here and fetch the viola. For you are going with me, my beauty, she told the trashed treasure.

*

He was unprepared for the violence of the welcome.

'What the hell do you mean by locking me in?'

Freya was flushed and angry and beautiful. Mark was the manblob who could do nothing but whimper and cower. He was the human version of Pearl, beaten to within an inch of her life. The manblob was slavishly sorry, he hung his head, he tried to explain to the irate woman that earlier she'd nearly passed out on the stairs and he'd helped her into the bedroom, but he'd needed to go out and worried that she might stumble down the stairs.

'Yeah, right.'

His guest stalked towards him like an adolescent who is prepared to bump straight into you if you don't shift out of the way.

'Really, I'm so sorry, Freya. I hope you weren't frightened.'

'It's OK,' she said, containing her wrath. 'I'm going home now though, Mark. Thanks for the visit.'

'Are you sure ... you're well enough?' And again, this was not how the day was meant to unfold. Mark seemed powerless to prevent its unravelling. And the haughty way Freya looked at him as she swept past was an echo of an echo of an echo.

'I'm fine, thanks. I'll just pick up my backpack and call a taxi.'

They were halfway down the stairs. He followed like a spaniel.

'I'm sure you have plenty to do here. Now which room did I leave it in?'

He realised she'd lost her bearings. In the panelled hall, which branched crookedly in a nod to the principle of a labyrinth, all the entrances must appear identical.

'It's in here,' Mark said courteously. 'With your coat. I'll drive you home as soon as you—'

'Oh my *God*!'

As he opened the door, Freya had got a view of what lay in the lounge. He led her into the space where he'd arranged the roses. Armfuls of blossom. The swooning scent enveloped them. All for Freya.

'What's all this?' She gaped at Mark as if he were mad. He might as well have gone and dug up a field of turnips and stuck them round his lounge for all the comprehension she showed.

'I thought you'd enjoy them, Freya. They are for you.'

'They're for *me*? Listen, Mark, it's good of you to go to all this trouble and I – admire your house – but –'

There was always the big biting *but,* the caveat. Any minute now she would say that she liked him as a neighbour (he read her eyes) but as for anything more serious, that was out of the question, she wasn't attracted to him. On the other hand, she seemed to be wavering, presumably embarrassed.

'That's all right, Freya. I understand. You don't like roses. Of course. It's too conventional of me.'

Perhaps she would like me to dump them on the compost heap,

Mark thought, riled and concealing it. Or burn the whole lot to ash, since roses offend her. Did his *guest* have the slightest idea what work of enrichment went in to their cultivation? The mulch, the spray, the feed, the pruning? Not that he had done much this summer, having been turfed out of his own property by a dope of a girl who – you may be sure – waltzed around the flowers like a wasp, without lifting a finger to nurture them (although the comparison was specious, since wasps are useful pollinators). But all this was irrelevant, it was the principle.

He went on mildly, 'Is it the colour or the scent you dislike, Freya? Or – oh dear, I hadn't thought – do forgive me – perhaps you're allergic.'

Freya was picking up her backpack and looking round for – he guessed – her phone. Mark's jaw set. He wasn't about to help her with that one. He'd switched off her mobile and placed it for safe-keeping in a drawer.

'Oh no,' she said, delving in the pockets of the backpack, 'it's not that I dislike roses – not at all – and I'm not allergic – it's just, well, way too much.'

She glanced up and blinked. She was wondering, doubtless, how to wriggle out of all this.

'I'm sorry you feel it's too much, Freya.' Mark was aware of speaking with dignity and tolerance. 'I wanted to please you. As your friend. And perhaps give you a nice surprise. You've been through such a rough time.'

She hadn't a leg to stand on. She murmured something about how of course they were friends; she wasn't feeling all that good; thought she'd mislaid something. Now she upended the backpack and her wallet clattered out. A hairbrush followed. Flakes of debris.

Mark stooped to pick up the wallet and brush; he returned them to Freya without comment, meanwhile drawing a mental circle round the fragments on the carpet and making a note to vacuum later. It was only a few specks but if you knew it was there, you'd keep noticing.

'What have you lost? Can I help?'

'Oh yes – thanks, Mark.' She smiled into his eyes for the first time since she'd woken. 'Would you mind just going and looking in the driveway? I think I may have dropped my house keys as we were coming in.'

Scouting around in the drive (surely they'd have heard the keys clatter as they dropped?), he glanced back. Through the tall window over the staircase, Freya was visible for a moment. She was running upstairs two at a time.

What the hell do you mean by locking me in?

The violence in her voice rang in Mark's mind again and awoke the echoes. Unsafe, unsafe. She had claws, they had claws. A neurotic musician – a ninny nanny – a hippie widow, they all had this in common: claws. They welcomed you into their presence and once they'd extracted what they wanted, they spat you out.

Take, take, take, had been his grandmother's refrain. But, in point of fact, Mark had *given, given, given.* With shortlived acknowledgment and nil recompense.

What on earth was the woman doing, racing upstairs the minute his back was turned? Perhaps she was looking for her phone? You won't find it up there, dear. And if she'd been caught short, he was sure he'd clearly pointed out to Freya the whereabouts of the downstairs loo.

There'd be no keys out here. And in any case, she knew Mark had a spare set for her house at the crescent. He could return them with impunity, for he had copies.

He was halfway up the stairs when it all came over him. It knocked him sideways. His knees gave. Nobody cared. He was unwanted.

19

She should have got out while she had the chance. Whatever had Freya been thinking of, haring up here to take a broken instrument that had nothing to do with her? And now this! Mark was prostrate. He'd come rushing in and taken one look at her, then hurled himself on to the bed, racked with sobs, with gobs of snot, eyes pouring tears, legs thrashing.

Easy does it, Freya thought. Just gently sidle to the door.

The viola was already zipped into the pack and the pack on her shoulders, before he'd burst in. He couldn't possibly have seen what she was doing. It was as if he'd scented something, nosed her out. For the first time, seeing Mark in the midst of this – this what? – Freya felt afraid.

All she caught of the storm was, *You don't want me!*

She'd patted Mark on the shoulder and murmured soothing words he couldn't have registered through his own noise. Flinging himself sideways across the bed, he'd shrieked louder. Freya crept towards the door.

You don't! I know you don't care!

Her head throbbed; she'd need to sit down before she fell down. Take some deep breaths, Freya told herself; calm the guy down; find the phone and leave. Had something happened to Mark between the moment she'd sent him out to hunt for the key she hadn't dropped and the moment he came plunging in, out of his mind?

And it's my own fault! I'm worthless!

She'd have to shout to make herself heard. 'Mark, whatever is the matter? Calm right down! Stop it – now!'

He stopped. Just like that. Freya was amazed. He just lay there, silent, as if he'd been switched off. Then one eye peeped out to assess the scene around him. His face was red as a radish.

'Sit up, Mark! Blow your nose!' she ordered him, in the same brusque tone, since it had worked the first time. 'Now whatever's the trouble?'

He blew his nose and wiped blubbered eyes. He hunched on the bed, elbows on knees, head in hands, shaking.

'It's the dog,' she thought she heard him mumble.

'Did you say *the dog*?'

'Pearl.'

'Who is Pearl?'

'My dog. She's dead,' he said with a kind of irritation, as if this fact must be patently obvious. 'Pearl's *dead*. They put her down.'

'When did this happen?'

'Do you care?' he accused her, drawing his sleeve across his nose like a kid and glancing up at Freya. 'Do you actually want to know?'

'Don't be silly. That's just silly.'

'Oh, so now I'm silly?'

'Well, yes, actually.' She censored the word *childish*. Also the word *performance*. And *tantrum*. 'I wouldn't have asked you if I hadn't wanted to know, Mark. Would I?'

Just leave, Freya told herself, get the hell out of here, the guy locked you in. He's totally unbalanced. Where was her damn phone? Somehow she stopped short of asking. What was she waiting for? Instead, she hesitated and perched opposite Mark on the edge of a chair, between him and the door.

'Pearl. They said Pearl was worrying sheep.' Tears bled out of his eyes. He thumbed them away.

'But when was this, Mark?'

'What does it matter, when it was?'

You're letting me down, Mark's irascible manner implied; you're missing the point. Try to keep up.

'You never mentioned a dog, Mark. Well, you did. You mentioned a dog called... I can't remember, but not Pearl. Beauty, or Bliss, or something like that. And your lodger said something about a Labrador. Was that the same dog?'

'That was another dog. But the real dog I loved, the dog that loved me, the dog that taught me everything I know of love, she was Pearl.'

Freya thought for a moment. He seemed to be in a muddle as to which dog was which and whether any of them were real. Mark had once praised a counsellor, Valerie or Nancy, who'd helped him in the past, in his bereavement. This was surely the person he needed to unburden himself to. Freya was not qualified to help. But how to indicate this now, how to slip away and run for safety, to Storm, to the crescent, she couldn't work out. It was leaving a wounded man to bleed out.

The night he'd fallen asleep on her settee came vividly to mind. The bellowing of an animal in terminal pain. A creature begging for the *coup de grâce*.

'Shall we go downstairs, Mark?' she suggested soothingly. 'And you can tell me about Pearl. Of course it makes no difference when you lost her. It's sad to lose a dog. It hurts so much, I know, I understand.'

'You won't leave me, Freya, will you?'

'Not until you're feeling better. It's all right.'

That did not satisfy him but it was the best he was going to get. In the kitchen, Freya made mugs of tea. Mark sat hunched at the window, looking out at the bushes. Occasionally his shoulders shuddered. But he was calmer now and so was Freya. In her mind, she had left him; bolted the door of her heart and quit. That recognition left her feeling easier. In future, she should and would avoid Mark. There was some toxic suffering within him that was trying to spread. The counsellor was his best hope. Poor guy, he must feel mortified.

She really should take off the backpack. It would draw attention to itself. She compromised by shifting it on to one shoulder, while she placed the mugs on a tray and found the biscuits.

'I'm sorry, Freya,' Mark murmured, back still turned, after-tremors shaking his voice. 'I don't know where to look, I'm your host and I meant to give you such a gentle day and I've made an absolute ass of myself. It all comes over me – not often, very rarely – as if I need to get it out of me, and then I'm fine again, and free, and the thing is,' he swivelled and eyed her, continuing more confidently, 'I can draw on this pain to help people. The youngsters who come to me at the gallery, for instance. That's the only positive about trauma, isn't it? It is experience, you examine and learn from it and pass on the wisdom. My counsellor –'

'You've mentioned her. Nancy, was it, or Valerie?'

'Val.'

'She sounds wonderful.'

'She is. She is what Pasternak calls "the good gift on the road to destruction".'

'That's good then. I hope this is not too strong? Or weak?'

He accepted the tea and refused the biscuits.

'Throw them away, Freya. Really, chuck them. They're stale. No, really, they're not appetising.'

Val was remarkable, he said, as they moved through to the living-room. Val could shine a light into the very depths of human suffering. He looked happier just for hearing and speaking the name Val. She meant wisdom to him, Mark explained; Val meant grounding in the here-and-now. And, yes, he and Val had gone over the subject of his dear old dog together – but, alas, a counsellor was not a magician! His voice had strengthened – he was authoritative now – and this would be how he'd be at the museum, Freya felt. He was explaining that no counsellor, even one as skilled as Val, could wave a wand to undo trauma.

Mark was staring, as he said all this, at the backpack. Freya placed it beside her chair, with her foot on one of the straps. He noticed that too. She saw him noticing. She saw him noticing that she had noticed him noticing.

'Perhaps,' Freya suggested, 'you might find it helpful to talk about this to Val again?'

'I know what you're thinking,' he said coolly.

She froze. 'You do?'

'Oh yes. You're wondering why a grown man would get so upset about a cocker spaniel that died over thirty years ago. What if I told you that my adored mother died the same year? She was twenty-six. I was seven.'

*

'Oh *no*,' Freya said, shocked. 'How terrible for you.'

He saw her taking it in, seeing what he'd intended her to see: the mother-loss not quite represented by Pearl but somehow covered by her. Poignant understanding flickered in Freya's face. She showed him the face he needed to see: the gentle and compassionate face he had fallen in love with when he first arrived at the crescent. She forgot to keep fingering the scruffy old rucksack and glancing towards the door. He had secured Freya's full attention. I have bared my heart to you, Mark said silently. Please don't let me down.

He began to quote Louis MacNeice, also forever a motherless child: *My mother wore a yellow dress – Gentle, gently, gentleness – Come back early or never come.* 'And, strangely enough,' Mark said, 'my own mother wore a yellow dress.'

'Did she really? You remember her?'

'For many years I didn't, Freya. I suppose I blocked her out. That's what Val thought, and it makes sense. But quite recently the memories began to surface. As much the sensation of her skin, the scent of her, as the image. They say our first memories are imprinted at the age of three. Mine seem to go back earlier. The yellow dress. More primrose yellow than buttercup, I'd say. It was sleeveless, with straps, and made of cotton, I think, quite thin fabric, a summer frock. She wore a locket with a curl of my baby hair in it.'

Mark's imagination began to paint his mother with such vivid brush strokes that he created her in his mind's eye: a quite commonplace woman, but not ordinary to Mark. She was bread and milk. She was the solid earth of belonging, where your first footsteps had been planted. Her hair was light brown, her eyes blue. She had loved wild flowers.

Liar, said Lily in Mark's mind. *You are incapable of telling the truth.* Lily seemed to swarm about his head, as she had on the stairs, accusing him. And saying she wanted a divorce, she didn't love him, had never loved him.

You must go, Mark.

What do you mean, I must go?

Leave, go. It's over.

I'm going nowhere. This is my home. You go. If you want someone to go, go yourself.

It's my house, my family's house. I was born here. I can't have you in my home any longer, Mark. You're dangerous.

Don't say that! I'm warning you, don't – say – it!

And he had run amok. What had she expected? She had spoken the curse which could not be retracted.

In point of fact Mark never lied. He excavated a form for deep truth. The form was a hollow in which a truth can lie. This was what people were too thick to understand. They took for dissimulation what was in fact an attempt to clarify a reality that lay beyond the scope of words. Yes, some of what one said might be metaphorical. But metaphor was not the same as mendacity. Mark lived on his wits, forever seeking to cover the void with something that could be visualised. What is one to say of a mother never seen? It was Mark's need that named itself by dressing her in a yellow frock, pale slip-on shoes, an Alice band holding back thin mouse-brown hair.

But the face? He could conjure no face.

'So who looked after you, Mark? Your dad?'

He shook his head and put out a hand as if to ward off the question. Freya took the hint and did not press.

Mark was going to say something more about the dress, or other dresses, how she wore her hair in bunches (for she was very young), how she used to sing 'Row, row, row your boat' when she bathed Mark, and lifted him out wrapped in a green towel which had a little hood on one corner (he must have been very small), and cuddled him dry, kissing his face all the while, and read him a bedtime story (his favourite was one about Bambi but all her stories were lovely and while they were being read, he'd look from the page to her face, from face to page, pointing at the pictures). He was going to let this stream of invented memory pour out, when the backlash set in, as it was always going to do when you dreamed these fond dreams.

For Freya said, kindly, 'I'm sure it's true that if you have been mothered in early life, that presence always stays with you, you can't come to grief, not ultimately. It is beautiful that you have these memories, Mark. Thank you for telling me about her.'

He rocked violently to and fro.

'Oh no, have I said the wrong thing?'

He shook his head, still rocking.

'Forgive me.' Freya reached out and took his hand. She squeezed it and let go, as they always let go. She tried again. 'My mum was just there, a given.'

She was compounding her error. Mark's pain intensified. They all boasted of having mothers, it was normal to have a mother, they wore their mothers on their sleeves. And if the mothers died, there'd be a dad to fall back on. He rocked harder and breathing could only be managed by concentrating on it. How come they could never intuit the truth behind the fiction? They were supposed to have intuition.

Freya went careering on down this false trail. 'I can hardly begin to imagine how it must have been for you, to lose your mum at such a young age.'

She seemed to recede. Her mouth was moving. Mark focused on the tip of her ear. A butterfly ear ring trembled there as she talked. He would have liked to snare it between finger and thumb, and pull, and rip the lobe. That would switch off her self-satisfaction. There was something perfidious about Freya. One discerned it in the way she sat, knees to one side, left hand half concealed in her shirt cuff. The other hand dangled over the chair arm, fingertips on the backpack. It was not a comfortable posture.

Something was different about the backpack. But what?

When she'd upended the thing over the carpet (he glanced with a forensic eye at the detritus), Freya's wallet and hairbrush had fallen out. And nothing else.

The bag had been empty.

Now it bulged, crammed to the gills, he realised, with a solid object, or a collection of solid objects. A very odd shape. My God, Mark thought, the woman's helped herself to something of mine! Never in a million years would he have suspected Freya of being capable of theft. Danielle Jones, yes. Freya Fox, no.

The rocking had ceased. Mark shook his head, incredulous, and whistled through his teeth. She stopped in mid-sentence.

Anxiety wrinkled the woman's forehead and it aged her. She put up her hand – the one with the blue stain – to her mouth. He was fascinated. Freya now appeared in her true light, as an unknown quantity. You did not know people, Mark thought. You only got a clue when you stumbled on some vital inconsistency. Whatever did he possess that, given her alleged unworldliness, Freya desired? Something poked out where the twin zips met – something jagged.

'Freya – oh dear – could you fetch me a glass of water?' he asked hoarsely, coughing and patting his chest.

'Are you OK?'

'Please. Water.' Mark tugged at his collar and pointed to the door, jabbing his forefinger.

And she was out. He heard her in the kitchen, running the tap. When she returned with the glass, he was positioned in the bow window with the backpack in his arms.

'Here's your –. What are you doing, Mark?'

'There's something of mine in here –'

'What do you mean, something of yours? Of course there's not. Give it back. I said – give it fucking back. What's the matter with you?'

'I will give it back. When I've checked.'

It was all over now, the gentle wooing, the roses, the yellow dress. Mark could see that it had always been over, from before the beginning. Her face was feral. She was a woman who habitually used gutter language. He smelt the sweat in her armpits as she lunged for the backpack.

Built on such a small scale, Freya was stronger than he could ever have imagined.

He hung on. And she hung on. It was ridiculous. They stood there yanking the thing this way and that, like angry kids in a playground. As they tugged and tussled, the zip that closed the thing split apart.

Some of its contents clattered to the floor and the window seat. He let go, contemplating them in wonderment.

'What's this mess? What have you broken?' he demanded.

'Nothing. It *was* broken.'

Recognition: Lily's viola. Of course. Lily had lied when she claimed to have thrown it in a skip. The horror of betrayal swept over him. It roared in his ears.

'Why have you taken this, Freya?' he asked quietly. 'Why?'

Her face was flushed and hot. She mumbled, 'Because of what your lodger told me.'

'My *lodger*?'

'Danielle.'

'Which was?'

'I want my phone back, Mark, and then I'm going.'

'You can go, Freya, when you have explained this theft. Of my property.'

'Oh? Is it yours? I don't think so!'

'You come here as my guest. You ransack my house. You steal something utterly – priceless. And you have the effrontery –'

She was leaving now, the woman insisted. Immediately. She hadn't stolen anything. And in case he'd forgotten, he'd locked her in his frigging bedroom! She'd come across this evidence of – she stumbled – evidence of – damage. She'd cleared it up.

She knew, she said recklessly, about his wife.

Don't say that, Mark thought, taking a step towards her. I really wouldn't, if I were you. Part of him felt for Freya Fox in her ignorance.

It didn't want her to head down that path, in the wake of *that woman*, from which there was no returning. He remembered – but as if it had all taken place years ago – his tenderness for Freya, the pitying kinship of his vigil, the roses he'd wanted to give her. Those roses would have cost a hundred pounds, more, from the florist.

'I'm sorry to have upset you, Mark,' she said, quickly backtracking, for she'd certainly read the look in his eyes, even if she could not decipher its precise meaning. 'I'm sorry about the viola. Really. I apologise. Nothing to do with me. Of course. It was on the spur of the moment.'

She took two steps back. Her breath came raggedly. She smelt of guilt.

'I don't know what came over me. Well, yes I do. I thought that if you came across the instrument yourself, the memory would be so painful – so I guess I felt I could spare you that –'

Good try, Mark thought. He caught the cajoling tone of her improvisation and was not deceived. She was emptying the backpack, laying the shards and splinters on a cloth before him.

'I think it's the grief,' she ad-libbed. 'For my husband. And obviously you have your own grief. For your wife. And there was a muddle between the two griefs. We are not good for each other, Mark, with all the grief we're both carrying. I think we can both see that now.'

She brought out the scroll of the viola. What remained of tuning pegs and pegbox came next. Strings. Neck. Bridge, fingerboard, chinrest. Scraps of ebony. The broken bow, like an impotent whip with its horsehair strings hanging.

This woman had no idea. None at all. Of what she'd done. Of what she'd let loose. Mark needed a cup of hot chocolate and a couple of codeine, or even a Xanax, needed them urgently. And where was today's newspaper? Had he even brought it with him? He hadn't done the crossword. No day had started properly if the crossword had not been solved. Or only one day. That day. Freya opened the neck of the bag so that he could see its emptiness.

'That's the whole lot,' she said. 'There wasn't any more. Could I have my phone back, Mark?'

He opened his hands to indicate that he hadn't a clue as to the whereabouts of Freya's phone. It was wherever she had put it.

'Mark! My phone!'

'Your phone?'

'Where is my phone?'

'How should I know?'

'Please. And then I'll – well, actually, I'll go now, and sod the phone.'

Mark didn't follow. He stood waiting, tapping the bow against the window frame. The woman was at the front door. It was locked.

He heard her flee through the house. Perhaps he had already done the crossword and just forgotten about it? Feeling in his trouser pocket, he located the emergency Valium: good. He would make a cup of chocolate shortly and take two.

Now she was at the back door, wrenching at the handle. There was a silence. He could tell that she was trying the window. No. Painted in. Every ground floor window was painted in. For obvious reasons.

Again, silence. She'd be taking stock, attempting to calibrate her mind so as to gain control over her situation.

Now that he had the prospect of the Valium and the hot chocolate, Mark already felt more tranquil. Ambling through the corridor towards the kitchen, he noted the gold-inlaid titles on the leather spines of his antiquarian books. The collection was worth tens of thousands. Well, that might be a bit grandiose: let's say thousands – and get a nice surprise on valuation. He ran a finger down the spine of a work of alchemy – third edition, mid-seventeenth century – when alchemy was really on its way out, so this rare book had been a golden find. There was no hurry. Mark felt a curious release from the throb of sorrow and rage. He walked into his own vacuum of emotion as into a safe-house. He hadn't yet done today's crossword: no, that was a smudge on the day. Generally, by this time, he'd completed the Easy Crossword in a matter of ten minutes as a warm-up exercise for the so-called Cryptic Crossword. But there was time.

'Unlock the doors, Mark,' Freya called. 'For Christ's sake, what are you on?'

'Yes, Freya, OK, I'm going to do just that.'

Her shoulders lowered. He'd changed his mind about the hot chocolate. Tea would be more soothing. Mark strolled to the kettle, checked the water level and switched on. He'd always liked this kettle, a burgundy red, the water level indicator a luminous blue. There was a speck of something on the handle, hardly more than a few molecules, but when you are aware of stains, you need to do something about them. He removed it with a piece of kitchen paper, then bent to observe the effect close to. Perfect.

'What the hell are you doing, Mark?'

'Making a cuppa.' He wondered why he'd started making tea when it was hot chocolate he craved.

'You've just said – you'll unlock the doors.'

'I will. All in good time.' Mark looked her in the eye with perfect equanimity.

'What do you mean – not yet? Why are you looking at me like that?'

'Like what?'

'Open the fucking door, Mark, I said open it and let me out! I'll call the police.'

She ran out into the corridor, kicked at the door and yanked the handle. Mark had seen it all before. How rapidly they abdicated reason and descended into childish tantrum. It was like watching a performance over his own shoulder.

Mark explained. Freya was his guest. As her host, one had done all in one's power to make her feel welcome. But perhaps she could understand that tampering with his property constituted an abuse of hospitality? They would be going upstairs together after they'd drunk their tea.

Now the woman really looked alarmed. She was going nowhere, she yelled, except out! Home!

When he could get a word in, Mark carried on. The reason they were going upstairs together was—

Again, the uproar. She wasn't going upstairs, was her theme.

The *reason*, he continued equably, was so that she could show him exactly where she'd found the instrument. Then he would let her out.

Freya shut up but remained standing by the open door.

She didn't want tea? Sure? No tea at all? He could make her Earl Grey, if she preferred? With lemon? Or camomile tea was calming? He thought he had a packet of green tea, if she fancied it? He could check? No?

Well, Mark, for one, was thirsty. He parked himself at the kitchen table, placed the pill on his tongue and swallowed it with a mouthful of tea. He took his time. At such rare intervals, he felt unselfconscious. No nervous tics. No jiggling of the foot as he crossed one leg over the other.

The humidity, he saw as he glanced out of the window, had broken and a fine rain was falling. Not enough to make a difference to the plants but it was a start.

Mark looked Freya straight in the eyes and kept the stare going.

20

Nobody at the crescent was about as Mark unlatched the back door and stepped out onto the moist lawn. There was an intermittent buzzing in his ears, like electricity on the blink. Think calm thoughts, he told himself, live in the present moment like the Buddhists. For in the moment was an eternity of peace. The grass could do with mowing when it had had a chance to dry out.

The cramped banality of the terrace had never fitted one's aspirations, but on the other hand, given that Tŷ Hafan signified a haven, one had always thought of the crescent as a refuge. A refuge from the Refuge, so to speak. It seemed so now.

He'd left a quandary sequestered at Tŷ Hafan. Here at the crescent, the little people went pottering about their business, narrow minds inhabiting narrow houses. Rather consolatory that they continued with their petty business, whatever was happening in the wider world.

Beside the fernery near the ornamental pond, he happened on the mess. Never mind. Omm. Think Buddha and send the crap home! Mark had to snigger as he took aim. The hilarity did him good. Up sailed Pansy's turds, high over Freya's garden, scoring a direct hit on Terence's plaster gnome.

Mark disinfected the trowel, stowed it away, washed his hands. But were they clean? He inspected them, holding his nails close to his eyes. A trace of dirt was ingrained but they would do for the moment.

The next thing on the list was making an appointment with Dr Lewis. Mark cajoled, then harangued the receptionist. Tomorrow morning, please, not next week. Yes, an emergency, of course it was an emergency! I'm in terrible pain! No, I don't need to go to A&E! When Mark hung up, he was assured of Lewis's first appointment of the day and the morphine prescription was as good as in his pocket.

Next thing: the dog. He'd seen Storm with his paws up on the window-sill, a patient sentinel, watching for his mistress.

Mark let himself in to Freya's house; the animal met him in the hall. It backed away, licking its nose, yawning. A growl rose in its throat. Mark stepped forward and stood over Storm, arms akimbo, silently reminding the animal who was pack leader in this house. You are the pack, my friend, and I am your leader. So I advise you to get into line. Got it?

The animal looked away.

Since there was no sign whatever of welcome or familiarity, Mark said nothing to the dog. Two can play at that game. Nevertheless, he filled the water bowl and Storm drank thirstily. Snapping on the lead, Mark opened the back door, to allow Storm to empty his bowels and bladder.

Was that another growl he heard? Storm stared, pupils dilated. When a dog threatens to turn against you, be oh so watchful, Mark reminded himself. Even a peaceable breed can challenge you for dominance. When Storm had done his business, Mark bagged the poop and pointed to the house to indicate that there was no walkies.

In, at once. That's right, slink in. Know your place.

When you show me a modicum of natural affection, Mark thought, I'll consider treats and din-dins. And not before.

Using Freya's laptop, he googled tinnitus. Apparently it might be the result of a change in stress levels – and was understood to be brain activity interpreted as sound. That sounded plausible. His stress levels were off the map, that was for sure. Mark had the impression that the high-pitched noise was blocking off something worse.

Sitting here in Freya's moth-eaten chair, the shock began to filter back: the violence of the irruption. The fractured body of the viola had exploded from the bag. The way Mark remembered it, a shrapnel of shards came bursting out. And look, a splinter had indeed grazed his wrist, where the veins fork close to the surface.

Superficial, yes, maybe. But he'd make sure to dab on zinc ointment: the smallest cuts turned septic on Mark.

What he could not get his mind round was the treachery. Freya had acted just like Lily! She'd even looked like Lily when he found her out. There was a vicious expression on that corporate face, call it fear if you like, but what is the root of women's violence if not fear? She deserved the penalty he had imposed.

Storm appeared beside the arm of the chair. The animal did not fawn or lick Mark's hand, just searched him over the parapet with sombre eyes.

'I expect you're hungry, boy, aren't you?'

Well, it was only a matter of time. Storm would get round to begging. The intelligence in the dog's eyes was unsettling.

'You shouldn't have been such a greedy boy, should you, snaffling up what she left you in the bowl all in one gobble? Naughty, naughty.'

He tapped the lab on the snout, in mocking reproof. The dog's nostrils pulsed. Storm was sucking up his scent, working out what the complicated musk of emotion and intention – that flowed on Mark's breath and in his sweat – might mean.

Mark stood up and ordered, 'Heel!'

Round and round the living-room they trekked, the puzzled dog walking (to do him justice) pretty well to heel.

'Sit!'

Storm sat. He lay down to order. The only thing he refused to do was roll over on his back, a vulnerable position. I will get you doing that, my friend, before you are allowed your meal, Mark silently told him. When he pointed to the door, Storm left the room.

'Basket!'

A scutter of compliant paws. It must be said, the dog knew who was master. But if he thought he was getting a treat, Storm was mistaken. He had to do more than obey orders. He must show love and affection.

How could Mark forgive the violence and betrayal? In the end, she'd followed him upstairs, superficially as biddable as Storm was now and just as dumbly hostile. She'd indicated the cubby he'd missed. Kneeling, he'd fished around in its bowels: nothing remained to be found.

However could he have missed that cubby in the first place? But he had. Mark had assumed he knew every inch of Tŷ Hafan – all its tricks and architectural jests, the *trompe l'oeil* that was its outward face. In this instance, the architect had outwitted him. And possibly in others. Danielle had stowed the horror in there, and now Freya had located the space and truffled out the relic.

She hadn't wanted to go upstairs with him. No, but what choice had she? Freya was compelled to revisit the scene of her folly and have her nose rubbed in her own mess. It was the way you trained recalcitrant dogs.

Mark had been glad enough to lock the front door behind him, buckle up in the car and glide out into the lane. Driving through a veil of drizzle, he'd been steadied by the certainty of return to the quotidian world. The windscreen wipers had thudded softly; he'd sucked a mint and played a Schubert CD. Meeting a car in the lane, he'd backed up courteously, responding to the guy's grateful wave as he passed. Back to civilisation.

He was aroused now from his reverie by a tapping sound from outside Freya's window. Eyes were gawping in through the pane, shaded by a fat hand. Of course. Mark had known it wouldn't take long for the worm to slime out of its hole.

'Terence,' he said, opening the front door. 'How are you? Oh, and Pamela too. How nice.'

Pamela seemed to be dressed in jodhpurs. Had the plump lady taken, in late middle age, to equestrian sports? Or were these pantaloons her version of Fashion? The Crouches' faces were stony. Where was Freya? they wished to know. They didn't ask aloud what Mark was doing in her house.

'Freya has asked me to take care of Storm for her,' Mark explained. Storm appeared, pat, at his side and he ruffled the animal's silky head. 'Did she not mention to you that she was going away for a week or so?'

'Going away?'

'That's right.'

'Away? Without mentioning it to anyone?'

'Well, she has told me. We discussed it, Terence. Don't worry.'

'I see.' The chap didn't see. He glanced at Pamela doubtfully.

'She has gone to stay with a friend, Terence. A friend from uni. I do think, all things considered, that it was the best thing. You know,' Mark confided, 'I had the feeling that we were crowding her here. Not allowing her to breathe.'

Had these net-curtain-peepers witnessed Mark taking her out in the car?

'I drove her to the station,' he informed them, just in case.

Storm pushed his way past Mark and dug his snuffling nose into Terence's corduroy crotch. He licked the chap's hands, wagging his tail. Black mark, Storm, thought Mark. Remember which side your bread is buttered. Your bone, rather.

'So – where precisely has Freya gone? Pammie has been ringing and ringing, haven't you, Pammie? It goes straight to voice message. And her brother has been phoning us. Everyone's worried.'

'Brother-*in-law*,' Mark corrected him.

'Pardon?'

'They're not blood relations, Terence,' Mark explained patiently. 'Brothers-in-*law,* I think you'll find.'

'Whatever. What the heck does it matter?'

There was all the difference in the world – but perhaps don't labour this point, Mark counselled himself. Pamela, one could see, was a beat away from going into fishwife mode. He felt the most rancid annoyance with the pair of them. Storm, meanwhile, had graduated from Terence to his wife and was rubbing his flank against her strange-looking legs. Perhaps she'd come across the jodhpurs in the bottom of her wardrobe and conscience had exhorted her, *Waste not, want not.*

'Oh, she's gone to Keighley.' Mark was mildly surprised to hear himself name this destination. Invention bubbled beneath the surface of one's brain, a fluent stream. 'Town near Bradford – moors.'

'I know where *Keighley* is, Mark,' Pamela said sharply. 'I'm not stupid.'

Oh, really? His eyebrows rose.

Refraining from comment, Mark assured the pair that Freya had arrived safely at the well-known northern town of Keighley, a place famous for cotton mills, steam engines and proximity to the Brontës.

'Quite a long and tedious journey,' he observed, with a tinge of a northern accent. 'Several changes of train are involved.'

From this new perspective, Mark seemed to see Freya meandering through purple moorland, dressed in a long skirt. The bilberries would be reddening on the bushes. One would see for miles across the heath. Like Emily Brontë, Freya could breathe the crystal air of freedom and dream of Things Wuthering.

'We'll carry on ringing her,' Terence said. He'd been signalling to his wife to keep her wrath under wraps. Did married couples really think folk didn't notice their minute head-shakings and elbowings?

'I'll give her your best,' Mark assured the Crouches. 'Can't invite you in, I'm afraid. Obviously. In charge of the house for the nonce.' The nonce: a term Terry wouldn't be familiar with, at least not in this connection. Good for the guy to stretch his tiny mind. 'Storm! In! Now!'

Closing Freya's door, Mark went rapidly back over the conversation. Am I getting reckless in my old age? he asked himself. Superior intellect had always provided a safety net, outwitting all and sundry. He'd often had to secure his inventions with secondary off-the-cuff inventions but in the end the web had held, more or less. And he'd carefully documented major innovations, noting the proliferating minor details on spider charts, as these were most likely to slip even a formidable memory. While in a way Mark enjoyed the element of risk, he'd always sought to buffer it. Was one getting careless? What about the brothers-in-law? They would not have heard of friends in Keighley. Well, the gym-bunnies could not expect to be party to every aspect of Freya's life. Others would be on her trail, for instance the hysteric dressed as a field of buttercups who'd ranted at the funeral – but Mark had not clapped eyes on her since the wake and was fairly sure she was out of favour. And there was Lawyer Lady whose kid had the bladder problem. But hadn't Freya said that Lawyer Lady was going on holiday to Parma or Las Palmas or some such tourist destination?

Then there was the lady herself. She was safe for now.

Mark took out the packet of dog food from the cupboard and shook it in Storm's face. The animal had been brought to heel, expeditiously. But Storm still had a way to go.

'Not yet,' he said, holding the packet high out of reach. 'You've got to earn your keep, my friend.'

Storm stared, not at the packet but at Mark, as if in disbelief.

*

He'd slept, somewhat against his will; napped, rather, for it was still early when Mark began to come to, tearful and alone in a house that was not his own, afraid for the creature that depended on him, and on him alone, for survival.

The two of them were grudgingly tolerated. They dared not put a foot wrong. But that was what they managed to do, at every turn. The laws of the house were stacked against them. Or, rather, they did not grasp the rules. If he could have understood the conditions of their existence (for he was a bright boy, the brightest in his class, even *she* recognised that), in this house, which was the world, the two of them could have made some adaptation. He was sure of that. The fact was, they both wanted to obey. They were eager, even. There was very little they would not do to obtain a smile from *her*.

The boy hated it that Pearl's ribs showed through. When he stroked her back, the spine rippled beneath his tender fingers. Despite all Mark could do, she was chronically underfed. But where *was* Pearl? Not in the house, not in the back yard. Where? Had something happened to her?

It was all right: here she was, she pattered in, he started to rouse and raise himself, here you are, my beauty, come to Markie, it's all right. He'd offer Pearl his porridge and she would lick the bowl clean. Yesterday, or the day before, or last week, Mark had been caught slipping out to the yard where Pearl, for some misdeed, was tethered, and he'd chucked the slab of congealed porridge on the ground for her, even as the hand gripped his shoulder and whirled him round. The glutinous mass slapped down in a dollop. He loathed the porridge anyway but Pearl did not mind, it filled her belly, she'd wolf it as if she'd dreamed all night of such a feast.

The paws came chasing across the linoleum and her breath was on his face, her beautiful breath. He opened his eyes.

'Of course – it's you. Darling Storm.'

Pearl was long gone and he had survived her death.

Listen, Mark told himself, sitting up and taking Storm's face in both hands, kissing the soft forehead, Pearl would have died anyway. She was not young. And *she* was safely underground, a pitiful, bitter, truculent pauper who'd never been given enough to have anything extra to give. Someone must have brutalised her before he was born. It was all a long time ago. His grandmother had been a woman wholly lacking in imagination. And he had always had too much.

It was Lily, darling Lily, in those early days his dearest friend in the world, who had taught him these truths and helped Mark to carry on living, for he hadn't wanted to live. She had opened apertures in his darkness and shone the light of her understanding through them. Lily had possessed wisdom, not only in her hands for the viola but in her heart for her friends. She had been the one who took both his hands and said, *Mark, you have survived all that. Let's live in the present moment now.*

But Lily had not been able to resist the warping of love that was his legacy.

In the kitchen, Mark fumbled the dog food down from the cupboard and tipped an ample helping into the bowl. What am I becoming, he asked himself, sitting cross legged on the tiles with one hand on the dog's back while he fed. Am I turning into Gran?

He offered a treat. As a kind of dessert. A little extra. There should always be extra. There should be some measure of extravagance. You don't have to do anything to earn this, he assured Storm. Just be. Who could ask you for more than that, you gracious animal? Storm made short work of the treat and Mark produced another. He wasn't hungry himself, not in any way that could have been assuaged by bread and cheese.

Bread and wine, perhaps. The priest had said ... what had the priest said? I'm so bad, he'd told the priest, like a child that has started to pee his pants and fears punishment and is hanging on to his squalid groin for dear life. *Lean in to love, my son.* So spoke the unseen northern baritone through the grille. But Mark had flinched from confessing the full truth. Perhaps nobody did tell the full truth, and the confessors knew that, and made allowance.

Besides, truth morphs, the more you ponder it. There are as many ways to tell a story as there are grains of sand. Grief twists into guilt. He was sure that Val, had she been real, would have counselled this. She would have said, *Your priest was right. Love yourself, Mark. Be merciful to yourself. This is the beginning of wisdom: the alpha that leads to the omega of universal charity.* Well she might not have referred to alpha and omega, since Val would not have known Greek. But she would have offered the same honey to his hunger.

As to his wife in their early days: how could he reconcile that person with the wreck she'd become? She was two people. No one could lay the killing of Lily's music at Mark's door. Could they? It must have been in her from the beginning. Surely it must. All he had done was to love her but their course must have been set from the start on self-destruction.

You are kidding yourself, she had accused him. *You are full of shit, Mark. Throw yourself out of the window, why don't you?*

She shouldn't have said that.

*

Tŷ Hafan was quenched: no light showed in any window. He'd been fearful on Freya's account; now he shrank with fear of her. If she'd injured herself in some way – what would Mark do? What could he say? Once is reckoned a tragic accident. But twice?

Twice, he thought, is Nemesis.

He had not pushed her, he was sure of that. And the medication had had no long-lasting effect. Mark had nothing to reproach himself with. But he continued to sit in the car, hunched, paralysed, gripping the hand brake. There was a *thing* in there. He could not go in and meet it. He ratcheted up the handbrake a notch. Stop that, you will break it, he told himself, and then what? He removed his left hand with his right.

'What shall we do, Stormie?' he whispered, seeking comfort in the dog's warm pelt. 'Whatever shall we do?'

Lips drawn back, Storm's head strained forward, over the passenger seat, and he panted. His body quivered. He took no notice of Mark. Could Storm detect her scent from here? Surely not. And the car must be swimming in it anyway.

What if Freya were lying where Lily had splayed herself, arms twisted like a puppet's?

What if she were dying and not dead?

*

He was plunging into the void, it was always there, his stomach lurched as he lost balance, it could not be otherwise, it was born with him, the void. It had happened before and it would happen again. This was predestined, he had always known there was no escape from the irony of infinite repetition.

301

He hadn't tried to minister to his wife: too furious after the row. Did she honestly think she could win an argument by staging a melodrama and flinging herself downstairs?

She lay with her legs disturbingly open.

Leave her where she was. Lily would surface in her own time. She'd done this before, he was sick to death of it, there was nothing physically wrong with her, she might be concussed and if so she'd vomit all over the carpet, she'd do that anyway, he loathed people throwing up, she was always at it, mixing wine and spirits in God knew what quantities. Put a bucket there? No, she would make sure to miss it.

*

She never cleaned up after herself. Was that too much to ask?

*

Edging down the stairs, he'd stepped in trepidation across her abject body, holding his breath. There was no blood that he could see. He only exhaled when he'd entered the living-room. The half-read Sunday papers were spread on the coffee table, lit up in a parallelogram of late afternoon light.

*

He'd cleared his throat. The shouting match having strained one's larynx, one did not want another bout of laryngitis. Straining the vocal cords and opening them to infection, as happened all too often, aroused the suspicion of throat cancer. There was always a fear tucked in behind the fear. Behind that cloaked fear would lurk another, worse, and so on, layer upon layer, leading back to the mother and father of all terror.

And so he'd stepped over her, cleared his throat, entered the silent room with the papers and the lozenge of brightness, and closed the door behind him. He'd gravitated to the window where, holding his specs up to the light, he'd huffed on the lenses and polished them with his handkerchief. He'd folded the handkerchief with care and restored it to his pocket. He'd patted the pocket. All done with deliberation.

*

The crossword. He remembered seating himself on the couch, reaching for the newspaper and a pen. Child's-play, all but a couple of answers, which Mark could not for the life of him figure out. And this was the so-called Easy Crossword, not the Cryptic!

He'd cudgelled his brain. No... no... nothing. A vein had throbbed at his temple. He'd glared at the crossword, personally insulted. The two answers had been on the tip of one's mind, they provoked one by remaining under cover.

*

There'd been an interruption, preventing Mark from solving the clues. He was aware of a strange noise, an agitation, a flurry – in the wall, was it? Hard to say where it was located.

Once a pigeon had got itself trapped in the chimney. He'd heard it die, the tiny tempest of an alien life. The RSPCA wouldn't come and shortly it began to smell. It had made him ill. He'd rung a man to deal with it, at his own expense, but as usual the man was slow to turn up. When eventually he did deign to appear, the man brought down soot into the living-room and a bird's blackened corpse. The man had not been careful enough in placing his sheets on the carpet to catch the mess.

*

So, on the day of Lily's leap –

– and really how could it be called a fall? – he'd many times counselled her about holding on to the banister when intoxicated – and he'd been thwarted by the crossword puzzle, which had never yet beaten him – given all this – and the concern about a trapped pigeon and the soot – it was natural, upon hearing the shuffling, fluttering, whatever it was, to suspect the presence of vermin. The thought of the outside getting inside always turned one's stomach. And his wife had turned it already with her hostility.

She had prostrated herself at the bottom of the stairs, as if to say, *Well, what are you going to do now?*

*

Given all these quandaries, Mark had felt he should swallow two tranquillisers and have a hot drink with plenty of sugar. In the kitchen, boiling milk for hot chocolate, whistling to himself, he'd done his utmost not to listen out for whatever-it-was in the chimney. The Valium had taken its time to kick in. He remembered shaking cinnamon on the froth and parking himself at the table, sipping, rubbing at the whorls in the blond wood as if they were blemishes. In the quiet, he'd concentrated on those whorls and the clock's tick-tick.

*

Sounds had intruded again. They were coming from the hallway. *Damn you, leave me alone!* In the end, but not until he'd finished the hot chocolate and rinsed the mug, he'd sighed and gone out to see to her, meaning to haul Lily up from her shameful degradation and drag her off to bed.

Stop – that – bloody – noise!

*

Sitting now, in the car outside a house so dark that it appeared windowless, Mark was aware of a seething beneath the mind's surface, mental magma, red-hot. There are memories that cannot permit themselves to be remembered. They are caught in an internal wall-space.

*

Mark switched his mind to the crossword, which had obsessed him then and whose obstinacy retained the power to distract, sitting here in the car outside Tŷ Hafan, staring at the blind windows. Whatever had been those clues that one couldn't solve? No idea now.

*

He'd bent to her, that was true; he'd shaken her shoulder.

He couldn't help remembering that the crossword answers had seemed to surface as he'd stumbled up from where she lay, and arranged his clothes, and tried not to look down at what she'd become.

It had been her choice. To abandon him. To forsake and desert him. To stab him in the back. Icy-calm, Mark had returned to the living-room to complete the puzzle.

*

To one's bafflement – and, almost, disgrace – neither of the puzzle answers had fitted, even on the second attempt. Over and over again he'd reread the clues. No synonym fitted the given number of squares. And Mark was a man who could have been a grand master, had he ever learned to play chess.

Perhaps the crossword-setter had miscalculated. It could happen. The world is riddled with human slovenliness.

Mark had given up trying: not a good day, not good at all. Twice he'd set his mind against the puzzle and twice he'd failed.

*

Round and round we go.

*

In a cold sweat and for the second time, he'd stepped smartly through the hall and hurried back to the kitchen, looking neither to left nor right.

Soon, he'd thought, soon, very soon, Mark would work out what to do about the situation in which he found himself. Call police and ambulance. And say? He could not decide. He remembered whistling the *Allegro* from *Eine Kleine Nachtmusik*. The puzzle had continued to irk him. When he'd stopped whistling, there came a buzzing sound. Where the hell did it come from?

A fluorescent strip had been on the blink. A couple of flies had somehow got trapped in there. Everything was sullied. The strip fizzed. The noise in Mark's ears swelled till it seemed like the wailing of fiddles in some woeful postmodern piece, which will never end except in the grave of music.

*

Apart from that, the house had been quiet.

Snuffed it, he'd thought, without emotion. She's snuffed it. At last. This had been Lily's stated aim in life.

Despite the tintinnabulation and despite needing to clean himself up, he'd repeated like a robot every compulsive action he'd already taken, since she landed at the bottom of the stairs. For if one could find a way to complete the crossword, things would slot into place. He'd be let out of the loop.

Accordingly Mark had made a second (or possibly third) cup of hot chocolate. Try to float the clue on the top of your mind, he'd exhorted himself. Don't labour over it. One has to trick one's brain.

Nothing had come of this. The clue had floated like scum on the surface. He'd tried the other clue, with the same success.

*

A wailing had gone up, like a distant siren.

Out there at the base of the stairs lay the source of the noise. Which. Would. Not. Die.

Hair on end, Mark had leapt to his feet and stood stock still. Another of him inhabited the bevelled mirror that distorted one's face. She had already been silenced. So the wailing must be in his head.

He was wrong. The thing at the base of the stairs had moved and it was moaning.

*

And after he'd dealt with this for the second (or was it the third?) time, he'd returned to the living-room and his hand had picked up the phone.

*

And what then? And what now? Memory burst up as if Mark were viewing these scenes for the first time, in the present moment – in the car, with his arm around the dog's neck, the dog that was not Pearl, for within this memory of Lily lay the curled foetus of every abortive event that had ever afflicted Mark. She encompassed every woman who had curdled love into detestation. His mother, who'd never worn a yellow dress, had sentenced her son to do the thing that arrested and incarcerated his heart without hope of remission.

No absolving priest existed behind the grille and there was no grille.

Storm let out a gruff bark. His ears and hackles rose. He snarled.

Moments later, a light went on in the hall of Tŷ Hafan. Relief flooded Mark. He wept. There you are, it's all right, Freya's all right. Of course she is. And he would find some way to explain why he'd fibbed to Terence about trains and Keighley and so on. Trivial fabrications, easily accounted for. He'd need to explain to Freya that the viola shock had tipped him over the edge, he'd had a terrible turn and said wild things and locked her in and bolted: could she forgive a grieving widower? He'd plaster over the cracks that had crazed the surface of reality and make things all right.

And then he'd leave her strictly alone. Freya Fox had been a mistake. An understandable mistake. Mark had done his best for this woman but she was not the One. She had thrust herself into his path and now must be eliminated from it. He'd email Janine and suggest a time for her visit to Tŷ Hafan. He would quit the crescent and the narrow minds of the little people.

Jesus Christ, someone was coming out of the door.

It was – could not be but was – Lily.

21

The guy's car had reversed at speed and taken off like a bat out of hell. She'd watched his departure from the window; sat down, stunned, gathering her wits.

As it turned out, all you needed was common-or-garden resourcefulness and a hairpin.

How could Freya have forgotten that she was a mechanic, an old hand at cobbling together any bits and pieces that came to hand? She had gone through every drawer in Mark Heyward's dressing table. Nothing. She'd groped in the cubby, without expectation, but – yes, out popped a scrap of hope. The wire mute that Lily had used for her viola was easily adapted and in seconds she'd fiddled the lock and freed herself from the bedroom.

Thanks, Lily. You're a friend.

Should have thought of all this before! You idiot, letting the creep get the upper hand. Shock and – what? Embarrassment? – had paralysed her. She could have been home hours ago if she'd had her wits about her. She ran downstairs and tried the wire trick on the front door lock. Stouter and more complicated, it refused to budge. The thing to do would be to locate the phone, if it was still in the house, and call for help.

You will be so fucking sorry you took me on, Mark Heyward, she thought. If she couldn't find the phone, never mind, she'd break a window. Never smashed one before: always a first time. The desire to smash something – preferably everything – seethed.

Rifling through the kitchen drawers, Freya tipped the contents on his lovely clean floor. You don't like pain, do you, Heyward, she thought, removing a knife from the wooden block. She'd known him whimper at a graze on his thumb. And, in point of fact, Mark wasn't physically all that fit. Listen, Freya told herself, you've never lacked resource or courage. You could have fought him but you gave in. You seem to have forgotten who you are. Now the little shit has helped you remember.

Thank you, little shit.

The backpack lay where it had dropped. When the damn thing had split open and revealed the viola fragments, she'd given in. She slipped the knife into the pack; found a hammer in his toolbox.

Maybe I'll smash this lovely, expensive Chinese-looking ornament.

Yeah, I think I will.

She brought the hammer down hard; stepped back as the shards exploded. I wonder what that cost you, she thought. Her head rang. Part of her was appalled but only part.

Standing back and throwing the hammer at a window pane would be safer than hanging on to it and getting your hand cut to ribbons. It would be an absolute pleasure to smash his bloody windows.

The remains of the viola would be going with Freya. I'm not leaving you behind, my beauty. No question. She retrieved the larger pieces and wrapped them in the cloth. Perhaps bury them somewhere. Give Lily's music a resting place.

'Did you think I was helpless, Heyward? Did you really?'

An old self – an old-young, never-say-die, fuck-you self – had blazed up: the spirit of revolt Mum and Dad had tried to tame. Why had Freya allowed this pathetic guy to threaten her? It came to her that not only the Crouches and the Foxes but her very dog had been trying to tell her. Storm had smelt the clues. He had information. If one could just interpret, in time, the language of an animal's eyes, human life would be easier to read.

Mark had often seemed wise and intuitive: *Storm is the life Keir has left to you.* Her neighbour had given her some hope when she was in need. He had the gift of the gab. He'd suffered. *My mother had a yellow dress.* In her mind's eye, she'd seen the mother. But didn't Mark trade on his woes? That didn't make them less real. It did make them predatory.

She'd turned to him when he turned to her, stoking her need, attracted by her helplessness. And all the time she'd intuited that he offered no refuge. Why had she often felt inexplicable guilt towards Mark, a repulsed desire to protect and solace him? He'd meant well. According to his lights.

But you are a parasite, she thought. You do nothing but suck. What are you but a sucker! She almost laughed. His mollusc mouth. His limpet hands. These were cruel thoughts. She let herself think them. It was a relief.

In fact, why not do some research? – although, if the guy came back, she'd need to be forewarned. Keep a look-out. Or go one better – barricade him out. She dragged a chest to the front door and the kitchen table against the back door. That would give plenty of warning. And Mark was easily frightened. His look when she confronted him, after he'd locked her in the first time, told her everything. She emptied out every drawer and cupboard in the living-room. No phone. Of course not.

Where next? An inconspicuous door stood flush with the hall panelling. This turned out to open into a store-room, or rather – good God – a pharmacy, with shelves of bottles and tubes for every malady under the sun. Eczema, halitosis, heartburn, fungal infections, diarrhoea, conjunctivitis – common complaints, ordinary remedies, but what took her aback was that there were at least ten of each packet or bottle. And literally dozens of boxes of paracetamol and codeine. Cupboards lined one wall, containing medications for rarer and more serious conditions. She pulled out Tramadol, diamorphine, liquid oxycodone, Xanax. Duplicates lined up behind them like toy soldiers. Powerful pain killers and a mountain of tranquillisers.

Was Mark seriously ill, then? Do I have to be sorry for the guy, after all?

He'd said he suffered from back pain. She remembered how he'd reached across and swept the morphine packet into the drawer, afraid it would remind her, he said, of Keir's illness. Jesus, he'd woken up and found her in his bedroom, stooping over him as he slept. She blushed at the thought of what he must have imagined at finding her there, sitting on his bed. Must have thought all his Christmases had come at once.

The dates on the stash of opioids went back and back. Where had he kept all this at the crescent? Perhaps he'd just locked it all up here.

Mark was ill, no doubt of that. He suffered. But this pharmacy did not contain the kind of drug the guy needed.

Another room was obviously his study: a grandiose space, more like a private library, with leather-bound books filling shelves on three sides to the ceiling. She wedged the door open. At the far end, a veneered wooden panel showed *trompe l'oeil* windows looking out onto some sylvan scene, golden – a castle, trees – rather lovely, but there were no real windows in the room. Before the hearth, a miniature sofa – its back ribbed like a shell – was flanked by twin armchairs. Over the mantelpiece, a concave mirror threw back a weirdly magnified image of a face, Freya's own.

The glass desk at the centre held Mark's computers and stacks of papers. A fountain pen lay parallel with a red leather-bound book.

I'm in now. I've got you now.

She'd been aware of Mark's comings and goings from the crescent, transferring books and papers. He'd moved his household gods, as he put it, to Tŷ Hafan, and then he'd sought to install her, as his – what? His household goddess? If Freya could get into the computer, she'd be able to email.

None of the possible passwords worked and she switched off. There were papers, cubbyholes, the filing cabinet to go through, and the laptop ... she had known the password because he'd parked it in her own study at the crescent and left it there. But he'd changed the password. Of course he had. Never mind. She started on the papers. Finances. Tax. Typewritten notes on Ancient Crete. Perhaps there was nothing to find. Still, she'd just glance into the alcoves.

Shoeboxes poured out a deluge of objects and information. She could hardly believe her eyes.

A teaspoon from her mother's cutlery set. It might have been anyone's. But not when it had been placed inside a slipper that had gone missing a while back. A white poppy. Her old silk blouse, stained.

A hairbrush with ... it had to be ... Freya's own hair in it. Mingled with – her stomach lurched – presumably his hair.

Item by item, with shaking hands, she exposed his trophies, tipped them onto the carpet. The boxes were systematically labelled and dated.

The earliest was 4th June, a week after Keir's death, the day of his funeral.

On that day, she'd entrusted Mark with her keys. She remembered how he'd promised to take Storm for a walk. And no sooner was I out of the house, Freya thought, than you were in and ferreting about.

A second box contained photographs, filed and documented. He'd charted her interior from front door to bedroom. In the bathroom, you could see the tip of Storm's tail, just in shot. Keir's fresco had been recorded in sections, ending with the cradle.

Nota Bene: dead baby = Larch Hardie Fox, he'd written on the back, with dates.

He'd found Larch's birth and death certificates. Otherwise how would he have known her son's middle name? He'd read the letters of sympathy. He'd snooped in the rainbow box of Larch's mementos.

The room grew cold, rage ratcheted. Keep going, Freya told herself. Reclaim it all. The rage went on rising and rising. It mounted independently of her will, with its own momentum.

He'd burrowed beneath her pillow, foraged, fished out her nightie, fingered it, laid it out on her bed and photographed it with – fuck – his hand in the bodice. He'd done – Christ knew what he'd done with it.

Just leave. Smash the window, get the hell out of here.

Stumbling to her feet in the obscene room, Freya came face to face with the reflection in the concave mirror. Throwing her face out of true, it warned her: what if you have another fit and he comes back? What will he do to you then? Hammer or no hammer, knife or no knife, you are done for. So, get out. Go. Now.

There will be no episode, Freya told herself. The medication seemed to have quelled the demon and she reassured herself: I am the person I used to be before I mislaid me.

Back at the desk, she opened the red book. Spider charts, labelled in miniscule writing.

Nomen: TANIA: *aetat* 7, red dress, saved from drowning Rotherslade.

Nomen: R VALERIE NILSSON (VAL), *nata* ? *Locus*: Stockholm, 1970 Cognitive Behavioural Psychotherapy PGDip (check awarding authority).

Nomen: LARCH HARDIE FOX, *diem mortis* 3 days // *Nomen:* FERN (any second name?) HEYWARD, *diem mortis* 1 week (say, 6 days), girl, hole in heart? Look up paediatric surgery, dead babies, how & where buried?

On the beach, he'd confided: Fern. A daughter. Died in my wife's arms. There are no words, he'd said, for that anguish. It leads to despair, he'd said. But we do learn to live again, our hearts in the grave, he'd said.

There was no Fern.

He made her up. He made it all up. And this book is his record, so that he doesn't lose hold of what he's said and who he's said it to.

He'd wept on Freya's shoulder for a child who'd never existed. His tears ran down her throat and shoulder. She'd allowed him to kiss her. She wiped her mouth with her hand, seated here at his desk, stalking him back, coldly sweating in the windowless room.

There was no Fern. It was a chronicle of lies.

At the back, under the heading 'My Pledges to Lily', she found jottings for letters or conversations, in minuscule writing. He acknowledged *malfeasance transgression trespass etc* and agreed to become *a different person*; to see a psychotherapist about his mood swings. He promised to do all to support and nurture his *darling tenderly precious sweetheart* whose fidelity he'd never doubt again *etc*.

Lily's darling hand would heal, he knew, and be good as new, better than new. He begged his Lily to keep him on track, remembering his *vulnerability etc, coalhole etc.*

One page was crossed through. ~~Want you to be free my angel & have friends of own men & women & live your life to full etc.~~ He appeared to have thought better of that, in the light of what it entailed for his own comfort – *opening door to endless comings & goings unwanted visitors ... promiscuity? Not say at all?*

Etiam: NOT SAY – imply / indicate.

As clearly as if he were physically present in the study, over there by the hearth, she saw Mark Heyward, slamming Lily's viola against the wall until it was shattered beyond mending.

It was you. You broke her priceless instrument.

She saw him doing the equivalent to Lily ... smashing her hand with some improvised weapon ... he wants to maim her, he envies her virtuosity, her reputation, he hates all the people who love and admire her. And then he cloaks his violence in fancy names. He placates, he fawns, he swears an oath to see a counsellor. Presumably that's the woman called Val – who doesn't seem to have done him much good. R Valerie Nilsson who came from '?Stockholm' ... Val who had done Mark no good whatever, mainly because ...

... it took a moment to get there ... because she might not even exist.

There may not be a Val. Or a Tania. Or a Fern. My God, Freya thought, it's all fiction. Between each fast pulse of her heart there intervened a long, ruminating gap. Every name shrivelled into a ghost of itself. Language collapsed into a common void. And yet it seemed incredible that Mark could have fabricated all this. Trust is the bedrock, she thought, it is a necessary habit or everything would fall apart. Mark's entire world was a tissue of fiction. There were so many names without people. How did you live with those hollow words?

At the centre of it all was the fact of Lily Himmelfarb. Lily, who had left to Danielle and then to Freya, the legacy of her viola. Lily who lay trussed at the dead centre of the spider charts.

What did you do to Lily, Mark, by *accident*?

The online videos of Lily playing at concerts had all been uploaded before 2009. She had faded from the public world. What other *accidents* had happened here? Freya saw Lily's isolation, wood-panelled walls closing in, burial before death in this mausoleum.

Once he'd caught you, but realised he'd never be able to possess you, Mark wouldn't care what he did to avenge himself. He'd break your hand. And your instrument. He'd lock you in. He'd lock you out.

You would not survive.

Freya shoved the red book into the backpack and started towards the door – and stopped herself. Finish the job, Freya told herself, be business-like. I'm not going to throw up, and I'm not leaving until I've seen everything. Her mouth was parched. In the kitchen she poured, with shaking hand, a glass of water. The fluorescent light picked out the blue stain of Keir's paint on her hand. In the garden, twilight was thickening. She forced herself back to finish the job.

More of Freya's possessions emerged; among them, an old broken lead of Storm's. She was working fast now, dumping stuff on the floor, a pile of rubbish – what did he want with all this junk? – until there just remained the filing cabinet.

There was no Fern. No Tania. No Pearl. There never had been. She had to keep repeating this, over and over. The thing was, though, there had been Keir, there had been Larch. These were real and true. Freya saw that with blessed clarity as she removed from the filing cabinet a tatty portfolio.

Meaning just to glance in, she opened it. Her heart stilled in wonder. How could Keir – how could anybody – have created these living likenesses with just a few scribbles of the pencil? His big old hand, so delicate.

So you found the studio, Mark? Of course you did. But this thought Freya lodged in a corner of her mind for future reference. The portfolio absorbed her entire attention.

She heard the whisper of each leaf as she lifted and turned it. She'd never seen them before. When did you make these studies, Keir? In one sketch, Freya was seated at the mirror, brushing her hair, head to one side, her body expressed in a kind of 'S' curve. It looked as if the brush had snagged on a knot and she was giving it a little tug. But how was it possible to glean all that information when there was no detail, just a few pencil marks? How did you even know that the portraits were of yourself?

Freya did know.

In the next sketch, she lay on her side, propped on one elbow and reading a book, though no book was shown.

It was as if Keir had left a message: go on living, Frey, go on brushing your hair like this – go on stepping into the bath like this – tie your laces, bending like this. Go on being yourself, Keir was saying, like the lilies of the field.

*

It had not been Lily.

Of course not, don't be ludicrous. Lily was long gone: a name without a person. How many times did Mark have to remind himself of this fact before it finally sank in? It was when the mind got caught in loops that one started to see things that weren't there and couldn't be there. The shadows of the japonica by the front door had been tossed about in gusts of wind; moonlight came and

317

went: easy, therefore, to imagine lights going on and a person moving in the doorway.

High time to go in and sort everything out.

The Foxes' dog strongly objected to being left in the car and only just missed having his snout trapped as Mark closed the door. One minute the animal was fawning and the next seemed ready to tear your heart out and eat it – which was not what you expected of a Labrador, bred for docility and faithfulness. The Foxes had failed to train Storm properly.

Mark strode over to his house with a sense of relief: once you were actively engaged in positive action, nervousness subsided. The whole sorry chapter would soon be closed. What a mess. He loathed mess. One had to admit, one had contributed – somewhat. Mark had been taken in by his neighbour's flattering reliance on his services. The sight of sheer need in another – someone you have the power to sustain and succour – produced a curiously consolatory effect. Compassion, however, was something of a trap. Empathy has no boundaries, Mark thought: it invites to its hearth any hapless ragbag of a human being.

Once his unwelcome visitor had been despatched and he'd addressed any consequences, Mark would reclaim his space, wait a while and then invite Janine.

The only thing that troubled him, as the warm thought of Janine flashed through his mind, was: what if some other fellow snapped her up in the meantime? He had ascertained that there was no boyfriend. *Oh no. I'm happily single, Mark!* Spoken with a lilting laugh. But singleness could change at any moment. And it seemed to Mark that the whole world must be gazing with lubricious eyes at Janine as she passed by, hips swinging. (Did her hips swing? He didn't know but the point was that this was how they'd see her). So the invitation had better be extended sooner rather than later.

First thing tomorrow, Mark would email Janine. He ticked it off in his mind. Just ask if she'd care to come round for lunch. She was the right age for a serious friendship: late twenties. He felt for his key and bent to insert it. And he and she had common interests and comparable aptitudes – without being competitive – for while Janine was up-and-coming, Mark could count himself without vanity as a world authority on the coded meanings of antiquities. The damn door refused to open; the lock was playing up. Try again. Janine was neither a vapid kid like Danny nor a woman in near middle age like Freya Fox and carrying a ton of baggage. He reinserted the key. It slipped in easily, and turned, so what was the problem?

Mark put his shoulder to the door and shoved. It did not budge. Presumably he'd used the right key? Yes, the right key. Try again. Nothing.

Put out, Mark retrieved his torch from the car boot, ignoring Storm's barking. And don't scratch my upholstery while you're at it, and don't pee, he told the animal, rapping the window with his knuckle in passing. He made his way by torchlight round to the back of the house.

The back door stuck fast. Mark had been barricaded out of his own house. Astonishment gave way to affront, as he imagined Freya Fox scraping the furniture over the parquet to block the door. She had got out of the bedroom. What the hell was she doing in there?

The fact was, he'd laid himself open to this. Not once but twice, women had taken over his home. And whose fault was that? It's your own, he scolded himself, too trusting by half, but never again.

Sweat beaded his forehead. Mark's heart hurt, his gut griped: I'm ill, Mark thought – no – no. He'd need to take – he wasn't sure what – there must be something in the cupboard to take. He propped himself against the wall, under the security light, and reached for his mobile. If this was a heart attack, he would die here, friendless and alone, for the ambulance would not arrive in time.

But, come on, perhaps it was just stress. Yes, it would be stress. There were plenty of Valium tablets. Xanax. Plenty, don't worry.

Mark drew in some faltering breaths. The pain levelled off. Perhaps he had fibromyalgia. That didn't kill you. Dr Lewis could run some tests. Mark would insist. And the pills were in the cupboard.

What the Fox woman couldn't know was that there was an entrance through the cellar.

Mark had sometimes wondered about getting that door bricked up. Stout and heavy, faced with metal showing geometrical patterns of the sun's rays, it was original to Tŷ Hafan. One had scruples about tampering with an original Art Deco feature. Besides, the cellar door was not a weak point in terms of security. It was just that he disliked the basement and tended to avoid it.

Needs must. He was in and passing through swiftly, not liking the smell, not looking toward the beams where *she* had threatened to hang herself. Halfway up the steps, his mobile rang. Damn, damn, damn. He felt in his pocket and, of course, it wasn't his phone, it was Freya Fox's. Fumbling it out, he glanced to see who was ringing. Wouldn't you know it: one of the brothers-in-law. Four hogs vying for the prize sow. Well, all four were welcome now to her, individually or severally. He switched the phone to silent. A text came through. *Where r u babes??? Get in touch!!! T says ur in Yorkshire?? Luv u Jamiexxxx.* Which one was this illiterate? No idea. Mark toyed with the idea of texting back some message to put them off the scent but – what message to send defeated him for the moment. Delete, delete, delete.

Turn off the light. Deep breath.

Mark inched the cellar door open. The hall lay in darkness. Perhaps somehow or other she'd managed to scarper. He hoped she had. But how could she have escaped from the bedroom in the first place? Lily had never managed it when he put her to bed. Standing in the black hall, he listened.

He heard himself whimper.

Stop that. Mark tried not to think the words *coal hole.* Close your eyes, he counselled himself, and you'll find when you open them that you've become accustomed: there'll be familiar shapes you can pick out. He released the breath he'd been holding. Just pull the cellar door to behind you! Very, very gently! You see, you see, you don't need to panic.

The latch clicked into place. He startled himself by lunging for the hall light switch and bellowing, 'Where the hell are you, Lily?'

A commotion: footsteps, a slammed door, a thrown bolt.

Where? Mark swung on his heel. He threw open the door to the living-room. The carpet was awash with red. The roses he'd cut for her – roses that would have cost the earth at a florist – lay strewn and trampled across the floor. The madwoman had upended a coffee table, the one with the inlay, it was scraped, it cost a fortune, she'd ransacked the cupboards – emptied the cubbies – she'd run amok –

– and oh, his Chinese vase – irreplaceable – the iridescent blue glass showing trees in moonlight, he could have wept for the vandalism. She had lost him five-hundred pounds. And she would pay.

In the kitchen, there'd been a whirlwind. Smashed eggs, the freezer door open, water pooling on the tiles, the meat would be ruined. Cutlery was everywhere, broken crockery and glass.

He picked up the shard of a bottle of milk the bitch had broken; stared at it. That would be coming with him.

Even in his outrage, Mark thought: careful now, don't let it cut you.

The pills, his pills. What had she done with the pills? Jesus Christ. If you've – if she'd dared to – my pills – *mine* – because he'd left that door open and his legs went to jelly, his mouth dried – was he having a heart attack? – worse –if she'd – bitch – if you've – my *pills*.

He reeled in to the store-room – and, oh sweet Jesus, thank God, yes, she'd been in and rooted out the medications but surely they were all or mostly here? He laid the shard on the sink and did a rough count of the Oramorph boxes. The Valium. It was all here.

My pills.

Mark stacked the boxes and bottles approximately where they

belonged, reminding himself to breathe. He pressed out a couple of precious tranquillisers from a pack and swallowed them. And a couple of codeine for the pain. Why had he left the woman in Tŷ Hafan in the first place? Sometimes he couldn't fathom himself. But how was Mark to know she'd get out and rampage through his property? He picked up the shard.

The study was bolted against him. He rattled the door handle which had – Mark remembered with a shudder – once come off in his hand. He'd stood there irresolute, clutching the handle which then he'd bowled over-arm at the door like a cricketer: in fact you could still see the dint where it had slammed against the wood and ricocheted off. Later, it had required a phone call to a handyman, who'd looked on Mark as a nincompoop and charged him £30 for restoring it, unaware that the house was a work of art, everything must be kept perfect. £30 for fixing a doorknob!

There was no earthly point in pulling at the handle in any case, and risking an expensive repeat. The lunatic had shot the bolt.

'Freya!'

He tapped, then knocked harder. He looked at the shard in his left hand. Careful with it, Mark reminded himself. There were no windows in there. She was trapped.

No response.

The top was spinning off his head. He should have taken double the Valium. But he did not want to weaken – emasculate – himself. Why was he thinking that? Don't think that. What had the bloody woman found in there? She'd not be able to get into the computer equipment. But had she damaged it? She would have to pay. He knew exactly, to the nearest pound, what was in her building society account.

He'd locked the Red Book away in the desk.

Had he?

'Please come out, dear,' he coaxed. 'We can talk. Or not talk, if you prefer it?'

Pause.

'You'll have to come out in the end, won't you? Think about it. I won't hold it against you.'

Was she thinking? Or was she just mindlessly waiting, twiddling her thumbs, imagining he'd give up and go away if she waited long enough? Mark was worried about the Red Book now. He might have left it out. The fact was, he'd just dumped it all on the desk when they'd arrived.

'There's no way out, Freya, is there? I'm sorry I locked you in and took off,' he crooned. 'It was because –' Because of what? – The word? The word? –

'It was *inadvertent*.' A downright stupid word.

'Look, dear, I was upset. It was – my darling wife – Lily – the grief, the loss, it all came flooding back,' he informed the door, and to his surprise Mark found that sincere tears had risen. He allowed them to overflow and more came. 'The trauma. You look so like her, you see, Freya. I've never explained that to you, my dear friend, and perhaps I didn't admit it to myself, I should have realised –'

In point of fact, Freya Fox looked nothing like Lily but she wasn't to know that. He continued in the same melancholy vein, unveiling his distress at the recovery of the viola, which had sent him into a version of his original grief – as when Lily smashed it, for she had been mentally unbalanced, she'd been bipolar and had suicidal tendencies, also aggressive tendencies – and his therapist – Val, his Swedish therapist – had told him his flashbacks were indistinguishable from those of war veterans, although of course he hadn't been on a battlefield … unless you saw the world itself as a battlefield … the train of thought seemed to have wandered, and Mark paused, ear to the door.

No response.

What if she'd had one of her fits and was lying there unconscious, having lost control of her bowels?

'Wake up!' Mark snarled. 'Wake up in there! I'm coming in anyway.'

There was much Freya Fox did not know about the house. He

crept, soft-foot, away from the door, so as not to betray the fact that he'd left it unguarded – although if she did sneak out, he'd hear and could return in seconds. In the kitchen, Mark silently cleared the counter top, replacing a loaf in the bread tin. As he did so, the thought travelled through him as clearly as if a voice, not Mark's own, were speaking aloud: *I asked for bread and you gave me a stone.* That was the long and short of it. A pastoral voice, the voice of one who comprehended the rage of an eternal hunger.

Centimetre by centimetre, Mark eased open the hatch. She wasn't in his line of view but he was sure he could hear her breathing. A little further along, the hatch door jammed. But now, squinting through the gap, he could get an angle on the woman.

For a moment she was anonymous, a stranger seated at his desk, reading in the amber light of the desk lamp.

Reading? How could she be reading?

No other lights were on and the room was dim. Was it the Red Book she was reading? He couldn't tell. Stupid, stupid, stupid to have left the door open and his precious records out. And it dawned on Mark that the filing cabinet was not locked. How could one possibly have foreseen that she'd get free and rifle through his private possessions?

She raised her head. How could the woman possibly have been concentrating, given her situation? As if he weren't there.

Or – as if *she* weren't there. Perhaps she was in some kind of fugue state? That might be it. Epileptics in such a condition suddenly get up and wander off, they catch a train or flag down a cab – they might go to Keighley and back but they'd not remember. How would she be able to prove, when she came to, that she *hadn't* been to Keighley? He stored this brainwave away for future use.

The hatch framed Freya Fox. And, very strangely, she did look a bit like Lily but of course it wasn't Lily, why always think of Lily? As she looked up, the top half of the Not-Lily's face entered the shadow; he couldn't see Not-Lily's eyes at all. How many times had Mark, in his infatuation, wished the wall away that lay between his own bed and this woman's pigsty of a bedroom? He'd wistfully imagined sliding it aside like a stage partition. Now he just wanted her gone, on any terms.

Idiot, he thought, it's not just the Red Book I've left in there – it's my everything, it's documentation for my whole life. My safety and peace of mind. He wrenched the hatch the rest of the way, obtaining a fuller view of the room. The figure gave a small start, before rising from his desk, with apparent composure.

Mark thrust his head and shoulders into the hatch. Done it before and I'll do it again. And watch out. He launched himself forward.

'Careful, it's a tight fit. You don't want to get stuck like that!'

It took Mark a moment to work out that the trapped female was mocking him, actually laughing aloud. Picking up something from the desk, she advanced towards him.

22

Freya had looked at her hand: the blue stain.

Keir had spoken through the paint. He'd said, I waited for you, my darling. I'm always here, not just in your memory but in my paintings, in our ideals and hopes, in these three letters I put aside for you, in Storm and our home, in your memory of the child we made, in every aspect of our shared life. Do not give up.

She'd rescued the letters from Heyward's trove of thefts and kissed them repeatedly. She'd glanced through one. It promised her – splendidly – irises.

Keir would leave her irises. Freya knew now exactly where to look.

Three letters? Two were in her hands but where was the third? Where was it? What had Heyward done with it? She'd heard him trying to force the front door; then the back. She ought to have been terrified, it was only sane to be terrified. She wasn't. You dug your nasty fingers into my entire life – like a rape, she thought – you had no qualms about removing Keir's letters. You've been snooping in the studio. You've laid yourself bare. And you will get what is coming to you.

For, written on the back of Keir's envelope in Mark's pedantic script, was the date of the theft, not of one but three letters from K Fox to F Fox, place found, to be opened posthumously, and the information that he'd destroyed one letter and retained two.

You destroyed my letter. I will kill you.

She'd looked again at her hand: the blue stain.

There had come a bellowing noise in the hall, sudden and brief. He'd got in. Of course he had. It was what he did, getting in. She'd rushed to the study door, shot the bolt. All quiet. She'd waited. He'd waited. Then, speaking through the locked door, his voice had begun to smarm. I really wouldn't, if I were you, Freya had thought coldly. Part of her had wished, from the point of view of Mark Heyward's safety, that he'd give up and clear off while he could.

She'd slipped the letters into her jeans pocket. The portfolio had gone into the backpack and the knife had come out. She'd slid the blade from its cardboard sleeve and laid it on the desk beside the hammer. Her hands hadn't trembled.

Someone was coming through the wall.

Shock had irrupted as a burst of hilarity. She couldn't help laughing, couldn't stop, at the sight of the writhing fool, a third of his body inside the room. He was shoving at the wall with one hand and twisting his torso, while flailing with the other hand, attempting to keep hold of something. It dropped.

Freya approached Mark, switching on the main lights. The guy was not going to make it through. Well, he might, but it would take one hell of a lot of effort. There was almost a fascination in observing him, an insect wriggling in a tight spot. It would shortly be impaled on a pin.

He looked up, drenched in humiliating light.

'Careful now, it's a tight squeeze,' Freya advised. 'I think you might be too fat.'

She stood with folded arms and her head at an angle, as if sizing up the relative measurements involved.

'I'm not sure you're going to make it, Mark. You may have miscalculated. Perhaps you'd be better sliming back where you came from. But maybe not. We'll see.'

She bent to retrieve what he'd dropped.

'Oh, a handy piece of broken glass. Nice. Thanks a lot for that.'

He was pouring out his regret, he'd been in the wrong, he was sorry, he'd never been so sorry, he was abject, how could he make amends? He could explain it all, he panted. His stomach muscles must be burning, his face was puce. His chest and hips hurt, he informed her feebly, he might have cracked a rib, he'd only wanted to come in and speak to Freya, he knew it looked farcical, he'd broken in (though it was his house, not hers) but it was grief that did it, terrible grief – and trauma, he wept – surely Freya understood about grief? – and if she'd just please help, he'd clarify everything.

'Hang on a minute. *You* want *me* to help you?'

'Please, dear lovely Freya. I know I don't deserve it.'

'What did it say?' Freya asked.

'What did what say?'

'Work it fucking out.'

'I don't—'

'Yes, you do, actually. I think you'll find you do know. And do you recognise this?'

He went still. He looked at what she was holding. He was a rat in a trap. She didn't pity him. In the past, Freya had been visited by suspicions that *he's fibbing or exaggerating*; the doubts had been clues to a suffering more acute than there were words to express. She'd half-consciously known this from the start. Now she didn't give a shit and she raised the hammer, not quite above his head but where he could see it – because he was going to suffer now.

'I asked you if you recognised this?'

'Yes.' Small voice. Scared, cowed little boy. Looking up, pleading eyes. Nowhere to go. Cornered.

'What is it?'

'Hammer.'

'And now you're going – to tell me – what it said.'

'What what said? I'll tell you, I want to tell you, but what do you mean?'

'You destroyed it. Like this! See?'

With both hands, she brought the hammer smashing down on the inlayed table, the mirror, the computer screen.

A woman, beside herself, was shrieking at the top of her voice. She was wrecking his precious stuff. Freya stopped and stood still, head spinning. Shattered glass and debris littered the room.

'Right? Right? You going to tell me now?'

He'd tell her, he sobbed, tell her anything, just explain what she meant—

'You stole my letters. From Keir. *From Keir! His letters!* You destroyed one. What did it say?'

'It said—'

'Stop fucking snivelling – what did it *say*? – and bear in mind, I'll know, Mark, I'll know if you're lying – you just lie and you lie and you lie – but not any more—'

'Don't, Freya, I'll tell you – I'm going to tell you – please, no! – it said, watch out for the – guy next door.'

He was making progress in squirming back into the kitchen.

'Watch out for *you*?'

'No, I think he didn't mean me—'

'So who the fuck did he mean?'

'He meant—'

She discerned the mental slither as the rat paused for the fraction of a second. She saw him wondering whether, having blurted something like the truth, he could somehow pin it on Terry Crouch.

Well, you had your fucking chance, pal. Her heart was huge in her chest. She brought the hammer down hard, shouting, *What did you do to Lily?*

*

His hand, his poor hand, she'd broken his hand.

The red bruise was turning purple under his eyes.

What to do, whatever to do?

Ice, he needed ice. He needed to get to A&E, his phone had been stolen, his house keys, his car keys; the computer was smashed, it was all gone. There was no way to contact the outside world.

How cold her eyes had been, utterly without mercy.

Even when he collapsed on the kitchen floor, curled around his damaged hand, she'd shown not a particle of remorse. *You're lucky I let you live.* She'd rifled his pockets and taken away all hope of help.

The ice in the freezer had melted and pooled on the tiles. So, come on, hold your hand under the tap, Mark told himself. But keeping it there was torture; he couldn't. His bones must be broken. He cried aloud and his voice bleated like a lamb. There was nothing and no one.

Medicine: he found the arnica and swabbed it on; swallowed hydrocodeine. That would help, give it a few minutes and keep the hand above your head. Nothing was happening. It wasn't enough. He took an Oramorph tablet. He retched and things began to blur. Fit to faint, Mark sank down on the living-room carpet, lay flat, hardly knowing where he was. He'd be found dead and no one would care. From the corners of his eyes, tears bled down his temples and he saw, through the tears, the crimson petals of scattered roses.

He held the pure pain of his ruined hand in the air above his head, using the uninjured hand to support it. Looking up at the maimed purple thing, he pitied it as though it were a creature distinct from himself. The arnica had dried.

After a while he became afraid of the hand and tried not to look at its misery. But the more he abstracted his attention, the more Mark's gaze was sucked back. When the pain drifted away, he carried the hand down to lie on his chest and let it rest there. He remained still until he could breathe more steadily.

The pain had not gone; it hovered over there, just beyond the horizon of his skin. It would seize him again in its jaws.

*

Mark's mind swam. Gran sat shucking peas at the kitchen table. She looked up and said, quite matter-of-factly, 'I had her put down, Mark. It was for the best.'

*

330

Later, he was cutting and knotting bandages, one-handed, and putting a torch in his pocket.

Later again, he'd moved the table that was blocking the back door and made an exit.

He thought he'd left Pearl in the car but there was no car.

And Gran had had his darling put down. Their world had ended. How could he live with the loneliness of his survival? What had Pearl ever done to harm anyone? He had never wished to outlive her.

Mark stumbled up the lane towards the village, the sling cradling the bundle of raging pain, which slowed him down with every jostling pace. He did not seem to be wearing shoes.

He waved a car down. It was when he saw the concerned faces and was helped into the back seat that the blank loneliness hit.

What happened? Whatever happened? the strangers wanted to know. Did someone attack you? Who has done this to you?

Mark shook his head. You can never tell people what happened. What happened is locked up inside, there is no way in and no way out.

23

She bounded into her home and up the stairs to the loft, Storm at her heels. With only one purpose. Over to the canvas with the confusion of marks.

Only the marks weren't random. They all belonged together. If you narrowed your eyes, you recognised the flower the wasted hands had intended to depict. It was the bearded iris that throve near the far wall and whose babies they'd buried last year around the mother plant. All but one had taken root and the mother had, against probability, blossomed vigorously despite the shock of division.

Keir had been watching Freya in the garden from their open bedroom window. So the letter told her: watching over her, loving her with his eyes, as he had done every day for twenty years. He'd seen her wander down to the wall and heard her chatting with Pammie Crouch over the fence. Mainly Pam had been doing the chatting and Freya, the listening. The word *rhizome* had floated up and Keir heard Pam say that the iris rhizome must be baked in the sun.

You've just giggled at thought of baked rhizomes, good to hear you laugh Frey cariad – I will leave you irises –- make one last try for that blue – Anyway I'll give it a go &

Unseen, Keir had left his death bed and made the epic climb up the loft stairs. How had he done that? He'd mixed these colours – she picked up tubes, ultramarine, phthalo blue. You could see and feel the indents where his thumb had squeezed them. On the palette was his mixture of blues, purples, green and a dot of yellow.

How Keir had managed this labour of love, three days before the end, Freya had no idea. It was an impossible feat. But it had happened. Keir's spirit had lugged the burden of his dying body up the Everest of the staircase, his decayed lungs famishing for oxygen. He'd handled this brush – she took it up, weighed its heft on the crotch of her thumb – he'd loaded it, made these marks for Freya.

The final weeks had bled into one another. The chat with Pam remained a blank, though maybe Pam would remember. Freya must have thought Keir was asleep. From time to time – at least once a day, more often, twice – she'd tiptoe out, half guiltily, to breathe in the scent of the garden and let the sun unknot her shoulders.

If only she could have Keir back for just ten minutes. Her heart twisted with longing. To say whatever had been left unsaid. Freya did not know what that might have been. She sank down on the modelling couch. If she could just hold Keir for ten minutes more, and live each second of those ten minutes – which we don't do, she thought, it's shameful how we waste time, fritter it so casually. If you could just be here with me, even as a hallucination, Keir, you don't have to be real – Rae had seen her dad a fortnight after his death, she'd been dozing in front of the television and woke knowing there was someone in the room, and she saw her dad and he said ... something about dolphins ... and he gave this odd salute before he turned away and was gone. Although Rae, a rationalist through and through, knew that this was the effect of her devastated brain beaming a film out onto the screen of reality, she'd said it affected her oddly, its uncanny rapture had buoyed her up.

If Keir would just come back and say something, anything.

It was all over. The paint was dry. Dry on the canvas, dry on the back of her hand, and she would scrub off the residue. She'd visited his corpse and that had been alien. It wasn't Keir. The memory sparked of spotting some insect, a money spider, on his wrist in the coffin, and she'd freed the insect, and left them. Keir lay underground.

And then again, Freya thought, when I had that fit, I did think he was coming through the wall, I did see him, didn't I? But it wasn't him. And it wasn't nice. It was an impersonator.

Keir would not come again. She did not want him to. He'd restored his atoms to the mother world. That was that. There was no afterlife. Freya would be satisfied to have the tenderness of irises.

You are home with me now, Storm's melting eyes seemed to say, as he licked the tears and snot off her face, and I shall never let you go again. He was the life Keir had left to her. Amongst all the untruths, that was sure. Freya cradled their dog in her arms, head against his substantial warmth, and let herself be crazily licked.

*

They'd fallen asleep up there together before dawn, to the sound of tawny owls calling back and forth to one another in Whitethorn Wood: the fluting male *hoo-woo* near at hand, and further off the shrill female *kee-wick*.

When Freya came to, the sickle moon had set, the dormer was a blank grey canvas, and somebody was in the house, moving around down there. My God, Freya thought, I never even locked the front door, how could I have just dashed in and left it ajar?

It couldn't be happening all over again, it just couldn't. She'd put the guy out of action. But maybe Mark hadn't been badly injured, when it came down to it. Perhaps the crunching sound she'd heard, which set her teeth on edge to remember – and the bedlam of his anguish as she brought the hammer down on his hand – had persuaded her that he'd been put out of action. She'd been out of her mind.

How could she have attacked him like that, how could she?

Drained now, spent and dark with the shock of her own violence, Freya levered herself up; her head swam, she might faint.

He was coming for her. And would Storm protect her? She didn't think so: the soft creature was snuffling at the studio door, looking round, pawing and whimpering. He should have been raising Cain.

The sounds downstairs paused, then resumed. They seemed to be coming now from the back of the house. She had the idea that someone was beating a carpet but why would they be doing that? It was nonsense. She swung her legs off the couch and held her body still.

But this was the crescent: there'd be folk around. He'd never dare assault her here. People would hear through the party wall. If I stood on the chair, she thought, I could get a better view from the dormer, I could call out for help. There's always someone about. She got to her feet but, shaking, didn't trust herself to climb on the chair. Peering out, she could see the corner of the street where last night she'd parked Mark Heyward's car, skewed, under the lamp post, the interior reeking of Storm's pee.

The car wasn't there. How could the car have gone?

How could she have brought the hammer smashing down on a person's hand? How?

Back again to the couch. It will be all right, he's not here, she thought, and the sounds had stopped. Perhaps they hadn't come from inside the house at all. She laid her head between her legs. It was what they advised you to do at the maternity hospital when you were pregnant and fainting all the time. *Let the blood flow to your head,* the nurse had said – *and take your time.*

The madness of yesterday rushed upon Freya full tilt. The locking in and the locking out. The viola. His collection of her underwear, toothbrush, slipper. The spider charts. Keir's letters. The obscene head poking through the hatch. Absurd, pitiful. Except that I didn't pity him, Freya thought: I trashed the bloke's house and then his hand. He'd sobbed, cradling the injury, face purple and crumpled, mouth squared up like an infant's. Freya hadn't cared. She couldn't remember the exact words she'd vomited but they were foul. Jesus, she'd morphed into another person. She'd thought, in so far as she'd thought at all: he deserves this.

She hadn't morphed. This must be who she was.

But I did actually swerve the hammer, Freya pleaded: I only hit his hand. Not his head.

You only hit his hand? Oh, wonderful. Actually, you wanted to batter and batter him until he was finished.

No, it had been self-defence. What was I supposed to do? Echoes of her own violence rang round her head, the smithereening of glass and the obscene bellowing. Rings of violent sound. And now he was here to finish her off.

With shaking hands, she picked up Keir's palette knife to defend herself, and – what else? – brushes, to stick in his eyes.

You are planning to stick the ends of brushes in someone's eyes? You would really do that? That is your intention?

She held on to the brushes, afraid that she couldn't do it, afraid that she could.

On the landing, hanging on to Storm's collar, Freya froze. Someone was on the stairs, creeping surreptitiously, pausing between steps to listen. Storm didn't bark. He looked up at Freya. She put down Keir's brushes: ridiculous idea. Just wait, Freya told herself, breathe, think. The other person must be saying the same to himself.

She edged forward. The intruder seemed to shuffle at the same time. Another pause. What Freya would do was – barge straight past him. He wouldn't expect that. She'd scared the guy rigid. At heart, Mark Heyward was craven. And in an odd way, not very bright.

On the quarter landing sat a little girl in a red dress, sucking an ice lolly. She had her back to Freya and appeared to be bum-shuffling slowly up the stairs.

'Haf!'

Haf twisted her head, the lolly sticking out of her mouth. She spoke round it. 'Hiya, Auntie Frey. Want a suck?'

'No, my darling. You enjoy it. Is it raspberry?'

'Strawberry. I got it out of your freezer,' she said with a guilty look.

'But I keep them for you, sweetpea. You can try all the flavours and let me know which one you like best.'

Haf wriggled sideways, patting the stair beside her. Freya plonked down, arm around the child's warm body. Safety and comfort flowed into her from Haf.

'Can I try all the flavours today, Auntie Frey?'

'Only if I can have the peach one.'

'You can.'

'Better ask Mummy first, if she lets us. Deal?'

'Deal.'

'Is she downstairs?'

'Yes, and Daddy. And Uncle David. And them ones next door.'

Haf's arm was round Storm's neck, as he licked at her ear lobe and sent the ice lolly skidding down her front. Freya rescued it and brushed the hair off her niece's face with her fingertips, kissing her forehead. Then she called out to Rae.

*

Blunt trauma.

Radiography. Wheelchair. Your husband is in shock. Don't worry. If you wait here – there's a coffee machine over there. We'll take good care of him.

An injection to numb the area. Yes, oh yes please, an injection.

That's the way. Don't cry. Here, have a tissue. The weary tears seeped out. How did this happen? Did someone do this to you? We can call the police. You fell? Really? You're sure about that?

He wanted to thank the heavenly nurse with all his heart for alleviating the pain but could not get the words out. Her uniform was pale blue.

Distal and proximate phalanx. Fracture of the metacarpal. He caught these alarming phrases.

But in conclusion, he was assured he had only sustained hairline cracks. However, the hand is one of the most complex and important parts of the anatomy, Mr Heyward, you don't need me to tell you that! After all, you use it to write, don't you, to button your shirts, and – although thankfully this is not your dominant hand – you don't want to live a one-handed life. Nurse will fix you up with a splint and you should keep the hand raised, can you remember that?

He nodded. They appeared unconvinced by his nodding. Mark would have preferred to stay in the hospital and be cared for. And be safe. But there were no beds available for the walking wounded. The medics were all pronouncing their words separately and emphatically, faces up close to his, as if addressing a child. Mark didn't mind. He carried on being mute, or rather the muteness that was in him had its say.

Acetaminophen for the pain. OK, dear? He nodded decisively this time. You must be careful not to overdose. Nod. Got that? Nod. We'll say a word to your wife about dosage.

And there's nothing you want to tell us about how you sustained this injury?

Mark shook his head.

Was he sure about that? Mark nodded.

Was he shielding someone? Mark shook his head.

A porter wheeled him back to the emergency room. Mark smiled bravely. He relaxed into his fate.

'Ah, Mrs Heyward. I'll just run through the treatment with you. Your husband's hand has hairline fractures. As you see, it's in a splint, and he must keep the sling on. Now, painkillers – antibiotics – and he must attend the clinic – on no account should he attempt to drive –'

'Of course not. I'll see to that.'

His companion stowed the box of medication in her handbag, with a secret smile, which he recognised, as she expected him to. Her whole demeanour implied, *I am a competent person, leave him to me.* She squeezed Mark's right hand. Her body was plump and comfortable. She had not denied the hospital's assumption of their marital relationship. Neither of them had. A whisper passed through his mind: *This was meant to be.* He'd thought this before and been disappointed – but this time was different. All previous betrayals had led up to this quiet illumination.

He had been passed from hand to hand and not fallen.

She settled the invalid in her car, arranging the safety belt so as not to jar his arm, climbed in and started the engine. Dawn was coming up as she drove him carefully back to her own flat. There were few cars on the road and the stars had not quite set. His mind swam in a haze of something like bliss.

'I don't know how to thank you,' he managed. 'I really don't.'

'Nothing to thank me for, Mark. You would have done the same for me.'

'I would.'

It was as simple as that. He rested his head back and surrendered to a pleasurable state of inaction.

Had she really said, 'I should be thanking you?'

Had she added that she was so proud that he thought of her as a friend?

'More than a friend,' Mark murmured. 'Far more. Oh Janine, if only you knew.'

ABOUT HONNO

Honno Welsh Women's Press was set up in 1986 by a group of women who felt strongly that women in Wales needed wider opportunities to see their writing in print and to become involved in the publishing process. Our aim is to develop the writing talents of women in Wales, give them new and exciting opportunities to see their work published and often to give them their first 'break' as a writer. Honno is registered as a community co-operative. Any profit that Honno makes is invested in the publishing programme. Women from Wales and around the world have expressed their support for Honno. Each supporter has a vote at the Annual General Meeting. For more information and to buy our publications, please write to Honno at the address below, or visit our website: www.honno.co.uk.

Honno, D41 Hugh Owen Building, Penglais Campus,
Aberystwyth University, Aberystwyth, Ceredigion SY23 3DY.

We are very grateful for the support of all the Honno Friends. For more information on how you can support Honno, see:
https://www.honno.co.uk/about/support-honno/